What the Dead Want

M J Lee has worked as a university researcher in history, a social worker with Vietnamese refugees, and as the creative director of an advertising agency. He has spent 25 years of his life working outside the north of England, in London, Hong Kong, Taipei, Singapore, Bangkok and Shanghai.

Also by M J Lee

DI Ridpath Crime Thriller

MJ LEE

WHAT THE DEAD WANT

© **CANELO**CRIME

First published in the United Kingdom in 2024 by

Canelo
Unit 9, 5th Floor
Cargo Works, 1–2 Hatfields
London SE1 9PG
United Kingdom

A CIP catalogue record for this book is available from the British Library.

Print ISBN 978 1 80436 255 6
Ebook ISBN 978 1 80436 254 9

Cover design by Tom Sanderson

Cover images © Arcangel, Alamy

Look for more great books at www.canelo.co

Printed and bound in Great Britain by Clays Ltd, Elcograf S.p.A.

1

For my brother Mike, who gave me the idea in the first place

Friday, May 8, 2020

Chapter ONE

It was just another summer's evening in Manchester.

She was lying in her small, thin bed, the night light throwing a grey shadow across her face.

I closed the door gently, ensuring the noise didn't wake her.

Standing in the entrance, I watched as she moved restlessly in her sleep, turning her face towards me, the small gold cross around her neck catching the light against her pale wrinkled skin.

The room was bare and functional, not decorated like the others; a small table with one chair, a dresser with one picture resting on top, and one armchair where she could sit and read. The walls were painted a light eau-de-nil green, a colour beloved of company bureaucrats everywhere.

I never understood why that particular colour had been chosen for all the rooms in the facility. Any colour could have been selected; a pastel blue, for instance, or a warm rich cream. But no, the company had chosen the official coldness of eau de nil.

Whatever.

I advanced two steps towards the bed. She turned over once more.

What was she dreaming? Of days gone by when she had raced up the hill of her beloved Yorkshire? Or her first kiss behind the bike sheds at school, her body trembling with delight? Or even her wedding day, walking down the aisle in her borrowed white dress, the out of tune organ playing the 'Wedding March' in the wrong key.

She had told me all about her life one day. An old woman lost in her memories. It was one of the reasons I had chosen her to die.

For a moment, I stood still and stared at the hands resting over the top of the white bedsheet. Wrinkled, liver-spotted hands. Hands that had once caressed babies, done the washing up, wiped a child's face, held a lover's hand.

She was still healthy though, despite her age.

Too healthy.

She had signed the form a week ago. I always got them to sign it before the cull, they never said no. Most times, they never even looked at it, just one more of those interminable pieces of bureaucracy. Signing their lives away with the stroke of a pen.

I took the hypodermic from my pocket, removing the cap covering the spike. She wouldn't feel a thing, a small prick and then a long, long sleep.

A forever sleep.

The hypodermic trembled slightly in my hand. This was my first time. But the Master had told me I was ready and the Master was always right. Praise his power.

I leant over the bed and lifted her thin arm. Her eyelids flashed open revealing blue, almost turquoise, eyes.

'Hello, is it morning already?' her sleep-drenched voice asked.

The voice was old, crackling with knowledge and the tannin of thousands of cups of tea.

'Not yet, but I thought I'd check on you. It's time for your vitamin injection.'

Before she could respond, I took the wrinkled hand and turned it over to reveal the soft, sagging flesh on the inside of the arm at the elbow.

'But I don't have vitamin injections, I have tablets and I've already taken them.'

Her head indicated the plastic pill box lying on the bedside table. Each small compartment of the box labelled with large black letters. SUN, MON, TUES, WED, THU, FRI, SAT.

'This won't hurt a bit,' I said ignoring her words.

I inserted the needle into the soft part of the elbow, making sure I found a lovely vein, as clear as a blue tunnel, beneath the paper-thin skin.

Even though I was nervous, I had done it perfectly, she hardly felt a thing.

'Aren't you going to give me a cotton ball? They always give me a cotton ball after an injection.'

I smiled at her. 'Not this time. It's not necessary this time.'

She didn't resist as I took her in my arms, feeling the fine grey hair resting against my chest, watching as her eyes fluttered and closed, the blue vanishing for the last time, eyes seeing no more.

The Master told me this would be my favourite time; waiting for them to die. There would be a point where one moment they were alive and the next they were gone.

The Master was right. It was the perfect moment. A moment to be savoured, to be enjoyed.

I was in control. I was the chosen one, the Master had selected me to do his bidding. I was his humble servant, his tool to be used as he saw fit.

I saw a shadow outside the window. Was somebody there? Was somebody watching?

I laid her head back on the pillow and strode to the window, looking out into the moonlit night. A thin, watery light from a crescent moon, filtered through the haze of petrol and diesel fumes hovering over Manchester, casting shadows across the old garden.

Nothing there. I must have imagined it. The Master said I would be nervous. Praise his power.

I was about to turn back when I saw a small figure dash from the left, run across the lawn and climb over the fence at the back.

Had he been watching? Or was it one of the peeping toms who haunted this suburb like thieves in the night?

No matter.

I turned back to stare at the old woman and I knew she was dead. There was something missing, something intangible, something no longer there.

If I were a Christian or a believer in religion, I would have probably said the soul had departed the body, leaving behind a shell with the life force no longer there.

But I didn't believe in anything.

Except the Master of course. Hadn't he told me everything that was going to happen? Hadn't he understood my pain? Hadn't he helped me rediscover my purpose in life?

The Master was my everything. My beginning and my end and everything in between.

He had told me I would understand the beauty of taking a life. The overwhelming power and control of deciding who should die and who should live.

I looked down at the old woman lying on her bed and knew she was dead, and I had taken her life.

An immense sense of power flooded my body. I closed my eyes, experiencing the austere beauty of it all. The Master had told me the depression would follow soon after, though. With the power comes the glory and the sadness. I couldn't have one without the other.

I took hold of the old woman's wrist and felt for a pulse.

Nothing.

I had chosen this woman because she was the most active of the residents. She was always full of life, greeting everybody with a cheery wave and a loud 'Morning'. She was perfect for what they needed.

I placed the wrist beneath the bedcovers, tucking her in and adjusting her clothes. She would be found by the morning attendant bringing her a cup of tea.

Another one who had passed in the night. The usual words of respect would be spoken. The door would be locked. The doctor called and she would be pronounced dead over the phone.

A death certificate would be issued and she'd be carried away quickly, before the residents were up and about, to lie on a cold, stainless steel table.

Her last resting place.

I noticed the cross glistening in the faint light. Reaching out I seized it and pulled.

The thin gold chain held firm.

I pulled harder, but still the chain held.

I tugged once more, sharply this time; the chain snapped leaving the small cross wrapped in my fist.

I wanted a keepsake from her to remind me of the feeling I had standing over her bed, helping her to leave this world. A small memory to keep me warm at night.

I took out my phone to take a picture of her lying on her deathbed. He wanted a picture of her dead, proof she had gone.

She was the tenth, but it was my first.

The Master would be pleased. He was always pleased when they were killed.

Praise his power.

Monday, February 5.

Present day.

Chapter TWO

Detective Inspector Thomas Ridpath approached the hospital bed. The coroner, Margaret Challinor, was still lying in exactly the same position as the last time he had visited three days ago.

Outside, the wind was howling and the rain lashed down against the walls of the old hospital building. The drive out had been difficult, but still he kept coming whatever the weather. He couldn't leave her now.

Inside the ICU all was quiet. Mrs Challinor's grey corkscrew curls lay sprawled across the pillow like the arms of an octopus. Somebody had combed and rearranged them since the last time he visited, probably one of the nurses.

A tube led from her nose, along her face, past her hair up to a bag hanging over her head. Her arms and wrists were covered in electrodes all connected to a variety of machines at the side measuring her vital signs; heart rate, blood oxygen levels, breathing, blood pressure and intercranial pressure.

She had been like this for the last eight months when Alexandra Orwell had attacked her one evening while she was walking her dog. There had been bleeding on the brain and an operation was performed in order to relieve the pressure. The doctors had been hopeful of a speedy recovery but then Orwell had attacked again, this time injecting her with morphine.

The doctors had resuscitated her one more time, but ever since she had lain there in a vegetative state.

The last time Ridpath visited he had talked to her consultant, Mr Pereira.

'Will she ever recover?'

'It has been known. Some patients remain in a coma for years, then wake up, ready to face the world. But…'

'But?'

'Statistically, the odds are not great.'

'She's a statistic now, is she?'

'I'm sorry, detective, it sounds cold and uncaring, but you have to understand how we assess Mrs Challinor.'

'How *do* you assess her?'

'Normally, I would not discuss a patient with a non-relative, but as you have been visiting her for the last eight months, I will make an exception in your case.' He took a deep breath. 'In this hospital, we use two assessments for coma patients: the Glasgow Coma Scale and the FOUR score. In both, Mrs Challinor is classified as having a severe brain injury.' Mr Pereira picked up the patient notes from the end of the bed. 'In her last examination, she received a GCS score of seven with specific indications of E2V2M3. Her eyes are closed with swelling, she is intubated but there is a motor score of three because she retains a small reaction to pain. The FOUR assessment gives us slightly more detail; her eyelids are closed, there is an extension response to pain but her pupil and corneal reflexes are absent and she breathes slightly above ventilator rate.'

'What does it all mean?'

'It means Mrs Challinor received severe brain damage in her attack and we don't know if, or when, she will recover.'

He tried to digest this information. 'Thank you for your honesty, doctor.'

Off to one side, a single chair lay parked against a wall, Ridpath pulled it across to her bedside and sat down. 'Hello, Mrs Challinor, it's good to see you again.'

She didn't react to his voice. There had been no acknowledgement of his presence for a long time.

No caustic remarks.

No blunt honesty.

No penetrating wit.

Nothing but the beeping and the whirring of the machines keeping her alive.

He no longer felt embarrassed at talking to somebody who never responded. The doctors said it was good for her to hear voices she recognised. One day, they hoped, one of the voices would cut through the fog of the coma into which she had fallen. One voice, one reaction, one hint that she responded, that's all it would take to bring her back.

God, how he missed her.

The words of advice she offered. The reminders of what he was required to do. The constant desire to be an advocate for the dead in the land of the living. Officially, she was his boss, but their relationship was more than that; she was a colleague, a mentor, a friend.

'Not a lot has happened since the last time we had a chat.' He stopped for a moment realising 'chat' was hardly the right word for what was happening. 'Monologue' might be more appropriate.

He began again. 'Not a lot has happened since the last time I visited. Eve is doing well at school. I think she has a boyfriend now but she won't tell me who it is. I don't want to come over as the heavy-handed dad, but she's only fourteen so I think I have a right to know. What do you think?'

He glanced over at Mrs Challinor. The skin was still as perfect as ever, an almost quintessentially English peaches and cream, but there was a sadness to her face which Ridpath had never noticed before. Mrs Challinor was always so alive, so animated. Now she seemed a shell of the person he had once known.

He carried on. 'Sophia and Jenny send their love. Sophia is engaged to be married to her Irishman. Apparently, the parents have met him and reluctantly agreed. He seems a lovely man and she is deliriously happy. Jenny has taken to wearing black to the office, gone are her Fifties orange dresses. Apparently, Clarence Montague took her aside one day and told her such clothes weren't in keeping with the image of the coroner's office so in true style, she has gone from one extreme to the other. Montague is still the same, managing to annoy anybody and everybody on a daily basis but we've all become used to handling his particularly prissy ways.'

For a moment, he thought he saw a movement of her eyelid but after staring for a while, realised he had probably imagined it.

He continued on. 'He's removed all the Section 28s you signed and has vastly reduced the number of inquests we hold.' Ridpath imitated his voice. '"Our role is not to question the departments of government but to ensure the smooth, efficient and economical running of the coroner's department."' Ridpath coughed twice. 'I often think he would make a better accountant than a coroner. At the moment, he's on an economy drive, turning down the heating in the office and switching it off at night. The old building isn't the warmest place to work at the best of times and now we all wear coats inside. It's so cold in Court 1, I saw a polar bear yesterday wearing a jumper in the witness box.'

He looked for a reaction to his joke but there was none.

'Helen Moore has been promoted to Senior Coroner and is supporting him in his efforts to reduce the costs of running the office.' He took a deep breath. 'We all miss you so much and can't wait for the day you return.' Another breath. '*I* miss you so much…'

A woman stood at the entrance.

'Hiya, Ridpath. You're here again.'

It was Sarah, Mrs Challinor's daughter.

'Thought I'd visit before heading off to work. She's still the same though.'

Sarah Challinor stared at the woman in the bed. 'I wonder if she'll ever be the same again. I mean, if she comes round…'

'She's a fighter, she won't give up easily.'

'I know, but it's been eight months now. How…' Her voice broke.

Ridpath stood up and put his arm around her. 'It's okay, she'll come through this. You need to be strong for her.'

They pulled apart, embarrassed by their closeness. She placed her bag down on the table and pulled out a large book.

'Still reading it to her?'

'Mother's favourite, *War and Peace*. Trust her to love one of the longest books ever written. I said she'd be out of the coma before we finished it and now we have just one hundred pages to go.' She stared at the cover. 'I don't know if she'll ever come round, Ridpath.'

A nurse bustled into the room. 'Sorry, I need to turn the patient now, can't have her suffering from bed sores, can we?'

'I'll go, I have to get back to work. A meeting at Police HQ.'

'Meetings, don't talk to me about them,' answered the nurse. 'It's a wonder we get any real work done.'

He leant over and touched Mrs Challinor's white hand in a voiceless goodbye.

Picking up his briefcase from the chair, he walked towards the door. 'See you again, Sarah.'

She held up the book. 'I'll still be here, reading this to her.'

Ridpath attempted a smile. 'She'll come back to us.'

'I hope so. I do hope so.'

Then he left the room without looking back.

He could never look back. It was too upsetting seeing Mrs Challinor lying there on that hospital bed surrounded by wires and machines, not moving.

A husk not a person.

Chapter THREE

The afternoon meeting at Police HQ started on time at 2.30 p.m. Steve Carruthers, the new DCI in charge of the Major Investigation Team, had made it a less formal affair than in the days of DCI Turnbull. Because of those changes, it was infinitely more productive.

The seating was no longer the usual theatre style. Carruthers had decided instead all the detectives and civilian personnel should sit around a square table formed by the small desks. It led to quicker, more conversational meetings where information was exchanged without the usual grandstanding or – heaven forbid – the PowerPoint presentations beloved by Turnbull.

Ridpath sat in his usual corner and was soon joined by DS Emily Parkinson and Chrissy Wright, a civilian researcher, wearing her usual Manchester City scarf around her neck.

Carruthers called the meeting together in his inimitable Glaswegian accent. 'Right, ye lot, we are all busy and we don't have much time, so let's get down to it. James, why don't you go first, and remember to be brief.'

DS James Schneider coughed twice. He was another new import into MIT, this time from the divisional CID in Bolton, but had soon established himself as a rising star. 'We've been working on the stabbing in Chorlton and have a suspect in the frame. DFIU have been brilliant tracking the movement of the suspect's phone on Apple and Google maps.'

'Digital Forensics finally got back to you then?' asked Carruthers.

Schneider smirked. 'Thanks for the kick up the arse, boss. Since your phone call they haven't been able to do enough for us.'

'So when are we going to see an arrest?'

'The suspect is banged up in Strangeways at the moment on another charge and he ain't going anywhere soon. We want to make sure this one is trussed up better than a treacle pudding before we move forward.'

'I asked when we were going to see him being arrested and charged, I didn't want your granny's recipe.'

'End of the week, boss, at the latest.'

'I want to review what you've got with Claire Trent before we make any move.'

'Of course, boss. Where is the guvnor?'

'London, I think, on some anti-terrorism course at the Met. Rather her than me. I hate London, it ain't a patch on Glasgow... or Manchester,' he added as a nod to his present location.

'The problem with London is it's full of Londoners,' said James Schneider.

'He's quick this afternoon, you been on the Mars bars, James? Don't bother answering. Harry, what do you have for us?'

Harry Makepeace had been in MIT for almost as long as Ridpath. Six months ago he had been slated to retire, but Claire Trent and Carruthers had persuaded him to stay on until she had rebuilt the team. It had given him a new lease of life, proving once and for all there is always life in an old police dog.

He adjusted his tie, laid his notebook on the table and began reading from it. 'Yesterday, I travelled down to Surrey on the train...'

'Harry, Harry, just the top line not a bloody novel. We haven't got till next Christmas.'

'Sorry, boss, we're getting close on the Ryman brothers—'

'What does "getting close" mean exactly, Harry?'

'We're liaising with the National Crime Agency and Kent Police. Plus, we have decrypts from their phones. Our end is all tied up. We know where they take the illegals, where they keep them in Cheetham Hill and we even know the code for the safe where they stash all the documents.'

'Were they another set of idiots using Encrochat?'

'Yeah, even better, they carried on using it even after it was decrypted by the French.'

'So what's the hold up, Harry?'

'As you know, NCA are leading this and they've decided to wait for the next lorry load of illegals to arrive in Folkestone before the Rymans pick them up and bring them to Manchester. They want to get both ends of the line, boss.'

Steve Carruthers harrumphed. 'Or end up with both ends of nothing.'

'There's an added complication…'

'Which is?'

'The Rymans seem to be working with people traffickers across the Channel.'

'The small boats?'

'Right, so now the Home Office is involved with Border Security.'

'Lord help us, those radges couldn't run a piss up in a distillery. Okay, Harry keep at it and good work on the Manchester end.'

'Thanks, boss.'

'Finally, for the ongoing investigations, we have Sandra.'

'Ta, boss. We're working with a local CSE team in Salford, looking into a gang of men exploiting young boys hanging around Peel Park. They caught one of them with his pants down in the toilets, checked his home computer and found over thirteen thousand images on it. He hasn't stopped talking since. He's given up fourteen other names across Greater Manchester.'

'Who's involved?'

'A couple of teachers, a car mechanic, a doctor, we're looking into them now.'

'Tread carefully, Sandra, but make sure you nail the bastards. We don't want another Rochdale on our hands. The chief, and therefore Claire, will be looking at this one through a microscope. Have our "friends" in the press cottoned on to the investigation yet?'

'Not yet, boss.'

'Keep them away for as long as you can. This stuff is like meat on a bone for reporters, and inevitably they'll get in the way in search of a "story". I don't know who is worse.' He clicked his tongue. 'On that note, we'll go round the table. Any major problems? Issues coming up? Wee shenanigans that might bite us in the bum?'

Everybody around the table shook their heads. Only Chrissy raised her hand.

'A little warning, boss. HOLMES is a little glitchy at the moment so it might take a while to get intelligence.'

'When is it not glitchy, Chrissy? When Scotland is bathed in tropical sunlight?'

'Funny you should say it, boss, the techies are blaming sunspots.'

Carruthers stared out of the windows at the vast expanse of grey cloud stretching over Manchester away to the Pennines. 'Sunspots in this fair city in February? Wonders will never cease.'

Chrissy shrugged her shoulders. 'That's what they said, boss.'

'Aye, and the new yellow buses might fly. Anyway, let's leave our computer systems for the moment and find out what DI Ridpath has for us from the coroner's office.'

Ridpath opened his pad and read the figures Sophia had sent him. 'One hundred and eighty-nine deaths in Greater Manchester last week, two murders which you know about and a body found in the hills above Oldham.'

'Murdered too?'

'No, the initial medical examiner thought it was a heart attack while the man was out walking but we're waiting on confirmation from the pathologist. We are looking at four inquests from the 189 deaths.'

'Only four? The number seems low. I remember seeing figures of twenty to twenty-five inquests.'

'That was under Mrs Challinor. The new temporary coroner is less keen on investigating deaths. He's on a cost-saving drive...'

'Another one of those. When will they realise they save money in the short run and then spend millions rectifying the errors they made to save pennies.'

'You're speaking to the converted, boss.'

'Aye, I'll save my breath. So you're not busy at the moment?'

Ridpath hesitated before answering. Was this a loaded question?

'We're busy, boss, but not over-committed.'

'A wonderfully noncommittal answer, Ridpath, are you taking lessons in how to manage upwards?'

'When you work with Clarence Montague, boss, you learn to hedge your bets.'

'Good, well stay behind after this meeting, I may have something for your undoubted talents.'

Ridpath closed his eyes. Here it goes again, he thought.

Chapter FOUR

He lay on his bed in the cold cell, hands clasped behind his head, staring up at the ceiling. Somebody had written in pencil: *What are you looking up here for, the joke's in your hand.* He'd been meaning to wash it off for the last couple of weeks but hadn't done it yet.

Somehow, in here, time ran away from him. The days merging together, punctuated only by the usual chores; slopping out in the morning, breakfast, taking his drugs, planning his escape, back to his cell (he preferred to call it a room), lunch, a walk round the exercise yard, reading scientific journals, more planning, dinner, more reading and lights out.

Every day the same.

Every day, just as the last.

The only exceptions were Tuesday and Thursday when he met with his clinical psychiatrist. A ridiculous man with an over-inflated belief in his own divine wisdom and a neatly trimmed, poseur's beard.

What fun it was to stroke the man's ego; burnish his self-belief, play into his earnestness. One doctor to another, two intellectuals talking as equals.

His ridiculous dickie bow, corduroy trousers and brown brogues, a parody of a working psychologist. He had caught him once preening and combing his beard in front of the mirror in his office, his intellectual vanity almost as strong as his love for his appearance.

An idiot, but a useful idiot. A man he unfortunately needed, and one who had proved immensely valuable in the last few months.

He knew they were talking about him, having meetings in his absence, discussing his 'case', calibrating his 'mental health', evaluating his fitness to return to 'society', whatever that was.

One more meeting, one more session and he would be free. It had all been planned to the minutest detail. Nothing could go wrong. Nothing would be allowed to go wrong.

Then he could take his revenge on all those who had placed him in this hellhole. How had he survived being cooped up with 200 violent offenders in this place they called a hospital, but was actually a prison with wards?

He didn't know and he didn't care any more.

But now he'd set the wheels in motion, laid the trail leading to his trap. His adversary couldn't resist, there was too much at stake.

He felt his body beneath the thin cotton blanket. His ribs were sharp against his skin, the hip bone jutting out. He coughed twice, a harsh wracking cough. It wouldn't be long now.

A shadow appeared at the door. 'Exercise time, Lardner.'

The attendant – aka a prison officer – stared down at him. 'I'm not feeling too good, Mr Harrison.'

The officer moved into the cell. 'Stop faking it, Lardner, time for your exercise.' The voice was a little too loud in case other prisoners could hear, then a whisper. 'It's all arranged.'

'Good. All according to plan?'

'As you ordered. You need to be ready on Thursday.' Then louder. 'Lardner, I'll put you on a charge for refusing to exercise.' Another whisper. 'I've changed shifts according to your orders.'

'Good. Thursday it is.'

'Right, Lardner, you're on a charge.' The attendant stomped out, leaving the door open.

Harold Lardner smiled and stared up at the ceiling. Harrison was easy to manipulate, the death of his wife three years ago making him susceptible to a sympathetic doctor who understood the stages of grief and could help him through the bad times.

The man soon became as loyal as a pet dog, and, for a little extra remuneration, provided all those extra perks that made life in prison comfortable; a mobile phone, notice when his cell was being searched, a secure delivery service for his messages, security from the other prisoners and, more importantly, the other guards.

Noises from outside of his 'ward' echoed through the cell: the slamming of doors, the rattling of keys, the quiet swoosh of the drugs trolley along the linoleum floor, the constant chatter of the other inmates – some mad, others simply going mad.

On Thursday, he would be out of this place. For him, it couldn't come a moment too soon.

He sat up in bed. Time to check his notes once again, written in code of course. Harrison had warned him that they searched his room twice a week when he was in his sessions with the psychiatrist.

Idiots.

Even if they read his notes, they didn't have the intelligence to understand them.

He picked up the pen, studying his right hand with its swallow tattoo between the index finger and thumb. Prison ink blue but competently drawn, even if he did say so himself.

Perhaps, he should add a few more words to the graffiti on his ceiling before he left.

The Beast of Manchester was here might be apt.

Chapter FIVE

Ridpath remained behind as the other detectives left the room.

'How is Mrs Challinor?'

'Same as before, unfortunately. No change.'

'How long has she been in a coma now? Eight months isn't it? What's the prognosis?'

Ridpath shrugged his shoulders. 'Nobody knows, least of all the doctors. We're just waiting for her to come out of the coma.'

'Let's hope it happens soon. She's a good woman.' He opened a file and took out a sheet of paper. 'This has landed in our lap and we're giving it to you. This is all the information we have at the moment. As you heard at the meeting, everybody else in MIT is up to their necks in work.'

He passed over the paper and Ridpath glanced at the heading.

ANDREW GOLDING, AGED 14. MISSING SINCE MAY 22, 2020.

Beneath the headline was a picture of a young freckled-faced boy with ginger hair and a winning smile, the front tooth missing on the left of his mouth.

'I've seen the campaign run by his mother. Shouldn't this be handled by Missing Persons?'

'Normally yes, but you've put your finger on it. The campaign run by the mother has been effective at keeping the boy's disappearance front and centre. They are looking for answers and, so far, we haven't been able to give them any.'

Ridpath read the short description at the top of the report:

Andrew Golding left his house at 11.15 a.m. on May 22 telling his mother he was going out for a walk. This was during the height of the Covid-19 lockdown period in Manchester. He was told not to go far but, as he had been confined at home, she decided to let him go out.

He was wearing navy blue shorts and a striped T-shirt, carrying a Nike Merlin football. He was last seen close to Southern Cemetery. It is presumed he walked around this area and has not been seen since.

Posters and flyers were put up in Withington, Didsbury and Chorlton but no responses were forthcoming.

At present, he is still missing.

If you have any information regarding his disappearance, please contact Missing Persons at the following number: 0161 800 523

Ridpath looked up. 'What about CCTV? He must have been spotted, the streets were empty.'

'There's the problem: the mother didn't report him missing for two days.'

'Why wait so long?'

'They had an argument and he stormed out. She presumed he had gone to stay with his grandad.'

'Didn't she check?'

'Apparently not.'

'Why didn't she ring him?'

'She did but his phone was off. And before you ask, we haven't found it.'

'Surely Missing Persons tracked the number. They will have been able to follow his route through the number of stations he pinged.'

'They did… eventually. The phone was switched off close to the house at 11.24 a.m.'

'You still haven't answered my question, what about CCTV?'

Steve Carruthers held his hands up. 'We screwed up. Either we were incompetent, too lazy or too slow, but by the time the detective went looking for CCTV, the only image they could find was the one at the bottom of the report, taken from an ATM close to Southern Cemetery.'

'So he vanished roughly ten minutes after he left his house., nearly four years ago. No contact with the parents since?'

'None.'

'No sightings?'

'None.'

'No CCTV?'

'None.'

'Nothing since then?'

'Not a sausage.'

'What do you want me to do? You know the chances of finding him after nearly four years are slim to negligible?'

'I know, but Claire promised we would look into it.'

'And I'm the "we"?'

'Got it in one.'

'Clarence Montague isn't going to be a happy camper.'

'He's still giving you problems?'

'Like a rotten tooth that's been extracted but still aches.'

'No worries, let me handle him. He needs to remember *we* pay your salary and you are still officially employed by MIT.'

Ridpath realised this was his chance to address something that had been nagging at him for a long time.

'You realise I am still a probationary Inspector?'

Carruthers managed to feign ignorance by saying 'Really?', not very successfully in Ridpath's eyes.

'I was appointed just before I fell ill.'

'Cancer wasn't it?'

'Myeloma. Not the happiest day in my life. Anyway, I must now be the longest serving probationary Inspector at GMP. Normally, confirmation of the promotion happens within a year. For me, it's been far longer.'

'The cancer is in remission?'

Ridpath knew Steve Carruthers was deflecting from the issue but he answered anyway. 'Complete remission. I only have to take a pill every day and go for a check-up every three months. Apparently, I'm one of my consultant's most successful case studies. But when am I going to be confirmed as Inspector?'

'You're like a dog with a bone. Let me have a chat with Claire Trent and HR and we'll see what we can do. Yours is a difficult position, caught as you are between the coroner's office and MIT.' He stood up. 'Meanwhile, what resources do you need for the Golding case? The usual suspects?'

Carruthers was leading him out of the meeting room.

'Emily and Chrissy would be great if they are free?'

'You've got them. Plus I'm going to give you one of the new recruits, Helen Shipton, she's just come on board from CID in Oldham. She's a fast tracker and has a reputation for being a bright bunny. I want you to assess her for me. Let me know what she's like and what are her strengths or weaknesses. But I would advise you she is one of Claire Trent's hires – understood?'

'Enough said. I'll start straightaway on the Golding case. When do you want the report?'

'I didn't mention a time, did I?'

Ridpath arched an eyebrow. 'No, you didn't.'

'It would be great for your first report to be on Claire's desk when she gets back.'

'But that's in three days' time.'

'There you have it. Three days. Good luck, Ridpath. If you need anything, let me know.' He checked his watch. 'I've got a meeting with the deputy mayor in charge of policing and crime. Wish me luck? At least, she's another Scot.'

'You lot are taking over Manchester.'

'About time if you ask me.'

And with that, he disappeared down the corridor leaving Ridpath standing at the door.

'Good luck,' he whispered to the retreating back.

Chapter SIX

At the end of the corridor, Emily and Chrissy were waiting.

'You've got a job, haven't you?'

'Are we in on it?'

They were both standing in front of him, eager to get started.

'We have a job, but you're not going to be pleased when you hear what it is.'

Chrissy scratched her head, ruffling the short hair. 'Listen, Ridpath, I'm fighting with every computer system used by GMP at the moment and the computers are winning. Anything is better than dealing with the techies. Why do they have an answer for everything but none of them solve any of the problems, only creating at least three more?'

'And I'm with Harry on the Ryman case at the moment. It's going to be at least four weeks before the plods in Surrey are ready to move. Honestly, it's like working with zombies but without the energy.'

'Let's find a room and I'll brief you both. We're also supposed to work with a newbie, Helen Shipton. Do you know her?'

Both their faces fell.

'She's been dumped on you now? Has everybody said they don't want her?'

'What's wrong?'

'What's right?' Emily began to count on her fingers. 'Arrogant. Ignorant. Pushy. Selfish and stuck up. And those are just her good points. Everybody knows she's Claire Trent's blue-eyed little girl. Harry got rid of her like a shot and it sounds like Sandra has had enough too. Do we have to work with her, Ridpath?'

'Apparently we do, but she can't be that bad.'

'Wait till you meet her.'

Ridpath didn't have to wait long. A tall woman with flowing black hair appeared at the end of the corridor. 'Detective Inspector Ridpath? DCI Carruthers told me I'm supposed to run a case with you?'

'Helen Shipton?'

'The one and only.'

'Great, let's find a room and I'll brief you. Have you met Emily and Chrissy?'

The greeting was coolness personified. A quick wave of the hand followed by an even quicker, 'Hi.'

'This one's empty Ridpath, shall we use it?'

Emily pushed open the door and they all trooped in. Emily pushed a few tables together to form a rough square.

Ridpath took out the document given to him by Carruthers and passed it across. It was quickly snatched by Helen Shipton.

'We are tasked to look into the disappearance of Andrew Golding, aged fourteen, last seen on CCTV in the area near Southern Cemetery.'

Ridpath gently took the paper back from her and shared his briefing from Steve Carruthers with the group.

'Missing for four years, it's going to be tough, Ridpath,' said Chrissy.

'No CCTV. No phone records. No witnesses. Not a lot to work with,' added Emily.

'If it was easy, we wouldn't get it. Chrissy, can you get the Misper files for the case and find out exactly what they did and when. Also check up on HOLMES for any missing children in Manchester for this period.'

'Will the Home Office computer be any use?' asked Helen Shipton.

'It may show us if there were a pattern of disappearances at the time,' replied Ridpath.

'You're thinking it might not be a one-off?'

'I don't know, honestly, but a child doesn't just walk out of his house and disappear.' Ridpath tapped the photo. 'Helen, can you check the area around and within Southern Cemetery for CCTV cameras and plot them on a map, particularly the route from the boy's home.'

'Why? What's the use of that? The boy disappeared four years ago. It's grunt work, can't Emily do it?'

The other women's mouths opened wide.

'No, I want you to do it. We need to know the possible routes the boy took after he was last spotted on CCTV.'

'But there could be thousands of cameras and Southern Cemetery is immense.'

'It was once the biggest cemetery in Europe,' said Chrissy with a twinkle in her eye, 'little known fact.'

'What's Emily doing?'

'She's with me. We're going to visit the family. I want to know why they didn't report their fourteen-year-old child was missing for two days. And I want you to map the CCTV. Clear?'

There was no response from Helen Shipton.

'Am I clear?' he repeated.

'Yes, sir. I'm to map the CCTV around Southern Cemetery.'

Ridpath sighed. Should he tell her why? He hated explaining what he was thinking all the time. He had worked with Chrissy and Emily and they no longer asked him what was going through his head.

He decided to give Helen Shipton the benefit of the doubt this once. 'In previous investigations, we discovered banks and financial institutions keep their ATM footage for ninety days and then archive it in the Cloud. Manchester Council keeps it for thirty-one days and then overwrites it. But – and it's a big but – if there was an incident, for example, a theft, credit card fraud or a traffic accident, the footage will be kept for much longer.'

'*Soooo*, if we map the presence of CCTV and then cross-reference it with police reports and council traffic data for the day, we may find retained footage.'

'Got it in one.'

'It's still a long shot. The boy would have to be in the footage at the exact time there was an incident.'

'Not necessarily at the exact time if the footage is retained for the whole day.'

'I get it. Still a long shot.'

'After four years, we don't have much to go on. Right Emily, now we have convinced Helen we know what we are doing, let's go and see the mother.'

'I didn't mean to question you…' Helen stammered.

'You may not have meant to, but you did. We work as a team, Helen. That means everybody does their job no matter how dull or boring. Clear?'

'As Tetley's.'

Chapter SEVEN

'What did I tell you about Helen Shipton? She's managed to put the back up of everybody she has worked with. She even annoyed Harry, who's so laid back and ready for retirement he wears his slippers to work.'

'She's bright and she's quick, Emily, give her a chance. Remember what you were like when we first started working together?'

Emily thought for a moment. 'Aggressive, opinionated, bolshie.'

'And I'm glad to say, you haven't changed. She just wants to prove herself. Let's see how she gets on with the job I gave her.'

They had parked in an empty space on the street and were now walking to Andrew Golding's house. The neighbourhood had once been a medium-sized council estate famous for being the home of one of Manchester's most ruthless gangs. Now, they were long gone; either dead or in prison.

These days, the estate had been gentrified by people buying up the old council houses and selling them on to young couples no longer able to afford the rarefied prices of nearby Didsbury. The home they were visiting was a classic example; an old council house, modernised by the addition of an extension built to the side and rear, extending the liveable area.

Ridpath rapped on the door. And stood back, pulling his warrant card out of his pocket.

The door was opened by a young boy. Ridpath was startled to see he possessed an amazing resemblance to the missing child, ginger hair and freckles included.

Had the boy returned and nobody told them? Then logic took over and he realised that the child had disappeared four years ago and would now be eighteen. This must have been a younger brother.

'Mum, it's the coppers again.' He turned away and vanished back inside leaving them standing at the door.

After a few seconds, a grey-haired woman appeared, wiping her hands on an apron. Her face looked far younger than her hair. Overall, the effect was disconcerting as if she had prematurely aged.

'You lot again, what do you want this time?'

The voice was curt and aggressive.

'I'm DI Ridpath and this is DS Parkinson. Could we come in Mrs Golding?'

'It's not convenient, I'm cooking Alan's tea.'

'We won't be a moment, we'd like to ask you a few questions regarding Andrew.'

'It's Andy. I keep telling you people his name is Andy.'

Ridpath noted the use of the present tense in describing her son. He would have to be careful how he approached this woman.

'It won't take more than a few moments.'

She rolled her eyes and stood back, opening the door wider. 'You'd better come in then.'

As they followed her into the front room, she shouted upstairs. 'Alan, keep an eye on the steak and kidney pies, don't let them burn.' An unintelligible grunt from upstairs was the only response.

The woman shook her head and sat down on the sofa facing the television. Ridpath sat to one side on a chair and took out his notepad. Emily remained standing next to the door. The delicious aroma of cooked pie wafted through from the kitchen, Ridpath's stomach rumbled reminding him he hadn't eaten since breakfast.

'Right, Mrs Golding, I'm DI Ridpath—'

'You already told me your name and your rank.'

He ignored the interruption. 'I've been tasked to look into the circumstances of your son's disappearance in 2020…'

A long sigh. 'No offence but you are the fifth lot of coppers that have come to the house about Andy. First, there was the uniformed sergeant. He filled out a lot of forms. Then there was a keen young woman, Fiona, I liked her but she stopped coming after she got Covid and was moved to Eccles. Then there was the old guy who smelled of tobacco, what was his name, Bert something or other...'

'Bert Ramsden?'

'That's him. He never had a pen, I had to keep giving him one.'

Bert Ramsden was local CID. He'd now retired, spending most of his time on the golf course.

'Then there was the young copper, barely out of school, I can't even remember his name. And now there's you? I guess you've come because of the article in the *Evening News* at the weekend?'

Ridpath looked quizzically at her.

'You haven't read it? I am surprised. Your bosses did though, and it's why you've been sent here.'

Ridpath held his hands up. 'I haven't read the article. I'm sorry you feel you haven't been treated well.'

'It's not about being treated well, it's because my son's disappearance was never investigated properly.'

The voice rose at the end of the sentence and Ridpath could feel the anger.

'I'm here to investigate your son's disappearance, Mrs Golding, I promise you. Can I ask you a few questions?'

A sigh again, longer this time. 'Ask them.'

'When was the last time you saw Andy?'

She exhaled a frustrated breath and rolled her eyes, answering in a monotone. 'Like I've said a thousand times before. He left the house at 11.15 a.m. on May 22.'

'Did you see him leave?'

She stopped for a moment, surprised by the question. 'I heard the door slam shut and I looked out of the window to see him walking down the path to the front gate, carrying his ball.'

'You didn't stop him?'

'Well… no.'

'Did anybody else see him leave?'

'John was with me.'

'John?'

'You haven't done your homework, have you?'

Ridpath reddened. He should have done more research before coming to see this woman. 'My apologies, Mrs Golding, I wanted to move as quickly as I could to look for your son.'

'He's been gone nearly four years, a few hours wouldn't make much difference.'

She had a point. He needed to get up to speed on this case asap. 'My apologies once again.'

She smiled. 'To answer your question, John is – or was – my partner.'

'Could we speak with him?'

'If you can find him. He left a couple of years after Andy disappeared. Couldn't handle the stress or the strain. And before you ask, he was with me all the time after Andy vanished. We were in lockdown in Manchester, remember?'

'He never left the house?'

'No, and I didn't either. We'd been to Tesco's a couple of days earlier with some money Andy had given me—'

'Your son gave you money,' interrupted Emily, 'where did he get it?'

'I don't know. His grandad was always giving him money for doing errands. Anyway, that has nothing to do with it. We stayed in, didn't go out.'

'Even though your son was missing?'

'We'd had an argument, I thought he had gone to his grandad's.'

'You didn't ring him?' asked Emily.

The woman scowled. 'What are you inferring? I should have checked up on my son? It's my fault he disappeared? Don't look down your nose at me, you bitch. Don't you think I've asked myself again and again why I didn't ring? Why I didn't check earlier?'

Her voice rose and she seemed to be on the point of tears.

'I sat here and I expected him to walk through the door at any second with his usual swagger.' A long pause as she stared into mid-air before her eyes refocused again. 'I didn't know I'd still be sitting here waiting four years later.'

Ridpath glanced down at his notes and pulled out the picture of the missing boy. 'Is this a good likeness of your son?'

She stared at the picture and a smile slowly spread across her face. 'That's him, that's my Andy. This was taken a month or so before he...' She didn't finish the sentence.

Ridpath leant over. 'I couldn't help but notice he's wearing a medallion around his neck.'

She smiled again. 'His grandma gave him a St Christopher for his birthday. He never took it off, not even when he was taking a bath.'

'Right.' Ridpath made a mental note to follow up on this medallion later. For now, he had to confirm the details of the disappearance. 'So, the last time you saw him was before 11.15 a.m. on the 22nd? The reports say you argued with Andy. What about?'

'Nothing. We argued about nothing. He was sick of being cooped up in the house day after day. Andy loves going out, playing football, he isn't a stay-at-home kid. The lockdown was hard for him. He likes being outside.'

'Can we talk to his grandad?'

The woman shook her head. 'He died in 2020. Covid. Same as my nan.' A long pause. 'Nobody left now. Just me and Alan.'

A smell of burning pie wafted from the kitchen; Sharon Golding jumped, shouting, 'Alan, what are you doing?'

She rushed out of the lounge. From where they sat, Ridpath and Emily could hear the banging of oven doors and the crash of dishes into a sink. The smell of burnt pie became even stronger.

The door slowly opened and Mrs Golding came back in. 'It was my nan's recipe. I used to love her pies when I was growing up.' She sat down again facing them.

Ridpath glanced across at Emily. 'I think I have enough to be going on with. Anything you'd like to ask us?'

She stared at them both for a long time. 'When are you going to find Andy?'

'We'll keep looking, Mrs Golding, I promise you we'll never stop.'

'That's what Fiona said and the other copper, the one who stank of cigarettes. But they did stop, didn't they? Everything stops eventually. Nothing carries on.'

Chapter EIGHT

Outside, Ridpath took a deep, cold breath. And then another. It was as if the atmosphere in the house had made him physically sick. He had to get fresh air into his lungs to rid them of the weight of the sadness.

Emily shook her head. 'Poor woman. Lost her son, her partner and both her parents in the last couple of years. I don't know if I could handle it.'

Ridpath was still inhaling the freshest, lead-laden air Manchester could offer as they walked back to the car. 'Get on to Chrissy, we need the present address of the partner, John. We have to interview him as quickly as possible.'

'Will do, Ridpath.'

'Plus, find out when the nan and the grandad died of Covid.'

Emily nodded, scribbling away in her notebook as she walked.

'And I need the full case notes to read this evening. I don't want to meet Mrs Golding again without knowing all the details.'

'I'll ask Chrissy to get a move on and send them to you. We probably went to see her too quickly.' It was a mild rebuke for Emily.

'No, we *definitely* went to see her too soon. My fault, it won't happen again. Carruthers is rushing us to reach a conclusion. It's time we ignored him and did our job properly.' He thought for a moment and then spoke again. 'It's time *I* ignored him and did my job. Could you get me a copy of the *Evening News* article?'

She reached into her bag. 'I have a copy, picked it up from Chrissy.'

Ridpath scanned the headline and subheading:

MOTHER GRIEVES FOR LOST CHILD: WHY DIDN'T THE POLICE DO MORE?

An investigation by our Chief Crime Reporter, Alice Reynolds, into more police incompetence, this time involving the disappearance of a young boy, Andrew Golding, in 2020.

'Is this as bad as I think it is?'

'Worse.'

He folded up the cutting, placing it in his notebook. 'I'll read it later after I've looked at our reports.'

As they reached the car, his phone buzzed with a text.

> Where are you? His Lordship is demanding to see you.

'Sorry, Em, I need to go to the coroner's office. Clarence Montague wants to see me. Can you get back to HQ on your own?'

'Let me get my stuff out of the car and I'll call an Uber.'

He opened the door and she grabbed her haversack from the back seat.

Ridpath stood there for a moment staring into mid-air.

'Earth to Planet Ridpath, come in Planet Ridpath.'

He shook his head, refocusing his eyes. 'I don't have a good feeling about this one, Em. Something is wrong here, but I can't put my finger on it.'

'More than us screwing up?'

'A lot more. I wish I knew what it was.'

Chapter NINE

I walked among them, smiling here and there, nodding occasionally. They all recognised me in the home, looked forward to seeing me, smiling back when they saw my face.

'Good afternoon, Mrs Moorcroft,' I said to the old woman playing patience in the corner on her own. She looked up briefly from her game.

'Three times today. I've done it three times.'

She spends hours each day trying to get the cards to come out correctly. Sitting there on her own at the table, not speaking to anybody, only stopping when it was time to eat.

'Well done, Mrs Moorcroft, only four more to get out.'

That's her target; seven times a day, she has to complete the set and then she stops playing.

'Could be my earliest finish yet,' she answered, still turning over the cards, her eyes flitting rapidly from row to row looking for an opening.

I once tried to get her to do something else – play a game of bingo – but she wouldn't have it. No sooner had she sat down and begun to mark her game than she was up again and back to her usual place, turning over the cards.

What a pointless existence. Perhaps, she should be next. She has lovely eyes.

Or perhaps it should be Mr Owens? The one staring out of the window not moving, trapped in his own little world.

I tapped him on the shoulder. 'Would you like to sit down, Mr Owens?'

He ignored me. He always ignores me even when we are changing his adult diaper every night before he goes to bed, he never responds.

Never says thank you.

Never acknowledges our presence.

Never shows we are here.

Another pointless existence, waiting for the end to come.

Well, it will be soon, Mr Owens. I guarantee it.

I'd checked the man's files. No close relatives and no visitors since he came here. The Master's instructions were clear after we screwed up the first time four years ago: 'Make sure there are no mistakes. Mistakes will be punished. The selection must have no ramifications. Understood?'

The Master was right. Praise his power.

Mr Owens looked the perfect candidate. Healthy as a butcher's dog, the doctor had given him a clean bill of health just three weeks ago.

Perfect.

It's decided then, Mr Owens it is. I'll alter his file and get him to sign the release form. Silly chough will sign anything as long as I promise not to disturb him.

I won't do anything until I receive his orders, though. The Master will decide when it is time.

I will simply enjoy the kill.

It was then Mr Owens looked directly at me for the first time. A look saying: I know what's happening, I know what's going on.

Then the old man turned back to stare out of the window again, not moving.

Had I imagined it? Did Mr Owens know what I was planning?

'Don't be silly,' I whispered to myself, 'you're imagining things.' He was an old man deprived of liberty, stuck in here until he died or was helped to die.

He couldn't know what was happening, could he?

Chapter TEN

'Sorry about the text Ridpath, but he's been on the warpath for the last hour.' Sophia was sitting at her desk facing his, a venti Starbucks latte in front of her.

'Doesn't he know it's my day with MIT?'

'Of course he does.'

In the last six months, and with the absence of Mrs Challinor, Ridpath had instituted a new work schedule. Mondays and Thursdays were spent at MIT, with the rest of the week in the coroner's office. In the main, it had worked well. But occasionally, Clarence Montague – Mrs Challinor's temporary replacement as Head Coroner – threw his toys out of the pram. This was one of those days.

'Do you know what it's about?'

'Haven't a clue. Way above my pay grade,' she answered with heavy irony. 'I did ask if I could help, but was told "I need to see Mr Ridpath, not his clerk."'

'Sorry, Sophia.'

'Look, Ridpath, I don't know how much more of this I can take. I know I'm fairly junior and low down on the pecking order but to be constantly reminded of it?'

He sat opposite her. 'You know how valuable you are to me and to the coroner's office. Without you, we simply couldn't function. Let me talk with him again.'

She leant forward. 'It's not just him, I've got my wedding to arrange and everything. Do you know what it's like to get four thousand aunties to agree on anything? And Ronan not being Muslim adds to the pressure. I don't know if I can handle all of that and Clarence Montague at the same time. The place is not the same since Mrs Challinor...' Sophia tailed off.

'I know, we all miss her. But I don't want to lose you. It's purely selfish of me, but I can't manage without you.'

'I'm sorry, Ridpath, I have to start thinking of myself, my own mental health.'

Clarence Montague appeared in the doorway. 'Ah, Ridpath, you're finally here. Can you come to my office... Please.'

The temporary coroner was the only man Ridpath knew who could make the word 'please' sound like a rebuke.

'I'll be there shortly, Mr Montague. I have something to finish with Sophia first.'

The coroner stood there for a moment, harrumphed and turned away to return to his room.

Sophia watched him go. 'He's like a child thinking only of his needs and his wants. Jenny has had enough, too.'

'She's not leaving?'

'She's thinking about it. Been here since she left school. It's the only job she's ever had.'

Ridpath shook his head and stood up. 'Let me talk to him. But promise me you won't do anything rash without telling me first. Promise?'

She smiled. 'Cross my heart and hope to die.'

'Not the sort of thing you say in a coroner's office, Sophia. And anyway, if you left, who would do your paperwork?'

'Not you, Ridpath, that's for sure.'

Ridpath gestured over his shoulder. 'I'll go and see him now.'

'Good luck.'

'Will I need it?'

'Probably. Everybody else does.'

He walked down the short corridor and knocked on the door, waiting five seconds for the perfunctory word, 'Enter'. When it didn't come, he walked in anyway.

Clarence Montague was exercising in front of the large picture window by swinging his arms backwards and forwards and bending his knees slightly.

'You wanted to see me? But if you're busy I could come back later.'

Montague's face reddened and he moved quickly back to the safe area behind his desk. 'No, come in and sit down.'

Ridpath did as he was told, sitting opposite the man as he rearranged the papers on his desk.

'I've been looking for you all day, but you weren't around.'

'It's my day at MIT, but you know that. It was the arrangement.'

'This "arrangement" as you call it, is no longer the most efficient for the coroner's office. As I am sure you are aware, being a coroner's officer is a full-time role, but it is one you have decided to perform in a part-time capacity.'

'It was agreed with Mrs Challinor. It worked well under her.'

'As you may have noticed, Mrs Challinor is no longer here. I have been given responsibility for the efficient and professional running of this office and I see it as my duty to ensure it carries out its duties and responsibilities to the people of Manchester with alacrity.' He smoothed down the outsides of his grey moustache. 'I have spoken with the Chief Coroner and he has agreed the running of this office is my responsibility until Mrs Challinor returns to the office – if that happens at all.' The last words were added as an aside.

Ridpath was sick of constantly arguing in circles with this pompous old man but he couldn't let such a snide remark go unchallenged. 'I'm sure Mrs Challinor will be coming back to work as soon as she recovers from the attack.'

'We will see. Anyway,' he continued quickly, 'I haven't called you in here to discuss Mrs Challinor.' He picked up a sheet of paper and passed it across. 'This arrived on my desk this morning.'

The paper was from an ordinary writing pad. At the top in the centre, the words: *SunnySide Residential Home for the Aged* in a bright green cursive script with a stylised drawing of an Edwardian house and garden. Beneath the logo, someone had scrawled.

They are killing us. Help us. We don't want to die.

'Is this all?'

'Yes, that's it.'

'No envelope?'

The coroner looked surprised for a moment. 'It came in one. I have it here somewhere.' He scrabbled beneath his desk, rooting through his wastepaper basket. 'Here it is.' He held it up triumphantly.

Ridpath took his handkerchief out of his pocket and held the corner of the envelope with the cotton guarding his fingers. He laid the envelope carefully down on the coroner's desk next to the letter itself.

The envelope also bore a smaller version of the green logo on the top left-hand corner. Below, somebody had scrawled an address in the same pen as the message.

The Head Coroner

East Manchester Coroner's Court

Manchester

'Is this real?' asked Clarence Montague.

'It exists, whether it's real or not. The rest I can't answer. When did you receive it?'

'This morning with all the other post. I opened it up and was shocked by the contents.'

Ridpath glanced at the envelope again. There was no stamp but it had been run through a franking machine and given a first class mark. Next to the franking lines was a round date stamp from the post office.

'Received yesterday and delivered this morning. First class post works for once. Interesting about the address.'

'What do you mean?'

'It's generic, not addressed to you or anybody in particular, just to a "Head Coroner". Plus, there's no street address.'

'Meaning?'

'Whoever sent it, didn't know this address. They tried to guess it and relied on the Post Office to deliver the letter.'

'I have received an instruction from the Chief Coroner, who has made it clear all whistle-blowing letters must be treated and investigated in the strictest confidence. I think it's a reaction to the lack of action following bullying complaints in the civil service.'

'I don't think this is a whistle-blower's letter.'

'How do you know?'

He pointed to the letter. 'The message talks about "us". They are killing *us*, but the headed notepaper is from the SunnySide Residential Home, suggesting it was sent by one of the residents rather than a member of staff.'

'We should forget it then.' He went to take the letter and the envelope.

Ridpath reached out and stopped him.

'No, I think we should look into it. Mrs Challinor was always clear that, after Harold Shipman, any allegation of death amongst old people or at hospitals or surgeries needs to be investigated.'

The mention of Mrs Challinor's name annoyed Montague.

'It reads like the words of a madman. "They are killing us. Help us. We don't want to die." Those are hardly the words of a sane man.'

'Firstly, we don't know if they were written by a man. And secondly, they are a cry for help. We cannot ignore it.'

'I'm not having you wasting my department's time and money traipsing around Manchester following up some madman – or madwoman's – letter.'

'But what if it's true?' Ridpath challenged. 'The lack of action during the Shipman killings led to a parliamentary inquiry about failings in the police and in the coronial service. We wouldn't want that to happen again, would we?'

Montague thought long and hard, obviously weighing up the pros and cons of investigating this letter. Before he answered, Ridpath asked him one more question. 'Why did you show it to me?'

'I thought it… I… I don't know, I found it… disturbing,' he blurted out finally.

'And that's why we need to look into it. As a coroner's office, we need to know.'

He stood up, pushing the chair back under the desk and placing the letter and the envelope into an empty clear file scrounged from Montague's desk. 'I'll start straight away.'

The head coroner said nothing, but nodded once. Ridpath took the nod as a go-ahead.

Now he had two investigations when he had had nothing this morning. He walked to the door, turning as he touched the handle.

'One final thing. I've talked with some of the staff. There is a deep unhappiness at the way you are treating them and their work. You could have resignations if you are not careful.'

A smile crept across Montague's face like a thief in the night.

'Frankly, I am not surprised. For too long the staff of this office has ignored the sensible precepts of the government and its legal entities, being run expensively and inefficiently. You should remember, Ridpath, change is good. If we have to change staff to achieve greater efficiency and save money, it will happen. Nothing must stand in the way of progress.'

'But you will lose years of institutional knowledge and experience. It will be like the police where we lost twenty thousand experienced officers and replaced them with people who wouldn't know their arse from their elbow.'

'I'll thank you not to use that sort of language in my office, Ridpath. You should realise change is coming. Are you going to stand in its way or are you going to join it? It's the choice you need to make.'

Ridpath had had enough of this insufferable man. He turned to go.

'One more thing I think you should know. The Chief Coroner has decided this office has lacked a leader for far too long. They have decided to appoint a head coroner to replace Mrs Challinor.'

'But they can't do that, she wants to return.'

'Has she told you? Last time I checked, she was still in a coma. Anyway, the position will be advertised shortly and I have decided to apply. I will look forward to making this office the best and most efficient in the coronial department.' He looked down at his desk diary. 'You can leave now. I have to interview a Mrs Johnson, a possible private secretary for my office.'

Ridpath was still fuming as he walked back to his office. In the corridor, he bumped into Helen Moore, the deputy coroner.

'What's this I hear about Mrs Challinor being replaced?'

She frowned. 'What? First I've heard about it. Anyway, they can't replace her, she's still on medical leave.'

'Montague has told me they will be advertising the position soon. Apparently, they can't wait for Mrs Challinor to get better.'

'They have to wait. Mrs Challinor *is* the East Manchester Coroner's Court. She's been here more than twenty years.'

'Not according to Montague.'

'Let me check it out. I know one of the clerks in the Chief Coroner's department. It can't be true.' She made to walk on then stopped. 'Oh, and Ridpath, have you investigated the death of Mr Frederick Means yet? The inquest opens in two weeks and I haven't seen your report.'

'Sorry, I've been out all day. It's on my laptop. I want to give it one more read and then I'll send it to you. You'll get it first thing tomorrow.'

'The pathologist's report has come in?'

'Dr Schofield's report is included along with toxicology. Apparently, Mr Means had smoked cannabis before his death.'

Her eyes rolled upwards. 'That complicates the case. Could his fall from the roof of the building have been a result of his cannabis use?'

'According to the doctor, the man did have THC in his blood-stream at the time of his death. But the direct cause of death was the failure of the safety harness. The Health and Safety expert, Josh Harley, is firmly of the opinion the harness wasn't fit for purpose.'

'Right, thanks. The cannabis use does muddy the waters though. The barrister for the builders will argue the case and cast doubt in the mind of the jury. Why is nothing straightforward any more?'

She wandered off back to her office at the end of the corridor.

'I'll get it to you first thing tomorrow,' Ridpath shouted after her.

She waved her thanks without turning around. Ridpath continued to his office. Sophia was no longer there but a note affixed to the screen of the computer said:

> Chrissy called. All the files are in your Dropbox at MIT. If you need anything, call me.

What would he do without all these women who made his life possible? Chrissy, Emily, Sophia.

And then it hit him. What would he do without Mrs Challinor?

Chapter ELEVEN

Ridpath stepped into the hall of his house and called out, 'Eve, I'm home.'

There was no answer.

'Eve, I'm back.'

Still no answer.

He frowned. Where was she? He was about to ring her best friend Maisie's home when Eve appeared behind him out of breath.

'Sorry, Dad, late this evening.'

She pushed past him, hanging her coat on the stand in the hallway.

'Where were you?'

'At Maisie's, doing homework. Lost track of time. I'm starving, what is there to eat?'

'I ordered pizza on the way back. Should be here in a minute.'

He followed her into the kitchen where she was already rooting in the fridge looking for something to nibble.

She held up a bit of Cheshire that had seen better days and a carrot on its last legs.

'Sorry, I'll get to the supermarket tomorrow. No time today. The pizza will be here soon.'

He looked across at her. When had she become so tall? She was now the same height as the fridge. He remembered when she could barely open the door and certainly couldn't reach the top shelf. She was looking more and more like her mother. Her nose had a slight upturn and her eyes had a glint of devilment he used to love in Polly. At least she hadn't started dyeing her hair.

Not yet.

Her eyes lit up and she pulled out a jar of peanut butter.

'I wouldn't eat that. You don't know how long it's been there.'

She checked the lid. 'The sell-by date says... 20 September 2021. Only three years ago and peanut butter doesn't go bad, does it?'

She grabbed a slice of bread from the bin. Ridpath heard the crunch of the crust as it hit the chopping board.

'I wouldn't eat the bread either, the pizza—' He was interrupted by the sound of the doorbell. 'What did I tell you?'

He grabbed his wallet and went to the front door, expecting to see Uber Eats with his margarita pizza held in front of him. Instead, a young, rather spotty man, stood there.

'Eve, forgot this.' He held out a pencil case which Ridpath took. 'Are you her dad? She talks a lot about you and the police.'

Ridpath stood there, not saying anything, words refusing to leave his throat.

'Well, tell her I'll see her tomorrow. See ya, Mr Ridpath.'

With those words he turned and walked down the path.

'I didn't catch your name,' shouted Ridpath.

'It's Billy to my friends. Tell Eve I came round.'

Ridpath closed the front door and went back into the kitchen.

'Who's Billy and why does he have this?'

Eve looked down at the bright green pencil case and blushed, the heat starting at her neck and rising slowly up her face.

She sucked in air. 'I was going to tell you about Billy...?' she finally answered.

'Go on, I'm listening.'

'Well, we met a few times on the tram. He's at college and we got talking.'

'I thought you said you were studying at Maisie's tonight?'

'Did I?'

'Yes, definitely.'

'So what are you going to do now, Dad, rewind the tape and point out my mistake? But you haven't read me my rights yet.

"Eve Ridpath, you do not have to say anything. But, it may harm your defence if you do not mention when questioned something which you later rely on in court. Anything you do say may be given in evidence.'" She held out her arms in front of her. 'You going to handcuff me now or later?'

Ridpath recognised the tactic from countless police interviews: when under threat, go on the attack.

'Don't be silly, Eve. I'm simply pointing out you said you were at Maisie's when it was obvious you were with this... boy.'

'He has a name you know, it's Billy. And I'm simply pointing out I feel like I'm being given the fourth degree here.'

Ridpath smiled. 'It's the third degree and it comes from the questions given in Freemasonry when a person wants to become a master mason.'

'Whatever. Are you going to give me one of the funny hand-shakes now?'

'Eve, you know I'm not a Freemason. The police have been handicapped for too long by their peculiar form of insularity. But let's not change the subject. Were you or were you not with this boy this evening?'

She stood up. 'None of your business,' she shouted.

'It is my business, I'm your father.'

'Exactly, you're my father not my copper, my inquisitor or my jailor. Don't you trust me or something?'

'It's not about trust...'

'Oh, it is Dad. It's all about trust.'

The doorbell rang loudly. To Ridpath's ears it sounded exactly the same as the bell at the end of the first round of a boxing match.

'The pizza is here.'

'I'm not hungry.'

She stormed out of the kitchen and stomped up the stairs in the manner only a teenager could stomp.

He was left sitting in the kitchen.

The doorbell rang again.

'Round Two,' he muttered to himself before going to the door.

Chapter TWELVE

He'd gone to her bedroom door twice over the last hour to ask her to come down to eat the pizza. Each time he was met with a firm, 'Go away.'

Finally, he put four slices on a plate and left it outside her door. At least, if she was hungry she could eat when she wanted.

He realised he hadn't handled the whole conversation well. He'd been both flippant and demanding. Not the right way to deal with a teenage girl.

But why hadn't she told him the truth? Why had she lied to him? They had always been honest with each other in the past, why had she suddenly started to lie?

He tried to think back to when he was the same age: spotty, unkempt, obsessed with football and totally lacking in any consideration for anybody but himself.

Eve was different. She seemed more aware of the world and its issues than he had ever been. More conscious of those around her, less selfish, far more aware. A function perhaps of growing up in a world surrounded by social media, 24/7 news, and Covid.

He settled down at the kitchen table and logged onto his laptop. He couldn't solve the problem with Eve at the moment, he'd try to have a word with her in the morning.

Right now, he had to get on top of the missing child case.

He checked his emails and found Chrissy had sent him the initial police missing person report. He scanned through the initial blurb at the head of all misper reports and then turned the page to the completed form, checking the signatures at the end first. The investigating officer was a Sergeant Aiden Markham and the duty inspector was Stephen Warner.

PERSONAL DETAILS AND DISAPPEARANCE CIRCUM-
STANCES

W1 British Male ANDREW GOLDING, aged fourteen last
birthday, reported missing, last seen 11.15 a.m., May 22,
2020. Report made at 12.55 p.m. on May 24, 2020 by his
mother, MRS SHARON GOLDING. Andrew went out of the
house at 11.15 a.m. and never returned. Mother thought he
had gone to stay with his grandad. She checked later and
when she discovered he hadn't been there, she reported it
to the police. Due to operational conditions, we went to the
house on the following day, May 25 at 2.15 p.m.

Ridpath shook his head. A child is reported missing and the
police don't arrive until the following day? He wrote a note to
himself.

What operational conditions? Why so late?

**CLASSIFICATION OF RISK AND RESPONSE (ACPO
Manual of Guidance 2005 – Para 3.5)**

High: There is an immediate risk and definite grounds for
believing the missing person is at risk through their own vulner-
ability or mental state, or there are grounds for believing the
public is at risk through the missing person's mental state.
Such cases should lead to the appointment of a senior investigating officer (SIO). There should be a press/media strategy
and/or close contact with outside agencies.

Medium: The risk posed is likely to place the missing person
in danger, or they are a threat to themselves or others. This
category requires an active and measured response by police
and other agencies in order to trace the missing person and
support the person reporting.

Low: There is no apparent risk of danger to either the missing
person or the general public.

After consultation with Inspector STEPHEN WARNER, ANDREW GOLDING's risk was assessed as HIGH.

MISSING PERSON REPORT

Section 1 – Administrative details

Surname/family name: GOLDING

Fore/given name: ANDREW

MP Reference No.: 1007/2020/APC2W3UUHJ9

Div/Area: SOUTH MANCHESTER

Website consent signed: YES

OIC/IIO name: AIDEN MARKHAM (SGT 1007)

DNA source available: YES

If YES – give details: HAIR BRUSH

DNA source current location: MFH FILE

Blood group: A+

Dental chart available: YES

Dental chart sent to MFH sect: YES

Mobile phone no. available: YES

Photo available: YES

Photo sent to MFH sect: YES

Section 2 – Misper's personal details and disappearance circumstances

Age: 14 YEARS OLD

DOB: 20 June, 2006

Ethnicity: WI

Hair style: SHORT. PARTING ON LEFT

Glasses: NO

NI no: NONE

Sex: MALE

Religion: CHRISTIAN

Last seen on: May 22, 2020

Transgender: NO

Build: SLIGHT

Disability: NONE

Eye colour: BROWN

Nationality: BRITISH

Sexuality: N/A

Mental impairment: NONE

Place of birth: MANCHESTER

Marital status: SINGLE

Relationship of informant to misper: MOTHER

Surname: GOLDING

Forename: SHARON

Date of Birth: 14 August, 1973

Information: GRANDFATHER – ERNEST GOLDING. 12 BRINDLEY STREET.

Details of clothing and jewellery believed to be worn or in misper's possession: STRIPED T-SHIRT, BLUE SHORTS, NIKE SNEAKERS. ST CHRISTOPHER MEDALLION ROUND NECK. MAY HAVE BEEN CARRYING NIKE MERLIN FOOT-BALL AND MOBILE PHONE.

Last seen location: HOME. 11.15 A.M. MAY 22, 2020

Last seen by: MOTHER

Who are they missing with? ALONE

Reason for disappearance: POSSIBLE ARGUMENT WITH MOTHER. RUNAWAY?

Venue searched by: AIDEN MARKHAM (SGT)

Known mental health issues: NONE

Previous history of wandering: NONE

Address previously found: NONE

Garden/garage/outbuildings searched? YES

Local parks/fields/school grounds/vehicle searched? NO

Search authorised by: SHARON GOLDING (MOTHER)

There it was, the bare outlines of the disappearance of a young boy. He always found these misper forms incredibly sad. In the last figures he saw, over 200,000 incidents of missing children were reported in England. Most were found quickly but over 1500 were classified as long-term missing. In other words, they had simply vanished and had never been found.

It appeared Andrew Golding was one of those 1500. And for each of them, there was a form lying in some police archive somewhere, gathering dust, unsolved.

He stood up and stretched. Just three more reports to go through to bring himself up to speed.

Above his head he heard the floorboards creaking followed by the bedroom door closing. Should he go upstairs and check on Eve?

Probably not. His presence was about as welcome as a City fan in the Stretford End. He opened the living room door and listened.

All quiet.

He crept up the stairs to the landing and peered around the corner. The pizza plate was sitting outside her bedroom door with only two slices still remaining. At least she had eaten.

He crept back downstairs as quietly as he could, so she wouldn't think he was checking up on her, even if he was.

Chapter THIRTEEN

After making himself a pot of tea, he sat down and thought about switching on the television to watch something mindless.

Outside, the wind was blowing through the leafless trees and the next door neighbour's garden gate was banging. Should he go out and close it for him? Eve wouldn't be able to sleep if it banged all night.

And then the noise ceased. He heard his neighbour's voice carried on the wind. 'I've closed it now, love. Bloody thing was driving me potty.'

Me too, Ridpath agreed.

He glanced at his laptop with his notes lying next to it. He had to finish reading the reports. As senior officer, it was his duty to know the ins and outs of the case off by heart. He couldn't rely on anybody else, it was his job, his duty.

He sighed loudly and sat down at the table to log on.

He checked the pages attached to the Form 737. The first was a report from Fiona Barton, a detective constable in West Didsbury who had been appointed as the SIO on the case.

27 May, 2020

Appointed SIO into the disappearance of ANDREW GOLDING on May 22 at 11.15 a.m.

Immediately instituted following actions:

Searched local area for CCTV

Interviewed family

Checked his room for diaries/notes. None found

Visited grandfather of missing boy

Tried to visit grandmother, but passed away three weeks ago

Discussions with misper team

Actions going forward:

Press release with image of missing boy

Check HOLMES for disappearances of similar young people

Visit school and talk to teachers

Exactly the steps Ridpath would have followed, straight out of the police manual. But why was she only appointed to look into the disappearance two days after the police visited the family's home?

They had missed the golden hour, the special time around the disappearance when memories were fresh and CCTV even fresher.

He yawned and checked the time: 11.30 p.m. He'd push through as there were only four more reports to read.

The next one was shorter and even more concise. DC Barton wasn't one for long-winded reports. A woman after Ridpath's heart.

28 May, 2020

Actions:

Discovered CCTV of ANDREW GOLDING. Near Southern Cemetery at 11.23 a.m.

No other CCTV available

School says he was a quiet boy, bright, sporting on school football team

Revisited family. Mother admitted argument on morning of disappearance

Press release: two positive sightings both in Southern Cemetery

Actions going forward:

Issue another press release

A walk-through of his last journey?

Check misper files

Check discovered bodies

Check morgues

The last two notes suggested to Ridpath DC Barton believed Andy wasn't a runaway. She had obviously come to the conclusion he was dead.

Why was she so certain? He needed to talk to her if he was going to get anywhere in the investigation.

He found another note in the file from a week later. This time in a different type font.

DATE: 4 June, 2020

I, Albert Ramsden, Detective Constable, have taken over the case from DC Fiona Barton.

I visited the family. Nothing to report.

I circulated the information and misper report to the UK Missing Persons Unit at the National Crime Agency, uploading data to HERMES, the MPDD and POLKA.

DATE: 25 September, 2020

Reviewed case with Inspector Stephen Warner.

Nothing to report except death of grandfather, Ernest Brindley, on 12 September, 2020. Have tried to find witness statements from Fiona Barton but appear to be missing.

Checked misper report at the UK Missing Persons Unit at the National Crime Agency. Updated HERMES and POLKA.

DATE: 25 October, 2020

Reviewed case with Inspector Stephen Warner.

No new leads or information.

In the absence, nothing to report.

Checked misper report to the UK Missing Persons Unit at the National Crime Agency. Uploaded latest details to HERMES and POLKA.

No leads from MPDD.

The case was then reviewed on the same date each month with exactly the same note attached each time.

DATE: 25 March, 2022

Case transferred to probationary Detective Constable Agnew, J.

Reviewed case with Inspector Stephen Warner.

Visited family on 31 March, 2022.

No new leads or information.

Checked misper report to the UK Missing Persons Unit at the National Crime Agency.

No leads from MPDD.

After Bert Ramsden retired, the case was passed to a new detective who'd just come out of the academy. He only visited the family once, a week after he had been put on the case. It was obvious the police had already given up on finding Andrew Golding and put the case in the 'too difficult to handle' box, simply passing on bits of paper from one unit to another.

Ridpath would have to check with Chrissy what MPDD, HERMES and POLKA were. These days there were more police acronyms than he'd had hot dinners.

He turned over the final page, finding a last unsigned note.

DATE: February 7, 2024

Case and notes transferred to Major Incident Team following report in the Manchester Evening News. Contact now DCI Steve Carruthers.

So that's how it had landed up in Ridpath's lap. The GMP didn't come out of this smelling of roses. Too late to start investigating, heavy churn of investigating officers, missing key evidence, lost witness statements and CCTV, plus lack of communication with the family.

He shook his head. That poor mother. Not only had she lost her mum and dad, and her son, the investigation had been shoddy from the start.

He took out the folded newspaper report from his notebook. It covered virtually the same ground as the internal reports, with the added perspective of the family's reactions to the lack of progress in finding Andy. It looked like the reporter had access, had done her research and had also spoken to somebody at GMP.

A disgruntled clerk?

Somebody looking for a back hander?

One of the investigating officers covering their backside?

Whatever.

It had created a stink amongst the senior management and the old adage held true: shit always flows downhill and he was the one left to clear up the mess.

Ridpath sighed. It was the family he felt sorry for. Imagine losing your fourteen-year-old son? How would he feel if he lost Eve? Devastated and unable to continue.

These people deserved better. He would try to make it right for the family, but after such a long time, he wasn't certain how much he could do.

What he was sure of, though, he would not allow this investigation to become a face-saving exercise for his bosses. He'd use all the resources at his disposal to find out what had really happened. It's what Sharon Golding and her son deserved.

Nothing more, nothing less.

He was about to close his laptop and go to bed when he remembered the report for Helen Moore into the death of Frederick Means. He read it through carefully. The safety report was damning but the cannabis use would muddy the waters. How would Helen handle it during the inquest? Would she be as tough as Mrs Challinor on a company who didn't maintain their safety equipment?

He didn't know, but he would have to find time to attend the inquest when it happened. Luckily, it wasn't for another two weeks yet.

He sent the report to her with a note attached asking for a meeting to take her through the contents and the statements from the various witnesses.

Another meeting.

He yawned and closed his laptop. Wearily, he climbed the stairs to his bedroom, noticing as he passed Eve's room the two last two pieces of pizza were now missing from the plate. At least she'd eaten that evening.

He would have to try to repair bridges with her tomorrow but he was still annoyed she hadn't told him the truth about the boy.

Enough, Ridpath. Let it rest. That was a problem for tomorrow.

He opened the door to his bedroom, seeing the unmade, empty bed from this morning. For a fleeting moment, he experienced the most awful pang of loneliness.

Polly wasn't there.

Tuesday, February 6.

Chapter FOURTEEN

The following morning Ridpath was up bright and early. He made coffee for himself and some toast for Eve. After checking the clock at 7.45, he called upstairs.

'Eve, time for school.'

No response.

'You'll be late if you don't hurry.'

Still no response.

He ran upstairs and knocked on the door. 'Eve, it's time to go.'

The door opened sharply and she stood there fully dressed and ready to leave. 'Keep your hair on, I'm ready.'

'Don't you want to eat breakfast?'

'I'm not hungry.'

'You've got to eat something.'

'I said I'm not hungry.'

Ridpath rolled his eyes. It was going to be one of those mornings. 'Okay, let's go.'

He went downstairs, finished the last of his coffee, packed up his laptop and briefcase, and put on his jacket.

She was waiting for him at the door, silently tapping her fingers on the newel post at the bottom of the stairs.

'Just take me to the tram station.'

'No worries, I can drive you to school this morning, I've got time.'

She opened the door and stepped outside. He closed it behind him and clicked the car key. The car answered with an approving squeak.

'No, I want you to drop me off at the station,' she spoke each word through gritted teeth.

'It's not a problem.'

'It is for me. I want you to drop me off at the station.'

'Suit yourself.'

'I will, thank you.'

She got in the car beside him and switched on the radio. Some inane announcer on Radio One was getting excited about a Mr Blobby costume she had bought.

He started the engine and drove off, reaching forward to turn off the radio. 'Can we talk about last night?'

'No.'

'You didn't go to Maisie's last night, did you?'

'I don't want to talk about it, Dad.'

'You have to talk about it sometime.'

'But not now. I have a history test this morning and I want to focus on that.'

Ridpath didn't speak. There was an even more deafening silence from her. Finally, he could stand it no longer.

'Who is Billy?'

'I don't want to talk about it, or him, Dad.'

'I need to know. Because it's important to me. You're still a young girl and I want to know who your friends are, particularly if they are older boys.'

She didn't say anything. At least that was a positive for Ridpath. If she had said 'no comment' he would have lost it completely.

'Who is he, Eve?'

'No comment.'

There it was. He gripped the steering wheel tighter. 'I'm entitled to know. I am your father.'

'You are entitled to nothing, Dad. And perhaps you should remember you are my father. I am your daughter, not a suspect.'

'Right, if you won't tell me who he is, you need to come home straight from school this evening. Do not go to Maisie's. Do not meet Billy, whoever he is. Come straight home. Understood?'

The station was up ahead.

'And if I don't?'

Ridpath thought wildly for a moment. How had he got himself into this ridiculous situation? 'You'll be grounded for two weeks.'

He stopped outside the entrance to the station.

'And how will you know if I go straight home from school? You're never there when I get home.'

'I've got a job to do, Eve.'

'But the job doesn't include interrogating me about my friends. I'm your daughter not one of your suspects.'

With that she took her bag from the back seat and opened the door without saying a word.

Ridpath watched as she walked away without looking back or saying goodbye.

'Well, Ridpath, you handled this morning particularly well. Ten out of ten for aggression. Nil out of ten for parenting.'

Chapter FIFTEEN

Ridpath's day looked a nightmare on paper. He decided he would go to Police HQ first to debrief Chrissy, Emily and Helen. Afterwards, he would go to the coroner's office, get Sophia up to speed with Clarence Montague's latest job, then head out to SunnySide Residential Home to check out the place and talk with the manager.

He had to finish everything and still be home by 5.30 to check on Eve.

He paused for a moment.

What had he got himself into? Why was he checking on his daughter? Was she right? Should he trust her? She was fourteen after all.

He decided to try again tonight to chat with her, avoiding confrontation if he could. It was strange, he'd never had any major arguments with his daughter before. Sure, they had minor disagreements and the occasional falling out, which usually ended with her not talking to him, but nothing serious. Why did this time feel different?

He put the blessed Bowie CD into the player and the strident guitar chords of 'Jean Genie' pulsed through the car. He drove onto the A56 and headed through the rush-hour traffic to Police HQ, singing the words loudly as he did.

It felt good to let go.

A half an hour and three stupid drivers later, he parked up and was swiping himself onto the MIT floor. Chrissy and Emily were already waiting for him in one of the meeting rooms.

'Where's Helen?' he asked.

They looked at each other and shrugged their shoulders.

'You did tell her about this meeting?'

'I sent her an email last night,' said Chrissy, 'along with the case files.'

The door flew open and a bedraggled Helen Shipton stood in the doorway. 'Sorry I'm late, bloody alarm clock decided to give up the ghost sometime around three a.m. I was woken up by the wet tongue of a dog at 8:30, desperate to go out for a pee.'

'You or the dog?' asked Emily.

'That sounds like far too much information, Helen,' said Ridpath quietly. 'But come in, we're just about to start.'

The detective constable bustled in, placing her computer heavily on the table along with a sausage bap from the canteen.

'Does anybody mind if I eat… I'm starving.'

The three others looked at her but didn't say anything.

Ridpath spoke first. 'I'll bring everybody up to speed. We visited Andy's mother, Sharon, yesterday. She confirmed the following facts for us.'

He began to write on the board.

ANDREW GOLDING

Left home at 11.15 a.m. on May 22.

Last seen on CCTV near Southern Cemetery at 11.23 a.m.

Police not called until two days later.

Police arrived the next day, May 25.

Investigation two days later, May 27.

Chrissy stood up and approached the board, placing more photographs next to the one from the files. 'This one was taken about a month before Andy went missing. Apparently, he was wearing the same striped shirt.'

She stuck the photo to the board with a pin. It showed a shy fourteen-year-old boy squinting into camera, his hand raised to cover his eyes from the sun.

Ridpath noticed he wore the St Christopher medallion around his neck. 'Don't we have anything better. A school photo?'

'I'll see if I can dig anything up. The case file is a bit thin.'

'Tell me about it. I've seen more information on a missing cat report.' Helen Shipton spoke with a mouth full of sausage bap. 'And what the bloody hell are MPDD, HERMES and POLKA?'

Ridpath was glad he didn't have to ask the same question.

'MPDD is the Missing Persons DNA Database, held at the Missing Persons Unit. I've checked and Bert Ramsden loaded the DNA to their files. DNA from hairbrushes is routinely added into the database and compared with other DNA from unknown bodies found at crime scenes or discovered by accident. And before you ask, there are no matches to Andy Golding anywhere on the database.'

'Right, good to know, I suppose,' said Helen. 'HERMES and POLKA?'

'HERMES is the Missing Persons Unit Case Management System.'

'I hope it works better than our bloody computer systems.'

'It's not bad, actually. At least when you search it, you can find information.'

'How did they get the name HERMES?'

Ridpath answered. 'He's the Greek herald of the gods. Also the protector of travellers, thieves, merchants and orators. His symbol is the caduceus, a winged staff intertwined with two snakes.'

They all stared at him.

'What? It's a common pub quiz question.'

'Anyway, that's what it's called for whatever reason,' Chrissy continued. 'POLKA is the Police On-line Knowledge Area.'

'At least the acronym makes sense...' interrupted Emily.

Chrissy carried on. '...It's a website maintained by the Missing Persons Unit, containing information and documents to help support the investigation of their cases and provide guidance surrounding obtaining samples.'

'So, looking at the case files,' said Helen, 'Bert Ramsden just uploaded files to these sites and checked them once a month.'

'Looks like it.'

'That was the extent of the investigation?'

'No point in criticising the previous casework, even though it was shoddy at best. We need to discover what happened to Andy Golding and quickly.'

'Why did it take him eight minutes to walk to Southern Cemetery from his house? Even if he was dawdling, it's only a few minutes' walk. What took him so long?'

Ridpath looked at the timings again. 'Good question, Em. Was he waiting around, deciding where to go? Did he meet somebody else? Or did he go to his grandad's after all?'

Ridpath wrote on the board.

Where did he go immediately after leaving home?

And followed with another question.

Where did he go after being seen on CCTV?

'I think I may be able to help with the second question.'

Helen Shipton put down her sausage bap, wiped her fingers on a tissue and took a large map out of her briefcase. She spread the map on the table in front of her.

'As requested, I trudged around the streets of the area yesterday mapping CCTV points. I've marked the ones I saw with a red X.'

Ridpath could see a lot of Xs marked on the main roads around the cemetery with fewer on the side roads.

'As you can see, I went as far as the McDonald's on Princess Road – they do a great Chicken McCrispy by the way – the Police Social Club on Mauldeth Road West and Albert's Restaurant in West Didsbury. I didn't have time to walk around on the side below the crematorium. Anyway, the picture shows him walking towards Didsbury, not going the other way to Chorlton.'

Ridpath raised his eyebrow. She had covered a lot of territory in a short time.

'You owe me a new pair of Nikes, Ridpath.'

'You didn't check out the cemetery itself?' asked Emily. 'According to the notes two people saw him there.'

'No point. I asked at their office and there are no cameras within the cemetery grounds, they think it would be intruding on people's grief.' She smiled quickly before continuing on. 'Now, some of these might not have existed four years ago, particularly those in domestic houses. The doorbell cameras are a relatively new phenomenon, but most of the businesses will have had cameras, plus I've added large black Xs for the road cameras operated by Manchester council. They are at the junctions here, here, and here.'

'The junction between Barlow Moor Road and Princess Road leads to the airport, it's always busy,' added Chrissy.

'Now I went into a few of the businesses and asked them about their footage. Most said they didn't keep it for longer than a month, but one IT company, here,' she prodded the map west of the Cemetery, 'did keep the footage in the cloud from four years ago. They have given me access to it.'

'Great, well done, Helen, great work.'

'That's not all,' she said smugly, 'I popped into West Didsbury nick, it's the new one next to the hospital. I asked the desk sergeant if they had been called out to any incidents on 22 May, 2020. He checked his logs and found they had been called to a domestic here,' she pointed, 'a road accident on Barlow Moor Road, and a disturbance at a care home here, SunnySide Residential.'

'What did you say?'

Helen Shipton checked her notes, 'A disturbance at a residential care home, SunnySide.'

'Strange… I wonder what happened?' muttered Ridpath under his breath.

'Why?' asked Emily Parkinson.

Ridpath shook his head. 'Probably a coincidence, but I have to visit there today for the coroner. I can kill two birds with one stone and find out what it was from them. But well done, Helen. Next steps?'

'I've arranged to view the footage from the IT company with digital forensics this morning.'

'How have you managed that? I thought there was a two-week queue for those guys.'

Helen Shipton tapped the side of her nose. 'Connections. I've also put in a request to see the casework on all three incidents. With the traffic accident, we may get some useable footage.'

'Good luck dealing with Traffic, it's like getting blood out of a stone with them.'

'They were extremely helpful and are sending across the footage, we should get the files this morning if the computers play nice.'

Emily raised her eyes as if to say 'that put me in my place'.

'Great. Anything from your side, Chrissy?'

'I sent everybody the misper files last night. There's not much for a missing boy. And there's nothing on HOLMES in Greater Manchester for other boys going missing at the same time. I've expanded the search to the North of England and should have something back soon. I also had a look at POLKA and HERMES. No leads on either of them.'

'Can you check with the National DNA Database? He may have been arrested for another offence somewhere else?'

'I'll do a non-routine speculative search in the DNA Database as soon as I have a second. It's a bit of a long shot though Ridpath, he was only fourteen. So you think he's still alive?'

Ridpath shrugged his shoulders. 'I don't know, but at this stage we have to keep an open mind. It's worth checking with all the DNA databases.'

'Okay, will do, Ridpath.'

'The notes also say he had a mobile phone with him. Can you check with the service provider? See if they keep the tracking information for their towers from 2020?'

'I don't think they will, Ridpath. It's too long ago.'

'Check anyway, we might get lucky.'

'Will do.'

'How about you, Em?'

'I followed up on the ex-partner, John Newton, he has a bit of form.' She tapped a key on her laptop and a police photo appeared of a man with a number beneath it. 'He was done for domestic abuse in 2003, sentenced to keep the peace. In 2005, he was given six months for receiving stolen goods…'

'What?'

'A load of high-end TVs. He said they fell off the back of a lorry. I'm not joking, it's what he actually said in court.'

'No wonder he got six months.'

'Afterwards he kept his nose clean until 2011 when he was done again for receiving, getting a year this time. After that nothing, clean as a whistle.'

'Or he's just never been caught.'

'Probably. Anyway, I now have his last known address so we can pay him a visit whenever you want.'

'Let's do it now, I can visit SunnySide this afternoon.'

Chrissy's phone buzzed with a message. 'It's Steve Carruthers. He wants an update at five p.m. this evening. Are you okay with the time, Ridpath?'

He closed his eyes forcing them to stay shut. He was supposed to be home to chat with Eve then. Her words from earlier came back to him: 'You're never there when I get home.' What was he supposed to do? Polly always understood the life of a detective was unpredictable. She wasn't happy but she understood. It was harder now she was gone…

'Are you okay with the time, Ridpath?' Chrissy repeated. 'Unfortunately, he's not free later on, some senior officer's get together apparently.'

Ridpath made a decision. 'Confirm it, Chrissy.'

'Will do.' She began tapping away on her mobile.

He would try to explain everything to Eve later this evening. Hopefully she would listen and understand. In the meantime, he would ask Maisie's mum to pick her up from school and he'd go round to their place after the meeting with Steve Carruthers.

He began to collect his papers and his laptop. 'Right, are we all clear on what we need to do? Let's meet up before we brief the boss. Em, it's time to go and see this John Newton.'

Chapter SIXTEEN

'Can I have a quick smoke before we leave, I'm gasping.'

Emily Parkinson hustled over to the smokers' area at the rear of Police HQ before Ridpath could raise any objection. By the time he joined her, she had already lit the cigarette and inhaled a long satisfying drag.

'God, I needed a fag. Simply being in the same room as that woman makes me crave the release of a good smoke.'

She took another long drag before expelling the smoke out of the side of her mouth away from Ridpath.

He had given up smoking for two years now, ever since Polly had died. It was his promise to Eve and one of the few he had managed to keep. He still enjoyed the vicarious pleasure of second-hand smoke though.

'You must admit her work on the CCTV was thorough and quick.'

'But why does she have to make such a song and dance about it. I find myself tensing up whenever I'm close to her.'

'You need to sort it out, Em. We can't have tension in the team, it's not productive.'

'There wasn't any tension before she arrived...'

Ridpath stared at his colleague, saying nothing.

'Okay, okay, I get it. Work with her. I'll *try* to do my best.'

Ridpath said nothing and he said it loudly.

'Okay, I'll make it work, Ridpath. Somehow or other, I'll make it work.'

'Good, that's all I ask, Em. Shall we get going or do you want another delivery system for carcinogenic substances?'

'Do you mean I can have another fag?'

'If you want, but then we have to move.'

She quickly tapped out another cigarette from the soft pack and lit it with the dying stub of the first one. 'What with Miss Clever Clogs grandstanding I forgot to tell you, John Newton didn't move far,' she said expelling the smoke at the same time as she spoke, 'just to a terrace in Chorlton.'

'Badly Drawn Boy country.'

Emily Parkinson screwed up her face. 'What? Badly Drawn who?'

'We're going to have to improve your musical education, Em. Badly Drawn Boy, Manchester's answer to Bruce Springsteen. *One Plus One is One* is one of the great undiscovered classic albums.'

'Right, Ridpath. Sometimes, I think you should get a life. I wonder how Eve puts up with you.'

'I think she's wondering the same thing right now.'

'Relationship issues?'

Ridpath nodded.

'The fierce fourteens. I remember I was a terror. It didn't help I was just discovering who I was, too.'

Ridpath told her all about the boy called Billy who came knocking at their door last night and Eve's reaction to his questions.

'Well, it sounds like you handled it with all the finesse of Norman Hunter. You should have waited until she was ready to tell you about Billy rather than charging in with your size nines.'

'Thanks for the encouragement.'

'And now you've reached a bit of an impasse. Personally, I wouldn't take on the self-righteousness of a stroppy teenager if I were you.'

'But she's only fourteen and he's much older than her.'

'Look, Ridpath, she's fourteen going on twenty-seven. Kids grow up far quicker these days, they've got far more to handle than I ever did. And I had a lot.'

Ridpath knew Emily was talking about discovering she was gay. She never talked about it and he felt it was her own business and nothing to do with her work.

'Sit her down, tell her you're sorry and start again. Even ask her to invite this Billy round to the house. That way you can check him out properly. That's my advice, take it or leave it.'

'I know it's what I need to do, but I can't let her see somebody who's far older than herself.'

'Better she see him openly with your knowledge than furtively when you're not there.'

'I know, I know.' He checked the time. 'We'd better be going.'

Emily took one last, long drag before stubbing the cigarette out in the ashtray. 'Lead on, Ridpath. Are you driving or me?'

'We'll take my car.' Ridpath smiled. 'One woman driving me crazy is more than enough.'

Chapter SEVENTEEN

'Thanks for this, Jasper.'

The digital technician quickly closed the door behind Helen Shipton. 'It's the last time you're jumping the queue. If my boss finds out, he'll kill me.'

'You shouldn't have drunk so much at the pub that night. Telling someone like me your little secret wasn't a smart move. And just so you know, it won't be the last time you'll help me, let's make it clear right now.'

Jasper sighed loudly and his shoulders visibly sagged. 'What do you want?'

'A couple of things. Can you access this footage in the cloud for me?' She handed across the file address and the password for entry.

'This is kosher, isn't it?'

'As a bacon sandwich. But if you mean the footage has been given to me and permission to access it granted by the owners, then the answer is yes. The search is also sanctioned by my SIO, Detective Inspector Ridpath. So I hope that keeps your little regulated life happy.'

Jasper glanced at the file address and began typing on his keyboard. 'You need to look at the screen.' He pointed to the left-hand monitor of the four on top of his desk. Another quick blur of fingers across the keyboard and a dark, street-lit image appeared of the road in front of a shop. It was raining heavily and a few drops of water appeared on the lens. 'Where is this?'

'Barlow Moor Road.'

He leant forward and checked the time code. 'Strange, it was taken four years ago. Didn't think anybody kept their footage so long. What month do you want?'

'What?'

'The footage, it's filed by month and sub-filed by day. When do you want?'

'May 22, 2020, roughly around eleven a.m.'

'Righty, coming up.'

Another blur of fingers and more footage appeared on the screen. This time, the image was a bright summer day, the sun was shining and a slight breeze rustled through the trees.

'What are we looking for?'

'A young boy. This one.' Helen Shipton showed him the photo.

'Righty.'

The image played on the screen. It was strangely empty. Hardly any traffic passed down the road and there were no pedestrians.

'Very quiet. Is it a Sunday?'

'It's the middle of the Manchester lockdown, remember?'

Jasper raised his eyebrows. 'Oh, I spent most of my time playing FPS games.'

'FPS?' asked Helen Shipton, immediately wishing she hadn't bothered.

'First Person Shooter. *Metro Exodus* had been released and I love a good apocalyptic story.'

She decided not to ask any more, even though she knew Jasper was dying to tell her. Why did men find playing video games so interesting? She'd had a boyfriend who insisted on playing them while she lay next to him in bed, unloved and unsatisfied. The relationship hadn't lasted long. She'd dropped him quicker than he could shoot a mutant zombie between the eyes.

The time code was ticking over at the top right of the screen. It had reached 11.42.46 when Helen shouted, 'What was that?'

'What?' Jasper had been fiddling with his phone.

'There.' She pointed to the screen. 'Top right, on the other side of the road.'

The image on the screen reversed back twenty seconds and then went forward again.

'See. It's him. Andy Golding.'

A young boy was bouncing a football at the edge of the pavement before walking on from left to right and out of the frame. He was wearing exactly the same clothes detailed in the misper report; a striped T-shirt, shorts and Nike trainers.

'Can you do me a printout of the image?'

'Even better, I'll zoom in a little and clean it up.'

More typing on the keyboard and the picture of Andy grew bigger and clearer. It was definitely him. The printer began to hiccup next to Jasper's desk and a screen grab appeared on a sheet of paper.

'We're done now. I have to get back to my day job. I've got a shitload of cell-mast data to go through for Sandra.'

'Not quite, Jasper.' Helen checked the printout he had passed to her. 'Can you access case files from here.'

'*Yesssss…*' answered Jasper dubiously, '…but I really need to get on with Sandra's job.'

'We won't be long. Can you access these files?' She passed along the three case numbers given to her by West Didsbury police yesterday.

'Do you have permission to access these cases?'

'Yes,' she said firmly. 'Come on, Jasper, it won't take long. And then I won't have to tell anybody about your little peccadilloes.'

'It's legal, there's nothing wrong with it.'

'Having a foot fetish and a desire to smell women's feet is perfectly legal, Jasper, but the lads in the canteen might find it a little strange… amusing, but strange.'

Once again, Jasper's shoulders visibly sagged and he began typing on the keyboard.

'When you go into the file, look for an attachment. It should be footage of the road taken from a traffic camera. There was an accident just after noon but I want to see the footage from before then.'

'We're into the file and here's the attachment.' Jasper spoke to himself as he typed. 'The footage is coming up on Screen Two.'

Footage of a road junction appeared on the screen with only the occasional car crossing it.

'Coming up, now.'

The speed of the time code on the screen increased as the picture blurred. Finally, Jasper slowed it down to 11.42.00 when they'd last seen Andy captured by the CCTV at the IT Company.

'Perfect, we'll watch from here.'

They both stared at the screen. Nothing happened for several minutes.

'What are we looking for?'

'The same boy, Andy Golding.'

The time code moved forward.

11.51.25

11.52.04

11.53.46

On screen, nothing much happened. The occasional car crossed the junction and a couple of buses but no pedestrians.

'How could they have had an accident, there's so little traffic?'

'I dunno. I think it was between a bike and a car. The bike shot through a red light. Can you fast forward to around 11.55?'

11.56.32

11.57.52

11.58.31

'There he is,' shouted Helen Shipton.

On screen, Andy Golding had stopped at the edge of the pavement, carrying the ball under his arm. He pressed the pedestrian button and waited for the green man to start beeping, occasionally checking for traffic.

'What's that?'

'What?'

'There, behind the boy.'

Jasper squinted at the screen. 'It looks like a shadow, somebody else is behind him.'

'Can you move the camera to the right. I want to see his face.'

'It's fixed, I can't move anything.'

'Can't you show me more? I want to see who is with him.'

'Hang on, they'll cross the road and then we'll see.'

As if on cue, the lights changed colour and the green man appeared allowing pedestrians to cross. Andy started across the road before a hand came out and pulled him back.

The boy was obviously talking to someone, then he shrugged his shoulders and walked away to the right, out of range of the camera.

'Go back, can you zoom in on the hand?'

The picture reversed and Jasper's hands tapped on the keyboard.

The image on the screen zoomed in to show a hand holding the shoulder of Andy Golding.

A male hand with a large blue tattoo of a swallow on the skin between the thumb and index finger.

'Got you,' shouted Helen Shipton.

Chapter EIGHTEEN

Pemberton Street on the border between Chorlton and Whalley Range was only a couple of miles from West Didsbury but, for Ridpath, it felt like he'd been transported back in time.

Either side of the road was lined with the kind of terraced houses that once stretched from here, all the way through Hulme, to the centre of Manchester. They were small, red brick terraces whose front doors led straight out into the streets and which were separated at the back by dark ginnels. No gardens, of course. Gardens had not been thought necessary by the Victorian builders. The Barratt homes of their day with a motto of 'build lots of them and build them cheap.'

Most of these old terraces had been demolished in the 1960s in the name of urban renewal, with new concrete, brutalist crescents being built to house the masses. Within thirty years, these new blocks had become infested with lice, drug addicts and crime. It was with huge cheers they were demolished in the early Nineties, loved by nobody and hated by those who lived there.

Pemberton Street had somehow survived the council-led vandalism. A throwback to an old time when community and shared poverty united everyone.

Nothing much had changed.

John Newton lived at Number 82. In the window, a yellowed and rusty blind was permanently closed. Ridpath knocked loudly on the door.

No answer.

He knocked again, even louder, shouting, 'Mr Newton, it's the police, we'd like to have a chat with you.'

At a house across the street, a curtain twitched and an old woman peered out from the dark interior.

Ridpath knocked for the third time.

Finally, the door opened and an unshaven man wearing a vest that had once been white, sleepily opened the door.

'Whaddya want? I ain't done nothing.'

'My name is Detective Inspector Ridpath and this is my colleague, DS Emily Parkinson. Could we come in for a chat?'

'What's it about?' The accent was pure Manchester; a high-pitched whine at the end of the sentence like a cheese grater on steroids.

'We're looking into the disappearance of Andy Golding and we'd like to ask you a few questions.'

'Does it have to be now? I've got company.'

Ridpath saw the fleeting back of a woman wearing a thread-bare slip scurry upstairs behind John Newton.

'I'm afraid it has to be now, Mr Newton.'

'He disappeared four years ago and you're only now investig-ating?' A long sigh. 'You'd better come in.'

He walked away leaving the door slightly open. Ridpath pushed it and stepped inside. The smell of dirty clothes and sweat struck him as soon as he crossed the threshold. He looked around for John Newton but couldn't see him anywhere.

A voice helped him. 'I'm in here.'

Emily closed the door behind them and they walked into the back kitchen. John Newton was sat at a table covered in glasses and empty bottles; beer, cheap wine and even cheaper whisky.

Without asking he lit a cigarette, depositing the spent match into the overflowing ashtray.

'We had a bit of a party here last night.' These were the only words of explanation. Upstairs, Ridpath could hear somebody heavily moving about.

He sat down at the table and took out his notebook, moving a few of the empty beer bottles to find space to write. Emily remained standing.

'You are John Newton who formerly lived at 27 Howsgill Road?'

'That's me. The formerly bit as well.'

'You were living with Sharon Golding and her sons in May 2020?'

The smoke of the cigarette rose to a tobacco-stained ceiling. John Newton's arms were covered in blue tattoos. Ridpath couldn't make out the designs but they were simple with only one colour: prison blue.

On the knuckles of his right hand the letters G-O-O-D were etched in the same colour. Ridpath couldn't see the left hand, but he'd lay a thousand quid it had E-V-I-L tattooed there.

Prison tattoos. Never the most original.

'I was living with her right until she chucked me out.'

'Really? She told us you left.'

'Nah, I was chucked out. She changed the locks too so I couldn't go back.'

'Why did she chuck you out?'

John Newton shrugged his shoulders again. It seemed to be his default response to life. 'I dunno, ask her.'

Ridpath scratched his head. No point continuing this line at the moment. He changed tack. 'What happened on the morning of May 22nd?'

'The day Andy disappeared?'

Ridpath nodded.

Another shrug. 'I dunno. I was in bed, I'd had a few the night before. I heard Andy and his mum arguing…'

'What about?'

'I dunno. Anything and everything. They were always arguing. Like cat and dog they were. I stayed out of it. Not my place to get involved, was it?'

'So what happened after the argument?'

'I heard the door slam and the place went quiet.'

'What time was that?'

'About eleven o'clock-ish.'

'And what did you do then?'

'I turned over and went back to sleep, didn't I? I couldn't be arsed dealing with their rows. Anyway, I told all this to youse lot already. First to the young woman and then to the older detective, the one who kept bludging fags off me.'

'We're relooking at the events,' Ridpath said blandly. 'Did you see Andy again?'

John Newton shook his head, the long grey-flecked hair becoming even more unruly. 'Nah, never saw him afterwards. Should have gone looking for him, I suppose, but I was knackered and I thought he was round at his grandad's. He were always going round there, spent the night there a lot.'

'So that's where you thought he went?'

'Yeah, the old man only lived two streets away.'

'Didn't anybody think to check up on him. He was only fourteen after all.'

'Andy was a strange boy, older than his years if you know what I mean. He used to go out at all times of the night and day, even in lockdown. Andy didn't see the rules applying to him. He was street-smart was Andy, knew what he was doing, knew his way around. Only thing he really cared about was his football. Loved the game. Well, all kids do at that age, don't they? Went everywhere with his ball.'

Ridpath remembered it was certainly true of him. His games of football were occasionally interrupted by the useless bits of life. Like sleeping, eating and school.

'And you stayed in the house for the next few days?'

'Yeah, didn't go out. We'd been to the supermarket a couple of days earlier and got all the booze, fags and food we needed. No need to go out. Sharon will confirm it. We watched the telly, and had a few drinks. It was always better when Andy wasn't around.'

'Why?'

'No arguments. No stroppy teenager slumped in the corner, moaning all the time.'

Ridpath thought of his stroppy teenager. He wasn't looking forward to the chat he would have with Eve later.

'What do you think happened to Andy, Mr Newton?' asked Emily.

Another shrug of the shoulders. 'I dunno, but I will say this. I think he's still alive somewhere, laughing at you lot, running around to try and find him.'

'A strange thing to say.'

'Is it?' Another shrug. 'Well, Andy was a bit strange if you ask me.'

'What do you mean?'

John Newton's eyes narrowed. 'I could never figure him out. Andy didn't trust anybody, he was a bit of a loner, even played football on his own. He thought he could sort everything out himself. He sort of scared me sometimes, he was so intense, unforgiving. That's it – Andy was unforgiving.' He laughed to himself. 'The only people who liked Andy were his nan and grandad. I don't think Sharon liked him much, if I'm honest.'

'Didn't she?'

'She never knew who his real dad was. Could've been any of three men, she told me one night after she'd had a few. Andy asked her of course. She was honest and told him she didn't know. That was the start of another bloody argument, a big one.'

'When did this argument happen?'

'A couple of weeks before he left. But by then it was one long row, almost non-stop, I switched off in the end. Well, you do, don't you?'

'What about Alan?'

'Who?'

'Mrs Golding's other child.'

'Oh him, didn't have much to do with him. Always in his bedroom playing video games.'

Ridpath glanced across at Emily to check if she had any more questions. She shook her head and looked down.

'Thank you for your time, Mr Newton. We'll be back in touch if we need anything else.'

'Is that it? You just asked the same questions as all the others.'

'Like I said, we'll be in touch if we need anything else.'

Ridpath stood up and placed his notebook back in his inside pocket. He made to leave when he stopped and said, 'One last thing, you mentioned Andy going to see his grandad, but did he also go to see his grandma?'

'Yeah, of course, but he couldn't stay the night there.'

'Why not?'

'His grandma was in a care home. Sunny-something, SunnySide, I think it was called, in West Didsbury.'

Chapter NINETEEN

Emily Parkinson was leaning on Ridpath's car smoking a Marlboro Light.

'What did you think of him? Did he have anything to do with the disappearance of our vic?'

Ridpath glanced back towards the house. A curtain at the upstairs window flickered briefly. 'A strange man. His relationship with Sharon Golding was interesting.'

'By "interesting" do you mean weird?'

Ridpath tilted his head. 'I don't know. He had an alibi for the weekend anyway. He never left the house.'

'An alibi provided by Sharon Golding and nobody else.'

'What a suspicious mind you have, Em.'

'Useful in a copper.'

Ridpath thought for a moment before coming to a decision. 'Right, we've got too much to do, let's split forces. I want you to run more checks on John Newton. Find out where he was working back in May, 2020 and what he's been up to since. Also discover where he's working now. You said you knew Fiona Barton from a course? Is she still in Eccles?'

'I think so, easy to find out.'

'Go and see her. I want her take on the investigation. There seems to be a lot of stuff missing or that wasn't done.'

'Like?'

'There's nothing in the files about checking the local pervs register. Surely, it would be the first thing to do if a child goes missing.'

'Don't you mean the Sex Offenders Register?'

Ridpath eyed her suspiciously. 'Don't go all PC on me, Em, not you too.'

'Pervs register sounds like Charlie Whittaker speaking, not you.'

Charlie Whittaker was Ridpath's first mentor in GMP, the man who had brought him into MIT when he qualified as a detective. An old-fashioned copper who didn't call a spade a digging implement.

'Yeah, well, Charlie got the job done.'

'And managed to piss off 99 per cent of Joe Public at the same time.' She glanced back at the house where the curtain had moved slightly again. Was somebody standing there?

'Should we have searched the house? I could hear somebody moving about upstairs.'

'We didn't have a warrant, Em, and it was just a friendly chat. If you find anything, we'll revisit Mr Newton again.'

Emily Parkinson had written everything down in her notebook. 'What are you going to do, Ridpath?'

'SunnySide Residential Home has come up twice now in our inquiries. I have to visit it for the coroner anyway. It might be useful to check up on Andy's grandma.'

Emily checked her notes. 'Irene Golding. And remember Helen saying West Didsbury nick were called to a disturbance there on the same day Andy disappeared.'

'I need to ask them what happened.' Ridpath made a note in his book of the grandmother's name. He stared at the words he had written down for a long time. 'Have you noticed, nobody has actually told us the date she died?' he finally said.

'Nor have they mentioned when the grandad passed away. But easy enough to check both dates.'

'I'll do it now.'

Ridpath pulled out his phone and rang Sophia. She answered after two rings.

'Hiya, Ridpath, are you coming in today?'

'Hi Sophia, you're on speakerphone. I'll try to come in later if I can.'

'His Lordship has been asking for you again.'

'Okay, I'll try to make time. In the meantime, I need you to do a couple of things for me. Can you find out information on the death of an Irene Golding? She was a resident of SunnySide Residential Home and died sometime in 2020. And also her husband, an Ernest Golding, he lived on Brindley Street and died in the same year I think.'

'Okay, will do, Ridpath.'

'There's one more thing, Sophia, can you check the numbers of deaths at the home?'

'Starting from when, Ridpath?'

He thought for a moment. 'Can you start from before the pandemic, say 2018. Get me the figures for the pandemic and the most up-to-date numbers you have.'

'The files are current till the end of last month.'

'Brilliant.'

'When do you want them? And don't say yesterday.'

'How about the day before yesterday?'

She laughed.

'But seriously, Sophia, I'm going to visit there this afternoon. You can message me with the details.'

'On it, Ridpath. Anything is better than what his Lordship has asked me to do.'

'Which is?'

'Compile a list of all the Section 28 notices submitted by Mrs Challinor in the last twenty years since she was made head coroner.'

'Why does he want the information?'

'Exactly the same question I asked him. His answer was "Just do it." Anyway, I'll do your stuff first. His Lordship can wait.'

'Thanks, Sophia. See you later.'

'Not if I see you first.'

The phone went dead in Ridpath's hands. 'We'll get the info before five, Em, if I know Sophia. How are you getting to Eccles?'

'I'll get the tram. The station is just around the corner.'

'Great.'

Ridpath opened his car door and slipped behind the wheel.

'But one thing, Ridpath, next time we take my car, okay?'

'Sorry, Em, rank has its privileges and one of those is I do the driving. See you at five.'

'To quote Sophia, "not if I see you first".'

Chapter TWENTY

'Do come in and sit down, Mr Lardner.'

The doctor's office at Ashworth High Security Hospital was as empty as the man's mind: a pine desk, two low Scandinavian chairs, a tall lamp from Ikea and bare brick walls painted white. Along one side, a row of bronze awards from the British Psychiatric Association were arrayed like soldiers at a funeral – a testimony to the man's love of himself.

It was all deliberately austere of course, as it meant all focus was on the man himself. His pudgy, self-satisfied, bearded face sat above a red spotted bow tie and green tweed suit.

Harold Lardner glanced down at the man's shoes. Black slip-ons. Should have been brown brogues.

He took his place on the left-hand seat, trying to get comfortable in the most uncomfortable chair imaginable.

Dr Mansell waved away Mr Francis, the guard who had accompanied Harold Lardner from his cell. The man closed the door without a word but his shadow could be seen through the plate glass, hovering still.

'It's good to see you again, Harold, I feel we have made tremendous progress over the last six months...'

The man's smug self-satisfaction was sickening, like eating two whole boxes of Cadbury's Milk Tray at one sitting. 'We' of course had made absolutely no progress at all. In fact, Harold Lardner had become even more convinced of the rightness of his pathology. It was the world that was wrong not him.

'...PTSD is one of the most difficult illnesses for us to treat and your case is particularly trying. Anybody performing over 12,000 post mortems in a career is going to be negatively affected by the process and the memories. I believe your work experiences lie at the heart of your negative attitudes to the human body and humanity in general. The experience of these post–mortems being the instigator of your antisocial personality disorder.'

God, he loved the sound of his own voice.

Negative attitudes?

That was a lovely way of describing the death of a police detective from anti–freeze dripped slowly into her veins. Harold had enjoyed her death. Lesley had been one of his more competent disciples.

'I saw them as experiments, they were no longer human beings, Dr Mansell,' he said blandly.

'When did that begin? I mean seeing people as experiments not human beings?'

Harold Lardner sighed. Here we go again, trying to find a motive for what he had done, missing the obvious one that was staring the stupid man in the face. He decided to lead him down a psychological garden path.

'The experiments began when I was young. I remember I used to set traps for birds and then put them in a cage.'

The doctor leant forward. 'And how old were you then?'

'About ten years old. Father had died and there was just myself and Mother living in the old house in Bowdon. Of course, she drank far too much.'

The doctor could barely contain his excitement. 'What did you do with the birds?'

I didn't do anything with them because I'm making it all up, thought Lardner but he answered, 'I used to put Mother's cat in the cage. I liked to watch the birds become more agitated, their wings fluttering wildly as they tried to escape. The cat used to just wait and watch. I remember the end of his white tail waving sensually like a snake before he pounced.'

'And what did you do with the bodies?'

'The birds' bodies?'

The doctor nodded.

'I used to cut them up, removing the heart and the liver and the other organs and laying them out on a tray next to their heads.' For once, he told Mansell the truth. That is exactly what he did, practising for later life.

Lardner finished and a long silence dragged on between them before the doctor asked, 'Did you enjoy killing the birds?'

'I think "enjoy" is the wrong word. It was just something I did, something I was good at.'

The doctor scribbled his notes in his blue book. 'And later when you were at school, did these experiments with the cats continue?'

'No, they had stopped by then.'

'Why?'

For a second, Lardner thought about telling him the truth. He stopped experimenting on animals and started on humans. School was such a wonderful place to be at that time. There were always vulnerable pupils to pick on and the teachers didn't care, particularly as he was always the top of his class.

Instead he answered, 'I don't know. I was being bullied remorselessly because I was bright. I went into my shell and just concentrated on my work.'

'And your mother was still drinking?'

'Like a fish. Usually a bottle of vodka a day, maybe more.' Actually, his mother was teetotal. The mere smell of alcohol made her sick.

More notes in his little blue book. 'And when your mother died, what did you do?'

'I watched her die. It took a long time, the cancer slowly spread throughout her body, absorbing her, killing her with its pain.'

'Was that when you became a doctor?'

But I didn't become a doctor, you stupid man, I became a pathologist. I loved death. Loved being surrounded by it, smelling it every day as part of my work.

'Was that when you became a doctor?' Mansell repeated.

'Yes, I wanted to help others, prevent the suffering my mother endured. But I found I was good at anatomy and pathology so that was where I specialised.'

The doctor smiled. 'Not surprising given your childhood. How many post-mortems were you performing each week?'

'Sometimes as many as ten a week.'

The doctor shook his head. 'No wonder the human body lost its essential humanity for you. These people became objects, you disassociated their bodies from their lives.'

The man took a deep breath and Harold Lardner knew he was about to embark on one of his interminable lectures.

'Freudian analysis centres its motivational theory on the pleasure principle, whereas Adlerian individual psychology focuses on what is generally called the will to power. I, on the other hand, have turned my back on both those eminent gentlemen, describing a new type or class of neurosis, a new sort of suffering that does not represent an illness in the proper sense of the term, I have called this new psychosis the egotistical vacuum, where life takes on a total lack, or loss, of essential and existential humanity. Now Cognitive Behavioural Therapy is usually used…'

It was at this point Harold Lardner normally tuned out from the doctor's voice, focusing instead on the pleasure he obtained from killing people or ordering others to do the work for him.

'Have the nightmares come back?'

The doctor was staring at him.

'Pardon?'

'Have the nightmares come back?'

'Not since I have been using the techniques you told me. I found them extremely useful, particularly listening to the meditation tapes of your voice before I go to sleep.'

The man beamed with joy. 'I developed those tapes for some of my other patients, obviously with far less stringent pathologies than the ones you display. But I am so glad they are proving useful.'

Harold Lardner didn't tell him he'd dumped the tapes in a bin weeks ago.

'I've written a book about the use of meditation in the treatment of PTSD and expanding on my theory of how it relates to the egotistical vacuum.'

'Really, I'd love to read it.'

This was probably the last thing he wanted to do. Toothache would be a much more preferable activity.

'Would you? I'd love to get feedback from somebody at the pointy end, as it were.'

God, the man was sickeningly stupid. 'The pointy end' for god's sake.

Lardner coughed twice. A harsh, wracking cough.

'You should get the doctor to check you out, Harold. You've had that cough for more than a month now.'

To be examined by a quack was the last thing he wanted. He quickly changed the subject. 'About the book, perhaps you can give me the manuscript if you want. I've nothing to do in here and I'd love to read your insights into my condition.'

A bit of flattery always worked on Mansell.

A broad smile crossed the clinical psychologist's face. He almost gushed gratitude. 'If you could, I would be most grateful. Any notes from you would be more than useful.'

'That would give me so much pleasure.' Lardner could hear the insincerity in his voice. The doctor, of course, couldn't. 'The manuscript would take a special space in my home library, up there with Freud and Jung.'

The man beamed another smile at him. Had his teeth been whitened recently?

'Talking of home, your case will come up at the monthly meeting tomorrow. I know you have wanted day release for some time already, but I'm afraid I cannot recommend you be allowed out of the hospital unsupervised at the moment. But...' he held a large, pudgy finger up, '...I am not disallowing it as a possibility in the future.'

For a second, the anger flared in Harold Lardner's eyes. No little pipsqueak with a bad degree from nowhere university was going to determine his life and what he did. Not now, not ever.

He gripped the arms of the chair, calming himself and regaining control. 'Whatever you think is right, doctor, you know best. I know I'm in good hands.'

The doctor stood up. 'Good, I'm so glad we have created such an honest relationship, Harold.'

He stepped out from behind his desk.

'You are one of my star—' He was about to say pupils, but realised that was the wrong word and switched to, 'patients. I think next time we should concentrate on the death of your wife, why that was so important to you. Why that was the catalyst for your PTSD.'

'I'd like to understand that too, doctor.'

'Together, we can do it.'

Harold stood up too, they were both the same height and build. Only the beard differentiated them and the fact one was wearing a tweed jacket while the other was dressed in a bright orange jumpsuit.

Mansell reached into a drawer and pulled out a manuscript, handing it to Lardner. 'We doctors have to help each other out don't we?'

The Beast of Manchester glanced down at the title. *The Egotistical Paradigm: Towards creating a theory of understanding for Post-Traumatic Stress Disorder.*

As he stood there, Harold imagined the immense pleasure he would take in pressing a sharpened scalpel against the man's pasty white neck and cutting into the carotid artery, watching the blood flow copiously over the hideous green tweed suit.

'You won't forget, will you? Insights from you may help to give my work the cut-through it needs. It's a dog-eat-dog world in modern clinical psychology.'

'I won't forget, doctor. In fact, I'll try to give a first read by Thursday.'

'Good. We do have to help each other, don't we?'

The man was as subtle as a kick in the teeth, thought Harold. Perhaps, that's what he should give him, right here, right now.

Harold resisted the temptation as Dr Mansell opened the door to reveal the guard waiting outside. 'You can escort Dr Lardner back to his cell now, Mr Francis. We'll see each other again on Thursday afternoon, Harold. I do look forward to our chats.'

'I look forward to them too, doctor. And thank you for everything you have done for me.'

'All part of the job, Harold, just taking care of people.'

'Such a good way to put it. "Taking care of people." There are some people I'd like to take care of too, doctor.'

'I'm sure you will be able to soon, Harold. Maybe in a couple of years you can enjoy day release from here. You'll have to be tagged of course, but at least it gives us both something to work towards.'

Lardner smiled. 'I'm looking forward to the day when I am well enough to leave the confines of these walls.'

'It will be soon Harold, don't worry.'

'I'm not worried, doctor, I know it will happen soon. See you on Thursday.'

Chapter TWENTY-ONE

Before going to SunnySide, Ridpath decided to get something to eat at Home, a small cafe in the area. It was carved out from the side of a church and he ordered a chicken salad sandwich plus a slice of lemon drizzle cake that looked particularly attractive.

In the last few months, he had become more aware of his food intake, making sure he ate healthily and regularly. In the years after Polly died, he had become careless about eating, losing weight and not looking after himself. A stern talking-to from Eve plus an even more stridently worded message from his doctor at one of his check-ups had finally hit home.

'Listen Ridpath, if you don't look after yourself, you'll only weaken your body and the cancer could return. If it does, I cannot promise our treatment will work again. Myeloma doesn't take any prisoners. We were lucky the first time, we might not be so lucky again.'

He'd finally taken the words to heart, eating better and, more importantly for him, regularly. He still couldn't stomach breakfast in the morning – except at weekends when Eve still made it – a cup of coffee was all he needed, but he made sure he always ate lunch and dinner. His belt had become a little tighter and he'd put on a few pounds, but he felt – and looked – far better than before. More importantly, he had more energy, particularly when the job became stressful.

Thinking about food reminded him the fridge was empty, time to order a delivery from Ocado. If he had time, he would even pop to M&S in Didsbury before going to SunnySide. At least, he could pick up some essentials like milk and bread. Perhaps, he could even stop by the cheese shop next door; a lovely slice of Wensleydale or Cheshire would go down a treat with a grumpy daughter.

He sat down at one of the tables in the glass extension, poured his tea out of the pot, and took a bite of the sandwich. He had started to enjoy quiet times like this. A time when he could just relax, 'chillax' as a famous ex-Prime Minister had once said, and smell the coffee. Or, in his case, the tea.

He ate slowly, trying to savour every mouthful. Another technique suggested by his doctor.

'Concentrate on eating, enjoy the sensation of eating, don't wolf everything down as quickly as you can.'

That one small tip had made an immense difference to his life. It was only fifteen minutes each day but he felt so much better for it. Indeed, his recent check-ups had been wonderful with the doctor complimenting him on his progress.

He finished the sandwich, took a large swallow of tea and contemplated the lemon drizzle cake. Time to make a few calls before starting to demolish it.

'Hi, is that Angela?'

Angela Knight was Eve's best friend Maisie's mum.

'Hiya, Ridpath. You want me to pick up Eve from school and bring her back here?'

'You know me too well, Angela. I think I'm going to be working late tonight but it shouldn't be too bad. I'll get to your place around seven.'

'No worries, she can help Maisie with her maths. My girl needs *so* much help. Do you want me to give her something to eat?'

'Don't trouble yourself, I'll feed her back at home.'

'A few snacks though. There's nothing hungrier than a teenager doing homework.'

'One other thing, Angela,' Ridpath paused searching for the words, 'Eve is a little difficult at the moment. I found she's been seeing some boy and we had a row about it.'

'You mean Billy?'

'You knew?'

'Maisie told me. Apparently, he's quite cute, a bit of a Harry Styles according to Maisie.'

It seems everybody knew about Billy except him. 'She didn't tell me about him.'

'Teenage girls like their secrets, Ridpath, I wouldn't worry about it. Maisie never tells her dad anything. He wouldn't be able to handle it if she did.'

Ridpath didn't know what to say.

'But no worries I'll pick her up from school with Maisie. See you later.'

Ridpath frowned. Was this relationship with Billy far more advanced than he knew? A sharp pain hit him between the ribs. For the first time his daughter was keeping secrets from him and he didn't like it. It almost felt as if their relationship had been betrayed.

Calm down, Ridpath, he counselled himself, *she's a teenage girl, of course she is going to develop relationships with young boys.* But still the nagging doubt remained.

He attacked the cake, wolfing it down and realising as he finished he'd broken his rule about being aware of everything he ate.

They would have to make time for their chat tonight. This had gone too far already.

He decided to message her. She wouldn't be able to read it on her phone while she was at school but she always checked her messages as soon as she left.

> Sorry, Eve, can't make it home at 5. Maisie's mum will pick you up from school and I'll see you there. We need to chat this evening.

She wouldn't be happy, particularly after their conversation this morning. He added another line to help assuage her anger.

I'm really sorry, something has come up at work.

He didn't know if it would help but at least he had tried. He finished the last of his tea and was about to leave the cafe, when he heard the familiar buzz of a text. Strange, Eve shouldn't be replying, she was supposed to be at school.

Luckily it wasn't from Eve, but Sophia.

Hiya, Ridpath, here's the info you wanted.

Irene Golding, died at SunnySide Residential Home on July 22, 2020. Cause of death: Complications from Covid.

Ernest Golding, died at home on October 10, 2020. Cause of death: Complications from Covid.

The SunnySide death figures are:

2018 – 6 residential deaths
2019 – 8 residential deaths
2020 – 17 residential deaths
2021 – 14 residential deaths
2022 – 12 residential deaths
2023 – 14 residential deaths
2024 to date – 4 residential deaths

The last reported death was a Mrs Elsie Meredith on Sunday, February 4 from a myocardial infarction. Death cert signed by a Dr Sanghera.

Hope this helps. See you later. Sophia.

Ridpath stared at the figures. Why hadn't the death rate come down after the end of the pandemic? It might just be the composition of the residents of the home. He'd have to compare the number of deaths with similar-sized residential homes in the area, but surely the death rate wouldn't remain as high as it was during Covid?

The words from the letter sent to Clarence Montague came back to him.

They are killing us. Help us, we don't want to die.

Chapter TWENTY-TWO

Emily Parkinson parked up outside the brick-built warehouse otherwise known as Eccles Police Station. Nearby she could hear the buzz of traffic roaring along the M60, racing to get nowhere fast. She picked up the phone mounted on the outside wall of the station next to a large blue sign which stated starkly: *There is no Public Inquiry Facility at this Station.*

Another successful engagement with the public, she thought. She picked up the phone and dialled 101. After seven rings a male voice answered.

'Yeah.'

'Detective Sergeant Emily Parkinson here to see Detective Constable Fiona Barton.'

There was no reply from the unseen male but instead a loud buzz suggested the door was unlocked.

Emily pushed it open and walked into a dull hallway with offices leading off to the left and stairs leading up. She hadn't a clue where to go. From the top of the stairs, a face peered over the balustrade.

'Are you Emily?'

'Hiya, you must be Fiona Barton. We met on a course about five years ago at Edgeley Park.'

A tall, dark haired woman bounded down the stairs and stuck out her hand.

'I remember it well. Probably the most boring thing I ever attended as a copper. Come upstairs to my pod. I'd offer you coffee but I think they pull it straight from the Ship Canal and stick it in the machine.'

'That bad?'

'Worse.'

They walked slowly upstairs, Fiona swiped the card around her neck and Emily was led into a large, open-plan office. Behind a series of scattered desks, a mixture of men and women, some uniformed, were staring intently at computers. Off to the right, a large map of Manchester adorned one wall while to the left, behind a glass wall, Emily could see large screens displaying images from traffic cameras all over the city.

'Welcome to Operation Wolverine.'

'What's that when it's at home?'

'Uninsured vehicles basically. All the cars come here when they've been seized because a driver has been unable to produce insurance, or if there's something dodgy about their licence. Either way, we deal with it.'

'Never knew it existed. How long's this been going?'

'It started in 2008 and hasn't been working ever since. I don't think it's ever going to end.'

'How'd you end up here?'

'Do you mean how did I end up in this dead-end role for the last three years basically chasing idiots without insurance?'

'You could put it like that. Personally, I wouldn't but...'

'I wish I knew, I think I must have done something bad in a past life. I've put in three requests for a transfer but I keep getting the "you're too valuable to lose at the moment and you are doing great work protecting the citizens of Manchester" speech. We occasionally have some fun though. One day, a berk driving a Lamborghini came here to pick up his uninsured car. Of course, he still wasn't insured so we seized the Lambo.' She laughed to herself. 'Word of advice. If you're going to turn up at the police station to reclaim your previously seized vehicle, it might be worth checking first the car you turn up in is covered on your policy.'

'Pillock.'

'The good days are few and far between though. After three years, I've had enough. I'll give it one more, go for another transfer, and then I'll jack it all in if it goes nowhere.'

Emily Parkinson looked around the office. 'What a waste.'

'You're telling me. Anyway, you didn't come here to talk about my career, or lack of one, how can I help?'

'We're re-looking into the disappearance of Andrew Golding four years ago. I believe you were the investigating officer.'

'I thought it might have been about Andy, given the piece in the paper at the weekend. The top brass covering their arses again?'

'Something like that.'

'What do you want to know?'

'Everything and anything.'

'Take a seat, I hope you have a couple of decades.'

Emily sat down in a seat opposite Fiona Barton, taking out her notebook and began writing.

'It was all a bit of a mess. From memory, the young lad had gone missing on the Friday, but it wasn't reported by his parents until the Sunday. We didn't go round until the following day, shortage of man power probably.'

'That's it. Friday the 10th and Monday the 13th.'

'Well, I wasn't called in until the Wednesday, the 15th.'

'Why so long? He was a young boy.'

'Shortage of staff? Covid? A cock-up? Take your pick. I remember I'd had my day off and was called in on my first morning back by Inspector Warner and told to look into it. I got the impression they thought he had just done a runner from the family but as he was under sixteen, they had to investigate so I was given the job.'

'Just you?'

'Me and my size sixes. I went around to see the family. The mother, Sharon, was distraught. The step-father hovering like a bad smell and stinking of drink.'

'What did you think of him?'

'A waster. One of those blokes who latches on to vulnerable women and uses them as a wallet, ditching them when there's no more money or it all becomes too hard.'

'You interviewed him about the disappearance?'

'I did, but he had a cast iron alibi, confirmed by the mother, they had been in the house all the time. I talked to the neighbours and they agreed, seeing them drinking in the back garden.'

'So what happened next?'

'I followed the misper manual on missing kids. Visited the grandad. A tough old bird he was, put out all the usual information for the press and the internet.'

'When did you check the local CCTV?'

'The following day, Thursday. Most of it had gone. I was lucky and found a bank near Southern Cemetery with some footage. I instituted all the usual procedures; put in a request for his mobile phone to be tracked on the day of his disappearance, checked with the school, child social services, and all the various Missing Person acronyms, then I caught Covid. I always thought I got it from the family or the neighbours. Anyway, it was pretty bad for me, this was before the vaccine, I was coughing and spluttering like an old miner for three weeks and off for another two recuperating. I didn't get back to the job for nearly six weeks. As soon as I did, they sent me here. Must have thought I was still infectious or something.'

'Sorry to hear it was so bad for you.'

'You win some, you lose some.'

Emily checked her notes from the briefing. 'Why didn't you check the register of local sex offenders?'

'I did. It's the first thing you do when a child goes missing. I even visited two of them living on the estate but both had alibis.'

'It's not in the case notes.'

'There's a lot not in the notes.'

'Why?'

'A combination of me falling ill and the new bloody computer system they implemented then. Half the time I couldn't log on.

But I passed my written notes to the officer who took over the investigation.'

'Ramsden?'

'That's him. Didn't he put them in?'

Emily shook her head.

'This looks bad, doesn't it?'

Emily didn't reply.

'I'm going to be stuck here until hell freezes over, aren't I?'

'If you have a record you passed your notes on, it shouldn't be a problem.'

Fiona Barton went straight to her notebook and then checked with her diary on the computer. 'There you are. I passed them across on June 14, two weeks after I went ill with Covid. I did it from home as soon as I was able.'

'Can you send me a screen grab of your diary and notebook?'

'Will do. What's your email address?'

Emily gave it to her and within twenty seconds Fiona Barton had said, 'Done.'

'Great. You'll also be helped by the fact the family thought you did a great job.'

'That's something, at least. But I didn't find Andy, did I? How is Sharon?'

'Holding up and still campaigning. Enough to put the wind up my bosses anyway.'

'Good, they need it. Anybody who was involved in introducing PoliceWorks before it was ready should have been made to apologise to each and every copper who had to use it.'

Emily closed her notebook. 'Anything else you can think of not in the files?'

Fiona Barton stared into the distance. 'Only one thing. The grandfather said Andy was close to the grandmother. Used to visit her in the residential home even though he wasn't supposed to go there during lockdown. I never got round to see the grandad again before I got ill. I always felt there was something there, a lead I could have followed up. I put it in the notes I sent to Bert Ramsden. I bet he didn't use it.'

'You'd be right. What was the name of the residential home again?'

'Sunny something. SunnySide that was it. Big old house in West Didsbury.'

Chapter TWENTY-THREE

Ridpath walked through the portico of the SunnySide Residential Home into the reception area. A desk was unmanned in the corner but a bell placed on top suggested he would have to ring it. He did and stood there, waiting.

The house was one of the classic big old Edwardian mansions built to house the rich cotton merchants who had made their fortune in Manchester. Of course, it had been extensively remodelled over the years plus an enormous concrete extension had been added at the rear.

At the front though, the house remained pretty much as it had been for the last hundred years. The gardens particularly had been well kept. Ridpath noticed a large Japanese maple and numerous multicoloured rhododendrons fighting for space in the large grounds.

'Can I help you?'

A young woman in a light blue uniform covered by a stained plastic apron and wearing a face mask and gloves had appeared from nowhere.

'I'd like to see the manager of the facility please.'

'Do you have an appointment?'

The last thing Ridpath wanted to do was make an appointment and warn people he was coming. 'No, but I'm sure he'll see me.'

'Mrs Staunton never sees anybody without an appointment.'

'She'll see me.' He passed over his card.

'Thomas Ridpath, Coroner's Officer.' The girl read the words aloud as if convincing herself. 'Shall I give this to her?'

'That would be a good idea. You might also want to add I'm investigating on behalf of the coroner.'

'Okay,' she said doubtfully, 'but I still don't think she'll see you.'

'Just give her the card.'

The girl vanished behind a large pot plant. Ridpath walked over and discovered a door hidden behind it obviously leading to the interior of the residential home. He was about to go exploring, when it opened and a large woman stood in the doorway.

'Mr Ridpath, how can I help you?'

'And you are?'

'Mathilda Staunton, manager of SunnySide. How can I help?'

'I have a few questions I need to ask, is there anywhere we can go?'

'Come through to my office, we can have a chat there.'

They walked down a short corridor. Immediately Ridpath smelt the aroma of the aged; a peculiar mix of baby powder, urine and disinfectant.

The corridor led to a large room dotted with comfortable armchairs and tables. Three staff stood to one side, two men and the young woman. All were dressed in the same blue uniform, wearing purple masks and plastic gloves. Only the girl wore the stained, plastic apron.

A few residents sat at the tables playing a card game. Others sat in front of a large television in the corner which was showing one of those interminable *Escape to the Country* programmes. Funny, Ridpath thought, these are the people who have no escape to anywhere, least of all some unattainable British countryside. A few more sat in their chairs staring into mid-air, their eyes blank and their mouths open.

'The resident bedrooms are off to the right.' She waved in the general direction of the extension. 'Each resident has their own bedroom and we are manned twenty-four hours a day. Most of our residents are DOLs—'

'DOLS?'

'Deprived of Liberty. In other words, a social worker and a doctor has made an order the person is no longer able to care for or look after themselves. Usually, it's because they have Alzheimer's, dementia or some other illness where they can no longer care for themselves at home safely.'

'So they are sent here?'

'*Placed* here and we look after them. The local council pays or, if they have assets of more than £23,000, then they pay. Most have no family members, or if they do, the family neither wants them nor can care for them.'

'It sounds depressing.'

'We try not to make it so. My staff work extremely hard to make sure they are happy and we have things happening most days. As you can see, people often enjoy better lives here than they would do alone at home.'

Ridpath scanned the room. The residents did seem comfortable even though the place had a terribly institutional atmosphere.

'This way, Mr Ridpath.'

Mrs Staunton opened a door on the right which revealed another short corridor at the end of which was a small but comfortably furnished office.

'Would you like some tea?'

Ridpath shook his head and made himself comfortable in one of the chairs facing the desk. It felt like the headmaster's study he had spent far too much time being told off in when he was young.

'How can I help you and the coroner?'

It was the third time she had asked the question. She was either extremely nervous or over-keen to help. Either way, Ridpath was going to string her along a bit more.

'As you know, the coroner takes a personal interest in all the residential care facilities in his area.'

Not exactly true, but she wouldn't know Clarence Montague was not at all concerned about the aged.

'Even more so since the pandemic.'

'We have been recently assessed by the Care Quality Commission and our facilities were rated as good by them. What can be concerning the coroner? There have been no inquests into any of our residents who have passed away. Certainly not while I have been in charge.'

It was time to put her on the back foot.

'There are a few matters I would like to discuss with you. Recently, the coroner received a letter which we believe to be from one of your residents. The letter made serious allegations about a situation in your home.'

'Can I see the letter?'

Ridpath passed over a copy made by Sophia.

Mrs Staunton looked at it before pursing her lips and exclaiming, 'This is ridiculous. Anonymous letters sent to the coroner. "They are killing us. Help us. We don't want to die." How can you take this seriously? Obviously whoever wrote this is deranged.'

'I'm afraid, after the Shipton case, the coroner has to take all allegations of this sort seriously. This is your headed notepaper, isn't it?'

'Yes, but anybody could have written this. We have thirty-eight residents in our facility at this moment in time. Clearly one of them has a grudge against this establishment or against me.'

Ridpath found it interesting how quickly she had made the allegations personal. 'But you do realise we have to look into this matter. Particularly when we see the number of deaths in your home has hardly changed from during the height of the pandemic.'

'Mr Ridpath,' she smiled condescendingly, 'this is an old people's residential home. People die all the time. They have had fruitful lives and then they pass on. To suggest either myself or any of my staff are killing them is absurd.'

Ridpath made a note in his book, making her wait for his next question. 'There is one other thing I would like to ask you, Mrs Staunton. It concerns the death of one of your residents, a Mrs Irene Golding.'

'The name doesn't mean anything to me, Mr Ridpath.'

'She died in July 2020.'

'Sorry, I still can't recall her. That was during lockdown wasn't it? We had many deaths around then.'

'Could you check your files? I presume you keep files on all your residents?'

'As we are bound to do by law.'

Ridpath sat silently, waiting for her to move. Finally, she got up and walked over to a metal filing cabinet in the corner. 'What name did you say?'

'Irene Golding, date of death July 22, 2020.'

She rifled through the files finally pulling out a thin brown folder and began reading it. 'Now I remember Mrs Golding. She wasn't with us for a long time and she died during lockdown. Another one of our Covid fatalities, I'm afraid.'

'Were there a lot of deaths during the pandemic?'

'No more than any other residential home. You have to understand it was a difficult time for the industry, Mr Ridpath, old people were being discharged from hospitals all over the country to make bed space. Most weren't tested before they were sent to us. Pretty soon, the disease made its way into the homes, leading to deaths. We weren't helped by blanket DNR notices issued by the government.'

'DNR notices?'

'Do not resuscitate. If our residents became ill, they weren't to be treated by doctors, just given palliative care. It's why so many died, particularly if they had co-morbidities such as diabetes.'

Ridpath shook his head. 'They weren't given medical treatment?'

She frowned. 'Come on, Mr Ridpath, you were a coroner's officer during that period. Are you telling me you didn't know?'

'I swear nobody told me. Nobody knew...'

She smiled, like a cat who had been presented with a bowl of cream. 'And how many inquests have you opened into those deaths?'

'There was a government instruction no inquests were to be opened if the cause of death was from Covid-19.'

'And you wonder why nobody knew?'

Ridpath pursed his mouth. He should have known what was going on in the care homes. Why didn't he know? Was it a sort of collective amnesia? And why hadn't there been any newspaper reports on what had happened? Didn't the nation want to know what had happened to our old people or was the truth too difficult to hear?

He made a mental note to do more research. Perhaps read the transcript from the Covid inquiry, particularly the section on care homes.

Mrs Staunton read more of the folder and said, 'Anyway, returning to Mrs Golding. I remember her. An older woman, always unkempt. Her grandson kept visiting here even though it was illegal at the time.'

'A grandson. Was his name Andrew Golding?'

She glanced at the file. 'We never found out the boy's name. A member of my staff had to escort him off the premises a few times. I seem to remember having to call the police once. By the time they arrived, the boy was long gone.'

'Can I see the file?'

She stared at him before closing it. 'I don't think I can allow it. These files contain confidential patient and resident information.' She stood up and walked back to the metal cabinet. 'Actually, I will have to get guidance from the legal department of my head office before I release any of them. I hope you understand.'

'I don't, *actually*. This person has already died, letting me see her file will not affect you, or her, in any way.'

Mrs Staunton's eyes narrowed. 'Why are you so interested in this particular death?'

And then her eyes flashed and a knowing look crossed her face. 'Golding? Golding? Wasn't that the name of the boy who went missing? Why would the coroner be interested in a missing boy?'

Ridpath knew he had to tell her. 'I am a coroner's officer but I also work for Greater Manchester Police. They have tasked me to look into this missing boy and the coroner has asked me to look into your residential home. Unfortunately, both investigations have brought me here.'

Mrs Staunton closed the file and placed it carefully back in the metal cabinet, locking it with a small key. 'I am going to have to ask you to leave Mr Ridpath. I need to hold discussions with my head office. You will have to get their agreement if you want to come here again.'

'Why are you being so difficult? I am here now.'

'I am not being difficult. I am protecting the rights and personal information of my residents. If you want to find out about them, please get permission from my head office. I think it is time you left.'

'I can get a search warrant, Mrs Staunton, but I wouldn't like to disturb your residents.'

'Are you threatening me, Mr Ridpath?'

'Not at all, but I will get that information. It is pertinent to my investigations both for the coroner and for Greater Manchester Police.'

'I will repeat myself, Mr Ridpath. Please leave.'

Chapter TWENTY-FOUR

As he left SunnySide, Ridpath checked his watch.

Three p.m.

Another interview he hadn't handled particularly well. Not like him at all. But he did need the information and nobody was going to stop him from getting it.

An allegation had been made against the residential home and it seemed Andy Golding had visited there. Two of his investigations had converged on one location. That immediately sent a red light flashing in his head.

He checked his watch again.

Did he have time to go back to the coroner's office before the meeting at HQ? His decision was helped by a text from Sophia.

His Lordship wants to know the outcome of your meeting at SunnySide. Can I tell him anything?

He immediately replied:

I'm coming back to brief him right now

He took one last glance at the residential home. The hair on the back of his neck rose. Something wasn't right there and he was determined to find out what was going on.

He drove back to Stockford, cursing the traffic lights, slow drivers and aged cyclists in skintight lycra who seemed to be hogging the road. What was it about seventy-year-old men and colourful lycra? It seemed to be the fashion choice of the prematurely senile.

Finally, he parked up at the Coroner's Court and immediately went to Clarence Montague's office, knocking on the door.

No answer.

He knocked again and heard a voice behind him.

'He's not there.' It was Jenny Oldfield, the office manager, who these days eschewed her usual colourful retro outfits and dazzling eye make-up in favour of black pinstripe twinsets. 'He's gone to get his teeth cleaned. Said it was urgent.'

Ridpath sighed. 'I've just driven like a madman to brief him on an issue that's come up.'

'He's back tomorrow morning and you know he won't answer his phone once he leaves the office. Insists we do though…'

She rolled her eyes and turned to walk back to her office. Ridpath followed her to the entrance.

'How are you managing, Jenny?' Ridpath asked her.

She stopped. 'I'm not. I put in my notice. I'll be leaving at the end of the month. I've had enough and a great job has come up in the Mayor's office. Apparently, they think I'm worth employing.'

The office was losing another key member of staff. Why didn't Montague understand what he was doing?

For once, Ridpath was at a loss for words. He mumbled, 'We'll all miss you, Jenny.' He took a deep breath. 'Do you have to leave now? The office needs you.'

'I'll miss you too, Ridpath.' She looked all around her at all the old files lining the shelves. 'This place has been my life for the last fifteen years and I've loved working here but I won't work for anyone who doesn't appreciate what I do or who I am. Life's too short to spend with arseholes. I've accepted the job with the Mayor.'

'I'm sorry to hear that, Jenny. I've loved working with you. Can I convince you to stay? Just till we find out when Mrs Challinor is coming back?'

The woman ambled over and gave him a hug. 'Thank you, Ridpath, your words have made my day. But I don't think she's ever coming back and I've just typed his lordship's application to become the head of this office.'

Then she stepped back obviously embarrassed. 'I shouldn't have said that, how indiscreet of me.' She indicated over her shoulder. 'I need to get back to my laptop. His Lordship wants an inventory of the office supplies on his desk by tomorrow morning. I'm now counting boxes of paper clips. Still, it keeps me out of trouble.'

She went back down the corridor and Ridpath was left on his own outside the door. He was suddenly painfully aware of the absence of Mrs Challinor. The glue holding them all together. In just a few short months, Montague had destroyed the work she had spent her life putting together.

He went back to his office and found Sophia.

'Hiya, Ridpath, how was SunnySide?'

'Not so sunny, but thanks for the information, it was extremely useful. His lordship has already gone for the day so I can't brief him.'

'He came in ten minutes ago and said he wanted a written report on your visit on his desk tomorrow morning.'

'I'll do it tonight. In the meantime, can you find out more about the home for me? Who owns it? Corporate structure, the history, all the usual stuff. Plus, can you take the mortality numbers back to 2015 and check the latest figures.'

'Something not right there?'

'It feels wrong, they're hiding something. We may have to apply for a court order to search the place and its records.'

'I'll start to prepare the usual documents. We haven't applied for a warrant in ages. I would be surprised if His Lordship knew what one was.'

Ridpath checked the time on the clock on the wall.

4.15 p.m.

Why was he always rushing to be late?

His phone buzzed with a new text.

> At Maisie's, I knew you wouldn't make it home.

The last thing he needed to deal with right now was a stroppy teenager. He texted back:

> We need to talk this evening when I get back.

He was tempted to soften the message with an emoji of a Snoopy talking to Charlie Brown, but he didn't, pressing send anyway. He wasn't in the mood for being playful and Eve would have to realise that.

Chapter TWENTY-FIVE

Everybody was already assembled in the meeting room at Police HQ when Ridpath walked in. It was obvious they had been waiting for him.

'Sorry I'm late. Traffic was a nightmare.' That was an under-statement. It seemed half of Manchester's roads were being dug up at the moment and all of them on Ridpath's route.

Steve Carruthers stared at him and shook his head. 'Let's get started, shall we? What do we have so far?' he said, looking to Ridpath as Senior Investigating Officer to begin the meeting.

'Right, well, we've been to see the family and checked the case notes from four years ago. If I'm honest, Steve, it looks a mess; the investigation was too slow to get started, turnover of officers, missed opportunities, badly kept case notes...'

'Yes, we know, Ridpath, but what have we discovered that's new?'

'Perhaps I can help here, sir,' Helen Shipton interrupted. She opened her laptop and turned it towards Carruthers. Ridpath had to lean over to see what was on the screen. 'As you know, we have this image of Andy Golding taken from a bank ATM opposite Southern Cemetery at 11.23 a.m. on the day of his disappearance. I created a grid of all the other possible CCTV cameras in the area and then cross-referenced it with incident reports at West Didsbury. I got two possible hits.'

Ridpath stared across at her, raising his eyebrow.

'Working with digital forensics, I isolated two additional images of Andy. The first was time-coded at 11.42 a.m. and was taken from the camera of an IT company. Luckily for us, they wanted to test the storage capacity of their machines and retained the images from four years ago.'

'Lucky for us,' Ridpath repeated.

Helen Shipton smiled. 'Here it is. As you can see, Andy is walking past the company here.' She switched to a map of the area with a red arrow pointing directly to the position on Barlow Moor Road.

'But it's four hundred yards from the last camera. Why has it taken him twenty minutes to walk the distance?' asked Steve Carruthers.

'Ah, I see you have spotted that as well, sir. I went back to the cemetery and checked recent burials with their office. It appears his grandmother was buried there six days before Andy went missing. Of course, the Covid restrictions meant only close family members could attend the actual funeral. Andy may not have been allowed to go.'

'Why didn't his mother tell us about this?' asked Ridpath.

Helen Shipton shrugged her shoulders. 'I don't know. I didn't go to the interview with the mother.' She pressed a key on her laptop. 'Here's a picture of the grave. I think Andy may have visited here between the two CCTV shots. I walked a possible route he may have taken through the cemetery, and if you add on five minutes for reflection at the graveside, the timings match pretty well.'

Ridpath glance at her and the other members of the team. Did they know about her discoveries before this meeting or was she grandstanding for Carruthers?

'Great, we're getting somewhere at producing a timeline for the day he disappeared. Well done, Helen.'

'But that's not all, boss. I cross-referenced the date against an accident on the incident list. As you know, they download and retain the footage from traffic and ANPR cameras in case of possible court proceedings. I found this.'

A still picture of Andy appeared, waiting to cross a road.

'There was an accident at this junction, two hours later. Luckily, they kept the footage for the whole day.' She leant forward to press a key. 'But this is where it gets interesting.'

The footage ran. Andy appeared into frame and waited at the traffic light. A hand came in and pulled him out of shot.

'What did I just see? Was he with somebody else?' Carruthers asked.

'He appears to be with an older male, sir.'

'Don't we have anything else? Can't we see who he's with?'

'I'm afraid the camera is fixed and there is nothing else. I had the forensic technician blow up the image of the hand.' The screenshot appeared in a tight, but slightly blurred, close-up. 'It doesn't give us much but we can say with certainty he was with an older male at 11.58 a.m. on the day he disappeared.'

Emily leant in closer to the screen. 'On the man's hand, there appears to be a tattoo?'

'I noticed too. I asked the techies to give us a close-up of it.' A new image appeared on the screen.

'It looks like a bird, a swallow.'

'Chrissy, can you check with HOLMES and Force Intelligence. Any records on such tattoos?'

'Will do, Ridpath,' she answered making a note.

'That means he must have met somebody in the time between the image being taken outside the IT shop and crossing the road,' said Emily.

'Exactly. This man.'

An image appeared of a map of the area already marked with a red arrow and a blue arrow. 'He met the man between Palatine Road and Princess Parkway.'

She sat back smugly.

'Brilliant work, Helen. Now, we're making some progress.'

But Ridpath wasn't looking at Helen Shipton, he was staring at the screen. Right in the middle of the map was SunnySide Residential Home.

Chapter TWENTY-SIX

All the staff were gathered in the common room by Mathilda Staunton as the day shift was ending and the night shift beginning. She clapped her hands loudly, forcing everybody to look at her.

'If I could have some silence. I have Mr Bruce Edwards from corporate affairs with me. He has an important announcement for all of you.'

A well-dressed man in his late forties stepped forward. 'Thank you, Mathilda. Some of you may know we had a visit today from a policeman masquerading as a coroner's officer, a Detective Inspector Ridpath I believe.'

He glanced across at the Mrs Staunton who confirmed the name with a slight nod of her head and crossed her arms across her chest.

'He was supposedly investigating a note apparently sent by one of the residents to the coroner's office. I won't repeat the allegations in the note but suffice to say it makes serious accusations of corporate malfeasance against SunnySide and its staff.'

A buzz went around the room.

He raised his hands to quieten the people. 'Naturally, we take such accusations seriously. Even more so at the moment as we are being taken over by the European Residential Homes Group, an important corporate development for the company. We believe,' another glance at Mrs Staunton, 'they have no basis in fact. I have already sent a stern letter complaining about the attitude of the officer concerned to the coroner and will follow up tomorrow with an urgent meeting with the corporate affairs people at Police HQ and with the coronial authorities in London.'

Another buzz went around the room.

'As this is an important, perhaps crucial, matter the company requires you report any and every approach by this coroner's officer to me immediately. Not reporting the approach or talking to this coroner officer will be grounds for instant dismissal as per section 3C of your contracts regarding actions likely to damage the reputation of your employers.'

He took time to stare at everybody in the room.

One of the staff, a young man employed as an admin assistant, put his hand up. 'Somebody from the coroner's office rang me about an hour ago. They wanted information regarding deaths in the home since 2015.'

'I hope you haven't provided the information.'

'Not yet.'

'Good. What was the person's name?'

'A Miss Rahman.'

'Thank you. Please refer all questions, phone calls or inquiries to me immediately. I will handle them for you. It will make your life easier.'

A man still wearing his mask and purple gloves put his hand up. 'What did the note say?'

The corporate affairs head thought for a long time before answering, as if weighing up the balance between honesty and confidentiality. He finally came down on the latter.

'The actual wording of the note isn't important. The allegations were serious and need to be handled by my office at this time.'

He stared around the room once more. 'Is everything clear? Good, thank you for your time. And please let me add, everybody in the corporate office is well aware of the great work you do day-in and day-out, looking after all our residents. I think I can safely say, with Mathilda's agreement, this is one of our most successful residential homes and is a shining star in the corporate portfolio. Thank you for your time.'

As the staff filed out to go back to work or go home, Bruce Edwards turned to Mrs Staunton. 'I think that went rather well, don't you?'

'We won't be bothered by Ridpath again?'

'Oh, I'm sure you will, but just pass him on to me. Our legal team will slap so many injunctions on him, he won't know whether he is coming or going.'

'He threatened me with a warrant to search the home.'

'I've already spoken to the head coroner for this area, it's unlikely to happen. The reputation of our company must be protected at this time. I'm sure you understand the financial implications of any scandal, Mathilda. We've worked too hard to let some pipsqueak of a coroner's officer spoil our rewards.' He put his arm around her shoulders. 'You leave him to me from now on.'

Chapter TWENTY-SEVEN

They finished taking Steve Carruthers through the rest of the investigation. Emily updated them on her interview with Fiona Barton while Ridpath added his notes from the meetings with the family, John Newton and at SunnySide Residential Home.

'I also checked up on John Newton. He was banged up in Preston both times, seemed to have kept his nose clean.'

'Thanks Emily, anything from you Chrissy?'

'The notes mention a mobile phone. It seems a request was made to BT to track the movements of his phone from their towers but nobody followed up. Unfortunately, they no longer retain the data from 2020, said I should have contacted them sooner. I hate being lectured by a bloody phone company.'

'Another missed opportunity?' asked Ridpath.

Chrissy nodded. 'We could have followed his movements through the phone on the day he disappeared but now the information has gone.' She paused for a moment. 'I looked at HOLMES and the NDNAD database. Nothing. One thing I did discover though, is we keep the DNA of over 300,000 kids between ten and eighteen on NDNAD. Surprised me, why are we keeping the DNA of children?'

'I guess they have been arrested and charged.'

'But kids?'

'I know, I know,' said Steve Carruthers looking at his watch, 'but this is not the time or the place to be questioning the policies of the DNA people.' He was silent for a moment, checking the information written on the boards. 'Great, well done, you've made real progress, but we still don't know what happened to Andy Golding. A young man can't just vanish into thin air.'

'My copper's nose tells me SunnySide has something to do with it. The manager said a boy had visited his grandmother despite the care home being in lockdown. I think the boy was Andy. They had to throw him out and call the police at one point.'

'That's all well and good, Ridpath, but I can't get a warrant to search the place on your "copper's nose",' he formed quotation marks with his fingers. 'We need evidence; hard, cold, pure as the driven snow evidence.' He stared at the people in front of him. 'Next steps?'

Ridpath took charge. 'Emily can you get Fiona Barton's notes and add them to the case. Plus contact the other detectives involved and the sergeant who first interviewed the family, what was his name?'

'Aiden Markham. He took early retirement last year.'

'Find him and see if there was anything he noticed not in the misper report.'

'Will do, Ridpath.'

'We need to show this new footage from Helen's work to the family to confirm it is Andy. Can you do that, Emily?'

'You want to show them he was with another male, Ridpath?' she asked.

'No, not yet. Use the footage of him standing at the kerb but edit out the presence of the man.'

'Sharon Golding might know who it is.'

'Ask her if she knows anybody with a swallow tattoo but don't tell her why. I don't want the papers to know.'

'Okay.'

'Last thing Emily, can you find out who were Andy Golding's mates at school and in his area? Check on his lifestyle. Was he involved in gangs? Had any arrests? You know the sort of stuff.'

'Wasn't it done at the time of his disappearance?' asked Carruthers.

'If it was, gaffer, we don't have any notes on it. My bet is Ramsden didn't bother, too much like hard work.'

'Jesus, if the papers ever get hold of this, we'll be toast. It's misper 101 to check on the lifestyle of any missing child.' He placed his hands on the desk in front of him. 'Thanks, everyone, you've made great progress in a short time. Let's meet up tomorrow at the same time so I can brief Claire when she returns from London. Ridpath, can you stay behind for a second?'

The others glanced at Ridpath as they packed up their files and laptops, gradually leaving the room.

When the door was closed, Steve Carruthers turned to Ridpath and spoke in his quiet, Glaswegian accent. 'Are you okay?'

'Fine, sir.'

'You don't look fine.'

'All is good, sir, we're making good progress with the investigation into the young man's disappearance...'

'Well, tell me, what just happened there?'

'What do you mean, sir?'

'Don't come the innocent with me, Ridpath. It was obvious to a blind sailor after a night on the pish you knew nothing about the CCTV discoveries.'

Ridpath realised he had to come clean. 'That's true, sir. As you saw, I was late for the meeting and didn't have time to get a briefing before we met you.'

'She didn't call you? Let you know by text?'

Ridpath stayed silent.

'And what about your team, why didn't they let you know?'

Ridpath remained silent.

'Or did they not know either?' Carruthers let out a long sigh and sat back in his chair. 'You are the SIO on this case, Ridpath, I shouldn't have to remind you. Yet you seem distracted, unfocused. I need a Ridpath on top of his game not somebody giving 50 per cent to the job.'

'That's unfair, sir. Myself and my team always give everything to every case we work on.'

'Well, laddie, you need to get on top of this one pretty quick.' He closed his eyes for a brief second before re-opening and speaking with a softer voice. 'Listen, I've worked with detectives like Helen Shipton before. They are good at their job but they are not team players. I didn't once hear her use the word "we". You need to make sure she understands you are the SIO,' a long pause, 'for her sake and for yours. Got it?'

'Of course, sir.'

Steve Carruthers stood up. 'We need this sorted and sorted quick, Ridpath.'

'Right, boss, it will be.'

'Good, I want—' before he could finish his sentence, his mobile rang. Carruthers held up his finger and mouthed the words, 'One second.'

'DCI Steve Carruthers.'

Ridpath watched and listened as he answered the call.

'Right, sir. Yes. Got it. On my way, sir.'

He switched off the phone and stood beside the desk, staring into mid-air. Then he spoke quietly. 'They've just found a body on a street corner in Withington. One of the coppers there says it matches the description of Andrew Golding.'

Chapter TWENTY-EIGHT

Harold Lardner looked up from the magazine article he was reading. Some researchers in Germany had written a hopeless paper on cryobiology. Too basic and too ill-informed. He had discovered more than those researchers years ago and still they were lagging behind.

He threw it into the bin in disgust. Outside his cell, the noises from the prison – otherwise known as Ashworth High Security Hospital – were at their height.

Always after the evening dinner, the inmates gathered to watch *Coronation Street*, chat about their meaningless lives or play an even more pointless game of table tennis in the games area.

He always retreated to the safety and peace of his cell at this time. He couldn't stand to be out in the corridors, listening to their inane chatter. The only time he felt lonely was when he was surrounded by other people. In his cell, he enjoyed the quiet of four walls, a rickety bed and his small desk.

Reading the magazine had taken his mind off the project for a moment. He had given the go-ahead to begin three days ago, but he had been planning it for six months now. The actual work had started a month ago, but soon it would be complete. He was running out of time, it had to happen soon.

He went through the details in his mind once again, mentally ticking off each step, each pressure point. All was good, planned down to the last detail. The disciples briefed on their duties, nothing left to chance.

After all, he had nothing else to do in this prison except dream of a bloody future.

It was one of the contradictions of the British penal system that prisoners came out of the jail better equipped to do damage to society than before their incarceration.

It was the same for him in Ashworth. Before, he had no time to plan his deaths properly, now he had too much time.

So it goes.

There would be no failure this time.

He would succeed or die trying.

He didn't mind death, in fact he welcomed it. Dr Mansell was right in one respect; 12,000 post mortems had affected him. They had convinced him we were all only a bag of cartilage, sinew, bones, blood, fat, assorted proteins and carbohydrates. Ashes to ashes, dust to dust, with a brief stop for a glass of wine in between.

Whatever the humanists said, we didn't matter.

God did exist and it was him. He decided if people lived or died. He decided the time and type of their death. He gave the thumbs up or thumbs down.

The meaning of life is it eventually ends. And he was the Angel of Death committed to making that happen.

And like the omniscient and omnipotent God of the New Testament, he would be terrible in his vengeance.

It was time to pay back those who had deprived him of liberty, thrown him in this place, sucked the life, and the death, from him.

The plan had started. A few more days and death would come to those who had wronged him.

Death comes as the end.

For some, the end would come sooner than they thought.

The Beast they called him. From today, he would live up to his name.

Chapter TWENTY-NINE

The crime scene had already been sealed off by the time Steve Carruthers and Ridpath arrived. They both signed in on a clipboard held by a constable at the outer cordon and walked towards the lights covering a tent erected by the CSIs at the corner of the street. The area was a quiet, leafy suburb with classic black and white painted Edwardian houses. Ridpath saw a street sign: Seagram Road.

Why did that ring a bell?

Before they had advanced more than ten yards they were stopped by a burly man in a coat two sizes too big for him. 'Where do you think you two are going?'

Steve Carruthers showed his warrant card.

'Sorry, sir, I didn't recognise you.'

'Were you the first person on the scene, detective?'

'DC Stan Jones, sir. I was. We got the 999 call at five thirty. A woman on her way home from work saw the young lad lying there. At first, she thought he was drunk or on drugs. She went to help him and then realised he was dead.'

'Who spotted he resembled the missing lad?'

'I did, sir. The picture is still up on West Didsbury's notice-board. The station is less than a mile over there.' He gestured in the general direction.

Ridpath looked around him. He recognised the neighbour-hood. They were in the neighbouring suburb to West Didsbury, slightly closer to the city. To think, he had been less than a mile away this afternoon interviewing the manager of the nursing home.

'Right, let's take a look at him.'

Carruthers pulled a pair of blue latex gloves from his pocket and approached the white tent covering the body. A CSI stood in his way.

'You can't go in yet. The medical examiner hasn't seen the body.'

'I know,' said Ridpath, 'I'm from the coroner's office, I just rang him. He'll be here in a few minutes.'

It was one of Ridpath's jobs to arrange medical officers to attend crime scenes like this as well as to commission a post-mortem if one was needed by the police.

'We won't touch the body, we want to make an ID.'

'Right, sir, if you could stay outside as I pull the flap back.'

The CSI lifted one side of the tent. Inside, Ridpath could see a young man lying on his back wearing a striped T-shirt and shorts. He looked exactly the same as the picture on the wall at HQ.

'What do you think?'

'It's him, Steve, I'm sure of it.'

'I agree. We'd better notify the mother to confirm the ID.'

Carruthers nodded once at the CSI, who closed the flap of the tent. Both men walked back towards the crowd being held back by a mixture of police cars and police officers. Despite the cold weather, people were filming the scene on their mobiles and the members of the press were hanging around the outside of the cordon like a pack of hungry hyenas.

'What I don't understand is how he looks exactly the same as the picture and the CCTV we saw this afternoon. He's still fourteen, he hasn't aged a minute since the day he disappeared.'

Ahead of them, a disturbance was happening as a man pushed through the crowd, shouting in a high-pitched voice, 'Let me through, let me through.'

He was briefly stopped by a copper before being allowed under the tape. He saw Ridpath and strode towards him.

'Brass monkey weather, Ridpath. This one of yours?'

'It is Dr Schofield. Have you met my boss, DCI Steve Carruthers?'

'We've already been introduced. A stabbing in Rochdale wasn't it DCI Carruthers? Victim bled out on the floor of an Aldi next to the fruit and veg.'

'We're still looking for the man who did it. He's done a runner to Thailand, but we'll get him eventually.'

'What have we got here?'

'A young man who disappeared four years ago.'

'Cause of death?'

'I was rather hoping you'd tell me, doctor.'

He bustled past them. 'I shall certainly try, Ridpath,' he said over his shoulder and he laid his bag down beside the tent. From inside he pulled out a white, one-piece Tyvek body suit wrapped in cellophane and proceeded to put it on carefully, adjusting the hood so no stray hairs escaped. He put white shoe covers on each shoe then pulled out a bright blue face mask, adjusted it to fit snugly over his mouth and nodded to the CSI. The flap was pulled back and he entered the tent, vanishing from view.

Ridpath and Carruthers waited for him to reappear. All around them the crowds were increasing, swelled by the news of the incident and the live broadcasting of the event by a reporter from the *Manchester Evening News*.

Carruthers strode over to the sergeant in charge and instructed him to extend the cordon by another seventy yards to the end of the street and create an inner cordon where only CSIs and dedicated investigators would be allowed.

Instantly, the sergeant assembled his men and began moving the crowds of onlookers, the news crews and the live reporter back from the scene. The reporters all went reluctantly, protesting they had every right to be there, but the sergeant was firm in his instructions.

While this was happening, Ridpath made a call to Angela Knight, the mother of Eve's best friend. 'Hi there, I'm sorry I have a favour to ask you. Is it possible for Eve to sleep over tonight at your house? Something has come up at work.'

The noise as the reporters were being pushed back became louder so Ridpath moved closer to the tent.

'It's no problem, Ridpath, Maisie will be so happy to have Eve here. I hope everything is okay?'

'It's fine, too much to do as usual and I've been put on a new job.' He was reluctant to talk about his work even with Angela. 'Could you put Eve on the phone and I'll explain it to her.'

'I'll get her.'

There was silence at the end of the phone, Ridpath wasn't looking forward to this conversation, particularly after his daughter's comments this morning.

A crackle on the end of the line followed by a surly, 'Yeah.'

'Hi, Eve, I'm sorry but I don't think I can make it back this evening, something has come up at work.'

'What's new? It's always the same old story. I thought we were supposed to have a chat this evening or had you forgotten?'

'I hadn't forgotten, and I'm sorry, but—'

'But it wasn't important enough for you to come home.'

'I'm dealing with a murder inquiry,' he snapped back, 'and for just once in your life I wish you'd think of somebody else instead of yourself for a change.'

As soon as he said it, Ridpath wished he hadn't.

There was a long silence at the end of the phone. 'Whatever, *Dad*,' was the eventual response.

'I'll try to pick you up from school tomorrow.'

'Don't bother.'

The phone line went dead. He was tempted to call her back but knew he didn't have anything to say. Accusing her of being selfish was stupid of him. What teenager isn't? It was like accusing a scorpion of being cruel because it used its sting.

He looked around him. The crowd had now been pushed to the end of the street and a feeling of relative calm shrouded the area. He wandered back to where Carruthers was waiting.

'Difficult call?'

'The daughter. I told her I'd be home this evening. She wasn't happy when I said I would be late back.'

'How old is she?'

'Fourteen.'

'Teenagers. Can't live with 'em, can't live without 'em.'

'Sounds like you've been through the same wringer?'

'And the washing machine, mangle and dryer. Two daughters, both at university now thank God, but they did try my patience. If it's any consolation, it gets better when they reach eighteen.'

'Only four more years to go then.'

'Aye, it's a long sentence. Four years of hard labour.' He scratched his nose and took a step forward. 'You know you can go home if you want. I'll handle here.'

'Thanks for the offer, sir, but it's my case, my responsibility. I'm the SIO.'

'Aye, you are.'

'I could say the same to you. Go home, no point in hanging round here.'

The DCI shuffled his feet and pulled his coat tighter around his body. 'I'll stay, if that's all right. Between you, me and the lamppost, this is the first decent piece of policing I've done since I came down from Glasgow. These days, I spend more time in meetings managing budgets, rosters and bloody overtime than I do being a copper.'

'The perils of being promoted, sir.'

'It's Steve, boss, or the useless git in the corner office, Ridpath. "Sir" makes me feel like my dad.'

'Okay... boss.'

At that moment, Dr Schofield came out of the tent, taking off his mask and removing his gloves.

'Well, gentlemen, from a cursory examination, I think the young man has been strangled. I'll confirm the conclusion during the post-mortem, but there is extensive bruising around the neck area and the hyoid bone appears to be broken. I'll perform the post-mortem tomorrow morning, right now I need the CSIs to take their pictures so my men can take the body back to the mortuary.'

Steve Carruthers coughed loudly. 'Can't you do the post-mortem earlier, doctor? We would like to know the cause and the time of death as soon as we can.'

'Normally, I would be happy to accede to your wishes and perform the post-mortem this evening, Chief Inspector, but there is a slight problem.'

'What's that?'

'I have to wait for the body to thaw out first.'

Chapter THIRTY

I watched from the crowd.

Nearby, a reporter from the Manchester Evening News was speaking on camera.

'This is Alf Cummings, live from Seagram Road in Withington. We're not sure exactly what is going on but police are out in force along with a team of CSIs. As you can see this is a quiet, suburban street which never sees this much activity. Talking with one of the policemen manning the cordon, it seems a body was found earlier this evening by one of the residents. We don't know any more at this time but we will remain live so you can watch as the events unfurl.'

I turned away from the reporter and walked to the edge of the cordon where I was stopped by the long arm of the law, this one belonging to a particularly broad-shouldered sergeant.

'You can't go any further, this area is cordoned off.'

'What's going on?'

'I'm not at liberty to say, please move back.'

Did all coppers talk like that? Or were they trained in police-speak at the academy?

I peered over the heads of the crowd, seeing the detectives stride to the white tent at the side of the road, exactly where I had dumped the body two hours ago.

The Master was right, they wouldn't move it until the doctor gave his permission.

I walked away from the cordon to find a quiet place in one of the side streets. I took out my phone and called the number on speed dial.

The Master answered after two rings, he must have been waiting for the call.

'Well?'

'They've found the body and he's here.'

'The doctor has arrived?'

'Late, as you predicted Master.'

'He would be late to his own funeral that one.' A long pause. 'Good. Go back to the home and carry out the next step in the plan.'

'Are you sure, Master, the police—'

'Are you questioning me?'

'No, Master, I—'

'Just do as you have been instructed.'

'Yes, Master. I will follow your instructions to the letter.'

'So you should.'

The dull buzzing of the end of a call echoed in his ears. *Should I stay and watch for developments?*

No. The Master had ordered me to the home and it was my duty to obey.

Chapter THIRTY-ONE

The rest of the evening passed quickly for Ridpath. After confirming with the Director of Operations that MIT was going to run the investigation, Steve Carruthers concentrated on managing the cordon and the coordination of the house-to-house inquiry.

'Get the teams to ask if anybody saw anything unusual in the local area and see if any of the houses have CCTV, particularly those new doorbell thingamabobs.'

'Video doorbells.'

'That's it, doorbell thingamabobs. We can follow up tomorrow with a more detailed house-to-house plan.'

'Thank you, Ridpath. I may be a chief inspector but I do know how to coordinate a house-to house.'

'Sorry, sir... boss.'

While Carruthers put it together, Ridpath sent a text to Emily Parkinson.

> Found Andy Golding. Can you go to see the family and warn them? We may need the mum to formally ID the body tomorrow.

> Already here. Showing her the photos from Helen Shipton's CCTV. Are we sure it's Andy?

Positive. Can you ask Helen to drop what she's doing and get over here?

OK, I'll message her. She vanished straight after the meeting.

Thanks. Meeting tomorrow at nine a.m. Please let everybody know.

Will do.

Twenty minutes later Helen Shipton arrived and elbowed her way through the crowds still hanging around.

'I'm here, Ridpath. What do you want me to do?'

'About time. Come with me.'

He walked over to where the woman who had found the body, a Mrs Anthony, had been quietly sitting in a police car.

'Hello, Mrs Anthony, my name is Detective Inspector Ridpath and this is my colleague DC Shipton. I believe you found the young man?'

'I was walking home from the shops and I saw the body lying in the streets. I thought it was one of the dossers you see in town. There's more and more of them on the streets these days, I don't know what the council is doing.'

'You saw him lying there, so what did you do?'

'Well, I walked over to him and said, "You can't lie here, young man, you'll catch your death of cold." He was only wearing a T-shirt and shorts in the middle of February, I was worried for him. He didn't answer so I told him again. I said, "You can't lie in the middle of the pavement." Still no answer, so I bent down and touched his shoulder. It was so cold and hard, like touching a block of ice. I knew he was dead then, so I called the police.'

'You touched his shoulder, nowhere else?'

'I didn't want to touch him again, not after the first time.'

'Did you see anyone near the body?'

She shook her head. 'I didn't see anybody. He was lying on the pavement all alone.'

'No cars or vans in the street?'

She shook her head.

'Did anybody pass you driving a car or a van?'

'Not that I remember. There's not much traffic on this street. Nothing much happens round here.'

'And you live nearby?'

She pointed to a house about ten doors down. 'Number 27, been there all my life.'

'Thank you, Mrs Anthony. DC Shipton will now take a formal statement from you and she'll get you to sign it.'

Mrs Anthony looked worried. 'Can't I go home now? You see, my Ron will be coming home from work soon and he likes his tea as soon as he comes back. Well, I haven't made it yet, have I?'

'Can't Ron make his own tea?' snapped Helen Shipton.

The woman looked aghast. 'That's my job. And Ron does like a hot tea when he gets home especially on nights like these.'

'Okay, Mrs Anthony. This officer will take you home and take the statement there. She can also explain the situation to your husband.'

A look of relief crossed the woman's face. 'A policewoman in my house. Ron will be so surprised.'

'As soon as you've finished taking the statement, come back here, Helen.'

'Will do.'

Ridpath moved away from the car and checked his notebook. A group of white-suited CSIs and a photographer walked past ready to go over the crime scene after the body had been removed by the men from the mortuary.

Ridpath heard a loud cough behind him. It was Stan Jones, the burly detective who had stopped them earlier. 'My gaffer has told me to hang around here, give you any help you need.'

'Great, Stan. My name's Ridpath. To bring you up to speed, we have been investigating the disappearance of the victim and now he's turned up on one of your streets.'

'Right, sir.'

'He was last seen about a mile away close to Barlow Moor Road. Problem is, the disappearance happened nearly four years ago.'

'What?'

'You heard me. Four years ago in May, 2020.'

Stan Jones frowned. 'What's he doing here now? Why? How? What?' spluttered the detective.

'The answer is we don't know, but we're going to find out. Do you know the area, Stan?'

'Like the back of my hand. I've been in West Didsbury nick for five years since the last "reorganisation".'

'Great. I want you to get as much CCTV footage as you can from the area before it's been overwritten or erased. Plus get onto traffic, and get all the footage from today at the major junctions.'

'You think the vic came by car?'

'Well, *he* wasn't driving, but somebody did bring him here and dump him.'

'Why here?'

'If we knew why, we might be closer to solving the case. Find me some CCTV, DC Jones.'

'I'm on it, sir.'

'It's Ridpath. And don't bother with this street, house-to-house organised by Chief Inspector Carruthers will cover it.'

'You've got a chief inspector doing a house-to-house, must be a world's first.'

'All hands to the pumps. Get a move on with the CCTV will you? I want to know where it is by tomorrow at nine a.m.'

Jones ran off to begin his search. Ridpath could see the crowds were thinning out now, off home to eat or off to the pub to gossip about what they'd seen. There were even fewer of the reporters hanging around. Only four or five were left with only one crew still filming.

The van from the mortuary pulled up beside the white tent. Two men jumped out and unloaded a gurney from the back before disappearing inside, reappearing three minutes later with a small shape covered in a green plastic sheet. Quietly and efficiently, they loaded the gurney into the back of the van and drove off.

Off to the right, four CSIs were combing the area around the crime scene, picking up everything and anything even if it looked like it had been there for years.

Ridpath walked over to the crime scene manager.

'Hiya, Hannah, got anything?'

'This one of yours, Ridpath? I thought the local nick would handle this not MIT.'

'We were already investigating. Got anything for me?'

'Not a lot, I'm afraid. We took swabs from the body and under the nails but they looked pretty clean. It was as if somebody had prepared the body before dumping it here.'

'Prepared it?'

'Yeah, the clothes had been laundered and placed back on the body.'

'You're sure?'

'Positive. If we get any forensics from the young man, I'll be surprised.'

'Anything from the area?'

'Nothing so far, except the usual leaves and street rubbish. We'll collect it all though just in case. Sorry I can't offer anything better, Ridpath.'

'No worries.'

She looked around her. 'Looks like it's going to be a cold one. Why can't these things happen in a nice warm office? I'll rig more lights, could be a long night.'

Ridpath checked his watch. 10.15 p.m. Where had the time gone?

'If you need anything, let me know.'

'Will do. But Ridpath, this one seems weird to me. Who dumps a frozen body on the street?'

'I don't know, Hannah, but we're going to find out.'

Chapter THIRTY-TWO

Ridpath finally arrived home at three in the morning. Without the presence of Eve, the place felt dark, cold and lonely. A house not a home.

He had stayed on coordinating the investigative effort until there was nothing left to do. Unfortunately, all his work produced little in terms of concrete results.

The house-to-house inquiry produced nothing. In such a quiet suburb, with the houses well back from the road, nobody saw or heard anything.

There was no local CCTV covering the corner or the street where the body was found. Stan Jones had recovered footage from a few shop cameras and from the main junctions along Princess Parkway, but without knowing what sort of car they were looking for, it was like searching for a herring in the North Sea. Nearly 15,000 cars an hour used the road in both directions, it was one of the major routes in and out of the city.

The CSIs had gone over the crime scene with a fingertip search but they hadn't found anything of interest. A couple of Vimto ring pulls, a few dead crisp packets and a pile of old fag ends were the result of two hours' work. It was one of the cleanest crime scenes Hannah Palmer had ever worked.

'Give me the inside of a house with lots of blood splatter and I'm as happy as a dog with a bone. But out here on the street, even if we do find anything, it's difficult to pin it down as being part of the crime. Sorry, Ridpath.'

Emily had stayed with Sharon Golding until a family liaison officer had arrived at eleven p.m. She had rung him from outside the house.

'How did the mother take the news, Em?'

'I was surprised, Ridpath. I thought after we met her yesterday, there would be histrionics; shouting, screaming and wailing. But there was nothing. When I told her, she nodded and walked away, going back into the kitchen to finish the washing up.'

'People take bad news in different ways, Em. Is she willing to ID the body tomorrow?'

'She said she wanted to see the body straight away. I said it wasn't possible at the moment but I would arrange it for her tomorrow. She finally agreed to wait.'

'You didn't tell her any details?'

'No, just that her son had been found deceased in Withington.'

'Good, I don't want anything in the papers at the moment. The only people who know the details are ourselves and the killer. Let's keep it that way.'

'Right, do you need me to come to the scene?'

'No, we're packing up here now. Go home and get some rest. I need you fresh tomorrow morning.'

'Right. And Ridpath, I was thinking, isn't it a bit of a coincidence as we start investigating, the body turns up?'

'You know I don't believe in coincidences, Em.'

'Did we panic the killer and so he dumped the body?'

'It's one possibility, but let's talk about it tomorrow at nine. Go home, get some rest, that's an order.'

'Yes, sir.'

Helen Shipton had stayed with him to the end, remaining as the CSIs packed up their gear, leaving the tent, the police tape and a solitary copper to guard the scene overnight.

He debated with himself whether to talk to her after her performance at the meeting with Steve Carruthers. There was a time and place for grandstanding and in the middle of an investigation wasn't it. But he decided now wasn't the time to criticise her. He would have a quiet word tomorrow.

He placed his coat and jacket in its usual place on the metal hat stand in the hallway. Polly had bought it years ago from some flea market. He hated the thing himself but couldn't bear to throw it away, it was Polly's.

He switched on the heating in the house and debated with himself whether he could be bothered to make a sandwich. He opened the fridge and realised it was still empty. He needed to find time to get to a supermarket or at least organise a home delivery.

Instead of eating, he moved to the living room and poured himself a large shot of Glenmorangie. As the burn of the whisky seared his throat, he slumped down in the armchair.

Within two minutes, he was asleep, the crystal glass still gripped tightly in his hand.

Chapter THIRTY-THREE

The orders were clear: return to the home and carry out the next phase of the plan. My job was to do what I had been ordered, not to question why, or how or when.

Just to do as I had been tasked.

Quickly.

Efficiently.

Precisely.

The Master was always right. Praise his power. I was his right arm, the instrument of his will. His weapon to do with me as he wanted. I had given myself to him unreservedly. It was the least he deserved.

Soon he would be with us in person and my world would be complete.

I entered Mr Owens' room using the pass key. I'd expected the old man to be fast asleep but instead he was sitting up in bed.

'I was wondering when you would come.'

I didn't know what to say so I kept quiet.

'It's my turn, is it? I was wondering when you would get round to me. Getting me to sign those papers yesterday was a bit of a giveaway.'

'How did you know about the papers, I thought you—?'

'You thought I was another one of your DOLs didn't you? Deprived of Liberty through an inability to make my own decisions and the prevention of serious harm.'

'I checked. You had a DOL order last year, reconfirmed by the social worker and the doctor last month.'

The old man shrugged his shoulders. 'It was easier that way. I couldn't take care of myself any more. Too much of a hassle. Decided to come here instead.'

'But you spend all day staring out the window, not talking with anybody. And when we put your incontinence pants on in the evening you still don't say a word.'

'What would you do in my situation? I can't stand bingo and the inmates in this place can't hold two thoughts in their head at the same time. Better to stare at the garden, watch the birds, remember the past.'

Then it all clicked into place. 'You wrote that note to the copper, didn't you?'

The old man smiled. 'No. I wrote a note to the coroner's office. I was surprised they reacted so quickly. Is that why you're here?'

'It's one of the reasons.'

The man rolled up his sleeve. 'You'd better get on with it. A quick injection, isn't it?'

'How did you know?'

'It's logical. You don't want any marks on the bodies, so a quick injection seems the most likely. What do you use?'

'A mixture of Pentobarbital and Phenytoin.'

'I should have guessed. Quick, painless and looks like a standard heart attack.'

'You seem to know a lot about it?'

'I was a pharmacist before I retired. Spent forty years dispensing medicines, of course I know.'

Again, I didn't know what to say.

'You should get a move on, it'll be light soon.'

I took out the hypodermic and walked over to Mr Owens. 'It won't hurt. You'll fall asleep and your heart will stop beating.'

'A better way to go than most.'

I hesitated. This wasn't how it was supposed to happen. They were supposed to be asleep and I woke them up, pretending to give a vitamin shot. This man was taking all the pleasure out of it.

'What are you waiting for?'

I tapped the man's vein in the crook of his elbow. It stood out bright and blue against the paper-thin skin. I removed the cap for the spike and pressed the plunger slightly to check the flow.

'I've had a good life, you know. No regrets. I'd rather it ended this way than a slow decline and pain. I had an aunt once who had a stroke.

Four years she spent in one of these homes; unable to move, or speak or communicate, but I could see in her eyes she knew everything going on.'

'Yet you still told the coppers.'

'I told the coroner. I wanted him to investigate all the deaths here. All the deaths you have caused. I don't care about me, but I do worry for the others. When are you going to stop?'

'When hell freezes over.'

I jagged the spike roughly into the man's vein, watching his face wince. That had shut him up. Slowly, very slowly, I pressed the plunger feeling the drugs flow into Mr Owens' body.

'I signed a donor waiver years ago. You didn't have to get me to sign another. What do they do with the bodies?'

'I don't know and I don't care.'

The old man nodded. 'I suppose I won't care either when I'm dead.' He closed his eyes and let his head fall back onto the pillow.

At least, he wasn't speaking any more. The room was silent now, just the quiet ticking of a clock next to the bed, counting down the seconds remaining in Mr Owens' life.

The breathing was raspier now, slower, as if straining for his last breaths.

And then he was dead.

The grey absence of life I recognised from all the others. One moment they were alive and the next they were dead.

So it goes.

I removed the hypodermic from the man's arm and rolled down his sleeve, checking the room, looking for a souvenir.

Nothing. The old man had nothing worth taking. It was almost as if he had given everything away already. What a shame. I liked taking souvenirs of those I helped to die.

I took out my phone and took a picture of the man, sending it to the Master.

I wouldn't tell him about what happened tonight though. The Master wouldn't want to know and he wouldn't care.

I checked the room one last time and then opened the door to leave. Outside, the first rays of dawn were beginning to peek through the trees in the garden. The attendant would discover his death soon and Mr Owens' body would leave the home in a couple of hours.

They had to be quick for the work they did. The schedule was always so tight.

I took one last look at Mr Owens lying in bed.

At peace at last.

Wednesday, February 7.

Chapter THIRTY-FOUR

Mornings didn't feel the same without Eve.

There was none of the shouting upstairs encouraging her to leave her warm bed. No grumpiness over a sodden bowl of corn-flakes. No last-minute rushing around looking for lost homework or forgotten pens.

Just him with a cup of strong coffee sat at the kitchen table, staring into mid-air. For a moment, his mind flickered back to the investigation.

Why was the body dumped now?

Was it the newspaper article which spooked the killer or was it his investigation?

And what about SunnySide Retirement Home, how was it involved? He was sure it was connected to the disappearance of Andy Golding but he didn't know how.

Thinking about the retirement home reminded him he still had to brief Clarence Montague. He typed a quick text to Sophia.

> Can't come in this morning. Have to work at Police HQ. Will brief Montague this afternoon.

An answer came back almost immediately.

> He's not going to be chuffed. He's already set a time of ten a.m. for the briefing.

Not possible, change it to the afternoon at two thirty.

Will do. See you this afternoon.

Also can you open a file on an Andrew Golding, aged 14, vanished from home in 2020?

This was the case you were working on? You've found the body?

Unfortunately, I have. I'll inform Montague this afternoon.

Ok, done.

Ta, Sophia.

He checked the time: eight a.m.

He would leave now and get to Police HQ early. Time to prepare and check if anything had come in overnight.

He threw the half-drunk coffee in the sink, packed up his laptop and notebooks, picked his jacket and coat off their usual place in the hall.

He sniffed the air twice. There was the aroma of wet dog even though no canine lived in the house. Eve had asked him multiple times if they could get a dog but he had always said no. He had enough problems caring for himself and Eve without looking after another animal as well.

He went to the kitchen closet and searched for the air freshener. There it was hidden at the back. It was obviously a long time since he had last used it.

He took it back into the hall and sprayed everywhere, concentrating particularly on the area around the coat rack. A fine mist hanging in the air before gradually descending to the carpet.

And then the smell hit him.

Fresh roses with just a hint of blackcurrant.

Polly's smell.

She used to buy tins of this stuff, spraying the house with it liberally.

'I can't stand the dank smell of winter in Manchester, Ridpath, this always reminds me of long, hot summers.'

A lump constricted his throat and tears appeared in the corner of his eyes. She would have known how to deal with Eve now. How to sit her down and chat without the inevitable fight or harsh words.

He grabbed the newel post for support.

God, he missed her.

Nobody had come into his life since Polly had died. Mainly, because he hadn't allowed anybody in. Ridpath realised he had put up an emotional Hadrian's Wall to keep women out, a defence mechanism he rationalised by saying he didn't have time for an emotional or physical attachment. There was work and there was Eve, and they both filled up his life.

But he knew it wasn't true.

He hadn't allowed any other woman to get close to him because he was afraid of losing Polly. Or more accurately, losing the space she still occupied in his heart and in his mind.

Nobody could take her place.

He breathed in deeply and stood up straight. 'Get yourself together, Ridpath, there's work to be done,' he said out loud to the empty house.

He placed the can of air freshener on the hallway table, picked up his briefcase, took one last look at the painted white walls, remembering if he had locked the kitchen door, then left.

He couldn't bring Polly back no matter how hard he tried.

Chapter THIRTY-FIVE

The usual suspects were already waiting for him in the meeting room when he arrived at 8.50.

'How was it last night, Ridpath?' asked Emily Parkinson. 'You saw Andy's body?'

'He looked exactly the same as the photo, even down to the striped shirt and shorts. What time is the post-mortem, Chrissy?'

'Dr Schofield sent a note in this morning. Apparently, the body is taking longer to defrost than he thought. He will start at noon.'

'Defrost?' asked Emily.

'I'll explain at the briefing. Chrissy, did you get the map of the area I asked for?'

'Done, Ridpath. I'll put it up now.'

'Em, can you get onto to Sharon Golding and the liaison officer. If she could ID Andy at eleven before the post-mortem would be best. I'd like you to be there.'

'I'll arrange it, Ridpath.'

Emily Parkinson wandered over to a corner of the room before she dialled the number.

Ridpath checked the boards as they had been updated by Chrissy. A larger picture of Andy Golding had been placed in the centre with the information from his disappearance at either side including pictures of his clothes, the football, a mobile phone and the St Christopher's medallion. Chrissy was putting up a map on the left and four crime scene photographs were arrayed in a vertical line on the right.

Emily finished her call. 'It's all arranged, Ridpath. Do you want to be there?'

'Not really, but I will. I'll stay on for the post-mortem.'

He stared at the boards as the other coppers and the crime scene manager wandered into the room, taking their place at the desks.

Finally, Steve Carruthers joined them. 'I'm here to watch not to run this investigation. The SIO is DI Thomas Ridpath and will remain so until further notice. Ridpath, we have arranged additional support from digital forensics.'

A large round man in the corner raised his hand. 'Jasper Early, I worked on the CCTV.'

'I've also asked Stan Jones and his team from West Didsbury to join us. They will provide on-the-ground support.'

Stan Jones nodded to the rest of the team.

'I can't tell you how important this investigation is. We are being watched not only by the people of Manchester and the honourable members of the press, but by our revered leaders. Let's clear this one and clear it quickly. Over to you, Ridpath.'

'Thanks, boss. At 5.30 p.m. last night the body of Andy Golding was found on Seagram Street in Withington.'

As he said the name of the street, a strange feeling of déjà vu washed over him. Something flashed across his mind: an image, a memory, he didn't have time to process. And then it was gone, like a whisper on the wind. What was it he was missing?

He coughed twice to cover his unease. 'From the initial medical examination, it would appear the young man had been strangled. But we will know more after the post-mortem at noon.'

One of the detectives from West Didsbury put his hand up. 'How sure are we the victim was Andy Golding?'

'Ninety-nine per cent certain but the mother will make a formal ID at eleven o'clock. Those are the basic facts about the case. Then it becomes a little strange. Andy Golding disappeared from his home on May 22nd in 2020. He has not been seen since.'

Ridpath pointed to the CCTV photos. 'We have him near Southern Cemetery at 11.23, caught by a camera outside an IT shop at 11.42 and finally sixteen minutes later at the junction of

Palatine and Barlow Moor roads. This is the most interesting shot as he appears to be in the company of an adult male.'

The whole room buzzed. A detective put his hand up. 'Why can't we see more of the image, more than just the hand?'

Jasper Early answered as if explaining to a child. 'I've tried to get more but that's all there is. It comes from a fixed traffic camera pointed at the junction. We were lucky to get this.'

'We know he met somebody between the location of the IT shop and the road junction, both marked with arrows on the map. His body was found last night less than a mile away from the area he disappeared.' He walked over to the new map Chrissy had put up. 'Exactly here.'

'You said you were 99 per cent certain it was him. How can you be so sure?'

'This is where it gets strange. He was dressed in exactly the same clothes as the day he disappeared and he hadn't aged at all.'

'Hadn't aged? What does that mean, Ridpath?'

'It means he was murdered at roughly the same time as he disappeared four years ago. It appears his body has been kept frozen all this time.'

Another buzz around the room.

Ridpath raised his arms. 'Quiet people. This is what we need to do. Chrissy, I know you've been through other disappearances four years ago but go through HOLMES again looking for people who have been found dead recently.'

'Will do, Ridpath. I'll cross-reference the Missing Persons register and new discoveries.'

'Also, can you check the Sexual Offenders Register? Has anybody moved into the area recently with a history of attacks like this. You might want to check it from four years ago too.'

'Will do, Ridpath.'

'Stan, can you organise a house-to-house inquiry team from the place he disappeared to the crime scene, taking in Princess Parkway on one side and Palatine Road on the other, going all the way out to Whitchurch Road.'

The copper whistled. 'Over two thousand houses, Ridpath. It'll take years.'

'We still have to do it and we might extend the area later. Ask them if they saw anything last night or four years ago.'

'I can't remember where I was four years ago,' said one of the coppers.

'You were skiving like you always do,' answered another to laughter.

'Can we get some extra bodies?'

Ridpath turned to his boss. 'Steve?'

The chief inspector stared into mid-air for a long time. 'I'll arrange it with the assistant chief. You'll get your bodies.'

'Why don't we do a television appeal instead of asking every single house in the area,' asked Jasper Early.

'Firstly, because not everybody watches television. Second, such an appeal will bring out every nutter from Manchester to Outer Mongolia tying up resources looking into leads. And third, and most importantly, I want your men to visit every house, to see if anything looks, or smells, odd. I trust the nose of a copper far more than some nutter ringing up a phone line. I'm convinced it's no coincidence the body was found close to where he disappeared.'

Ridpath glanced around his team, making sure the point was understood.

'Helen, can you work with Jasper Early to check the CCTV Stan found last night.'

'What am I looking for?'

'Use the ANPR to see if any cars and vans re-appear in the area more than once. Plus look for anything out of the ordinary. Whoever dumped the body at this location, knew there was no CCTV here. They must have been there before.'

'We could end up with a long list of delivery vans?'

'Then we'll exclude them one by one. Clear?'

'Clear, Ridpath.'

'Em, I'd like you to be evidence officer and manage the case files, as well as being my number two.'

'Got it, Ridpath. I also checked with Andy Golding's school like you asked. It's pretty much as John Newton described. He was a bit of a loner but he loved football. Often played all by himself against a wall rather than with other people.' She glanced at her notes. 'One thing, his friends told me the Nike ball was new. He bought it online just a week before he vanished. Back then, it cost over one hundred quid.'

'Phew, I wonder where he got that sort of money?' said Chrissy.

'I'll ask the mother,' said Emily making a note in her book.

'Right, people, as Steve said, there's lots of people watching this. I want us all to be on our toes and sharp. A young man has been murdered and our job is to find out who did it.'

One of the detectives from West Didsbury spoke to his mate loudly. 'What kind of sick fuck keeps a body on ice for nearly four years?'

'What did you say?' asked Ridpath, staring directly at the man.

'Sorry, I didn't mean anything from it.'

'No, what did you say?'

The man looked around for support from the rest of the team, but everybody was looking elsewhere. 'I just said what sort of sick fuck keeps a body on ice for nearly four years?'

All the strength seemed to leave Ridpath's body, he suddenly needed to sit down. The question had made him flashback six years ago to the snarling face of a killer he had put inside.

Then, like a double whammy, he suddenly understood why the name of the street had scared the hell out of him.

Chapter THIRTY-SIX

Sarah Challinor placed her bag in the seat next to her mother's bed. As usual, she leant over and kissed her on the forehead before removing her coat and hanging it on the coat rack in the corner.

She'd already had a word with a nurse. There had been no change in her mother's condition overnight.

She was still the same. She was always the same.

The machines keeping her alive kept whirring. The monitors kept showing each beat of her heart. The drips above the bed kept feeding her saline and drugs.

And her mother remained in her coma.

She settled down in the chair, taking out her battered copy of Tolstoy's *War and Peace*. It was one of her mother's favourite books but when she was working she had no time to read it. Over the last six months, Sarah had read a few pages each day to her mother, hoping against hope she would somehow react to the spoken words.

But there had been nothing. Not even the flicker of an eyelid.

She had promised herself, when she started, her mother would come out of her coma before she finished. It was a long book and now there were fewer than forty pages left. What would she do when she finished reading it?

She didn't know and she didn't want to think about it.

Not now. Not ever.

She opened the book taking out the paperclip marking the last pages she'd read. 'If you remember, Mother, Natasha has married Bezukhov and Count Ilya Rostov has passed away. I'll begin where I left off.'

But she didn't start reading, instead she stared at her mother's face. Her skin was still as clear as a young girl's, her grey hair laid out like a mane across the pillow.

'Please wake up, Mum, come back to us,' Sarah whispered.

She looked closely.

Had her eyelids moved? And had the crease on her forehead been there before?

She stood up leaning over her mother, staring down at her face.

But there was no movement. Just the endless whirring of the machines behind her bed.

She sat back in her chair, and taking up the book, began reading again. "'At the beginning of winter Princess Mary came to Moscow. From reports current in town she learned how the Rostóvs were situated, and how 'the son has sacrificed himself for his mother,' as people were saying…'"

Behind her mother's bed, the machines steadily droned on.

Chapter THIRTY-SEVEN

'Are you okay, Ridpath?' asked Steve Carruthers.

He breathed in and out. 'Fine, sir, I've realised something has been staring me in the face. I'm amazed I haven't noticed it earlier.'

'What?'

The rest of the room was watching the both of them.

Ridpath took a deep breath. 'This murder bears all the hall-marks of the Beast of Manchester, Harold Lardner.'

The chief inspector's eyebrows rose upwards. 'That's a long shot, even for you.'

'Hear me out, sir. Lardner froze his victims, keeping then in a cold storage at the University of Lancashire body farm.'

'But didn't you put him away? Isn't he in the high-security wing of Ashworth hospital? And he was already in prison when Andy Golding disappeared.'

'True, sir, but listen, he strangled some of his victims just as Andy Golding was strangled.'

'We don't know the cause of death yet. We haven't had the post-mortem.'

'But I trust Dr Schofield's first instincts. Plus Lardner operated in this area. His first victim was found only 400 metres away.' He strode to the map, prodding a point on it. 'Here. Finally, and this is what's been bothering me for the last day: the body of Andy Golding was found on Seagram Street. The name of one of Lardner's victims was Alice Seagram.'

'It's a coincidence, Ridpath, you're reading far too much into this.'

'It could be a copycat killer, sir. There have been many books about Harold Lardner and his crimes, most focusing on how a former pathologist became a serial killer,' said Emily Parkinson.

Steve Carruthers stroked his top lip, deep in thought. 'It seems a long shot to me, Ridpath, but what do you want to do?'

'I'd like to go to see him.'

'In Ashworth?'

Ridpath nodded.

'When?'

'Tomorrow.'

Steve Carruthers sighed loudly and closed his eyes for a long time before suddenly opening them wide. 'Right, make it happen. But not a word of this is to get out, understand?'

He turned to the rest of the group. 'Don't speak about this to anybody. Not your wives. Not your lovers. Not your best mates. Not even your Highland terriers. If word of this leaks out, we'll be crucified in the press. Understood?'

There were mumbled noises of agreement.

'Understood?' Carruthers said louder, his broad Glaswegian accent becoming much more pronounced.

'Yes, sir,' was the chorused reply from everybody.

He turned back to Ridpath and stared at him for a long time. Ridpath understood he was on thin ice. Perhaps he should have kept his mouth shut until he had more evidence.

As everybody filed out of the room, he was left behind with the core members of his team; Emily, Chrissy and Helen.

'What was all that about, Ridpath? And who is this Beast of Manchester?'

'It was before you joined the force, Helen. In 2008, after I finished my training, I arrested a man called James Dalbey who we thought had been responsible for a series of murders of young women, including Alice Seagram. He was sentenced to thirty years. However, he kept protesting his innocence and finally convinced the Seagram family he wasn't guilty. They pushed for a review of the conviction. One of my first jobs in the coroner's office in 2018 was to disinter the body of Alice Seagram from its grave in Stretford cemetery. When we opened the coffin, we found it was empty.'

'What? An empty coffin? Jesus, sounds like something out of a horror movie.'

'Anyway, the discovery eventually led us to the real perpetrator, the real Beast of Manchester, Harold Lardner, a pathologist working for the local authority. He kept the bodies of his victims frozen in a body farm operated by the University of Lancashire.'

'I read about him. Didn't he murder a copper who was working on the investigation?'

Ridpath nodded slowly. 'Sarah Castle was his last victim. It was her death that finally helped us crack the case.'

'I was working here at the time,' said Chrissy. 'Everyone was devastated. It led to the chief super at the time, John Gorman, losing his job, and Claire Trent taking over.'

'What happened to Lardner?'

'He was found guilty of only one murder: Alice Seagram.'

'But I thought you said there were multiple victims and he murdered a copper?'

'The Crown Prosecution Service decided the evidence was only strong enough to charge him on one count. He was eventually found guilty of diminished responsibility and sentenced to serve his time in a high security hospital under section 37 of the 1983 Mental Health Act. His barrister argued performing over 12,000 post-mortems had affected him profoundly, creating a form of PTSD, particularly after the death of his wife.'

'But surely PTSD wouldn't cause him to murder young women?'

'That was the barrister's argument and the judge and jury believed him.'

Helen Shipton snorted and scratched her head. 'But what's all this to do with Andy Golding?'

Ridpath went quiet. 'I don't know. But I feel there is a connection, something we are missing. Too many coincidences...' He reached for the words to describe his intuition.

'Did Lardner kill young men?' asked Helen Shipton.

Ridpath shook his head. 'He concentrated on women, vulnerable women.'

'Did he strangle his victims?'

'At least one of them that we know, possibly more. He used to perform experiments on them, like Dr Mengele. One was beaten to death, one was garrotted. We don't know how Alice Seagram died.'

'And Sarah Castle?'

'She was murdered by having anti-freeze dripped into her veins. A method Lardner picked up from a Russian serial killer.'

They all remained quiet. Eventually, Helen broke the silence by saying, 'So the only real link is the fact the victim was frozen.'

'And the name of the street where Andy Golding's body was found,' added Chrissy.

'That's a stretch even the most gullible judge would find difficult to believe.'

Ridpath held his hands up. 'I know, I know, it's a long shot. But for the moment, it is one of the channels of inquiry we need to follow.'

'Are you sure we won't be wasting time and resources on a wild goose chase?' Helen Shipton was blunt in her assessment.

'I am sure it is not a waste of time and resources,' replied Ridpath firmly.

'On your own head be it.'

'Thank you, Helen, as SIO I will take complete responsibility but it will be one of the lines of inquiry we will follow.' He stood up. 'Let's get on with our jobs. Helen, isn't it time you were looking through the CCTV footage with Jasper Early?'

'We don't even know what we're looking for?'

'It's your job to find something. Now go and do it.'

Reluctantly, she began to pack her laptop and notebook.

'Em, you're with me.'

'Where to Ridpath?'

'I think we need to pick up Sharon Golding and ask her to ID the body of her son.'

'Some jobs I'd prefer to avoid, Ridpath.'

'Unfortunately, this is one we can't. You don't have to attend the post-mortem though.'

'No, I want to.' She paused for a long time staring into mid-air before finally looking back at Ridpath. 'I don't know if it makes sense, but if I didn't it would somehow dishonour Andy. Do you know what I mean?'

'I understand, Em, to me it makes perfect sense.'

Helen Shipton finished packing her things.

'This time, Helen, message me and the rest of the team immediately when you find something. I don't want to come to another meeting not knowing what is going on. Understand?'

She nodded and walked towards the door.

'Is that absolutely clear, Detective Constable Shipton?'

'Yes, sir,' she said over her shoulder as she closed the door behind her.

Emily Parkinson raised her eyebrows. 'I told you she would be trouble.'

Chapter THIRTY-EIGHT

They strode into the reception area of the mortuary. A place as cold as the charity of a miser. Despite himself, a shiver ran down Ridpath's back and scuttled out through the door.

Emily was holding Sharon Golding's arm with the duty FLO, a police constable called Rachel Lynch, bringing up the rear.

'This way. If you wait here, I'll see if they are ready.'

Sharon Golding nodded saying nothing. She'd hardly spoken since they had picked her up from her home thirty minutes ago. She was dressed and waiting for them when they arrived, only speaking to her son as she left. 'I'll come back to cook your tea later, Alan. Make sure you tidy your room?'

'Yes Mum,' the boy said wearily as he closed the door.

Now they were standing in the cold embrace of the reception area. Ridpath could see Mrs Golding nervously biting the skin from the tips of her fingers, the stress of the occasion etched into every line of her face.

Emily appeared at a door on the side. 'They're ready for us. If you could come this way.'

Ridpath followed Sharon Golding and the FLO into a small, dark, maroon-painted room. Four mahogany chairs were lined up in front of a glass window covered on the inside with a curtain.

Emily spoke into a microphone mounted next to the glass window. 'We're ready, Mr Higgs.'

The curtain opened. Behind the window, he could see a small room with a long steel table, a white sheet stretched over it. Under the sheet, the barely discernible shape of a small body lay unmoving.

A sharp cry came from Sharon Golding and her hand shot up to cover her mouth.

Emily spoke again. 'If you could remove the top half of the cover, Mr Higgs.'

The lab technician didn't reply. Instead he leant over the small shape and carefully folded the white sheet down from the top, revealing the boy's face, serene and un-aged.

'Is this your son, Andrew Golding, Sharon?' asked Emily.

The woman nodded, tears beginning to run from the corner of her eyes. 'It's Andy.'

'Are you sure?'

'I know my own son!' She snapped before softening her voice. 'It's Andy, he hasn't changed. Why hasn't he changed? He looks exactly like the day he walked out of the house.'

She turned directly towards Ridpath and repeated her question. 'Why hasn't he changed?'

'We believe your son was killed on the day he disappeared, Mrs Golding.'

'But that was four years ago. He still looks exactly the same...' Her voice trailed off.

'We believe your son was kept somewhere cold which prevented the body from deteriorating. But we will know for certain after the post-mortem.'

'I don't want any post-mortem. I don't want them cutting my son open. You can't cut him open.'

She began to shout and scream. The FLO moved forward to comfort her, but she only shrugged her off. 'I DON'T WANT NO POST-MORTEM.'

'I'm afraid as a coroner's officer I am required by law to carry out a post-mortem when a death is suspicious, sudden or unnatural. We need to catch whoever did this to Andy. The post-mortem may give us valuable information to help us in the investigation.'

'What are you, a police officer or do you work for the coroner?'

Sometimes Ridpath asked himself exactly the same question.

'I am employed by GMP and presently seconded to the coroner's office.'

'I do not want Andy's body cut open, is that clear?'

'I'm sorry, Mrs Golding. I will note your concerns and ask the pathologist to make the post-mortem as minimally invasive as possible. But I am legally obliged to conduct a post-mortem when somebody has been murdered.'

Ridpath nodded at Emily Parkinson.

'Mr Higgs, please close the curtain.'

Sharon Golding flung herself at the glass window. 'No, no, I want to see my son, I want to feel his face one last time, to hold him. He's *my* son…'

Both the FLO and Emily took hold of her by the arms and gently pulled her away from the glass towards one of the chairs. At first she struggled, then all the strength seemed to leave her body and she collapsed into their arms.

They both lifted her onto the chair and Emily knelt beside her, one arm around her shoulders.

Ridpath shook his head and hardened his voice. 'I'm sorry, Mrs Golding, but as Andy was murdered and I am certain a criminal offence has been committed, I cannot allow his body to be touched before the post-mortem in case evidence is lost.'

He stared through the glass at the lab technician, indicating with a sweep of his arms the curtain should be closed.

Mrs Golding sat in the chair, her head bowed and her shoulders slumped. 'I just want to hold my son one last time.'

Emily Parkinson looked up at Ridpath, asking, almost begging him, to agree.

Ridpath thought for a moment. How would he feel if it were Eve lying on this cold slab in an even colder mortuary? The body had already been dusted for fingerprints and the scene of crime manager said they had found nothing on it.

'I just want to hold my son.' Sharon Golding's voice came from some vast pit of despair.

Sometimes, this was the worst job in the world.

Ridpath nodded towards Emily.

'Come this way, Sharon. You can see your son.'

She helped the woman to her feet, while Ridpath opened a door to the right of the window. Inside the small body lay beneath the white sheet, Mr Higgs standing to one side.

Sharon Golding sucked in air as if she was taking her last breath, covering her mouth. She staggered two steps to the steel table. 'Oh, Andy, what have they done to you?'

She reached out her hand to stroke the boy's hair.

Up close, the boy's face was unlined and unworried, as if he had fallen into the most peaceful sleep. Except, the eyes were open; cornflower blue eyes with a hint of grey.

'He's cold. Why is he so cold?'

'Like I said, Mrs Golding, we believe the body has been kept in some sort of freezer after death, that's why there has been no deterioration after four years.'

But Sharon Golding wasn't listening. She was slowly stroking her son's hair as if comforting him as he slept. She bent over and rested her head close to her son's face, whispering endearments Ridpath couldn't hear.

Then she surprised them by leaning over and kissing her son full on his lips and wrapping her arms around his body. Neither Emily Parkinson nor Ridpath moved.

After a minute, he said, 'It's time to go now, Mrs Golding.'

'Can't I stay longer with him?'

Ridpath shook his head. 'I'm sorry.'

She let go of her son still staring down at his face. 'Where's his St Christopher medallion?'

'What?'

'The medallion he wore round his neck. He never took it off even when he showered.'

Ridpath glanced at the attendant who shook his head.

'It wasn't found when we discovered Andy, Mrs Golding.'

He took her arm and gently led her to the door.

'Andy would never take his medallion off, never. It was a gift from his granny.'

Emily took over and led her back into the room.

'When she is ready, take Mrs Golding home, DS Parkinson.'

Emily lowered her slowly to sit in the chair. The woman leant forward, covering her face with her hands, her shoulders slumped over, her chest gasping for air.

He stared at the hunched figure of the mother of the victim.

This was definitely the worst job in the world.

Chapter THIRTY-NINE

The post-mortem began punctually at noon, with Dr Schofield speaking to the microphone above his head. 'It is noon on February 10, 2024 and I am about to commence the post-mortem on the body of Andrew Golding, aged fourteen at the time of his death. With me, assisting, is Dr Niamh O'Casey from Liverpool. I hope I pronounced your name correctly this time.'

'Nearly, John, it's Neeve. In Gaelic, the i–a–m–h is pronounced "eeve".'

'I'll get it right eventually. The laboratory technician is James Higgs and representing the coroner's office and GMP is DI Thomas Ridpath.'

At the mention of his name, Ridpath looked up. Andrew Golding was lying naked on the stainless steel table. His small white body dwarfed by the cold metal surrounding it. In the clinical surroundings of the pathologist's mortuary, he looked even more vulnerable and trusting than he had in his photograph.

'The parent of the deceased child has requested a minimally invasive post-mortem and I will attempt to conform to this request. Unfortunately, we have no Magnetic Resonance Angiograph available so I am unable to examine the body using a machine. In addition, as we believe this person was murdered, I must put the search for clues to his death and the perpetrator of it, above all other considerations. With those caveats, let me begin.'

Through all this introduction, the lab technician had been placing a series of saws, electric drills and knives on a small stainless steel table next to Dr Schofield, while Dr O'Casey had been leaning over the body examining the eyes, the throat and the hair closely.

Dr Schofield continued. 'The body is slightly small for a male fourteen-year-old child with an undeveloped musculature. Puberty has not yet begun with neither of the scrota having descended. On visual examination, there are no scars or marks on the body and he does not seem to have suffered any major injuries in his relatively short life. There seem to be several extensive lesions on the skin which were probably caused by the freezing and thawing of the body.'

'They weren't caused by somebody striking him?'

'I don't think so, Ridpath,' answered Dr O'Casey. 'I have examined a section of the cells under an electron scanning microscope and they show no evidence of haematoma. In addition, this morning I tested the same cells by measuring the activity of an enzyme, short-chain 3-hydroxyacyl-CoA dehydrogenase. This technique was initially designed to test meat quality in the food industry but it has been successfully transferred to the work of pathologists. The test shows post-mortem freezing of this body.'

'It was also why we postponed the post-mortem until today, Ridpath,' added Dr Schofield. 'The research told us we needed to slowly thaw the body in a refrigerated morgue before performing any tests on it.'

After a short pause, Dr Schofield continued. 'The effects of freezing and thawing cells have been well studied by Mazur, Pegg, and Diaper, Scott and others. It is widely recognised freezing results in cell damage, cell lysis, and in the accumulation of extracellular fluid. The macroscopic and microscopic differences between frozen and unfrozen tissues can be distinguished histologically. There's even a whole new area of investigation being developed in relation to the fundamental laws of cryobiology.'

'And of course, I couldn't miss the opportunity of meeting you again, Ridpath.' Dr Casey laughed, pushed her glasses back onto the bridge of her nose and continued speaking. 'There are a few conclusions we can make. First, the mechanics of freezing leave behind both macroscopic and microscopic signs in the tissues which can be detected if one knows what to look for. If the freezing rate is fast, for example using liquid nitrogen, the water will not be able to flow over the cell membrane before ice crystals form intracellularly. Subsequent thawing will partially return the tissue to normal, but there will be evidence of damage, mostly due to the changes in osmotic pressure on the cell. However, in slow freezing for example in a domestic freezer, the temperatures do not go low enough or fast enough to cause intracellular freezing.'

Dr O'Casey paused waiting for Ridpath to ask the obvious question.

'What was it in this case, doctor?'

'Actually, my official title is professor, but you can call me Niamh. In this case, the freezing was slow with a non-industrial freezer being used. There are another couple of things we can conclude from the microscopic examination of the cells. First, the presence of the surfactant-protein-A helps to differentiate between ante- and post-mortem immersion. In this case, the body was frozen post-mortem. Secondly, there is relatively little degradation of the cell structure involved in the decomposition of the body suggesting it was frozen soon after death. My guess, but don't quote me, was within one hour.'

Ridpath stayed silent. It must have been planned. The killer had a freezer ready and waiting to receive the body.

Dr Schofield took over. 'You're going to ask us next the inevitable police question: "What was the time and date of death." And the truth is we haven't a clue. Freezing makes any such determination impossible. We don't even know how long the body has been frozen, the literature is contradictory. It could have been four days or four years.'

Ridpath scratched his head. This was becoming difficult.

'But, from his physiological development and given he disappeared at...' Dr Schofield checked his notes, 'age fourteen years and eighty-seven days, plus Dr O'Casey's observations on the freezing process, I would guess his death happened soon after he was taken.'

'Could you be more exact, doctor?'

'Sorry, I can't. Humans develop and grow individually. He could have been killed immediately after he vanished or a month later, we have no way of knowing. But, in this case, we can be certain freezing must have taken place immediately after death because of the absence of any signs of decomposition.'

'Thank you. Can I ask how he died?'

Dr Schofield switched off the microphone for a second. 'Niamh, have you finished your examination of the face and neck?'

'I have.'

The mike went back on. 'Dr O'Casey has been examining the head and neck region.'

She began to speak, her strong, lilting Irish accent soothing to listen to even as she described the damage to the young man.

'I concur with your initial examination, Dr Schofield. This body has petechiae in the eyeball and eyelid which are still visible despite it having been frozen. The hyoid bone in the neck has been damaged and there are still bruises around the front of the throat and at the back of the neck. This young man is also missing patches of hair with additional petechiae on the scalp.' She bent down examining the back of the head closely. 'Extensive bruising and a haematoma to the forehead suggest he was struck by a blunt instrument before he died. We will have to examine the brain itself to see if this injury caused a contusion or subdural or epidural haematoma.'

'In words of less than one syllable, what does that mean, Dr O'Casey?'

'It means the boy was manually asphyxiated – strangled, in the common parlance – after being hit on the head. When we look at the brain, we will have a better idea of the damage caused by the blow.'

'Thank you. Anything else you can tell me?'

'I think we have covered most points so far. There are no defensive wounds or signs he was bound or gagged. I wonder if he may have been drugged, but in that case why was he struck? We will know more when the toxicology results come back from the lab.'

'Thank you.'

'Any other questions?' asked John Schofield.

Ridpath shook his head.

'Good. I think we should take a look at the brain first, don't you, Dr O'Casey?'

'I agree.'

When the noise of the electric saw bit into the young boy's skull like a power drill through brickwork, Ridpath decided he'd heard, and seen, enough.

'I'll go back now, doctor, send me the full report as soon as you have it.'

Dr Schofield stopped drilling, lifting the plexiglass shield covering his face. 'Going so soon, Ridpath, we still have a lot to do.'

'Unfortunately, I have a live investigation to run.'

'You'll miss the most interesting parts. The histology of cell damage after freezing is a new science in pathology, we'll be breaking new ground today.'

'Thank you, Dr O'Casey but I'll pass.'

'Suit yourself, we'll get the final report over to you by tomorrow morning, minus the toxicology results, of course.'

'Of course,' he replied, heading as quickly as he could without running. The last words he heard before the saw starting whirring again were, 'A rather thin skull wouldn't you say, Dr O'Casey. The saw is cutting through it like a knife through butter.'

Chapter FORTY

Outside on the street again, Ridpath sucked up gallons of fresh air. Or at least what passed for fresh air alongside one of Manchester's busiest roads.

Images of Andrew Golding's small white body lying naked on the stainless steel examination table flashed through his brain.

Why had he insisted on the post-mortem? Could he have avoided it, found some reason not to have cut open the child's body?

But he knew these were pointless questions. He had no choice. The law was clear on the matter. If a person died in suspicious circumstances, as a coroner's officer, he had to order a post-mortem. And, as a police officer, he had to use all the tools at his disposal to discover how Andy Golding died and who killed him.

He had no choice.

But it could have been Eve lying on the cold metal slab. She was now the same age as Andy when he disappeared. The thought sent a shudder through his body. What would he do if something similar happened to her? Would somebody like him have to order her body to be cut up?

He was desperate for a cigarette. Anything to help remove the cloying smell of death clinging to the mortuary like a drowning sailor holding on to a plank of wood. Across the road, two women were chatting together around an upright ashtray filled to the brim with cigarette stubs. One raised her Marlboro Light to her lips and expelled a long plume of grey smoke into the air, joining the overcast grey clouds covering Manchester.

For the first time in a long time, he was tempted to ask them if he could borrow a fag.

They saw him staring at them and both turned their bodies away. He must have come across as some strange stalker or cigarette fetishist.

Luckily, their reaction helped make up his mind. He headed back to his car parked nearby, and switched on the engine. The banal comments of a local radio station DJ talking about jam doughnuts filled the car.

The ordinary, mundane world of normal people, he missed it so much.

Sometimes, he would have preferred never to see another dead person for the rest of his life. Certainly, never to see another dead child.

But he had no choice. Death was the life he had chosen.

He checked the car clock. 2.12 p.m. Where had the time gone? Had he been in the post-mortem for over two hours? Time flies when you are having fun.

Where to go next? Back to Police HQ and check up on the investigation? He had received no messages from anybody so far. No news was good news, wasn't it?

But then he remembered he had to brief Clarence Montague at two thirty. He was going to be late. Shame.

Afterwards, he had promised Eve he'd pick her up from school. This time, he'd keep his promise, taking her home and then going back to work.

Time to trust her.

His phone beeped. More figures on deaths at the home from Sophia. What would he do without her. He quickly messaged thank you and decided to contact Chrissy.

> Have you heard anything so far?

The reply came instantly.

Nothing. The house-to-house is ongoing. Emily is still with Sharon Golding. HOLMES is acting up. No news from Helen Shipton.

Let's get together at 6 p.m. in the operation room to bring everybody up to date. Can you tell them?

Will do. How was the post-mortem?

His fingers hovered over the keyboard before he finally typed.

Harrowing.

He switched off his phone, put the car in gear and drove off. It was the life he had chosen.

Chapter FORTY-ONE

'I was expecting to be briefed by you first thing this morning, Ridpath.'

Clarence Montague sat behind his desk, Mont Blanc fountain pen in hand, poised over an arctic-white notepad.

'I came back to the office to do it yesterday afternoon at four but you had already left for the day.'

'I am the coroner, I decide when I receive these briefings not you. I wanted it first thing this morning.'

'I wasn't available, I had to be at Police HQ.'

'If you are to continue to do this job, you are going to have to manage your time better. I expect you to be available when I want you.'

Ridpath had had enough. 'That is not possible when I have a live investigation on my hands.'

The only response from Clarence Montague was a loud snort.

'Would you like to hear my report or not?'

'I suppose you should give it to me. I also have something for you.' He tapped a folder in front of him.

Ridpath opened his notebook. 'I visited SunnySide Retirement Care Home yesterday afternoon. There, I met the manager, a Mrs Mathilda Staunton, she refused to let me look inside the home or give me access to any of her records. I suggest in the face of such a refusal we need to apply for a warrant to search the place and a subpoena to examine the records for the last ten years.'

Clarence Montague frowned. 'You do know the use of such extreme judicial measures by a coroner is extremely rare.'

'Mrs Staunton was adamant she wasn't going to allow me to examine her records or the home itself.'

'I see,' Montague said slowly making a note on the pad in his trademark vermilion ink. 'And the reasons for using such judicial measures?'

'Other than the letter you received?'

Clarence Montague nodded.

Ridpath checked his notes again. Sophia had sent him the information this morning. 'The home is owned by ChromaEstates Ltd, a division of ChromaIndustrial, a diversified conglomerate with interests in hospitals, nursing homes, prisons, retirement villages and refugee centres.'

'I have heard of them.'

'When they took over running SunnySide in 2015, deaths at the home were running at four people per year. This number remained relatively constant until 2020 when it shot up to seventeen deaths.'

'Understandable given the pandemic. Deaths in all care homes increased after patients were discharged from hospitals into them to free up beds.'

'The number of deaths has remained constant since then. Fourteen deaths in 2021, twelve in 2022 and fourteen in 2023. So far this year, there have been five deaths, with the latest happening this morning. A Mr Albert Owens.'

'Perhaps, the residents had been weakened by Covid. After all, old people do die.'

Ridpath was stunned into silence by this last statement. Then he coughed twice and continued on. 'The reasons given for the deaths are always the same; old age and pneumonia before 2020. After that, Covid or Covid-related illnesses.'

'But no evidence of anything untoward on the death certificates?'

'There was no evidence in the Shipman case either. And besides, Sophia hasn't examined each death certificate, these are the collated statistics from the home.'

Clarence Montague hummed and aahed, staring down at his notepad before continuing. 'Who is the doctor who signed the certificates?'

'A Dr Sanghera. But he was not present at the time of death. Most of the recent deaths happened in the middle of the night. Only one happened during the day.'

'Perfectly normal when old people are concerned. Personally, I would like to simply fall asleep and never wake up when I die. Makes everything so much easier.'

'It is convenient, isn't it?'

'Have you interviewed Dr Sanghera?'

'Not yet.'

'I suggest you do so with alacrity.'

'There is one other thing you should look at.' He turned his laptop around so Montague could see it. 'Sophia created a spreadsheet comparing the seven other residential care homes of a similar size and demographic as SunnySide.'

'And?'

'See for yourself. SunnySide is the only home reporting such high mortality figures. Everywhere else has seen a decline in deaths since the end of the pandemic, some more than others.'

Montague put the end of the Mont Blanc in his mouth, realised what he was doing and stopped immediately. 'Ms Rahman's work is certainly interesting, but I wonder if it merits the extreme judicial measures you are suggesting. After all, the home has been rated good by the Care Quality Commission.'

How did Montague know that? The information wasn't in Ridpath's report or Sophia's. 'But the mortality figures themselves would merit an investigation and, in the absence of any compliance by ChromaEstates, we can only visit the place with a warrant.'

'Hmm…' was Clarence Montague's response, followed by, 'Let me take it under consideration. I usually find when I sleep on a problem, it either goes away the following morning or a compromise is reached.'

'And if somebody else dies in the meantime?'

'I hardly think one day will make a difference, do you?'

'I think it will. We need to look into the home immediately. Something is going on there, I can feel it.'

'Your feelings are the least of my concerns, Ridpath.' Montague raised his voice and pushed the folder on his desk towards Ridpath. 'This however is of concern to me. ChromoEstates has raised a formal complaint against you. I received it from their senior legal counsel this morning. Apparently, the manager of the facility, Mrs Staunton has accused you of trespassing on her facility, being rude, aggressive and overbearing.'

Ridpath picked up the file and began to read the legal letter. 'It's all bollocks,' he finally said.

Clarence Montague winced visibly at the swear word. 'Nonetheless, Mr Ridpath, I must respond to these allegations. I have asked for an independent investigation by the Judicial Conduct Investigations Office.'

'That's rubbish, a waste of time.'

Montague smiled briefly before continuing, 'Nonetheless, given the modern climate against such behaviour, and the fact a Manchester coroner was suspended last year for similar reasons, I must support them when they investigate formally. Until then, you are suspended from duty with the coroner's office.'

'But… but you can't…'

'I just did. I require your coroner's officer ID and the keys to your office.'

'But who is going to do the work?'

'I believe Ms Rahman is more than capable. Now are you going to give me your ID and keys or do I have to call a security officer?'

Ridpath took out his coroner's ID and keys and passed them over the desk.

Clarence Montague put them in the top drawer. 'When I become the head coroner, Mr Ridpath, I will make certain you never see these again. Such aggressive behaviour is unbecoming for a coroner's officer.'

For a moment, Ridpath wanted to reach over the desk and pound the man's pudgy face into a bloody red pulp. Instead, he clenched and unclenched his fists, feeling the bone bite into the skin of his knuckles.

'What are you going to do about SunnySide Residential Home?'

'I don't think it has anything to do with you any longer but I am going to call the legal office of ChromoEstates, explain the situation to him and request access to his files and to the home itself.'

'And if he doesn't give them to you?'

'Well, I have fulfilled my duty. But, as I said, the workings of the coroner's office are no longer your concern.'

Ridpath stood up suddenly and Clarence Montague flinched, moving his chair backwards. The detective leant on the desk and spoke softly. 'The workings of the coroner's office may no longer be my concern as you say, but as a serving police officer I am duty bound to investigate when I believe the law has been broken. In the case of SunnySide, I believe it has.'

He took his weight off his hands and stood upright, looking down at the coroner. 'So when you have your friendly chat with the legal officer of ChromoEstates, do tell him I will be looking into his organisation and particularly how it runs SunnySide Residential Care Home.'

He put his laptop back in his briefcase and popped his notes under his arm. Stopping at the door, he said, 'You won't forget, will you?'

As he closed the door to Clarence Montague's room, Ridpath leant on the door frame and took three deep breaths. Once more, his mind drifted back to Mrs Challinor lying on her bed unconscious, tubes leading out of her body and throat to the inexhaustible machines behind her bed.

How he wished she were here right now. She would know exactly how to deal with places like SunnySide.

He walked slowly down the corridor and opened the door to his office. Inside, Sophia was staring at her computer.

'Ridpath, you've been suspended.'

'How do you know already?'

She pointed to her computer screen.

He strode to her desk and looked over her shoulder. A memo had already been written and sent out by Clarence Montague to all staff and the deputy leader of the local council and copied to Claire Trent.

Dear Staff,

In recent months, I have become increasingly concerned at the behaviour of our coroner's officer, Thomas Ridpath.

He has often treated the post as a part-time position, turning up late for meetings or not all. His work has had numerous errors and his supervision of his junior staff has been remiss, bordering on neglectful.

I have received numerous complaints about his work attitude and demeanour. Yesterday, I was made aware of his misconduct in a formal complaint made by a company running many successful residential and care homes. This complaint alleges rude, arrogant and aggressive behaviour on the part of Mr Ridpath, along with trespassing on their property, refusing to leave when requested and threatening legal action in the form of a warrant and subpoena of documents. All these actions were taken without my sanction or approval.

I am now concerned Mr Ridpath has possibly committed gross misconduct of duty. I have asked the Judicial Conduct Investigations Office to conduct an independent inquiry into his conduct.

While the inquiry is being conducted, Mr Ridpath will be suspended from duty herewith.

Clarence Montague, Head Coroner (temp.)

Montague had worked quickly. There was no way he could have written the memo in the short time it had taken Ridpath to walk down the corridor. It had obviously been prepared in advance. Had the coroner set him up?

Probably.

'What am I going to do, Ridpath?'

'You need to stay here and do the work in my absence, Sophia, people depend on you.'

'But I don't want to stay here any more, he's poisoned the atmosphere. Everybody knows you are good at your job and have managed to balance the demands of GMP and the coroner's office so well.'

The door opened and Jenny Oldfield stood in the doorway. 'I've been told to make sure you leave the building forthwith, Ridpath. I mean nobody uses the word "forthwith" do they? Can I leave with you?'

'Please don't Jenny, without yourself and Sophia the place couldn't function.'

'I can't stand it any longer.'

She walked into the room, all her usual ebullience and happiness gone, a spirit whose energy had been sucked out of her.

'Let me sort this out, Jenny. But in the meantime, yourself and Sophia need to keep going, people are dependent on you.'

She stared down at the floor before slowly raising her head and nodding. 'I only have seventeen more days till I take up my new job anyway.'

'Have you heard anything from Mrs Challinor?'

'Her sister rang this morning. No change, I'm afraid.'

Somehow or other, Ridpath would have to make time to visit her in hospital. At least now he wouldn't have to come into the coroner's office for a while.

'He also asked me to search for a locum coroner's officer to take over your job temporarily until he can find a permanent replacement.'

'So the result of the suspension has already been decided, has it?' asked Sophia.

'In his mind, it has,' replied Jenny.

'Look on the bright side, you won't have to get me coffee any more,' he smiled.

Neither of them laughed at his joke. His mobile buzzed with a new text from Chrissy.

> UPDATE: I think Helen Shipton has something but she won't tell me what it is. Saving it for the 6 p.m. meeting apparently.

That was disappointing. He thought he had explained the importance of teamwork to the detective constable. Obviously, the message had fallen on deaf ears.

He texted back.

> Thanks Chrissy, I'll handle it when I get back. Meeting at 6 p.m. still on.

He switched off his phone, time to get moving. 'I'll get my things and be on my way in a few minutes, Jenny.'

'What are you going to do, Ridpath?'

'Obviously, defend my reputation, but right now, I promised my daughter I would pick her up from school. And this time I am going to keep my promise.'

Chapter FORTY-TWO

Eve was surprised to see him standing at the gates of her school.

'Dad, I didn't think you'd come.'

'I promised I would and so I'm here.'

She waved at Maisie who was walking away.

'Can I give you a lift home?' he asked his daughter's best friend.

'Thanks, Mr Ridpath, but I'm meeting Mum at Sainsbury's. She's doing the weekly shop.'

They walked towards Ridpath's car parked on one of the side streets.

'It's good to see you, Dad. I wasn't expecting you to come.'

'Too many broken promises, huh.'

'Something like that.'

She went silent for a long time until they reached the car. The electronic beep as it opened seemed to wake her up.

'Dad, I…'

'You don't have to say anything, Eve. I've been a bloody idiot. Even worse, I've been an arrogant idiot.'

'You don't have to—'

'But I think I do. You're old enough to decide your own friends now. I should trust you more, particularly when I can't be there all the time. I tried to smother you, control you, but you're becoming your own person.'

She leant over and kissed him on the cheek. 'Thanks, Dad, I should have told you about Billy, but in my head it was no big deal, he was just another friend. Should have told you though.' A short pause. 'And in some ways, I'm sort of glad you got mad, it shows you still care, like when I was little.'

'I'll always care, Eve, no matter what happens or what you do, I'll always be here for you.' He snapped his fingers. 'I've got an idea, why don't we invite him round one night.'

She rolled her eyes extravagantly. 'Yeah, that would work... *not*. "Come and meet my dad, the policeman, he wants to check you out. Oh, and don't be surprised if he frisks you when you walk through the door, asks to check your ID and performs a quick stop and search."' She laughed. 'Anyway, Billy's not that sort of friend. He's gay for a start and somebody I like to talk to.'

'Okay, bad idea. Let him know he's always welcome though.'

'I will.' She paused. 'You're still going to frisk him though, aren't you?'

'When he comes in and when he leaves. Just in case he nicks the silver spoons.'

'We haven't got any silver spoons.'

'He's already been there, has he?'

She was silent for a moment, then after realising he was joking, laughed with all the joy of a teenager let loose in H&M with a credit card. When she'd finished, he spoke again. 'I've some bad news though. I have to go back to work tonight.'

'The boy found in Withington?'

He nodded. 'How do you know about it?'

'Duh, it's all over the papers. Everyone in school is talking about it, even the Maths teacher, Miss Sellars. Normally she doesn't know anything about the world outside trigonometry.'

'Sorry, I have to go back tonight. Will you be okay in the house on your own or do you want to invite Billy to join you?'

'You'd better put away the spoons first, but no, I'll be okay. I've got lots of Miss Sellars' maths to do. She thinks everyone is as excited about the beauty of the area of a triangle as she is.'

'Anyway, what do you fancy to eat? We can get it on the way home.'

'Pho, I fancy pho.'

'You can't eat fur.'

'No, pho, Dad, the Vietnamese soup.' She saw he was smiling at her and banged him on the arm. 'Stop teasing me, Dad. It's not funny.'

He started the engine. 'Pho, it is then. A big, steaming bowl from a tropical country, perfect for a cold February day in sunny Manchester.'

He started the engine.

'Weird that.'

'Weird what?'

'A tropical country creating food perfect for cold weather.'

'You mean like curry from India? Chilli from Mexico? Jerk chicken from Jamaica? I remember as a kid we didn't have such a variety of food to eat. Your grandmother, bless her soul, would cook egg and chips, sausage and chips and, if we were really lucky, chips and chips.'

'No pho? You had a deprived childhood, Dad.'

'Tell me about it.'

Chapter FORTY-THREE

Ridpath dropped Eve off at home, apologising again about not being able to stay with her. He raced down the A56 to Police HQ, finally arriving at 6.10 p.m.

He ran upstairs instead of waiting for the lift and strode into the meeting room reserved for the inquiry.

Empty.

No people. No buzz. No sign of life.

Chrissy had updated the wall with the latest information from the house-to-house team and from her searches on HOLMES, but where was everyone?

He messaged her.

> In the meeting room, where are you?

He sat down at the table and stared across at the face of Andrew Golding in its place at the centre of the wall.

Why was the body dumped now, four years after he vanished?

It didn't make sense. The young lad's body must have been kept in a freezer all this time, why not leave it there forever? After four years, it was hardly likely to be discovered.

And why keep it there in the first place?

Was it a memento, a souvenir of the killer's work? Or was there another reason? Something they knew nothing about?

And how was SunnySide Residential Home involved? Had Andy Golding gone back there? But why? His grandmother had died over two weeks before. Had he made friends with one of the staff? But he was told Andy had been thrown out and they all hated him.

And what about Harold Lardner, where did he fit in? Or did he have nothing to do with it?

He shook his head. Too many questions and too few answers. None of it made sense.

His phone buzzed.

> We're all in digital forensics. You'd better come. Helen's found something.

He ran up the stairs to the digital forensics department, quickly realising how out of shape he was. Too many late nights and too little exercise. After this case was over he would go back to the gym. At least he now had time, as he was no longer working for the coroner's office.

As that thought hit his brain, a wave of sadness washed over him. He had put so much effort into his work, as had Mrs Challinor and all the others. Now it was being destroyed by a jobsworth in a business suit.

He badged his way through the main door, asking a civilian officer, 'Jasper Early?'

'Second editing room on the right.'

He followed the man's pointing hand and knocked on the door. It was opened by Emily Parkinson.

'Great, you're here, Ridpath. Helen's spotted something interesting.'

He walked in and took a seat next to the large, bearded editor.

'Roll it back to the beginning, Jasper,' ordered Helen Shipton.

A blur of images appeared on the central screen.

'We did as you said Ridpath, checking all the traffic and CCTV from the area. There's obviously no CCTV of the body actually being left at the corner, but we thought it can't have been left where it was for more than ten minutes before being discovered.'

'A reasonable assumption. People walk along the street all the time.'

'So we checked traffic footage along Princess Parkway, which is only one hundred yards from where the body was found.'

'And?'

'Through ANPR we found two cars and a van which appeared more than once on this section of the road. Play the footage, Jasper.'

The civilian researcher pressed a button on his console and the footage on the central screen began to play.

'Here's the first car.'

Ridpath frowned. 'It's a police car.'

'Right, not surprising as West Didsbury nick is nearby. Cops would use this road all the time. It turns out the other car was a police vehicle too. But the van was different. Play it Jasper.'

Again, the rattle of keys on the console and the footage changed.

'This is the white van. It's a Renault Trafic, registration number WTR22XD. I don't know who comes up with the stupid names. What's a Trafic when it's at home?'

'A white van like that,' said Emily.

On the screen, a van was driving on the inside lane and signalling left.

'See it's going into one of the connecting streets where the body was found,' said Helen Shipton.

'The number plate?'

'We checked with DVLA in Swansea. No such number was ever issued.'

'Fake?'

'As a pair of Nikes in Cheetham Hill.'

'Interesting, so either this van is up to no good for something else, or he's our killer?'

'Our thoughts exactly. Through the wonders of modern science, we checked the same ANPR camera for hits from the same vehicle and came up with this two hours earlier.'

Again, more footage appeared on the screen. The van was in exactly the same place, signalling left to go into Edgar Street.

Ridpath peered at the screen. 'What's he doing? Recceing the place?'

As he spoke, Steve Carruthers entered the room.

'Don't mind me, youse lot continue what you're doing.'

Helen continued speaking. 'It looks like it. And there's more footage from an hour earlier. This time he's on the same road in the outside lane but going the opposite way.'

'Can we see inside the van?'

'Not from this angle, Ridpath, plus the camera is focused on the number plate.'

Ridpath continued watching the footage.

'Isn't a police car going the other way?' He pointed at the screen. 'Could we look at the dashcam footage and see if we can spot the occupants.'

Helen Shipton smiled. 'Great minds think alike, Ridpath. Jasper managed to get the footage from OS16, the police car involved.'

The screen to the left began showing footage of a windscreen and the inside of a police car. In the top right-hand corner, graphics showed the time, date and speed of the vehicle.

'We matched the time on the ANPR camera with the police car. At exactly 14.09 and 36 seconds, the van comes into view.'

The screen showed dashcam footage of a van coming towards the police car and going past it. The whole sequence lasted less than one second.

'Obviously, we could see nothing when it happened so quickly so Jasper slowed it down.'

The same sequence appeared again on the screen in slow motion. Ridpath saw the car coming towards him with one person in the driving seat. Unfortunately, the light struck the windscreen at the wrong angle to see inside. All that could be viewed was the top of a steering wheel with two hands holding it.

'Is there a tattoo on the man's hand?' he asked.

'The wonders of modern science.'

A still image appeared on the screen.

'Now Jasper uses the optical zoom and we can get even closer.'

The image began to zoom in, the hand becoming bigger and bigger until it filled the screen, the blue ink beginning to fade.

'Is that a swallow tattoo on the hand?' Ridpath squinted his eyes. 'Is it?' he repeated.

Helen Shipton leant forward. 'We all think it is, Ridpath. Our man with the swallow tattoo makes another appearance.'

Chapter FORTY-FOUR

The nurse popped her head around the door. 'It's time to go home, Sarah.'

Mrs Challinor's daughter checked her watch. 'Thank you, Angie, I lost track of time.'

'Easy to do in here,' she said closing the door.

Sarah put down *War and Peace*. Only thirty pages left to go. She looked at the book, staring at all the pages she had read to her mother over the months. A vast tome of well-thumbed pages from one of the longest books in literature. She had read it all aloud from beginning to near the end and her mum was still in a coma.

A tear came to her eye. 'Come back to us, Mum. We – I – miss you,' she whispered.

She marked her place with a bookmark realising, not for the first time, it was one her mother had given her a long time ago, bought at some coroner's conference in Lancaster. A picture of a foreboding castle etched in gold leaf against a black background.

She always bought these little presents back from her travels around the UK. A tradition that had started when Sarah was a small girl and had continued for all these years.

It had taken Sarah a while before she had realised why her mother did it, but finally the penny had dropped; it was her way of saying, I remember you even when I am away from home. I'm always thinking about you even when I'm not there.

'I miss you, Mum,' she whispered again.

Was her mother thinking about her now? Did people in comas have dreams? She had asked the doctor once and he had tried to answer.

'Whether they dream or not probably depends on the cause of the coma. If the visual cortex is badly damaged, visual dreams will be lost; if the auditory cortex is destroyed, then they will be unable to hear dreamed voices. We won't find out until she wakes up and tells us.' He smiled ruefully. 'I'm sorry I can't be more precise. There is so much we don't know about the coma state, a lot more research needs to be done.'

Packing up the rest of her things in her bag, she stood up to put on her coat, wrapping it around her body ready to face the winds of a cold February in Manchester.

Still the machines whirred on behind her mother's head as they had done for the last eight months. The tube in her mum's throat still giving her the oxygen that kept her alive.

She went over to the bed and bent over to kiss her mother's forehead. The skin was hotter than usual. Was her mother getting a fever or was this normal?

She leant in closer trying to feel her mother's forehead with the back of her hand. As she did, she knocked over a metal bowl at the side of the bed. It fell to the floor, hitting it with a loud clang.

As she bent down to pick it up, the sound of the monitor behind her mother's bed began to change, the rhythmic beat of the last eight months increasing in intensity.

She stood up, the bowl in her hand. Had her mother's eyes just flickered? On top of the bed sheet her mother's index figure was tapping away making a hollow sound.

She was about to call the nurse, when her mother's eyelids both opened wide, revealing those cornflower blue eyes she knew so well.

'Mum, are you awake?'

She pressed the call button beside the bed, again and again.

Chapter FORTY-FIVE

After the excitement of discovering the CCTV images of the white van, Steve Carruthers rapidly brought them down to earth.

'The work is good, but…'

'Don't you hate it when there's a "but"?' whispered Chrissy to Emily.

'First, you still haven't established any link between the white Renault van and the dumping of the body. You have them in the area and you have them using a false number plate but that's it. Secondly, there is no link either between the man with the swallow on his right hand and Andy Golding.'

'But we have him on CCTV holding the boy's shoulder before he disappeared,' said Helen Shipton.

Carruthers' Scottish accent became more pronounced. 'I'm sorry your honour, I thought the wee young laddie was going to get run over at the traffic lights so I cautioned him to be more careful. No, I've never met him before and I don't know him.'

'But that's not true. Andy Golding was never seen again after this picture on CCTV.'

'It doesn't have to be true, a jury just has to believe it. Our job is to find enough evidence to link the two of them together and to show he was involved in Andy's death.'

Ridpath interrupted. 'The boss is right. We need to place the van at the scene of the crime and we need to show swallow man and Andy Golding have a direct connection.'

'How do we do that?'

'Simple. We find the van. If the body was transported in it, there will be DNA evidence. Plus, if it has a satnav we can correlate its movements with ANPR and place it at the corner where Andy Golding's body was left.'

'How are we going to find the van, thousands of them were probably sold in the UK?'

'Chrissy, how many Renault Trafics were sold in the UK?'

'Just googling it, Ridpath. Over 250,000 since 1980 but this is the third version, introduced at the end of 2022. I'm going to have to check with the manufacturer but I'd guess about 10,000 vehicles to date.'

'So, we look for 10,000 vans. Can you break it down by region?'

'I'll get onto the importer. He can also give us the names of all the buyers in the UK but obviously not those who bought their vehicle second hand. We'd have to collect the data from DVLA in Swansea.'

'You mean you want us to go through every van like this sold in the UK?'

'That's about it, Helen.' Ridpath stood up and walked over to the printout of the van placed on the board. 'We're lucky it has some distinguishing features. The rear left light isn't working.' He tapped the photo. 'Here, there's a dent at the top of the van, right where the doors meet.' He moved across to the picture from the front and side. 'There's the shadow of a decal on the driver's side panel.'

'Those are buggers to remove,' said Carruthers, 'I had to do one for the missus. What a pain.'

'The mark where the square decal was is still there. Finally, there is a dent beneath the handle of the driver's side door. Those are the four features we are looking for.'

'But what if the van has been sold on more than once?'

'Then, we trace all previous owners.'

'Jesus, that's a lot of work, Ridpath.'

'Has anybody got any better ideas? Door-to-door has given us nothing. Helen has exhausted all the CCTV available. HOLMES is as dead as Manchester City centre on Sunday. The only thing we have is the man has a swallow tattoo on his right hand. Anything from HOLMES or Police Intelligence about the tattoo, Chrissy.'

'Nothing, Ridpath.'

'So, with no other leads so far, we have to eliminate this van from our inquiries. Was it used to transport Andy Golding's body? We won't know until we find it.'

He stepped away from the boards and moved closer to the team. 'Let's not forget, a young boy was strangled. He was then kept in a freezer for four years before being unceremoniously dumped on the street, fly-tipped like an old fridge. We need to find this van and find it quickly. Chrissy, can you get on to traffic police? See if we can track the van's movements on ANPR? Helen and the West Didsbury lads, can you start creating a database of all owners of this van since 2022?'

'You're putting all your resources into the search, Ridpath?' Carruthers questioned.

'We don't have anything else at the moment, boss. For me, it's too much of a coincidence a vehicle with false number plates is operating in the same area where our body was found. We need to find it.'

Ridpath's phone rang. He glanced down at the display and saw it was Dr Schofield. 'I should take this boss.'

Steve Carruthers nodded.

'Dr Schofield, how can I help you?'

'I think this time, it's me who can help. Niamh and I, actually. We found something that may interest you. It certainly shocked me when I saw it.'

'I'll be right over, doctor.'

Chapter FORTY-SIX

Ridpath was on his way to the mortuary in Emily's car when he received the message:

> Mum is awake.

It took him a few moments to work it out. Who was Mum? Then it hit him. He typed back:

> Mrs Challinor? She's come out of the coma?

> The doctors have examined her. She's a bit confused and agitated but otherwise seems ok.

> Great news, after so long.

> The doctors say she needs rest and recuperation but she's already asked about you.

> Should I visit her or give it a few days?

> Come as soon as you can, I'll be spending the night here.

> Will visit early tomorrow morning before work.

> Great.

Ridpath stopped typing and smiled broadly.

'You look happy, you just won a million quid on the lottery?' asked Emily.

'Nah, much better. Mrs Challinor has come out of her coma.'

'That's brilliant news. I always said she was a fighter that woman.'

It *was* brilliant, thought Ridpath. He had so much to tell her about the last eight months, so much to update.

They parked up and strode over to the mortuary. Inside, Ridpath's mood was instantly depressed by the sterile stench of the place.

'Come in, come in.' The doctor greeted them in his high voice. 'We are extremely excited by this discovery, aren't we, Niamh?'

'We are indeed, John. Even the normally taciturn Ridpath may be excited.' She looked up from the body of Andrew Golding still lying on the stainless steel table, in exactly the same position Ridpath had left it five hours ago. 'But you seem to be smiling Ridpath, first time I've ever seen you so happy, it suits you.'

'Mrs Challinor has come out of her coma, Dr Schofield, isn't it good news?'

Ridpath could see the doctor's eyes shining with pleasure above his face mask.

'It is, we've been waiting for so long for her to rejoin the land of the living.'

Ridpath thought it was an interesting choice of words for a man who spent his days surrounded by the dead.

'And who have you brought with you to our office?'

'This is DS Emily Parkinson, my number two on the case. Emily meet our pathologists, Professor Niamh O'Casey and you already know Dr Schofield.'

'Nice to see you both.'

The two women eyed each other like two prize fighters from across the vast expanse of a boxing ring.

Ridpath rubbed his gloved hands. 'Now we have the introductions over, what do you have for us?'

'Well, this could be the second good news of the day. We had nearly completed the post-mortem when Niamh decided to check the epiglottis.'

'I wanted to see if it too had been damaged during the manual strangulation. I looked inside the boy's mouth and to my surprise found this tucked between one of his pre-molars and his cheek.' She held up a small red and orange gel cap.

'Are you saying he was drugged?'

'We think he probably was, but this is far more important.'

'Why?'

Dr Schofield took over. 'You see if the boy had been given the gel cap before he was dead, his body heat and saliva would have dissolved it.'

'And it would have been impossible to have given it to him after he was frozen because the jaw would have been unable to open.'

'But you know, Niamh, the body could have been unfrozen, the gel cap placed in the boy's mouth and then refrozen again.'

'Interesting John, but we found no evidence the body had been slowly frozen twice. The cell damage of such an act would have been catastrophic. No, I think our only conclusion is the gel cap was placed in the mouth after the body was unfrozen but before it was dumped beside the road in Withington.'

It was as if Ridpath and Emily Parkinson weren't there.

'Yes, I must agree, Niamh, it's the only logical conclusion.'

'But why does it matter when the gel cap was placed in the mouth? You said he was probably drugged.'

'Oh, but it does matter, DS Parkinson, it matters very much. You see you are making some obvious assumptions about our little gel cap.'

He held it up between his index finger and his thumb.

Ridpath thought for a long time. What assumption had they made about a gel cap? And then it hit him like a double decker bus. 'We're assuming the gel cap contains drugs.'

Dr Schofield turned to his colleague. 'I told you he was good, Niamh.'

She tapped her hands together in quiet applause.

'So what does it contain?'

Dr Schofield placed the gel cap on a small white tray, pulling the two halves apart with a small pair of tweezers, talking as he did. 'When we opened our little friend, we discovered this.'

Inside the gel cap, was a small roll of onion paper. Using the tweezers and the blade of a scalpel, the doctor unrolled it and gestured for them to join him.

Looking over his shoulder, they could see it contained a single stark word in black, capital letters.

TRACE

'I haven't a clue what it means. Is it a child's game? Does it mean the killer is leaving something behind on his victim, teasing us about Locard's theory about forensics?'

'Every contact leaves a trace.'

'Exactly DS Parkinson.'

Ridpath had been quiet, staring at the single five-letter word on the paper. A word which had sent a stab of fear down his spine.

'It's not either of those possibilities,' he finally said. 'I know exactly what this new discovery means. And it's not good news. Not good at all.'

A silence hung over the examination punctuated only by the sound of the air conditioning.

Finally, Emily asked, 'What do you mean, Ridpath? I don't understand.'

Ridpath closed his eyes briefly. An image of frozen corpses lying in a freezer flashed through his mind. 'TRACE is the facility near Preston run by the University of Lancashire. It is the nearest thing the UK has to a body farm.'

'I've been there and worked there. But they only use animal parts in their scientific work not human cadavers,' said Niamh O'Casey.

'It was where Harold Lardner kept his victims. Hidden in plain sight. We discovered them by chance.'

Emily Parkinson was silent for a long time before saying, 'But I thought Lardner was only convicted on one count of murder.'

'True. But we tied Lardner to at least five other murders of women. However, the Crown Prosecution Service decided, in its infinite wisdom, only one count would generate a failsafe conviction. In their opinion the evidence wasn't strong enough to convict him of the other murders and they didn't want to "confuse" the jury.'

'So Lardner killed more women, concealing their bodies at TRACE?'

'That's about it. He was far too clever to leave forensic evidence on the bodies tying him to the murders.'

'Yet here we are having discovered a piece of paper linking this murder with Lardner. And one of the few people who would recognise the clue happens also to be the Senior Investigating Officer looking into the case.'

'It would point to two conclusions, Dr O'Casey.'

'Which are?'

'Either Lardner is active again, coordinating the murders from his cell in Ashworth High Security Hospital—'

'The whole point of having such strict security for people like Lardner is they are continually watched by a team of profes- sional prison officers, psychiatrists and security staff. It would be extremely hard, if not impossible, to arrange a murder four years ago, for the body to be kept frozen and now left by a road in Manchester.'

'Everything you said is true, doctor.'

'Plus, you said yourself Ridpath, Lardner didn't kill men or boys, he focused on women.'

'Also true, Emily. But we do have a murder which seems to link back to the MO of Harold Lardner, unless...' Ridpath stopped speaking, staring into mid-air.

'Earth to Ridpath. Come in Planet Ridpath.'

He snapped out of his thoughts. 'Unless, we have option two: a copycat. A killer who is trying to replicate the murders of the Beast of Manchester. And wants to show his adulation by leaving clues behind on his victims.'

'You said victims, Ridpath,' Dr O'Casey's voice cut through the hum of the equipment, 'but we only have one victim. This boy.'

'I'm sure he has killed already. We just haven't found the other victims yet. But maybe, doctor, he's telling us where they are with your small piece of paper.'

'You think they are at TRACE?'

'It's the first place I would look, wouldn't you?'

'There is one other possibility, a third option you have over-looked, Ridpath,' said Niamh O'Casey.

'What's that?'

'Lardner is operating from Ashworth, directing the copycat to commit crimes on his behalf.'

Ridpath stayed silent for a long time before saying, 'You're right, Niamh, that is a third possibility. He did use stooges before to do his bidding. One even killed herself rather than be arrested by us.' He stopped again, lost in thought before suddenly saying, 'I need to talk to Steve Carruthers.'

Ridpath strode down to the other end of the post-mortem facility, calling his boss. The overpowering pickle-like smell of formaldehyde hung around the area like rotting kimchi.

Carruthers answered after four rings. Ridpath explained the situation to him and requested Police Tactical Unit support plus a team of search officers.

'What exactly are we looking for, Ridpath?'

'I'm not certain, sir, but I suspect we will find more bodies.'

'I'll have to contact Lancashire Police, it's in their area.'

'Try Detective Superintendent Hollis. We've worked with him before and he knows the case.'

'Will do, what time do you want to go in, Ridpath?'

'As soon as we get the team together, boss, let's say ten o'clock tomorrow morning.'

'Not earlier?'

'Those bodies aren't going anywhere and it will take a long time to put a team together. I also want the manager of the facility to be there.'

'Right, consider it done. I'll message you the details as soon as I have them.'

Ridpath switched off his phone and walked back to where the three others were gathered around the body of Andy Golding.

'It's on, tomorrow at ten.'

'Can I go with you?' asked Niamh O'Casey. 'If you discover bodies, you are going to need a pathologist on site. At least I know the case.'

'I'm not sure, Dr O'Casey. Lancashire will want their own pathologist and coroner involved.'

'But that would take time. And, I should remind you, if there is another Beast of Manchester out there, time is the one commodity you don't have.'

Chapter FORTY-SEVEN

After explaining the latest discoveries on a conference call with the rest of the team, Ridpath decided to head home.

The call had been short. Chrissy was to continue tracking the van using ANPR and Helen and her team were to contact possible van owners first in Greater Manchester and then expand the search to the rest of the North. It was going to be a painstaking and detailed operation.

'I don't think I'm the right person for the job.'

'Why Helen?'

'I've never done anything like this before.'

'You'll have a team to support you. It's important, Helen, we need to find the van and tie it to the death of Andy Golding.'

She finally acquiesced. Ridpath thought she was in love with the exciting, derring-do aspects of policing, not realising it was the hard grind of detailed evidence recovery which led to breakthroughs.

'And Chrissy, can you organise a warrant to search the SunnySide Residential Care Home and its files? West Didsbury were called to the home on the day Andy disappeared. I am still convinced the place has something to do with his disappearance.'

'Any reason, Ridpath?'

'You could use a series of unexplained deaths in the last year.'

'Isn't that the coroner's territory?'

'Probably, but he's not doing his job so we'll have to do it for him.'

'Right, I'm on it, Ridpath, I'll find a friendly magistrate to sign it.'

'Finally, Em, you're with me on the raid at TRACE tomorrow. And did you organise the visit to see Harold Lardner?'

'You still want to go, Ridpath?'

'Now more than ever.'

She checked her notebook. 'Right, it's arranged for four p.m. tomorrow but the deputy governor is insisting on a meeting before we see Lardner.'

'Why?'

'He wouldn't say, but he won't let us meet Lardner unless we see him first.'

'Confirm it, Emily. We need to see him.'

'Right people, we are getting close, I feel it in my water. Let's keep pushing now, and we can nail this case.'

He wished he could have used better speech to inspire the team but the words hadn't come to him.

After the meeting was finished, it was ten fifteen before he arrived home.

As he put his key in the door, he shouted, 'Eve!'

There was no reply.

He looked around the hall, glancing upstairs. 'Eve!' he shouted again.

Still no answer.

Then the door to the kitchen flew open. 'Surprise.'

The table was set and a steaming bowl of lasagne stood in the centre along with a large salad and two place settings.

'I thought you'd be hungry when you got home.'

'You shouldn't have bothered, a sandwich would have done.'

Her face fell.

'But thank you, it's a lovely surprise.'

A broad smile. 'It's the last frozen lasagne though, you're going to have to make some more.'

The lasagne was Polly's recipe. Once a month, Ridpath made a whole batch, keeping them in the freezer until they were needed.

'We'll do it at the weekend. I'll organise a delivery from Ocado for the stuff and we'll be ready.' He made a mental note to do it later.

'Promise?'

He held out his hand with the thumb and forefinger extended. A strange teenage ritual she had taught him. 'Promise.'

He took off his jacket and sat down.

'Sorry about the salad. It's a recipe from TikTok. We didn't have any mustard so I used lemon juice and oil. I hope it's not too sour?'

'I'm amazed we had any salad ingredients in the fridge.'

'We didn't, I walked to the local Tesco Express. Couldn't get any wine though.'

He was about to reprimand her for not staying in the house as he had instructed, when he realised this was not the time or the place.

'Well let's get stuck in, I'm starving.'

'So am I, the pho didn't really fill me up.'

'Fur never does.' He began eating, the lasagne was good, even if he had made it himself. 'What did you do waiting for me?'

'The usual; finished my homework and watched a bit of telly. *Digging for Britain*. Alice Roberts is so cool.'

'So you're thinking about becoming an archaeologist?' He spoke with his mouth full of cheese sauce and salad.

'She's not an archaeologist, she's an osteologist. She specialises in anatomy and has a medical degree.'

Ridpath's mind flashed back to the body of Andy Golding lying on the stainless steel table.

'I'm thinking of doing a medical degree and specialising in pathology.'

Ridpath said nothing. He couldn't imagine his beautiful daughter being surrounded by dead bodies for the rest of her life, having the single-minded focus of Niamh O'Casey.

'But it may be just a phase. I might go back to wanting to be an MP next week.'

The wonderful freedom of the young. At that age, they had lots of choices. His job was to help her realise her ambitions.

'I have some good news. Mrs Challinor has come out of her coma.'

'Great, can I go and visit her?'

'Probably not yet. Let her recover for a few more days.'

'Perhaps on Sunday? I'd love to see her again.'

'I'll check when I see her tomorrow morning. Now the not so good news…'

'You mean the bad news, Dad.'

'I'm going to be busy tomorrow, I have to go up to Preston.' She didn't need to know he was going to a body farm. 'So I may not be back early and won't be able to pick you up from school. I'll call Maisie's mum and ask her to look after you till I'm free.'

'I'd rather you didn't, Dad. I can look after myself now. I'd prefer to come home on my own and do my homework here. I can let myself in and, after my visit to Tesco, we've even got some food.'

Ridpath thought for a long time.

'I did it this evening, Dad, and I was okay. Trust me.'

He nodded agreement. 'But you must come straight home, do not pass Go and do not collect 200 quid.'

'Fat chance.'

He changed his tone. 'I am serious. I might be late. Just come home, lock all the doors and stay inside. No more visits to Tesco.'

'Not even if I need something?'

'Not even if you need something.' He held up his finger. 'Plus, I have to leave tomorrow morning at six, it will be too early to take you to school or the tram station…'

'I can walk and I'll get up early to see you off.'

'I'd prefer you went to Maisie's and her mum took you. I'll make breakfast and leave it out for you. Agreed?'

He held out his little finger with the index extended.

She did the same. 'I'll get up before you go, but it's agreed.'

He changed the subject. 'You and Maisie not getting on?'

She shrugged her shoulders. 'We're okay, it's just she can be a bit much sometimes. Everything is such a drama…'

'It comes with being a teenager.'

'Tell me about it. Seems like half the school has got the dreaded teen disease.'

'And you haven't?'

She stared at him. '*Daaaad, puhlees.*' She carried on speaking about her day and Maisie and the strange Chemistry teacher with one finger missing. As she talked, Ridpath zoned out. Something he had thought earlier as he spoke to Eve was nagging at the back of his mind.

What was it?

And then it came to him. The frozen lasagne. He made a batch and stored it until it was needed.

Was this what had happened to Andy Golding? But that raised a host of other questions.

Why store the body in the first place?

Why was it needed later?

And, more importantly, who needed it?

Ridpath's head spun with the questions flooding into his brain. He tried to focus back on to Eve again. What was she saying?

'Billy, messaged me. I told him about possibly meeting you. He said he couldn't face it, you scare him.'

'I seem to have that effect on people at the moment.'

She put her arms around his neck. 'Not on me you don't. You're just Dad, with all the clumsiness, silliness and total uncoolness that involves.'

'At least, I don't dance badly.'

'Only because you don't dance at all.'

'True, my legs weren't made for it. Sorry about Billy, maybe he'll change his mind later.'

She stood up and placed her empty plate into the sink. 'I doubt it, but never mind. I've decided you were right after all, he is too old for me. If I'm going to be the next Alice Roberts, I can't be distracted by insignificant things like boys.'

With that, she flounced out of the kitchen and clomped her way upstairs.

Ridpath was left alone with his questions.

Still too many, with too few answers.

Thursday, February 8.

Chapter FORTY-EIGHT

True to her promise, Eve was up at 5.30 and ate breakfast as Ridpath gulped down the extra strong coffee he had made for himself.

'What time are you going round to Maisie's?'

'Eight o clock.'

'What are you going to do till then?'

'Read. I'll use the time to catch up on my reading.'

He placed the half-drunk cup in the sink. 'You can do the washing up before you go...'

Eve ignored him.

'It's not going to happen, is it?'

'You know me too well, Dad.'

'Right, I'm off.'

'Give my love to Mrs Challinor.'

She stood up to kiss his cheek. Once again, he was surprised at how tall she had grown recently. She hardly had to reach up any more.

'See you tonight. And remember what we agreed.'

'*Daad.*'

He put on his coat, grabbing his briefcase and laptop. She came to the door, standing in the entrance to wave him off.

As he drove away, he looked in the rearview mirror and didn't see his little four-year-old girl any more; a gangly teenager had come in and usurped her place. Soon, the teenager would vanish and a young woman would be standing there. And then there wouldn't be anybody at all when she left home, leaving an emptiness where his heart should be.

He smiled to himself. You can't stop them growing up, just cherish every moment you can. It was part of being a parent, part of being a dad, and he hated every second of it.

He reached forward and tuned the radio to the classic Seventies station. Mott the Hoople's 'All the Young Dudes' blared from the speakers.

For the rest of the drive to the hospital he sang every song they played at the top of his voice, getting bemused stares from other motorists. He parked up and took the lift up to Mrs Challinor's floor.

She was sitting up in bed waiting to greet him with Sarah by her side. 'Good… morning… Rid…'

'Take it easy, Mum, the doctor said not to talk too much.'

She struggled to get the words out. After eight months in a coma, it wasn't surprising. Ridpath thought it was good to hear her voice again even though it was raspy and rough, not her usual tone. God, how he had missed it.

'It's great to see you again, Mrs Challinor.'

'It's good… to be back.' She swallowed and tried to talk some more, 'I was asleep…'

He sat down next to her bed, holding her hand. 'For eight months.' He finished her sentence for her. 'We were worried for you.'

She nodded her head. Her face was paler than normal and the eyes betrayed the exhaustion she felt. Still she tried to speak.

'Can't… remember… anything.'

'You were attacked near your home by Alexandra Orwell. Apparently you were getting too close in your investigation of the unexplained deaths of her husband's patients. She attacked you again in the hospital.'

'Where… is… she?'

'Now?'

Mrs Challinor nodded.

'On remand, awaiting trial.'

She seemed satisfied with the answer and then she frowned. 'I can't… remember.'

Sarah placed her hand on her mother's arm. 'Don't worry, Mum. Your memories will come back. Just don't push too hard.'

Mrs Challinor closed her eyes for a second and then her body stiffened as she summoned up all her strength. 'I hear... you've been... suspended.'

She was well informed. He glanced at Sarah.

'Sorry. Sophia told me.' She stood up. 'Do you want a coffee? I'll go and get one and leave you two to talk.'

When she had gone. Mrs Challinor indicated he should pass the pad and pen on the bedside table to her. She slowly wrote in rough, badly formed block capitals:

> DON'T BLAME HER. I FORCED HER TO UPDATE ME.

'I won't. How are you?'

She began writing again.

> MY HEAD HURTS. I HAVE SANDPAPER FOR A THROAT, I WANT TO PEE ALL THE TIME AND I CAN'T REMEMBER ANYTHING. BUT OTHER THAN THAT, I'M GOOD. HOW ARE YOU?

He didn't want to lay all his troubles on Mrs Challinor so soon after her recovery. 'I'm good,' he said eventually.

She wrote more quickly this time.

> RUBBISH. YOU LOOK WORSE THAN I FEEL. MONTAGUE GIVING YOU PROBLEMS?

He read the note and smiled. 'A few. Nothing I can't handle.'

> HE'S AN ARSEHOLE. WHY WERE YOU SUSPENDED?

He explained the message and his visit to SunnySide Residential Home without going into too much detail.

'You were right, he... wrong,' she rasped, ending with a bout of coughing. He poured some water into a glass from a carafe next to her bed and passed it to her.

She took a few sips and wrote again.

> BLOODY THROAT. FEELS LIKE I SWAL-LOWED A FACTORY OF RAZOR BLADES.

She took a few more sips of water before scribbling furiously.

> ALL UNUSUAL DEATHS <u>HAVE</u> TO BE INVESTIGATED.

She underlined the word 'have' heavily.

> YOUR JOB IS TO REPRESENT THE FAMILIES AND LOOK FOR THE TRUTH. WHO DIED? HOW DID THEY DIE? WHO WAS RESPONSIBLE?

She let him read her message.

'I understand, Mrs Challinor, it's what you told me all those years ago when I started working at the coroner's office.'

She then seemed to summon up all her strength to speak. 'Your job... is to be... an advocate for the dead... in the land of the living. That's what... the dead want. An advocate... Remember...'

She began coughing again, her chest heaving with effort. Dr Pereira appeared at the door.

'I think you'd better leave, Mr Ridpath. It's too early for Mrs Challinor to be speaking so much.'

'Of course, doctor, I'll go now.'

He stood up. As he did, she grabbed the sleeve of his jacket. 'Do... your... job, that's what the dead want.'

She collapsed back on the bed, her forehead and grey hair drenched in sweat.

Mrs Challinor was back in the land of the living.

Chapter FORTY-NINE

All had gone as planned so far.

The bait of the young boy had been taken. The van was spotted on CCTV. No doubt they were tracking the route on ANPR. They might even be checking up on every buyer of a similar make of van in the last three years.

Fat lot of good all that would do. The trail would lead to an offshore account in Belize.

He would decide what they discovered, when they found it and what relevance it had.

They were all so predictable, particularly Ridpath. He could forecast each of the man's moves at least four steps before he made them. It was so enjoyable leading him by the nose like a cow being led into an abattoir.

The end would be the same, too.

'Are you feeling okay, Lardner? You didn't come to breakfast this morning.'

He coughed, slid off his bed and limped to the door as if he were extremely sick.

'I didn't sleep, Mr Francis, the nightmares came back, I need to see Dr Mansell.'

'Your session is this afternoon, Lardner, wait till then.'

He made his voice sound desperate. 'I don't think I can wait, Mr Francis, it was a bad night.'

The door opened and two attendants stood in the entrance. Mr Francis and Robert Harrison.

'What do you think, Bob?' asked Francis.

Harrison scratched his nose with his right hand, showing the swallow tattoo in between the thumb and forefinger.

'He looks a bit agitated, Alan. I'd give it another hour and then see how he is.'

'Right Lardner, you heard Mr Harrison, try to get some rest. I'll check on you later.'

The door slammed shut, a key turning in the lock.

He smiled to himself. The seeds were now planted in the stupid attendant's mind. Harrison had played his part beautifully.

He checked the time. He would wait another hour before he started to bang on the door. The timing had to be just right.

He went back to lie down on his bed. In a few hours if all went to plan, and it would, he would be out of this pestilential place. This prison masquerading as a hospital, where patients end up sicker than when they came in. An evil place where psychopaths were treated by the terminally insane.

He laughed out loud thinking of a joke he had once told Dr Mansell: Two cops lead an unfortunate man into a padded cell. Instantly the men in white coats grab him, wrench his arms behind his back and, when he screams in pain, the psychiatrist tears down his trousers and jags him with a needle. As they're carrying the unconscious body away the younger of the cops, shocked, says:

'Was that necessary? He came along gentle as a lamb.'

The psychiatrist frowns and replies:

'This place is run rationally, with efficiency, everybody gets exactly what they need: the depressives get prozac, the manic depressives get lithium, the schizophrenics get chlorpromazine and the catatonics get ECT.'

'And what about people with conditions there's no treatment for like psychopaths and narcissists?'

The psychiatrist smiles and says, 'Oh, we get a job.'

Harold Lardner laughed out loud and then immediately crammed his fist into his mouth to prevent the attendant from hearing.

Mansell never did get the joke. He had simply frowned and asked, 'Why do you need to tell jokes about psychopaths and narcissists?'

Because they are everywhere, you fool. The Prime Minister, members of parliament, the so-called leader of the opposition, all narcissists, sociopaths and psychopaths, all standing for office, running the country, in charge of our lives.

Look at the world around you.

At least, he knew he was a psychopath and revelled in the knowledge. But Mansell had no idea he was a narcissist, he wallowed in a pool of his own self-satisfied ignorance.

He also didn't know his favourite patient was going to escape in a few hours.

Free as the proverbial bird and ready to settle a few scores.

Nobody was going to hurt Harold Lardner any more.

From now on, he would be the one doing the hurting. And he had so little time left to enjoy their pain.

Chapter FIFTY

Ridpath sat in his car waiting for the digital display to reach ten a.m. Next to him, Emily was coolness personified, staring out of the window, deep in her own thoughts.

Behind them in another car was Stan Jones from the West Didsbury team and the pathologist, Niamh O'Casey. Further behind was a transit van full of coppers from Lancashire Police.

For Ridpath, looking through his rearview mirror, it looked exactly like a modern version of the cavalry waiting to ride to the rescue of some isolated homestead.

Except it wasn't the wild west of America but the even wilder west of Lancashire.

He had already briefed all of them, everybody knew what they had to do, what to look for and what to avoid. They would bring in a cadaver dog later if he felt it was necessary.

They had been parked on a side road for the last twenty minutes. One car had passed them but, other than that, the place was as quiet as a graveyard should be. This part of rural Lancashire was just miles and miles of undulating fields populated by cows, sheep and the occasional human.

'Only five minutes to go.'

Emily looked at the clock. 'What's it like inside?'

'You'll see soon enough. Cold. Sterile. Scary.'

'Sounds like my sort of place.'

9.55

He picked up his airwave. 'Five minutes to ETA.'

'Roger,' answered the head of the search squad followed by the same response from Stan Jones.

'Do you think we'll find anything?'

'Honestly, I don't know. This could be the wildest wild goose chase we've ever been on.'

'Or?'

'Or we may find a serial killer has been operating in Manchester and we knew nothing about him.'

'Not great options.'

'They never are.'

The conversation ended.

Ridpath could feel the excitement building inside him, like a horse waiting in the stalls at the start of a big race. In his inside pocket, he could feel the search warrant nestling next to his heart.

He tapped the steering wheel nervously, beating out the rhythm of 'Jean Genie'.

'I do wish you wouldn't do that,' Emily said irritably.

He stopped tapping.

9.58

He picked up the airwave again. 'Two minutes people. Remember I will go first and show the warrant to the facility manager. You will only come when I call you forward.'

'Roger.'

He began tapping the steering wheel again, getting dubious glances from Emily.

9.59

'Sod it, it's close enough.'

He put the car in gear and stamped on the accelerator. They surged forward around the bend and the TRACE facility came into sight.

Ridpath could see it hadn't changed since his last visit here six years ago; an eight-foot high security fence topped off with three coils of razor wire surrounded the site. A thick electric cable and the ubiquitous red lightning flash of live electricity attached to the fence.

The research facility itself looked like all the other agricultural buildings in the area except instead of using the land to grow food, the land on this farm was used to bury dead animals and monitor their rate of decay.

He slowed at a thick red and white barrier which blocked the one road into the facility. A single CCTV camera stared down at him. A burly security man came out from his hut and walked over to them.

'Sorry, nobody's allowed in here. It's university property.'

He pointed to the single sign stating who owned the land.

UNIVERSITY OF LANCASHIRE

NO ENTRY

Ridpath flashed his ID followed by the warrant. 'We're going to search this place.'

The guard stared dubiously at the piece of paper in his hand. 'I dunno about that. I'll get Mr Richards to come out.'

He vanished back into his hut, obviously making a phone call to his boss. Ridpath began tapping on the steering wheel again.

Before he had even reached the second verse of 'Jean Genie', the security guard approached the car.

'Mr Richards says you'd better come in. Park behind the security building over there. Do not go past the red sign in the car park and please do not leave your car until Mr Richards comes out to take you into the facility.'

'I know the drill.'

The security guard raised the barrier and Ridpath drove through. He parked where he was told to and waited for Mr Richards. A man in a white lab coat soon came hurrying across to meet them.

Ridpath and Emily got out from the car.

'This is most unusual. Alan said you had a warrant to search the facility?'

'My name is DI Thomas Ridpath and this is DS Emily Parkinson, we are officers from Greater Manchester Police and we do have a warrant. We believe human bodies are being kept here.'

He passed over the paper again. The man glanced at it quickly.

'You can't come in here, it's a research facility. No human cadavers are kept at TRACE. But a search could endanger the experiments. Last time you lot came here, we lost two years of work.'

'And last time, we found human bodies.'

'But we have upgraded our security and procedures since then. They had been far too lax under the previous management.'

'Where is Patrick Downey now?'

'Mr Downey,' the man sniffed, 'the former manager of TRACE no longer works for the university. Anyway, you are not coming in here until I obtain clearance from my superiors.'

'I'm sorry we don't have time to waste. We have a warrant to search these premises and we're going to do it now.'

Two more burly security guards appeared out of nowhere and were joined by the one from the gate.

The man in the lab coat smiled. 'As I said, I'd like you to wait until I confirm it with my superiors.'

Ridpath looked at the security guards. 'Are you threatening me, Mr Richards?'

The same insipid smile. 'Not at all. But I am sure we do not want to lose two years' worth of work again.'

'And as I said, there is no time.' Ridpath held the airwave to his mouth and simply said, 'Now.' Within seconds, Stan Jones's car and a transit van full of coppers rounded the bend and approached the barrier.

'Unless you give us immediate access to all your buildings, I will be arresting you and charging you with obstruction. Is that clear?'

The shoulders of Mr Richards slumped forward and he nodded at the security guards who backed away.

'What do you want to see?'

'Well, we'll start with all your CCTV footage, your gate logs and all the specimen arrivals for the last four years.'

'Four years?'

'That's right.'

'I can get you the other documents but we only keep CCTV for a month before it's erased.'

Niamh O'Casey and Stan Jones approached them.

'Emily can you check the CCTV?'

'What am I looking for?'

'Our man or his van.'

'Where are the disks kept?'

'Please show the detective to the security room, Alan, and help her with the machines,' ordered Richards.

The burly security guard mumbled, 'This way,' and Emily followed him.

'You can show me your gate and specimen logs.'

Mr Richards sighed. 'Come to my office.'

'What do you want me to do?' Niamh asked.

'Wait here Dr O'Casey, I'm sure there'll be plenty for you to do later,' Ridpath answered, crossing his fingers.

If there wasn't, he would have a lot of explaining to do to his superiors.

Chapter FIFTY-ONE

I lowered my binoculars; my arms were tired from watching the police in the valley below. I was standing on a hill above the facility, hidden by a stand of old beech trees.

I'd been there since first light, accompanied only by a flask of lukewarm coffee. They'd arrived later than the Master had predicted but here they were. One car had gone first, presumably to execute the search warrant. A whole posse of them had followed later, emerging from their transit van, and then hanging around waiting for the signal to start searching.

I spotted Ridpath in the centre of it all with the stupid facilities manager by his side. A woman, probably a detective, went with the guard back to his post.

The Master was right again. They would check the CCTV at the entry first before doing anything else.

After ten minutes, the detective signalled for Ridpath to join her. Five minutes later they came out and began to head towards the storage room.

I picked up my mobile and called the number on speed dial. I had a signal despite being deep in the Lancashire countryside. The Master had said there was a cell tower built at TRACE for the use of researchers.

'He's started,' I whispered into the phone.

'Good, a little later than I thought but Ridpath was never the quickest of coppers. You can leave now.'

'Are you sure he'll find them?'

'He'll eventually get round to working it out. Is the pathologist with him?'

I picked up the binoculars with my free hand. 'An older woman with her hair in a bun?'

'That's her. Niamh O'Casey. She could never resist a chance to escape the lab. Right, they are all set. You can return to the safe house now.'

'You don't want me to stay and make sure they make the discovery?'

'No, you must return to the safe house, waiting for me when I arrive. I am about to begin. Do you understand?' The last words were a command not a question.

'Yes, Master.'

The phone call ended.

I wiped the mobile with an alcohol-based wet wipe and leant it against the tree, taking the flask of coffee with me.

The coppers would eventually find it but that was the whole point, according to the Master.

I never understood the plan the Master kept in his head. My job not to reason why, just to do what I was a told. To the letter. No exceptions.

It had worked so far and it would continue to work. The Master was always right. Praise his power.

I looked back to where I had been standing all morning. Nothing there except the glint of the sun against the mobile's screen.

I lifted my binoculars one last time, seeing them about to enter Cold Store 7. Would they find what had been hidden?

Chapter FIFTY-TWO

It didn't take Emily long to discover the footage she needed.

She asked the security guard if a man with a swallow tattooed on his hand ever came to the facility and he answered right away.

'You mean Frank?'

'Frank who?'

'Frank Desmond, works for Genepro. He comes here often in his van.'

'How often?'

'Every month or so. He always stays for a cuppa and a biscuit in the shed after he's delivered his load.'

'When was the last time he was here?'

The man tried to work it out using his fingers. 'About three weeks ago I reckon, just after the storm. Couldn't get here before then because a tree blew down blocking the road. I had to stay here overnight. The missus wasn't best chuffed, I'll tell you.'

'Can you show me the footage from your CCTV?'

He selected a disk marked January and inserted it into the machine, rapidly scrolling backwards, stopping a few times to check the date on the timecode.

'Here it is. Around January 13. As you can imagine, we don't get too many visitors. Can be a bit lonely stuck out here some-times with the nutty professors and the dead animals in the fridges. Problem is they pay so well...'

'Not a problem with the police.'

'I can imagine.'

He continued to scroll back until the time code reached 11.45 a.m. Emily watched as a white van drove up and stopped at the barrier. The driver hopped out of the vehicle and shook hands with the guard.

'That's how I knew who you were talking about. Always friendly was Frank and shaking hands. I noticed the tattoo. Asked him once why he had it done. He said it was about someone who'd gone away, but they'd be back soon, like swallows returning every year.'

'Can you zoom in on the van?'

'Sure.'

On the screen, the image of the van grew bigger. Emily could see the number plate was different but all the dents were in exactly the same places as the van in Manchester. And this van had one extra addition; a small sign on the side with big blue and red letters proclaiming the words, 'Genepro, a Medical Science company'.

'What does Genepro do?'

'Frank told me once. According to him, they do vaccine testing for the pharmaceuticals industry using animals; rabbits, monkeys, mice, hamsters, pigs, even ferrets.'

'Ferrets?'

'Saw more of them after Covid began. According to him, ferrets were used to study Covid-19 because they show similar symptoms to the disease as humans, their lung physiology is also similar to ours, and they can spread the virus to other ferrets through the air.'

'He seems well-educated for a driver.'

'He's not just a driver. Dunno what he is exactly but he knows his stuff, does Frank.'

'So after being used for testing, they bring the animal bodies here?'

'Yeah, always store them in the same place. Cold Store 7.'

Emily rushed outside and waved to get Ridpath's attention. 'You'd better come here, you're going to want to see this,' she shouted.

Ridpath ran over to the office where the machines were kept. Emily asked the guard to rewind the footage again.

Ridpath stared at the screen in front of him.

'It's definitely our man and the same van. When did you say he was last here?'

'Three weeks ago, on January 13, delivering dead animal bodies.'

'Can you match the delivery with your logbooks?'

Mr Richards already had the book open at the correct date. 'See, Genepro delivered six bodies to their store. A pig, two rabbits and three ferrets. All had been used for testing and were non-toxic.'

Ridpath frowned. 'What?'

'Non-toxic. If an animal's body has been tested using radio-active materials or viruses, we must be notified. One of the new procedures I put in place. During Covid, we took in a lot of the animal bodies used to test the anti-virals created for mass immunisation,' he said proudly. 'We store those in a separate area at the back of the Cold Stores.'

He stopped the video playback. 'Where did this man put his bodies?'

'For this delivery, Freezer 3 in Cold Store 7.'

'Do you have keys?'

'Of course, but—'

'Take us there now,' he ordered.

'But... I... It's a private store for Genepro, I'd have to ring them first.'

'You're not ringing anybody until we've checked what's inside. Emily, can you get Dr O'Casey and bring her along to Cold Store 7.'

'Will do.'

The DS ran out of the security building.

'Now, Mr Richards, please lead the way.'

'I don't know, it's most irregular.' He muttered as he walked out of the building, pulling a large bunch of keys from his trouser pocket.

Ridpath followed him and was soon joined by Emily and Dr O'Casey.

'You have something for me, Ridpath?'

'Perhaps, we'll know soon.'

They walked down the side of one of the long, wooden buildings. The cold wind roared through the gap, Ridpath pulled his coat around himself. In this weather, they wouldn't need cold storage.

They walked across to a large square, brick-built structure with a metal door at the front.

'This is Cold Store 7.'

'Please open it.'

Shaking his head, Richards fumbled the keys, finally finding the right one for the lock. He opened the door and they were immediately confronted by long sheets of plastic hanging down from the ceiling.

'Keeps the flies out in summer,' explained Mr Richards.

Ridpath expected the Cold Store to be freezing but it wasn't. Instead, six large coffin freezers were arrayed against the walls, their lids clamped and padlocked.

'The delivery was to Freezer 3 wasn't it?' asked Ridpath.

Mr Richards nodded and searched through the bunch of keys in his hand.

'Here it is, but are you sure you want to open this freezer? Genepro gave strict instructions their animals were never to be disturbed. They had to keep them for three years in case their clients asked them about the results.'

'Please open it, Mr Richards.'

Dr O'Casey moved to Ridpath's side and they both peered in as the lid was lifted. A sheet of frozen Perspex covered the contents.

'Shall I?' asked Dr O'Casey putting on a pair of bright purple latex gloves.

She removed the Perspex sheet, carefully examining it before laying it down on the floor.

'What have we here?' She leant in and pulled out a large plastic bag with a tag attached to it. Through the plastic, Ridpath could see a large brown eye with long eyelashes staring back at him.

'*Sus domesticus*, the domestic pig. They're often used for testing because their physiognomy is so similar to ours.'

She laid the frozen animal in its bag on top of another freezer. 'There's more, looks like *Oryctolagus cuniculus* to me, the European rabbit. Both of these have white fur. Quite cute, aren't they?'

She held up a plastic bag for Ridpath to see. It looked exactly like one of Eve's stuffed animals she slept with every night. Except it was dead and ice cold.

Dr O'Casey laid it next to the pig. She reached in and pulled out another bag which looked exactly the same. 'Mr Oryctolagus again. You did say there were two of them delivered?'

Ridpath nodded without saying anything. He was clenching and unclenching his fists and could hear the heavy breathing of Richards beside him.

Dr O'Casey leant in once more, pulling out three small plastic bags. 'It looks like *Mustela putorius furo*, the common ferret, the domesticated version of the European polecat.' She held up one of the plastic bags for everybody to see. 'You know one of my earliest memories is of one of my da's friends sticking one of these down his trousers. Didn't know then why he did it, still don't know now. They have these sharp little teeth and claws. I wouldn't put one of them anywhere near my naughty bits.'

She laid the ferrets next to the pig and rabbits and stared into the freezer. 'Well, that's it, nothing else.'

She checked the freezer one last time. 'I can take these back to my lab, Ridpath, but they look kosher to me.'

Mr Richards smiled broadly. 'I told you the records would match. Genepro is a reputable company, we checked them out before we allowed them to deposit their waste animals here.'

'Can you check the other freezers, Dr O'Casey?'

'Is it really necessary?' asked Richards. 'These freezers and their contents are the property of Genepro. They shouldn't be touched without their permission.'

'Fortunately, this warrant says I do have permission. Are you going to open them for Dr O'Casey or do we have to break the locks?'

Chapter FIFTY-THREE

While Dr O'Casey painstakingly went through each of the freezers matching the delivery log books with the contents inside, Ridpath watched the CCTV footage once more.

'Can you give me a printout of the man with the swallow tattoo, and another one of his vehicle?' he asked the security guard.

Richards nodded, approving the request and seconds later the printer had produced two full colour images.

Ridpath picked them up, examining both photos closely. The van was definitely the same as the one picked up by the traffic cameras on Princess Parkway at the time of the dumping of Andy Golding's body. In the second image, the man was wearing a nondescript green baseball cap, his face was hollow and pinched with a sharp nose and chin. To Ridpath, he looked like a human version of one of the dead ferrets Dr O'Casey had taken out of the freezer.

'And you say the man's name was Frank Desmond?'

'That's what he told me. And the same name was on the driving licence.'

'Driving licence?'

'Another new security protocol. We take photocopies of all the licences of the people who deliver here.'

'Why didn't you tell me before? Where is it?'

Richards went through his files, finally producing a sheet of paper. 'Frank Desmond, see the photos match.'

Ridpath was immediately on the phone. 'Chrissy, I want you to check with DVLA on the driving licence of a man called Frank Desmond.' He read out the number on the licence.

'Is he our swallow tattoo man?'

'We think so. I'll take a picture and zap it over to you now. Top priority, Chrissy.'

'On it.'

'I'm also going to send the address of the company he works for, Genepro. They are based in Bird Hall Lane in the Europa Business Park in Stockport. I want to know anything and everything about them. Who owns them? What do they do? Everything, got it?'

'Got it, Ridpath.'

Ridpath shot the driving licence and the Genepro address with his mobile and sent it to Chrissy. 'Now, Mr Richards, while we're waiting, take me through the security protocols again.'

Richards rolled his eyes. 'Once a consignment arrives, the materials are logged into the delivery log and a place of storage assigned. The drivers are then escorted to the storage area and watched as they unload their consignment and place it in the location. Afterwards, the freezers are locked again by our security guard and the driver is escorted back to the front gates. It's a foolproof system. After last time, we had to tighten up security.'

'So the delivery drivers are never left alone?'

'Never. They are escorted at all times.'

'And they don't have keys to the cold stores or the freezers.'

'No, only we have the keys.'

Dr O'Casey appeared at the door. 'We been though all the freezers, Ridpath, the contents match the delivery logs exactly—'

'See, I told you they would,' said Richards proudly.

'—But there are still two outstanding deliveries we can't find.'

'What? Give me that.'

Dr O'Casey handed the delivery logs to Richards, who scanned them quickly before smiling. 'These pigs are in the contaminated store. You won't find them in Cold Store 7. Remember we follow the Controlled Waste Regulations Act of 2012 and the Hazardous Waste Directive of 2011 religiously at TRACE, plus a whole host of other government and environmental regulations.'

'So where is the contaminated store?'

'Behind Cold Store 7, but you can't go in there unless you're wearing a biohazard suit.'

'So if a delivery is made there, both the driver and the security guard have to get changed into the suits before they enter.'

'That is the protocol.'

Alan, the security guard looked sheepish. 'I didn't do it,' he said softly.

'What?'

He looked straight at Ridpath. 'I didn't do it. I couldn't breathe in those things and afterwards my skin itched for days.'

'What are you saying?' shouted Richards. 'You didn't follow the protocols? They are the rules, man.'

The security guard didn't answer, staring down at his feet.

'But if you are following the protocols set down in the 2012 Act, it means anatomical waste arrives in a sealed container and is not examined by you?' said Dr O'Casey.

'Correct, but...'

'It also means you have no idea what is contained in the sealed containers delivered by Frank Desmond. Even if your security guard had accompanied Desmond into the biohazard area, he wouldn't have known what was in the containers.'

'True, but the protocol states a guard must be with a driver at all times.'

Niamh O'Casey shrugged her shoulders. 'Seems like a stupid protocol to me.'

'A rule is a rule. Bio-security protocols must be followed. Some of the animal bodies in the store have been subjected to radiation or injected with viruses or pathogens such as anthrax.'

'I am well aware of biosecurity protocols, Mr Richards,' snapped Dr O'Casey, 'I helped write the legislation.'

'Just making it clear—'

'So I understand,' said Ridpath talking directly to the guard, 'when Frank Desmond made these deliveries you didn't go inside with him?'

He shook his head without saying anything.

Ridpath's phone buzzed. It was a message from Chrissy.

> According to DVLA, Frank Desmond's licence doesn't exist. It's fake. Still looking for the Genepro info.

'It looks like you have another problem, Mr Richards,' said Ridpath quietly.

Chapter FIFTY-FOUR

Ridpath, Niamh O'Casey, and the manager of the TRACE facility entered into the changing areas next to the storage building. The bright yellow PVS hazmat suits were contained in sealed lockers against one wall.

'These are decontaminated after every use. They provide the highest level of protection against vapours, gases, mists and particles. The hazmat we use consists of a chemical entry suit with a face piece and self-contained breathing apparatus. There are also heavy boots with steel toes you must wear.' He glanced at Niamh O'Casey's feet. 'We may have your size. Finally, there are chemical-resistant gloves for an additional level of protection. If you would like to begin to get changed now, I will help you as necessary.'

'No need,' said Dr O'Casey already planting her legs into the bright yellow trousers of a suit.

'These are Level A hazmat suits. Selected the make myself after rigorous testing, best on the market.'

Ridpath struggled into the large yellow trousers before fitting the heavy PVC overcoat with its built-in face mask over the top of his head, ensuring the wrists and waist were firmly secured.

Richards, already in his suit, stepped over and gave him a last check, adjusting the angle of the face mask. 'Just breathe normally and you can fit the earpiece in your ear before you close the hood.'

The security guard was right, the suits were uncomfortable. Even in the dead of a Lancashire winter they were hot and stuffy. Ridpath had to continually resist the urge to scratch his arms and legs as the material itched unbearably. He put the earphone into his left ear.

Niamh O'Casey's voice came in immediately. 'The sound is voice activated. Speak normally and I will be able to hear you.'

'Right, okay.'

'Don't shout, speak normally. The oxygen system gives us twenty minutes of working time inside the biohazard facility.'

'What if we can't finish by then.'

'Make sure you do finish.'

After one last check by Mr Richards, Ridpath heard his voice through the system. 'Right, you're ready to go.'

Ridpath could taste the metallic tang of the oxygen, hearing the sound echo through the suit as he breathed in and out.

Behind him Niamh O'Casey had already finished dressing. She looked exactly like a preternaturally thriving Pokemon.

Richards' voice was in Ridpath's ear again.

'Just a last run-through on safety protocols. The suits are positively pressurised so even if they are damaged, hazardous material cannot enter, but I would advise you to leave the area immediately if you do damage the suit. Secondly, breathe normally, there is enough air in the system for twenty minutes and finally—'

'Let's go and stop wasting time,' interrupted Niamh O'Casey.

Richards opened the door to the biohazard facility. Inside, everything was clean and tidy, looking exactly like any other building in the TRACE facility. The one difference was the padlocked metal door with a large wheel in the centre.

'That's the entrance to the airlock and decontamination chamber before we enter the biohazard store.'

'Why aren't the bodies incinerated like all other bio-waste?' asked Ridpath. His voice sounded strongly Mancunian in his ear.

'Sometimes researchers want to retain the animals in case they need to re-test them again.'

'And this was the case with Genepro?'

'I don't know, they never said.'

Wearing the heavy gloves, he fumbled for the right key, finally selecting the correct one on his chain. He unlocked the padlock, turning the wheel clockwise and lifting the locking lever.

The door swung open slowly, white mist drifting out of the entrance. Even through the suit, Ridpath could feel the bitter cold of the air.

'We keep this storage area at a constant minus five degrees.'

'Just like a Manchester summer,' said Dr O'Casey.

As the mist cleared, another door similar to the first was revealed.

'We'll stay in here for five minutes as our suits are being disinfected from tiny aerosols set in the ceiling.' Richards pointed upwards, revealing a steady stream of a thin, blue vapour. 'The same procedure will be followed as we exit.'

'Where is the delivery stored?' asked Niamh O'Casey.

Richards checked his log details. 'Palette 5, Stack 2. It's on the left against the far wall.'

They stood there for five minutes, not saying a word to each other. Ridpath began to tap his fingers against the side of his hazmat suit. His throat was dry and he was desperate for a long cool drink of water. Then he realised he'd better not think of water. 'What happens if you want to go to the toilet in one of these things?'

The answer came from Richards. 'Hold it.'

He could swear Dr O'Casey was smiling broadly behind her glass face mask.

Richards took out a different key and unlocked the second door.

'Are we ready?'

'Ready,' answered Dr O'Casey.

'Ready,' croaked Ridpath.

Richards turned the wheel, the door swung open and another cloud of cold air bellowed from inside the storage room.

Through the glass of the face mask, Ridpath could see paletted containers of various colours and materials; blue, white and purple bins, red square tins, large black barrels and grey cardboard boxes. All were shrink-wrapped in plastic and had bright yellow biohazard stickers prominently displayed.

He could hear his breathing become faster.

Richards beckoned them forward and closed the door as they stood in the room, turning the metal wheel in the centre.

'Are you locking us in?' asked Ridpath.

'Protocol,' was the one-word answer.

His rate of breathing increased even more.

Shivers ran down his spine as he followed Richards down to the far wall. Either it was the cold air or it was the knowledge untold diseases, poisons, pathogens, viruses and bacteria were contained in these crates.

He didn't know which and he didn't care. He wanted to get out of there as quickly as possible. Niamh O'Casey on the other hand, seemed to be in her element, staring all around her, checking all the labels attached to each pallet.

'You have a treasure trove of research here, Mr Richards. I noticed a bin with a label saying it contained a rhesus macaque infected with bubonic plague.'

'That would be from Oxford. They are researching a vaccine against the plague. They only started sending us their animals six months ago.'

Another shiver went down Ridpath's spine.

Richards finally stopped in front of two pallets on the floor. 'These are the Genepro deliveries.'

On each pallet, a blue plastic container about four feet long and shaped like a miniature coffin was shrink-wrapped and stickered in at least four places with the yellow biohazard marker.

'We'd better get started,' said Dr O'Casey, 'no time to waste.'

'I urge you not to open these containers, we should contact Genepro first to discover what is inside.'

'No,' said Ridpath, 'I don't want anyone in Genepro to know what we are doing.'

'Your log says they contain pigs, Mr Richards,' said Dr O'Casey.

'But what did the pigs die from? You shouldn't open these containers.'

'These are approved hazmat suits?'

'Of course.'

'Then we should be safe. But Ridpath, if you want I could take them to a secure facility at my lab and X-ray them first?'

'How long would it take, Niamh?'

'That's the first time you haven't called me Dr O'Casey and you pronounced my name correctly. But to answer your question, about a week to organise the secure transportation and prepare the lab.'

'We don't have the time. Particularly as there might just be pigs inside.'

Dr O'Casey looked around her. 'The safest place to open these is here. It is biosecure after all.'

'If you are opening the container, I am not going to stay.'

'Suit yourself, Mr Richards, please go ahead, Niamh.'

'There it is again, music to my ears, Ridpath.'

'Please do not open it.'

Dr O'Casey took a scalpel from her bag and cut through the plastic wrap surrounding the first blue container.

Richards spluttered and stamped his foot, before shouting, 'I'm leaving, I've told you not to do it, you don't know what it contains.'

He strode back towards the entrance, almost running in the hurry to get out of the building. He turned the wheel on the door, took one glance back at them, opened it and fled through. Ridpath watched as the wheel turned anticlockwise as if by magic, locking them in.

'Ye man seems a bit worried, you still want me to go ahead?'

'It has to be done.'

'Famous last words, Ridpath.' She held the scalpel close to the seal on the side of the container and with one swift stroke cut it.

She reached into her bag and produced a pair of forceps. 'I usually use these to spread the rib bones during a post-mortem, but they'll work for a lid as well. You still sure you want me to proceed?'

Ridpath felt his mouth go even dryer. Of course, he wasn't sure. Was this the right thing to do? Should he have waited? What happened if there was only a pig inside, but a pig infected with an unknown pathogen?

He nodded anyway. They had to know now, not in a week.

Niamh O'Casey stepped forward, hooking the forceps under the lid and applying pressure upwards. 'Well, here goes. At least whatever's inside will be frozen.'

Her words didn't comfort Ridpath very much. Actually, they didn't comfort him at all.

'A little more pressure. It is like opening the sixth and seventh ribs...'

Before she could finish the sentence, the black lid popped off and slid slowly onto the pallet.

They both leant forward to look inside.

'Would you believe that?' Dr O'Casey said after a moment of silence.

Chapter FIFTY-FIVE

Harold Lardner banged on the door of the cell.

'Mr Francis, I need to see the psychiatrist *now*. I need to see Dr Mansell.'

The guard ambled over to Cell 23. 'What is it, Harold? You know you're all supposed to stay in your rooms till lunchtime. Just read a book.'

'But I need to see the psychiatrist, Mr Francis, I'm having flashbacks.'

'Relax, Lardner. Your appointment with him is this afternoon at four, wait until then.'

'But I can't wait. The flashbacks are getting worse. Please, Mr Francis, ask if he'll see me before noon.'

'I think you should ring the doctor, Alan.' Harrison appeared out of nowhere. 'He's sounding agitated. Don't want another person topping themselves, do we?'

'But it's my lunch break at noon, Bob.'

'Don't worry, I'll take him for you. I'll bring him back before my shift finishes.'

'If you think it's a good idea, Bob.'

'I do.'

'Even if I ring Mansell, he might not see him.'

'Please ask him. Tell him I've read his book and have a few comments.'

Mr Francis stood outside the cell wondering what to do. Lardner was an important patient in the hospital. The deputy governor had made it clear he was to receive special attention. If he didn't tell Dr Mansell and something happened, he would be for the high jump. But if it was all a waste of time, the doctor would be reporting him. What to do? His thoughts were interrupted by Lardner again.

'I have to see him this morning, Mr Francis, it won't take long, promise.'

'I'll take him, Alan,' said Harrison.

The guard remembered something his old boss in the army had told him long ago: 'Remember, the motto of the Army is CYA, Alan.'

'CYA?'

'Cover your arse. If there is a problem, cover your arse. If there isn't a problem, cover your arse. And if something looks like it might possibly become a problem in the future, what do you do?'

'Cover your arse.'

'Remember these words of wisdom and you'll go far.'

The advice had given him a twenty-two-year career in the army but, even though he was out now, he still found it useful.

He picked up the phone on his desk and dialled the doctor's number. 'Morning, Dr Mansell, Harold Lardner has been banging on his cell door, shouting he wants to see you urgently.'

'Has he had his medication?'

'This morning at the usual time.'

'So he should be fine.'

'He says he keeps getting flashbacks.'

'Perfectly normal in a patient with PTSD. Tell him to use the meditation techniques I taught him.'

It was obvious the doctor didn't want to see Lardner.

'He also said something about reading a book and having comments…'

'Did he?' The doctor's voice brightened on the other end of the phone. 'I suppose I could make time at noon.'

He looked across at his colleague. 'Mr Harrison will bring him at that time, doctor.'

The line went dead. The guard ambled over to Lardner's cell and banged on the door. 'He'll see you at noon.'

'Thank you, Mr Francis, I won't forget this.'

'Just doing my job. Mr Harrison will take you.'

'What was that, Mr Francis?'

'Nothing. Just keep quiet and don't disturb the other patients.'

'No problem.'

Inside his cell, Harold Lardner had a broad smile plastered on his face.

It had started.

Chapter FIFTY-SIX

They looked down into the open mouth of the containment coffin. Inside was another clear vinyl sheet.

'Shall I cut it?'

Ridpath paused for a moment.

'Shall I cut it?' repeated Dr O'Casey.

'Go ahead,' he finally said.

She sliced through the vinyl sheet and peered inside.

'There appears to be another plastic bag.'

She moved slightly back to allow Ridpath to look. Both of them stared inside the containment coffin.

It was the doctor who spoke first. 'Doesn't look like a pig to me.'

Ridpath didn't answer.

'If I was a betting woman, which I am, I'd say that was the top of somebody's head.' She shone her torch inside trying to get the light in as deep as possible. 'A male, I'd say. From the grey hair, an older male.'

Ridpath snapped out of his torpor. 'We need to get a scene of crime team down here as soon as possible.'

'Do you want to open the second one now?'

'No,' he said firmly. 'I don't want to destroy any more possible evidence. Can you put the lid back on?'

She did as she was asked. 'You'll need a specialised team, one with experience and training in handling biohazard material.'

'I've heard of biohazard crime scene clean-ups but not biohazard investigations. I'll check if we have one or if we have to bring in help from an outside force like the Met.'

'I'll hang around if that's okay with you, I want to be here when they pull this man from inside the container. I presume I will be doing the post-mortem with Dr Schofield?'

'I'll clear it with the Lancashire coroner. I'll leave one of the Didsbury sergeants with you.' Ridpath moved to run his fingers through his hair, but stopped short realising he was still in the suit. 'What a nightmare.'

'What are you going to do next?'

'Well the first thing to do is to get out of this bloody suit, it itches like mad and I'm starting to feel cold.'

He walked towards the now closed door and stopped suddenly, looking for a handle or an exit bar.

Nothing.

'How the bloody hell do we get out of here?'

A crackle on the radio mike in his helmet before Richards' voice came through. 'Give me a second DI Ridpath, the door is a bit stuck.'

Ridpath glanced across at Niamh O'Casey. She was staring up at the ceiling. He looked down at her hands and the fingers were crossed. Had they omitted to tell him something before they went in?

The door was still not opening.

'Mr Richards, what's happening?' A note of tension in her voice.

'Just a second,' came the reply.

Still no movement from the door.

Ridpath suddenly started to feel very cold. He thought about Andy Golding's body, frozen for four years. Had he been kept here? He heard his breathing becoming faster and shallower. 'Mr Richards, what's happening?'

He glanced across at Niamh O'Casey. Through her helmet visor, she looked concerned. She stopped what she was doing and strode over to join him at the door. 'Open the airlock now, Richards,' she ordered.

'Just a minute.'

Through their earphones, they heard the sounds of the man grunting.

'It seems to be stuck.'

Niamh O'Casey stared at Ridpath. 'Richards, we only have ten minutes left on our oxygen, you'd better get us out of here.'

More grunting and groaning before the wheel began to spin and the door suddenly swung open, revealing a suited facilities manager still in the airlock area.

'Sorry, I don't normally do this. I leave it to the security guards.'

Neither Ridpath nor Niamh answered him, moving quickly out of the biohazard room.

'I'll activate the decontamination procedure. It will take five minutes.'

A machine began to hum and a fine drizzle of disinfectant rained down from the ceiling.

'Well?' asked Richards. 'Did I hear you correctly?'

Ridpath decided to let the man stew in his own self-satisfied juices for a little while longer, as he stood under the stream of disinfectant.

Richards turned and repeated his question to Dr O'Casey. She took her cue from Ridpath and didn't reply.

'Tell me what's going on?' He stamped his foot like a child who couldn't get his own way.

Finally, Ridpath looked up at him. 'You've got another problem, Mr Richards. And now, so do we.'

Chapter FIFTY-SEVEN

Mr Francis came for him at exactly 11.55 a.m.

If there was one thing the security guard could be trusted for, it was his punctuality. Not a brain cell to rub together, but he was always on time.

'Come on, Lardner, you got your wish, the trick cyclist is waiting. Mr Harrison will take you to the doctor's office and bring you back. If you give him any trouble, you'll have me to answer to. Understand?'

'I won't be no trouble.' The double negative satisfied the guard. Lardner picked up his notebook and stood at the door with his legs and arms spread.

'Good, you're finally following the rules, no moaning this time.'

The guard searched Lardner's body, finding nothing.

'The book.'

He cracked the spine and checked under the cover for razor blades or sharpened bits of metal.

'You can't be too careful these days, Bob,' he said over his shoulder before handing the book back. 'You take him, Bob, he's clean. I'll go on my lunch break now, just put him back in his room when you return.'

'Come on, Lardner,' growled Harrison. 'You know the way.'

As soon as they were out of earshot, Harrison whispered, 'Are you ready, Master.'

'Let's do it.'

They went through three locked metal doors before finally arriving at the entrance to Dr Mansell's office in the new wing of the hospital complex. The guard rapped on the door.

'Come.'

'Harold Lardner for you.'

He pushed the patient into the room. 'Shout if you need me, doc.' He closed the door, standing guard outside.

'Come in and sit down, Harold.' The psychiatrist's voice was as smug and self-satisfied as ever. He continued writing in his notebook without looking up. 'Now what seems to be the problem. We were due to meet this afternoon, couldn't it wait?'

Harold Lardner adopted his usual submissive position; shoulders hunched, steps tentative, eyes cast down to the floor. He sat down opposite Dr Mansell, letting his fingers play with each other nervously in his lap.

The doctor looked up, taking in all the submissive clues and instantly relaxed. He took a pencil and inserted it into the sharpener on his desk. The familiar whirring sound filled the small room.

He took it out, examined the sharpened point and then paused, pencil hovering over the pristine white page of his notebook.

'The dreams have returned, Dr Mansell. Rather than dreams, I should call them memories.'

'The memories of your post-mortems? Which one is it this time?'

'The death of the police officer.'

The psychiatrist stopped for a moment, pencil hovering over the page. 'That wasn't a post-mortem.'

'It was a murder.'

'So you are finally admitting that you were involved in her death?'

Of course I am you fat fool, it's my last gift to you: the truth. 'I watched on the monitor as Lesley administered the anti-freeze into her arm.'

A smug smile crossed Mansell's face. 'We are making progress today, Harold. I always wondered why you acted through proxies to commit your murders.'

'It was about control and power. I enjoyed controlling people, making them commit the last taboo in human civilisation: to take the life of a human being.'

'Isn't that a—'

'Do not interrupt me when I am speaking,' he shouted. 'I controlled them. I'm still controlling them. They do my bidding out of love, for me and my work. They are still doing my work as I sit here and rot in this prison.'

'Let us get back to the matter at hand,' the psychiatrist said nervously. 'Why is this memory particularly troubling for you?'

It wasn't troubling, idiot, Lardner screamed inside his head. *It was pleasurable. I enjoyed watching her face contort in pain and agony.*

Instead he said, 'I don't know, it just is.'

'Did you try to use the tapes I gave you for when these memories come back? Going to your safe place for example.'

Lardner looked down, shaking his head and whispered, 'They didn't work.'

'They will always work if you do them properly and believe in them. Belief is key.'

'Perhaps I am not doing them correctly.'

'I will show you. There is so little time left to master these techniques to make the coming days easier. You do understand, don't you, Harold?'

'Of course, I do.'

The doctor stood up and taking up his notebook and pencil, walked round to sit next to Lardner. He made himself comfortable and began speaking.

'Now I want you to close your eyes and concentrate on your breathing, noticing how with each breath you can relax more.'

Lardner closed his eyes and breathed in, slowing his heart rate. It was important to be calm and dispassionate for what he was about to do.

'And as you continue to listen to the sound of my voice as you relax, I want you to move your attention to your toes and notice any tension and let it go. Aware that with each and every breath you can relax deeper and deeper.'

Lardner focused away from the voice to the sounds outside the window; the tweeting of birds, the faint buzz of traffic, the hum of the air conditioning.

'Now I want you to move your attention to your feet and let the tension go.'

Lardner did the opposite of what he was told, focusing the tension like the string of a cross bow being pulled back.

'Now, as you move up to your calves I want you to continue to relax as we move up to your thighs, continuing to breathe deeply...'

The time was now. The doctor was relaxed by the sound of his own voice. His eyes were even closed.

Lardner leant forward, snatching the sharpened pencil from the top of the notebook, grabbing the doctor's hair and holding the pencil against his throat.

'Shush, shush, it will be all okay, Dr Mansell.' He whispered into the man's ear. 'Can you feel the point of the pencil against your carotid artery?'

The doctor whimpered, nodding his head.

'I once performed a post-mortem on a man who had used a pencil to kill another prisoner in Strangeways. The details were fascinating. Of course, nothing happens when you push the pencil in, it's when you pull it out the fun starts. One hundred millilitres of blood spurts upwards with each beat of the heart. Each spurt as high as two metres above the head. The blood being heavily oxygenated is bright red and, in my particular case, we found spatter on a wall eighteen feet away. Imagine that, eighteen feet? All the while the victim is aware of life ebbing from his body. Do you want to die, doctor?'

'No, no,' the man whispered, his body shaking.

'A little louder for the guard.'

'No... no... no.'

'Good, I heard the fear in your voice. Now stand up.'

Lardner hauled the man to his feet, still holding his hair and the point of the pencil stabbing into his throat. 'Now, call the guard in.'

'Mr Harrison, I need you in here.'

'Louder.'

'Mr Harrison!'

The door burst open and the guard stood in the door. 'We need to move quickly, Master.'

Dr Mansell's eyes moved rapidly from side to side trying to work out what was going on.

The guard came into the room and closed the door behind him.

'We need to strip him,' ordered Lardner.

'No, I... please don't.'

Lardner pressed the pencil deeper into Mansell's neck. 'Don't make a sound, and take off your clothes.'

The doctor began to remove his tweed suit, whimpering all the time.

'You've got to hurry, we don't have much time, Master.'

'Get a move on, Mansell.'

When the man was down to his undergarments, Lardner began to dress in his clothes. The hideous garments fitted him perfectly.

Taking off his own belt, the guard used it to secure the doctor's hands, stuffing a handkerchief into his mouth. 'Lie still and you won't be hurt,' he ordered.

Mansell did as he was told.

'Now, you need to take my handcuffs and put them around my wrists. We have to make it look like you overpowered me and then killed him.' Harrison nodded towards Mansell, who began whimpering again. 'But first I need to clear your exit.'

He took the walkie-talkie off his belt. 'Harrison to Control, over.'

'Control here, Bob. Everything okay?'

'All good, Keith. Looks like Lardner will finish soon. The doctor told me he is going out for lunch afterwards.'

'Not like him.'

'Told me, he needs a break from the place.'

'Don't we all. I'll clear him through security.'

'Right, Keith. I'm taking Lardner back to his room in five minutes.'

'We'll keep an eye out for you, Bob.'

'Over and out, control.'

Harrison switched off the walkie-talkie. 'You have five minutes to get out. Don't forget Mansell's car keys and wallet. He's driving a BMW 640.'

'He would, wouldn't he.'

Harrison sat on the floor. Lardner took the guard's handcuffs and placed them around his wrists, ensuring they were snapped shut.

'You need to hit me now, make it look real. Don't hold back, Master.'

'I won't, Bob.'

Lardner picked up one of Dr Mansell's awards from the book-shelf. He thought it was the one from the British Psychiatric Association, and brought it down on the skull of the guard, feeling the crunch of the heavy bronze biting into the bone.

He lifted the award up and brought it down again, harder this time right behind the man's ear. Again and again and again he lifted the heavy bronze award, bringing it down on the man's head, feeling the thrill of pleasure as the metal crunched into the grey matter of the brain.

Finally, he stopped, breathing heavily, wiping a small piece of bone from his lapel. 'Sorry about that, Bob, but you've now outlived your usefulness. Shame really, I quite enjoyed our conversations. I've always wanted to bash someone's brains in with an award from the British Psychiatric Association. It feels apt, don't you think?

Dr Mansell was curled up in the corner of the room, whimpering like a baby.

'I'm afraid, doctor, it's now your turn.'

Chapter FIFTY-EIGHT

The long drive back to Manchester down the M6 was time for Ridpath to think. He'd asked Emily to get behind the wheel so he could spend time with his thoughts.

Before he left TRACE, the scene of crime team had arrived at the facility.

'We've got a biohazard team coming from the university in an hour,' the scene of crime officer told him. 'This looks like a long job but I'll let you know what we find as we discover it.'

'Use Dr O'Casey as your pathologist.'

'Niamh? We've worked with her before. Mad as a box of hammers but good at her job.'

All the additional expense had to be cleared by Steve Carruthers.

'Are you sure there are dead bodies inside those containers?'

'At least one, Steve, confirmed by Dr O'Casey.'

'So there could be more?'

'Probably. Frank Desmond made other deliveries we haven't opened yet.'

'Jesus.'

'There are hundreds of hazardous containers in the store, Steve.'

'You're not suggesting we open all of them, it could take years and cost millions.'

'Not yet anyway. I suggest we concentrate on those linked to Frank Desmond first. After that, people like yourself will have to make the decision, it's above my pay grade.'

'Above mine, too.'

'But it is the perfect place to store a body you never want found. Beats putting them in the foundations of a building or the stanchions of a motorway.'

'Jesus.'

'I don't think he's buried here, sir, but we can have a look if you want.'

'Very funny, Ridpath. Any ID on the body you saw?'

'Nothing, boss, but if I'm honest, we didn't spend a long time looking. Perhaps the SOCOs will find something.'

'Right, get yourself back here asap. I want a meeting with the team. This is getting far bigger than we ever thought.'

He'd put the phone down and packed up his things, bagging the TRACE logs and the CCTV disks to take with him. He walked back to the main office and was stopped by the sergeant in charge of the police search team.

'Do you need us any longer, sir? Only there's a big flap over some incident over in Merseyside and we're short of manpower.'

'Nothing your mob can do here until the SOCOs have finished. Leave a couple of constables to guard them. The rest you can send away.'

'Ta, sir. Control will be chuffed.'

He went into the main office. Richards sat in the corner of his office, head in his hands, whispering to himself. Ridpath had one last question for him.

'The logs state Frank Desmond made at least four deliveries to the hazmat store in the last six months. Did he ever take anything away? You said research scientists sometimes removed materials for further research?'

Reluctantly, Richards reached for another log book. 'These are the records of removals from the facility. Not that many as you can see.' He ran his finger down the columns. 'Three weeks ago, Frank Desmond removed one container. It was during his last visit here.'

In the car, Ridpath turned over this information in his head. Emily in the driving seat had the sense not to speak. Even the radio was turned off so as not to distract him.

What if, he asked himself, the container had the body of Andy Golding inside? Had he been stored at TRACE for the last four years? And then it struck him. If Andy Golding was removed from TRACE three weeks ago, Ridpath hadn't started his investigation by then. The *Manchester Evening News* hadn't even printed the story that led to him being put on the case.

So why had somebody placed the capsule in his mouth? Without that clue, Ridpath would never have gone anywhere near the place again.

None of it made sense. Ridpath felt he was running in a race where he was continually trying to catch up and the finishing line was continually being moved.

Outside, the grey tarmac of the M6 carved its way through the Lancashire countryside.

Inside the car, Ridpath forced himself to breathe deeply. 'Go back to basics,' he whispered.

Andy Golding disappeared on May 22, 2020, just after his grandmother had died at SunnySide. He was last seen in the company of a man with a swallow tattoo on the corner of Palatine Road, minutes from the care home. His body was found four years later in Withington, also not far from the care home.

And just two days ago, Clarence Montague received an unsigned note on headed notepaper from the home indicating the residents were being killed.

'Why does it all keep coming back to the care home?'

'I don't know, Ridpath, are you sure it does?'

Without realising it, he had spoken aloud. 'I think so, Emily, too many unanswered questions about SunnySide.'

'I hate to remind you, Ridpath, but we are supposed to be visiting Harold Lardner this afternoon. The meeting was set for four o'clock.'

'Damn, I'd forgotten all about it. We need to postpone it until tomorrow morning. I'll ring Chrissy and get her to do it.'

He dialled the number. Chrissy answered immediately.

'I was about to call you, Ridpath.'

'Chrissy, can you cancel the meeting with Lardner at Ashworth? Rearrange it for tomorrow morning.'

'I wouldn't bother if I were you.'

'Why?'

'Have you been listening to the radio?' she asked. 'Obviously not. Harold Lardner escaped from Ashworth at one o'clock today. Half of Merseyside and Lancashire police are looking for him. He killed a security guard and a prison psychiatrist in the escape.'

'Jesus Christ.'

'My words exactly Ridpath.'

'What do you want to do?'

Ridpath thought quickly. It would be pointless for the team to join in the hunt for Lardner, there was probably a thousand coppers already looking for him. 'The search for Lardner is Merseyside and Lancashire's problem for the moment, we have a job to do. We need to raid Genepro's offices asap.'

'This evening?'

'Exactly. Can you get Helen to work with Steve Carruthers on it? Hang on...' He turned to Emily. 'When will we be back at HQ?'

'Barring traffic, around five thirty.'

'Use the blues and twos.'

She pressed a switch on the dashboard. Instantly, the noise of a siren erupted from the front of the car. She opened the window, placing a blue flashing light on the roof and then moved into the outside lane as the car surged forward.

'We'll be back as soon as we can. Be ready to move with a tactical team when we do.'

'Will do, Ridpath.'

He ended the call. 'Get a move on Emily, we have work to do.'

As the sound of the siren cleared the cars in front of them, Ridpath thought about the latest news.

Lardner had escaped. Why now?

Was he linked to the death of Andy Golding? But he was locked up in Ashworth when the boy disappeared. Could he have used an accomplice? He had form for using proxies to do his dirty work before.

'We need to get back to Manchester asap, Emily.'

'I'm already doing 95.'

'Go faster, we haven't a second to lose.'

Outside the car window, the countryside of Lancashire blurred past.

Chapter FIFTY-NINE

Frank was waiting for him in the car park of the KFC close to the Concourse Shopping Centre in Skelmersdale. He'd parked at the Co-op Bank next door and ran across the road to his follower's car, diving in the back as it accelerated away.

'How'd it go?'

He ignored the question, concentrating on changing into an Adidas tracksuit left for him on the back seat, removing the doctor's tweed suit.

The man had absolutely no taste.

As planned, they drove along the M58 back towards Liverpool, past Ashworth again, changing into another car at the Asda Aintree store before heading towards Manchester.

On their way, they saw fleets of police cars, their lights flashing and alarms blaring on the other side of the road.

Lardner sucked air in between his front teeth. 'In answer to your question, it went even better than I planned. He called me into his office at noon. At precisely 12.10 p.m., after listening to the man's grating voice, I held the sharpened pencil to his carotid artery and asked him to call in Harrison. He complied of course. A sharp object held to the throat has that effect on a man.'

'I'd love to slit a throat.'

'One day, Frank, you will have the pleasure.' Another intake of breath. 'Harrison arrived, we tied up the doctor and I dressed in his clothes, putting on the beard you procured. Harrison arranged for my departure and I walked through the detectors and out the front door. One of the guards even said "Have a good day, doctor" as I left. Finding the man's car was easy enough using his key fob.

He had to drive a BMW 6 series of course. A big car for a little man.'

'Sounds like it went smoothly, Master. I listened to the radio, it said you escaped but there were no other details. What happened to Harrison?'

'I handcuffed him before I left and knocked him around a bit. I'm sure he's being questioned by the police as we speak,' he lied.

'And the doctor?'

Harold Lardner cackled. 'He won't be poking around in the heads of any of the inmates any more. In fact, very soon, a pathologist will be probing around his head, trying to put it together again.' He stared through the window, a beatific smile on his face. 'I'll always remember the doctor's eyes though, as he watched me put on his clothes. The fear in them was delicious when I stabbed him in the neck with one of his pencils. His blood didn't spurt as high as it should have done. Not a strong heart. After so long, it was pleasurable to watch someone die again. You have arranged Dr Sanghera and the safe house?'

'It is exactly as you ordered.'

'Good. Very good. Our friends from the police are going to enjoy a pleasant surprise. One of the many I have planned for them.'

Chapter SIXTY

It was 5.15 p.m. before Ridpath and Emily Parkinson walked into the situation room at Cheadle Police Station. Inside, he saw Steve Carruthers and a tactical sergeant, both hunched over a table, staring at a plan of a building, surrounded by the other members of the tactical unit.

'Glad to see you're finally here.'

Ridpath had been diverted from Police HQ after a call from Helen Shipton.

'They've moved to Cheadle nick as it's closer to the Europa Business Park. The boss has taken charge of the operation.'

Did he detect a hint of triumph in her voice? Was she still annoyed with him because he hadn't taken her to TRACE that morning?

'He wants you to join him asap.'

'So they're going in this evening?'

'I think so, but nobody tells me anything.'

Definitely a hint of annoyance.

'Anything from the CCTV, the house-to-house or the search for the van?'

'Nothing, it's all a bit of a wild goose chase.'

He decided to ignore the whinge. 'Keep going, Helen, something could turn up. I'll let you know if we discover anything at Genepro.'

He put the phone down and told Emily of the change.

'We'll be there in ten, Ridpath.'

Eight minutes later and they arrived at Cheadle nick, one of the new police stations built on the edge of the city, far away from any of the residents it served.

'Let me introduce you to Sergeant Anthony Connor, head of the Police Tactical Unit,' said Carruthers.

The two men nodded to each other.

'I'm going to be Gold Commander on this operation. Understood?'

'Of course, boss. You decided to act quickly?'

'After the discovery of a body and a strong link to Genepro we couldn't do anything else.'

The tactical sergeant pointed at the table. 'As you can see, we have the plans and layout of Genepro's operation. There is a security guard posted in reception but there doesn't seem to be any employees. We talked to the business park management and they told us Genepro keep paying the rent but they only occasionally see activity there.'

'As long as they keep getting their money, I presume they don't care.'

'Exactly, DI Ridpath. There are entry points to the building here, here and here with swipe cards,' he prodded the plan. 'We will enter through the front to neutralise the security guard and through the rear. Guards will be posted at these exits in case anybody goes out. I will lead the team through the front of the building while Dave will take a team through the rear. As the building appears to be empty, we are not expecting any resistance but we need to be vigilant at all times. Is that clear?'

The members of his team grunted approval.

'After today, we may require a scene of crime team to go through the building after it's been cleared by Sergeant Connor, can we have one on standby, boss?'

Carruthers frowned. 'After your efforts from today, Ridpath, we're short of SOCOs but I'll find some from somewhere.'

'Right, lads, everything clear. We'll force entry at 18.15 hours precisely. Please synchronise watches; the time is now 17.42. Be careful, we are not expecting trouble, but that is exactly when it is most likely to happen. Understood?'

'Understood.' They all chorused back. The officers, all wearing their protective gear – matt-black Kevlar helmets, NIJ level IIIA bulletproof vests, and black ski masks to cover the HOSDB-approved jumpsuits – moved away to perform last minute checks on their Heckler & Koch rifles.

'DCI Carruthers you will be in the command vehicle on Barn Hall Road, we'll patch you into our communications. Please wait for my all clear, sir, before coming forward.'

'Understood, Sergeant. DI Ridpath and DS Parkinson will be with me.'

'It'll be a tight fit in the vehicle, sir, but I'm sure you're used to it.'

'Right, people, final checks on the equipment. Dave, you and your team can commence moving out at eighteen hundred hours.'

'Roger that, Team Leader.'

'The rest of you with me.'

More grunts of agreement as they continued with their final checks.

'We're moving quickly, boss,' said Ridpath.

'After today, it was inevitable. The deputy chief and the rest of the management team were scared shitless by your discovery.'

'I thought you were management, boss.'

Carruthers ignored his comment. 'And then the news of Lardner's escape came through and everybody has been put on red alert.'

'I've been thinking about his escape, boss, and I have a few ideas.'

Sergeant Connor appeared in the doorway and waved them forward to join him.

'Tell me them later, Ridpath, we're a little busy right now.'

Chapter SIXTY-ONE

As they walked towards the command vehicle, they were buffeted by the cold wind and rain of February in Manchester.

'Snow is forecast for tomorrow, coming in from the Arctic apparently,' shouted Emily.

Ridpath glanced back towards the two tactical teams standing in the open air, oblivious to the rain and sleet pouring down on them.

'Not the best night for it, boss.'

'There's never a good night for things like this, Ridpath.'

One hundred yards away, three police cars were parked obliquely across the road, preventing any entry to the area around the building. Cars were being forced to U-turn and then diverted away from the scene. Luckily the building was on a cul-de-sac so the disruption to traffic was minor.

Ridpath pointed to a large van with a dish on the roof. 'Looks like the reporters have arrived, boss.'

'Last thing I need.'

They squeezed into the command vehicle, a converted police transit van. Two radio operators were monitoring the airwave traffic and the body cams of the team leaders appeared on the screens in front of them.

'Is this in real time?' asked Carruthers.

'As real-time as we can make it, sir, there's a slight lag in the picture. With better equipment, we could—'

'Don't go there, son, not now.'

The operator had the sense to shut up.

His colleague began speaking. 'Team B, where are you?'

'Moving into position now, Sarge. ETA, one minute. Over.'

'Right. On arrival hold until further orders. Over.'

'Copy that. Over.'

'Team A?'

'Ready to go,' answered Sergeant Connor. 'Will commence operation in sixty seconds. Over.'

Ridpath looked at Steve Carruthers hunched over the table, desperately trying to get closer to the loudspeaker. On the screen, the body cam of Sergeant Connor showed the edge of a watch.

'Thirty seconds. Ready, Team B? Over.'

'Ready. Over.'

'Twenty seconds.'

Another quick glance at Emily Parkinson. She was chewing the end of her fingertip. Steve Carruthers crossed his fingers.

'Ten seconds.'

Then silence. A seemingly eternal silence.

A loud 'GO. GO. GO,' exploded through the loudspeakers.

On screen, they could see shaky, blurred footage from the body cams.

The sound of an enforcer being smashed against a door, followed by the crash as it collapsed to the ground.

'GO. GO. GO.'

'Breaking glass.'

'What's happening, Team A?' asked the operator.

A security guard standing behind his desk, a worried look on his face. A black arm coming in and pushing him down to the floor, his face pressed into the ground.

'Team A, entry secured, over. Heading upstairs.'

'Team B, going up the rear stairs to first floor. All clear.'

More crashing as another door was knocked down.

'Team A, first floor stairway clear. Over.'

'Team B, rear stairway, clear. Over.'

The camera continued its shaky way forward down a corridor with rooms on either side.

'Clear. Over.'

'Clear. Over.'

'Something on the far side. Over. Come out with your hands up.'

A burst of light on the screen.

'Team Leader from Team B. We have a body. Over.'

'Confirm message, Team B.'

'A body. Deceased. Seems to have shot himself. Over.'

Steve Carruthers looked at Ridpath. 'Who the hell is it?'

'I don't know, boss.'

'Command Vehicle, the body is an IC4 male, shot through the head. Gun nearby, could be suicide. Over.'

'Make sure he doesn't touch it,' ordered Steven Carruthers.

The operator responded. 'Order from Gold Commander. Do not go near. Over. Repeat. Do not touch. Over.'

'Roger that, Command Vehicle.'

More noises of doors crashing open followed by shouts of 'Clear. Clear. Clear,' as the rest of the building's empty rooms were checked.

Finally, another door crashed open, and a male voice said softly, 'Oh, my God. You're going to want to see this.'

Chapter SIXTY-TWO

The traffic was backed up to the M60 as the police ran around like Keystone Cops setting a perimeter around the area.

I stood on the roof of Park Building, watching the activity beneath me through binoculars.

The Master was right. After visiting TRACE they would soon work out the connection to Genepro. Dr Sanghera had to be eliminated. He was the weak link in the Master's arrangements. He wouldn't have lasted two minutes in a police interview. He would have been spilling his guts out in the nick just as he was now spilling his brains out in Genepro.

Shame. I liked the doctor.

But the man had his weaknesses, the biggest of which was an inability to keep his hands off his female patients. It was almost a compunction with him, an addiction, like gambling or drugs. Dr Sanghera would be found out again soon, it was better this way.

A quick shot to the head, the gun smeared with his fingerprints. They might be able to work out pretty soon there was no gunshot residue on his hands but as the Master said, it didn't matter.

The point was to create a blue boat; a diversion for the police to focus on while they acted elsewhere. The Master carrying out his work and me doing mine. The clues were there, all the police had to do was find them.

The Master had thought of everything.

By the time the plod knew what was really going on, I would be sunning myself in Thailand and our enemies would be dead or at least mourning their dead.

As the Master predicted, they were moving in now. Two lines of heavily armoured police, guns at the ready. One to the front and the other to the back.

In the neon glow of the street lights, they looked like malevolent shadows, faceless in their black balaclavas and body armour.

They would find Mr Owen, of course, or what remained of him. The eyes, the heart and the spleen were already being used. The Master said to leave the kidneys in the fridge. A little discovery to get them excited.

I put the binoculars down and checked out the area. A small crowd had formed, mainly of office workers and warehousemen who worked in the district. Even the Outside Broadcast units for the press had arrived.

The Master said they would. 'Cockroaches after our droppings,' as he put it.

The Master did have a way with words.

I checked my watch. 6.18. Time to go and blend in with the crowd being held back by the police.

I left the binoculars on the parapet of the building. A little gift for the cops or whoever found them.

It was time to go to work. As the Master said, 'Everything as normal. There is safety in the usual.'

The Master was always right. Praise his power.

Chapter SIXTY-THREE

After the building had been given the all clear by Sergeant Connors, Ridpath, Emily and Carruthers were allowed in. They put on gloves and overshoes before entering to make sure they didn't contaminate the crime scene any further. Ridpath realised this was pretty pointless as twenty tactical officers had been through the building in their size tens only five minutes ago. Nonetheless, it had to be done.

The building itself was modern; a glass-plated facade, two storeys with a small, now shattered glass door at the front. The security guard was still sitting in reception being guarded by one of the tactical squad.

'Emily, can you question him. See what he knows about this operation?'

'Will do, boss.'

Ridpath and Carruthers climbed the stairs to the first floor. A long corridor led from a small foyer through a broken door.

They went into the first room on the left. It was a small office. In the corner, behind a desk, a man sat in a chair with half his face missing.

'This is how we found him, sir,' said Connors, 'the gun was at his feet. Sorry we had to neutralise it as a threat.'

'By neutralise it, you mean...?'

'One of my officers picked it up wearing gloves and checked the chambers, sir. One shot out of five fired. An American revolver, sir, a 38 Colt Special. Not a common armament in the UK but they do sometimes get over here through Ireland.'

Ridpath was going to ask a question but realised it could lead to a long-winded answer from the tactical officer about firearms, so he stayed quiet.

'When does the SOC team arrive?' Carruthers asked.

'They're already here, sir, getting ready as soon as we allow them in.'

'Do it now. The sooner they sweep this place, the better. When does the medical examiner get here, Ridpath?'

'Ten minutes, boss, it's Dr Schofield.'

'Good.' Carruthers turned back to Connors. 'Show me what else you've found, Sergeant?'

'This way, sir.'

He led them out of the room and down the long corridor to another room at the back on the left. A small antechamber led on to a large, brightly lit, sterile room with halogen lights above a stainless steel table.

On the table, the body of a naked white-haired man lay unmoving.

'Looks like a lab or an operating theatre, boss.'

They moved closer to the table, being careful where they placed their feet. The old man lay on his side with his back towards them. Two large incisions ran at oblique angles to the spine. Whoever had cut him had not bothered to sew the incisions back up again.

Ridpath moved slowly around the table. The man's face was old and wrinkled, his hair thin and grey. But something else made Ridpath flinch.

'His eyes have been removed, boss, the sockets are empty.'

'What?'

Carruthers moved next to him, staring down at the old man. 'Jesus, who would do something like that?'

'You might want to check the small room at the back, sir.'

Anthony Connors was pointing to the far side of the operating room. Ridpath walked over. Inside were four large stainless steel fridges, the temperatures displayed on the door panel. Beside them, three coffin-like chest freezers were arrayed against the far wall. He couldn't help but think they were the perfect size for storing the body of a fourteen-year-old boy. Perhaps, Andy Golding had been kept here and not at TRACE. If that was true, what – or who – had Frank Diamond removed three weeks ago?

He forced himself to concentrate on the task at hand, putting on his neoprene gloves and pulling open the door of one of the fridges.

Empty.

'You should look in the third one, DI Ridpath,' said Connors.

He moved along to the fridge the sergeant pointed to. The temperature on the door panel indicated it was kept at minus five degrees. Using his fingertips, he prised open the seal and the door swung open.

Inside, on the middle shelf, were two plastic bags each containing something small and red. He leant in closer without touching anything. The closest bag had a date: 07/02/24 on it plus the words *Renes Sinistre*.

'I think we've found his missing kidneys, boss.'

Chapter SIXTY-FOUR

'He looks like he's been tortured, doctor.'

The doctor was bent over the old man's body examining it in minute detail, wearing his usual head-to-toe Tyvek suit. Carruthers and Ridpath had been sent away to stand at the doorway of the room as the doctor worked. He finally stood up and spoke to them directly.

'Most medical patients do, DCI Carruthers. Many medical procedures are often more damaging to the body in the short term than the illness they are curing.'

The doctor bent over the body again, examining the wounds closely. 'This man wasn't tortured, his body has been harvested.'

'I don't understand,' said Carruthers.

'Essentially, his vital organs have been removed. I'll be able to know more once we get him back to the mortuary and perform a post-mortem, but from the incisions in his body, I would estimate the heart, kidneys and liver were removed, along with his eyes, perhaps the spleen as well.'

'But he's an old man, doctor, why would anybody want to remove his organs?'

'Firstly, he may be old but his organs are probably functioning perfectly. Secondly, a buyer won't know the age of the organs they are purchasing.'

'A buyer?'

'The laws of supply and demand, DCI Carruthers. There is a vast demand for fresh organs and a limited supply. Hence, the creation of an underground trade in body parts. It's been estimated approximately 10 per cent of the European population has some sort of kidney problem. There is no shortage of people looking for kidney transplants but an immense shortage of suitable donors.'

'But I thought there was a donor law now.'

'Yes, passed in 2020. People have to opt out if they don't want to donate their organs, but it doesn't solve the fundamental problem...'

'Which is?'

'Why wait two years for a kidney when you can get one now.'

'If you can afford it.'

'It's always about money, Ridpath. The waiting list on the NHS for treatment was at four million people before the pandemic. Now it's closer to eight million. Remember many operations, including transplants, were cancelled. But those patients still needed their new spleen, or skin, or kidneys. There are those who don't want to wait in the queue and are wealthy enough to make sure they don't have to.'

Ridpath stared at the old man's body lying on the stainless steel table.

'Any idea who he was, doctor?'

'Naked men don't normally carry ID about their person, DCI Carruthers. I thought most people, even policemen, would realise that. We may be able to make an identification through his dental records or if he has had an operation in the past. You may also check his DNA and fingerprints against the database if he had been arrested. But, as you can see, there are no tattoos or other identifying marks.'

Carruthers seemed annoyed at the doctor's patronising tone. Ridpath was used to it, however. And besides, Dr Schofield was good at his job, very good.

'Now, a couple of things you should understand about the removal of human organs which might be useful in your invest-igation.'

The doctor paused waiting for his cue. Ridpath, like Ernie Wise, provided it immediately. 'What's that, doctor?'

'The organs have to be recovered and transplanted as early as possible after death. The heart and lungs have short cold ischemic time limits, only four to six hours. The liver, intestine and pancreas only last on average for about twelve to eighteen hours. While kidneys can typically survive outside the body for twenty-four to thirty-six hours. However, bones, skin and heart valves can survive up to five years if kept in the proper conditions.'

Ridpath immediately thought of TRACE. 'Like a cold storage facility?'

'Exactly. It's why creating a tissue bank is possible but an organ bank is not at the moment. Although work by the University of Minnesota on cryobiology suggests the use of nanoparticles could be—'

'So you're saying this man had to have his organs removed quickly?' interrupted Carruthers.

'I believe that was what I said.'

'The kidney in the fridge is labelled with the date of February 7 so it means he must have died on the sixth at the latest,' Ridpath jumped in.

'You are presuming the kidney belongs to this man, DI Ridpath?'

'It could belong to somebody else?' said Carruthers.

The doctor shrugged his shoulders. 'We won't know until it is DNA matched.'

Dr Schofield was examining the right arm of the naked man. 'That's interesting,' he said slowly, bending down to take a closer look.

'What?'

'There's a puncture mark and bruising on the cubital fossa.'

'Where?'

'The inner elbow in layman's terms, often used for venous access in injections or blood tests. Now, he may have had an examination performed around the time he died or this may have been a lethal injection. We won't know until toxicology comes back.'

The doctor rolled the victim onto his stomach. 'Looks like I was right about the organ donation.'

'What?'

'A strip of skin has been removed from his right buttock down to the bottom of the thigh.' The doctor moved closer, staring at the red flesh. 'Skilfully removed, I might add.'

'Why would anybody remove skin from a corpse, doctor?' asked Carruthers.

'The most likely reason is for skin grafts. The skin is in fact the largest human organ, Chief Inspector. Each person has about twenty-one square feet covering their body with over eleven miles of blood vessels.'

'This man now has slightly less.'

'Quite true, Ridpath. Some of it has been removed, probably for a skin graft after a burn injury.'

'Is that common, doctor?'

'The skin graft or the removal of skin?'

'Both.'

'And the answer is yes to both, Ridpath. The skin is a valuable commodity in the organ trade, even from somebody as advanced in years as this man.'

'One more question, doctor.'

'Yes, DI Ridpath.'

'If the viability of organs outside the body is extremely short – four to six hours for a heart for example – how does the organ trade work?'

'Oh, I'd have thought that was fairly obvious, Inspector.'

'Not to me.'

'Nor to me,' echoed Carruthers.

'The organs are ordered before a person is dead. For example, if they are on life support before the machine is switched off and they have a donor card.'

'Was this man on life support?'

The doctor quickly examined the corpse. 'I think not, there are no signs on his body he was ever attached to a life support machine.'

'So that means...'

'He was killed to order, Inspector. He was killed for his organs.'

As the full import of what the doctor had just said was absorbed by the two detectives, the crime scene manager appeared beside them.

'We found this on the IC4 male, sir.' She held up a plastic evidence bag containing a leather wallet and its contents: forty pounds in notes, three credit cards, a driving licence, another three plastic cards and two passport-sized photos. 'The name on the driving licence is a Dr Sanjay Sanghera, sir. The other card with his picture is ID for a private hospital in Wilmslow.'

Ridpath recognised the name immediately.

'He was the doctor who signed the death certificates for the old people who died at SunnySide Care Home in West Didsbury, boss.'

'Another link to that bloody care home.'

'There's something else you should come and see.'

They followed her out of the operating theatre and into a store room at the end of the corridor.

'We did a quick search of all the rooms, this one was particularly interesting.'

Inside, Ridpath could see a series of blue, coffin-like containers. Exactly the same as the one he had opened in TRACE.

'They are all empty except one. This one.' She pointed off to her left at a container pushed against the wall. 'We looked inside. It has twenty-six bags, containing what look like people's personal effects; watches, jewellery and interestingly, purple name bands with a person's name and blood group on them.'

'Purple?' whispered Ridpath. He turned to Carruthers. 'I saw them when I went to—'

'Let me guess, SunnySide Residential Home.'

'But that's not all. I also found this.' She held up a clear plastic bag containing a Nike football, a mobile phone and a St Christopher medallion.

Chapter SIXTY-FIVE

'Right, everybody gather round.'

Steve Carruthers had collected everybody together for a debriefing at Cheadle Hulme nick after the raid on Genepro.

'It's late, so let's be quick, people. Here's where we are: Ridpath and Emily discovered at least one, possibly more, bodies hidden at TRACE. Any news from Niamh O'Casey?'

'The SOC team has released one body to her from the cold store. She has performed a quick evaluation and found the same organs missing: the heart, eyes, kidneys and liver. No skin was taken this time. She'll know more when she completes the full post-mortem. She estimates it will take another week just to search all the Genepro containers.'

'Shit. How much would that cost?'

'An arm and a leg and a kidney and a spleen,' answered one of the detectives from West Didsbury.

Everybody laughed except Steve Carruthers. 'Let me remind you, we are dealing with human beings here. Mothers and fathers, aunties and uncles, sons and daughters, whose bodies have been defiled. This. Is. Not. A. Laughing. Matter.'

He stared at everybody in the room, his jaw clenched and anger flaming in his eyes. 'Anything from the security guard, Emily?'

'He was a proper Manuel, "I know nothing". Employed by the building management as a service to Genepro, he slept there every night. He works for an insurance company during the day.'

'Didn't he hear or see anything?'

'Not a lot, boss. Says he never went upstairs. The place used to give him the willies apparently. About once a month, he noticed signs of activity when he clocked in to work at six p.m., but he never actually saw anybody.'

'Signs of activity?'

'Coffee cups and used food containers in the pantry.'

'He never went upstairs to check?'

'Apparently not.'

Steve Carruthers ran his fingers through his hair. 'I think we've just found the world's most useless security guard. Where is he now?'

'We're holding him at Cheadle nick pending inquiries.'

'Okay, I want you to check up on him, find out if he's got any form.'

'Will do, boss.'

'Helen, anything?'

A long sigh. 'A day watching CCTV and nothing new, boss. My eyes have gone square. Nothing to report, the van seems to have vanished. We've checked the first 150 people who bought that model of the van, just 7473 to go.'

Carruthers seemed annoyed at her response but didn't say anything. 'Right. Anything from the house-to-house, Stan?'

'Nothing, sir. Nobody saw or heard anything. Not surprising really, it's one of those suburbs.'

'Shame, a witness would have been useful, but we've made progress here. Tell them, Ridpath.'

'We found the body of another unknown vic at the Genepro headquarters.' Ridpath pointed to a crime scene photograph of the old man lying on the stainless steel operating table. 'His fingerprints are currently being checked on IDENT1, with his DNA waiting to be analysed and compared on NDNAD.'

'Give them a kick up the arse, Ridpath, we need to know who this man was yesterday.'

Ridpath glanced at Emily. He'd never known Carruthers so upset before. His DCI was normally so calm and composed.

'Another body was found at Genepro. From his ID, it seems to have been Dr Sanjay Sanghera, a consultant physician. He

291

was employed at West Yorkshire and Humberside Hospital Trust until six years ago when he was asked to leave after allegations of inappropriate behaviour with patients surfaced.'

'He was never charged?'

'Apparently not, just quietly removed. However, his signature has appeared on all the death certificates from SunnySide Residential Home for the last five years.'

'There it is again,' said Emily, 'the bloody home.'

'There's more, Em. We found a container full of personal effects, including purple wristbands that look exactly like the ones the residents wear in the home. In the same box we also found this.' He held up the bag containing the football, a mobile phone and the St Christopher's medallion.

'Are those Andy Golding's?'

'I think so, Em. We'll need to get a proper ID from his mother and check the phone but we can safely assume that these are his missing effects.'

'Anybody else?' He scanned the room. 'Where's Chrissy?'

'On her way, boss,' said Helen. 'She was finishing something when we got your call to come in.'

Carruthers frowned. 'I'd like all of us to be here when we have these briefings.' He looked around making sure they got the message. 'Okay, we're finally getting movement on the case—'

Ridpath stuck his hand up. 'What about the link to SunnySide Residential Home, boss? Dr Sanghera signed the death certificates for all those who died there. Andy Golding's things were found in the same container as effects and wristbands from the home. Surely that shows a link between the two cases. It would also explain where the bodies came from, if this is an organ trafficking case. The two we have at the moment are both old people.'

'I need more evidence before I can go in there with our size nines. I've already heard about your argument with them, your other boss phoned me.'

'Clarence Montague?'

'The one and only. He accused you of having a vendetta against SunnySide and their owners, ChromaEstates.'

'What? I'm just doing my job.'

'The man's a gowk, we all know.'

'A what?'

'A gowk, a bampot, a choob, doaty.'

Ridpath looked at him as if he was speaking a foreign language.

'A tosser, now d'ye ken? Anyway, I want to make sure I have all my Is dotted and Ts crossed before we steam in. It's too late to move now, I want to think about it overnight. Can you get copies of all the death certs signed by Dr Sanghera from SunnySide?'

'No problem, the coroner's office will have them. I'll get Sophia to look them up.' While Ridpath messaged Sophia asking her to go through the records, Carruthers was addressing the team.

'It's been a long day and I want everybody to go home and come back fresh tomorrow. I'll be briefing another crew to do some of the legwork overnight. The deputy chief is throwing resources at this. He wants to get it solved whilst the region's press are obsessing about Lardner.' He held up a copy of the *Evening News*. Across half the page in big, bold, black letters, the headline said:

THE BEAST ESCAPES

'One of their more literate efforts,' said Helen.

'I never thought I'd say this, but I feel sorry for the scousers,' added Emily, 'they're going to have hundreds of bloody reporters watching their every move.'

'Back here at nine a.m. tomorrow and get a good night's sleep, tonight.'

Chrissy appeared at the door. 'Sorry I'm late, had to finish something off.'

Carruthers beckoned her to come in. 'Try to be on time, Chrissy.'

'Sorry, boss, but it was important I finished the research.'

'What d'ye have?'

'According to Companies House, Genepro were formed seven years ago as an organisation specialising in the sourcing of data and biological samples for health researchers. They operated for two years successfully but have not filed any company reports or accounts for the last five years.'

'Their offices aren't cheap, who has been paying the rent?'

Emily answered the question from Carruthers. 'According to the building's owners, it's paid out of a company in the Cayman Islands, Genedata Research. The money arrives on the dot at the beginning of the month and they've never been in arrears.'

'There's something else you should know, gaffer…'

'Go on, Chrissy.'

'I checked out the registered owners of Genepro, a Mr Ryan Chettle and a Mr Owen Scrimshaw, cross-referencing their pass-port details and addresses with the Register of Births, Marriages and Deaths, and guess what?'

'I give in, Chrissy.'

'Both men died seven years ago before the company was registered.'

'What? How can dead men be company owners?'

'Very simple, if you steal their identities. Nobody bothers to verify the identity of owners at Companies House, they don't have the time or the resources.'

'But surely, they would have had to register for bank accounts, electricity, water and everything else.'

'True, but nobody actually checks the details. As long as the passport and address are valid, then bob's-your-uncle, you are as kosher as gefilte fish.'

'We need to find out more, Chrissy. See if you can contact any former employees. Somebody must know what they were doing there,' said Carruthers.

'Will do, boss, but there was something else I discovered. Genepro has one other registered director.'

'Who?'

'A Dr Harold Lardner.'

Chapter SIXTY-SIX

Harold Lardner stood in the living room of the house in Withington. It was not decorated to his taste at all: an orange carpet that had seen better days, a dresser which was old in the Sixties, a skein of pottery ducks desperately trying to escape on one wall, brown and white psychedelic curtains and Anaglypta wallpaper painted the colour of soured milk.

'How can you live here Frank? I thought the hospital was bad, but this is worse.'

Frank Diamond looked around the room. He couldn't understand what the Master was talking about. It was perfect for him.

'Anyway, enough design chit-chat, has everything been prepared?'

'To the letter.'

Frank strode over to the table, reached out with his tattooed hand, carefully removing the blanket like a magician revealing his best trick.

A small digital clock sat on top of a metal lid with wires leading from it to a metal tube. One end of the tube was inserted into what looked like a lump of plasticine sitting in a metal tin. The outside of the tin proudly displayed the words 'Huntley and Palmers' with a picture of a Dickensian London scene on the side.

'A biscuit tin?'

'It's an old IRA trick. The metal container makes a perfect case for a portable bomb. You simply set the timer by pressing this button here.' He pointed to a small, innocuous-looking red switch on the top. 'That starts the countdown.'

'How long do I have once I press the switch?'

'I've set it for three minutes but I can change it if you want?'

'Three minutes will be plenty of time.'

'To prime the bomb, simply press the button to start the timer. Three minutes later… Boom.'

'That's it?'

Frank shrugged his shoulders. 'Couldn't be simpler. The IRA weren't renowned for making stuff complicated. I've added a few little touches myself.'

'Have you?'

'There's a layer of metal nuts, screws and ball bearings in the tin. They give it weight and stability but the main reason is when you set it off, they become like thousands of pieces of shrapnel flying around and ripping into flesh.'

'Perfect.'

'I've also added a rocker switch. Another little Irish touch.'

'A rocker switch?'

'Like I said, once you've planted it, press the button on top of the tin. It will light up red, meaning the bomb is armed and the rocker device is ready. If anybody tries to move the bomb, the rocker closes the circuit and… Boom.' He made an exploding noise and spread his arms wide.

'What happens if I drop it accidentally.'

'I've added a delay into the rocker switch. If you drop it, you have five seconds to get the hell out of Dodge.'

Lardner nodded, approving the design. 'The explosion will be big enough to wreck the Coroner's Court and kill everyone inside?'

'There's enough Semtex here to blow up three coroner's courts. Happy?'

Lardner leant in to look at the device more closely. 'Very happy, your time in Northern Ireland wasn't wasted. The schematics of the Coroner's Court?'

From a bag, Diamond pulled out a set of blueprints. 'These were in the local library.'

'Good, we're ready and set, all we have to do is go.'

Diamond stroked his chin. 'There is the matter of my payment.'

'You've been extremely well paid over the years we've worked together, Frank.'

'I have been, but as our arrangement is coming to an end and this is a special device, I need the extra hundred thousand. We agreed.'

'What are you going to do with the money?'

'Myself and my son are planning a trip to the tropics. Apparently, Thailand is rather warm at this time of the year.'

'Certainly better than Manchester in February.'

'Not one of my favourite times of the year.' He rubbed his hands together. 'The money?'

'How do I know your device will work?'

'Have I ever let you down in the last seven years?' Frank Diamond stepped forward, prodding his chest angrily. '*I* was the one who killed Andy Golding after he saw the murder of his grandmother and started blackmailing us. The little bugger was a greedy sod but I did as you ordered.' He moved even closer to Lardner. '*I* was the one who took those bodies up to TRACE, getting into those bloody suits each time, not to mention taking the parts all around the North and on to the continent at short notice. *I* even gave my son to you.' He turned away, pacing up and down, agitated now. 'I was messed up for a long time after Northern Ireland but now I'm back to being me.' He moved back to confront Lardner, his face inches away. 'I'm not going to use the "Yes, Master" bollocks any more. This me wants his money, and he wants it now.'

Lardner adopted his submissive pose and softened his voice. 'Of course, you will get your money, Frank. Log on to your laptop and I'll transfer it to your account.'

A large smile crossed Frank Diamond's face. 'I knew you'd listen to reason… Master. I'll get it.'

The man left door open as he went to the back of the house.

How the worm has turned, thought Lardner. *At least, he has proven useful over the last seven years. Shame it has to terminate this way but all good things must come to an end.*

Frank bustled back in carrying his laptop. He sat down at the table and began entering his password.

Lardner patted the back of the man's neck with his left hand in a show of affection, gently feeling for the small gap between the C1 and C2 vertebrae, between the Atlas and Axis bones.

As the home page on his screen formed, the news headlines popped up.

THE BEAST OF MANCHESTER KILLS GUARD AND DOCTOR IN DARING ESCAPE FROM HIGH-SECURITY PRISON.

'But... you said Bob Harrison was alive when you left him...'

'I lied, Frank.'

Before the man could say any more, Lardner plunged the screwdriver he had taken from Dr Mansell's car into the back of Frank's neck, instantly severing the spinal cord.

Frank Diamond slumped forward, his head hitting the screen of the laptop, the screwdriver still buried in the back of his neck.

Lardner used the flat of his hand to force the screwdriver even deeper into the gap between the bones.

'I think you can hear me, Frank. I've just severed your brain-stem. Your body is beginning to shut down. In a few moments you will lose consciousness. You may already be finding it difficult to breathe. In roughly one minute you will be dead. I do enjoy this method of killing somebody, it's a relatively clean death; no blood or pain. I felt I owed that to you.'

Frank Diamond's eyes fluttered and closed.

'Enjoy your last minute on Earth. And while you do, please remember nobody is indispensable, even you. I would like to thank you for your work. You have made everything possible.'

Lardner waited one more minute before checking the pulse.

Nothing.

'Dead as the proverbial dodo. I think you forgot, Frank, pathologists always know the best way to kill people. It comes with the
territory. Now, I wonder what you have in your fridge. Killing
people always makes me so frightfully hungry.'

Chapter SIXTY-SEVEN

When Ridpath arrived home at eleven, the house was quiet.

He padded silently up the stairs to Eve's room. She was fast asleep in bed, one arm around a large stuffed elephant and the other still holding a pen. The book in which she had been writing her history notes lay open on the floor next to the bed.

He tucked her in, kissed her forehead and picked up the history book, placing it on the bedside table, switching off the reading lamp her mother had given her on the Christmas before she died.

She slept on through all this, no doubt exhausted after a tiring day at school. He took one last look at her sleeping. Her face a picture of serenity; no lines on her forehead, no tenseness about the mouth, her jaw relaxed and unclenched. A person at ease with the world.

Every child should sleep like this. It was a shame many of them didn't.

He closed the door and crept back downstairs. In the kitchen, the dishes from this morning had been rinsed and placed in the dishwasher, along with a plate and bowl from her evening meal. From the look of it, she had finished the leftover lasagne. He would have to make a new batch this weekend.

At least she had managed to feed herself. He thought about making something to eat for himself but couldn't be bothered.

After pouring a large – probably too large – glass of Glenmorangie, he slumped into the chair in the living room.

Outside, the wind was whistling through the trees. The promised Arctic storm arriving from the north to invade Manchester. There was no snow yet, later in the morning according to the weather forecast.

He didn't like snow; cold, wet stuff that looked pretty for ten seconds before a combination of cars, people's feet and Manchester turned it into a dirty, grey slush. He hoped the schools weren't going to close. The last thing he needed at the moment was Eve at home all day while he still had this case to crack.

He sipped the whisky feeling the honeyed fire singe the back of his throat. The drink was one of the most important inventions by man; a little could make anybody's troubles and problems go away. Too much and they would just be beginning. He had too much on his plate to get drunk tonight. One glass would be enough to relax him.

A lot had happened since that morning. They had made real breakthroughs in the case, why then did he feel so uneasy?

And then he knew instantly why.

Harold Lardner had escaped. Would he come back to Manchester or flee abroad? Would he seek revenge on those who had put him away all those years ago?

The memories of their encounters came back to him. The icy calmness of the man. The threats spoken in the quietest of voices. The intensity of the eyes. The bodies of the women he had killed in cold blood. The total lack of empathy for anything living. Or dead.

Ridpath put his glass down and checked every window and door in the house. Tonight, he would put the alarm on before he went to bed.

Just in case.

Should he move out of his home into a hotel? Just until Merseyside recaptured Lardner? But how would he explain it to Eve?

He settled back into his armchair and picked up his whisky. Was he overreacting?

He decided he wasn't. Tomorrow was Friday. He would go away with Eve for the weekend tomorrow night, perhaps up to the Lakes. Tell nobody where they were going. He could convince her it was a treat because he had been working so hard. Time for them to spend together. He'd have to get Steve Carruther's agreement and explain everything to the team; their SIO suddenly leaving for the Lakes in the middle of an investigation would go down like a cup of cold sick.

But it was more important that they should be safe until Lardner was caught. He couldn't risk Eve's life, not with that madman on the loose.

His phone buzzed with a message making him jump.

Is it ok to call?

It was Sophia. He'd forgotten he'd sent her the message to check the death certs earlier that evening. He dialled her number.

'Hi, Sophia.'

'Hiya, Ridpath, I've got the information you asked for.'

'You're not still in the office, are you?'

'I went back after I received your message. My mum and her sisters were arguing about the food at the wedding reception. It was a question of whose samosas were better. I couldn't take it any more. Your text was a godsend.'

'Are you there on your own? Let me drive over and pick you up.'

'It's okay, my mum is going to pick me up soon. And besides you are persona non grata, remember? Good news about Mrs Challinor though.'

'I saw her this morning, she's recovering well.'

'Great, it'll be wonderful to have her back.'

'I think she has a long road to recovery yet, Sophia.'

'Anyway, I dug deeper into SunnySide and retrieved all their signed death certificates from our files from 2018 to this week. There were sixty-eight in total.'

'And?'

'All of them were signed by Dr Sanghera, usually on the morning of the death. He seems to have been very efficient.'

'More than usual?'

'Definitely. Most doctors aren't renowned for their bureaucratic prowess.'

'Great, and before that?'

'In 2017, the certificates are signed by a variety of doctors from hospitals and clinics in Manchester. At least, five different ones. But 2015 to 2017 is different again.'

'How?'

'All the certs were signed by one doctor.'

'Who?' Ridpath could hear the tension in his voice.

'The guy you put in jail. The pathologist, Dr Lardner. But why he was signing death certs for a small residential home in Withington is anybody's guess.'

'I have a pretty good idea, Sophia.'

There was silence on the end of the phone. 'You're not going to tell me, are you?'

'Not yet, I will later.'

'Okay, but I do want to know, so I'll hold you to your promise.'

Ridpath imagined his assistant holding up her little and index fingers to the phone like Eve.

'It's a deal.'

'What were the causes of death?'

'Before 2020, a variety of causes; heart attacks, pneumonia, old age, dementia, Alzheimer's. The most common was pneumonia.'

'And after 2020?'

'Almost exclusively the cause of death was Covid-19 or Covid-related illnesses.'

'Not surprising, given the impact of the disease on care homes.'

'There's one other thing I noticed.'

'What?'

'The same company was used every time for mortuary services. The weird thing is the firm isn't one of those we normally deal with. It doesn't even sound like an undertaker at all.'

'Let me guess. The company was called Genepro and they collected the bodies within hours of the death being discovered.'

'How did you know? Have you got somebody else doing this, Ridpath?'

'A wild guess.'

'I can hear my mother beeping me from the car. I'd better go.'

'One last question, were any inquests convened on these deaths?'

'Let me check.'

Ridpath could hear her turning over the pages of her printout. 'No inquests ordered on any of them. It was an old people's home and most of the deaths happened during lockdown.' A short pause. 'Oh, that's interesting.'

'What is it?'

'I've just noticed. All of these people opted in to donate their organs to science.'

'Why's that interesting? The law changed in May 2020 didn't it? After that, everybody was considered to have agreed to donate their organs unless they opted out.'

'But there were excluded groups, and those included people who lack the mental capacity to understand the new arrangements and take the necessary action. But everybody who died at the home agreed to opt in.'

'Mathilda Staunton told me a lot of her patients suffered from Alzheimer's or dementia, how would they have the capacity to opt in?'

'Exactly.' A shuffling of pages. 'Even more interesting, most of them opted in a few days before they died. A couple even agreed to donate their organs on the day they died.'

'Very convenient. Too convenient.'

'I've got to go now. Hope the info was useful.'

'You don't know how key it was, Sophia. Take care and don't let the wedding arrangements get you down. See you soon.'

'Not if I see you first.'

The phone went dead.

Ridpath sat back in the armchair. How had they missed so many deaths at the same care home? Why were no inquests convened? Why had all those old people opted in to donate organs if they were incapable of making a sound decision?

Then he saw the brilliance of the scheme. If you were going to harvest organs from people, where better to start than at a care home in the middle of an epidemic?

He finished his whisky and was about to check the windows and doors one more time when his phone rang again.

He picked it up without looking at the number. 'Hi Sophia, you forgot to tell me something?'

'I didn't forget to tell you anything, Ridpath.'

The voice wasn't Sophia's. It was deep and male. 'Who is this?'

'I thought you would have recognised me, Ridpath.'

'Who is it? How did you get this number?'

'You're the coroner's officer, the number is easy to find.'

As the man spoke the words, Ridpath realised exactly who he was.

'Lardner? Is that you?'

'So you do recognise me? How flattering. I just thought I'd call to let you know I have left Ashworth. I'm sure you've heard that already, the police radio has been full of it. "They seek him here, they seek him there, those Frenchies seek him everywhere." But they won't find me, Ridpath, I'll make sure of that.'

'What do you want, Lardner?'

The man laughed. 'What a question. But the simple answer is I want you, Ridpath. I want you.'

The phone went dead in the detective's hand. A frisson of fear ran down his spine. For the first time in a long, long time, he was afraid, very afraid.

Friday, February 9.

Chapter SIXTY-EIGHT

'What? Lardner rang you?'

'Late last night.'

'Where was he? What did he say?' Carruthers babbled, trying to understand.

'He made a direct threat. I asked what he wanted and he said, "I want you".'

'What does that mean?'

'I think he wants revenge for putting him away all those years ago.'

Ridpath sat opposite Steve Carruthers in his office. He'd arrived early, ready to ambush his boss when he came in. He'd been up since six a.m., not having slept at all, listening to every creak and squeak in the house, fearing the worst.

He'd woken Eve and made breakfast for her.

'Do you want to miss school today?' he'd asked.

'I can't, Dad. I've got a test,' she answered between bites of toast. Then she eyed him suspiciously. 'Why? You never want me to miss school.'

He couldn't tell her the truth, not yet. 'I just thought I'd been working so hard recently we should spend some time together, go to the Lakes.'

She looked out of the window. 'It's supposed to snow today, are you sure?' Then she shrugged her shoulders. 'The Lakes would look cool in the snow... literally. Let's go tomorrow, Dad, okay?'

'I'll book a nice hotel near Elterwater.'

He had driven her to school. 'Are you okay going in this early?'

'The Breakfast Club will be there plus the history teacher, Mr Thomas, gets in at seven every morning for some obscure reason. I don't think I'll ever understand grown-ups. Why would you leave a nice, warm, cosy bed to go to school early?'

'You do.'

'Only because I have to. If I didn't, the repressive forces of the state would be down on me like a ton of bricks.'

'I suppose I'm the "repressive forces of the state"?'

'Got it in one, Dad.'

'Good to know. I'll pick you up from school this evening but if I'm not there, get a lift with Maisie's mum. Go straight home, do not pass Go, do not collect 200 quid, do not let anybody into the house—'

'Fat chance.'

'I'm serious, Eve, just go straight home and don't let anybody into the house. Understand?'

'I get it. Why are you so nervous? You're not normally this bad.' She took her school bag from the rear seat and leant over to kiss him. 'You need to relax, Dad, a weekend away will do you good.'

She opened the door and was gone, without looking back.

Now here he was, sitting opposite Steve Carruthers.

'Shit. Do you want protection? I can arrange a safe house.'

'I'm okay. Anyway, what place could be safer than a building full of hairy coppers.'

'What about Eve?'

'She'll be safe at school, I dropped her off this morning. I'll leave early and go to pick her up if I can. We'll go away for the weekend. Hopefully, Lardner will be captured by then.'

'I can handle the case while you're away. Nothing is more important than the safety of yourself and your family, Ridpath.'

'Thank you, boss, I appreciate the concern.' Ridpath took a deep breath. 'Meanwhile, have you thought what to do about SunnySide?'

Carruthers nodded. 'I've prepared a document for the assistant chief and I'm due to meet him this morning after we've finished the briefing.'

'We'll need to get a warrant to search the place.'

'I asked Chrissy to get one just in case. The assistant chief isn't going to be a happy bunny but I didn't come down here from Glasgow to make people happy, I came to do a job. ChromaEstates have been in his face for the last two days, threatening law suits, actions for misconduct and God knows what else. They don't like you, Ridpath. According to them you are the devil incarnate.'

'A repressive force of the state actually, boss.'

'What?' Carruthers shook his head. 'Sometimes I think they may have something. I also have a feeling the funny handshake mob are mixed up in this.'

'The Masons?'

'Their sticky fingerprints are all over it.' He glanced at the clock. 'Let's do the briefing and see if anything else has come up. Then I'll go to meet him.'

'Aren't we wasting time, boss?'

'It will only take ten minutes. I'll need more ammo if I'm to convince him.'

He stood up. 'Come on, let's get it done.' He stopped for a moment. 'We won't tell anyone on the team about your phone call from Lardner, not yet anyway. But I'll let the scousers who are looking for him know. They'll probably want to question you.'

'I agree, boss, let's keep the team focused on the case.'

The team were already waiting for them in the situation room. For once, Helen Shipton was already there, munching on a sausage bap.

'Right, everybody. Let's do this quickly, I want to go and see the assistant chief this morning; Chrissy, did you get the warrant to search SunnySide?'

'Done, boss. The magistrate wasn't chuffed but he signed.'

'Anybody else have anything to add?'

Chrissy put her hand up. 'Helen asked me to check the mobile phone we found last night. They confirmed the number was registered in Sharon Golding's name. They don't keep data from their cell towers so we can't track his movements, but they confirmed the last call was on May 22, 2020. Even better, they gave me the number that was called…'

'Go on, Chrissy.'

'It belongs to a Frank Diamond.'

'Frank Diamond. The name is pretty close to our Frank Desmond who works for Genepro?'

'That's what I thought, Ridpath, so I checked his driving licence with DVLA in Swansea. They had this picture on their records.'

On her laptop, a driving licence appeared.

'That's him. That's our man from the TRACE CCTV. Does he have a swallow tattoo on his hand.'

'That sort of information isn't available at DVLA…'

'But I bet you've checked him out.'

'His last known address was a house in Withington.'

'How does a driver afford a house in Withington?' asked Stan Jones. 'I can't even afford a parking space there.'

'I haven't a clue, but more importantly, he was nicked in 2016 for drunken driving. The description on his charge sheet lists a tattoo of a swallow on his right hand as a distinguishing mark.'

'Bingo,' shouted Carruthers. 'Well done, Chrissy. We've finally got our man. His real name is Frank Diamond.'

The civilian researcher was beaming from ear to ear, as if Haaland had just scored a hat trick in the European Cup Final. She stuck a printout of the driving licence on the case wall.

'Helen, you're off searching for the van. I want you and Stan Jones to raid the address. Chrissy, you need to get another warrant before lunch.'

She stood up, taking her files. 'On it, boss.'

'And get anything and everything you can on this Frank Diamond. I want to know want size and colour keks he's wearing.'

'Will do.'

'Helen and Stan, get a team ready with backup from West Didsbury nick. I want Frank Diamond in custody asap.'

'On it, boss.'

'Anything else?'

Emily raised her hand. 'I went to see Sharon Golding and asked her about the money Andy gave her before he died. She said it was 300 quid.'

'Where does a fourteen-year-old get so much money unless he's selling his tail in Piccadilly Gardens,' said Helen.

'His mother said she didn't know where he got the money. I think she couldn't be bothered to ask, just glad it was there.'

'She didn't think this was important information for the police?'

'Apparently not.'

'Can you look into it, Emily? I want to know where Andy Golding was getting his money?'

'Will do, boss.'

'Meanwhile, let's focus back on this man.' Carruthers pointed to the picture of the man's hand with the swallow tattoo. 'It looks like we've discovered who it was.'

'But Frank Diamond worked for Genepro not at SunnySide, how did he know what was going on there and how did he have access to the home to murder the residents?'

'We're going to have to go there and find out.' He stood up and gathered his papers. 'I'm off to see the wizard, also known as the assistant chief. Carry on with the preparations to raid the two addresses at precisely noon... Unless you hear from me to the contrary.'

'Surely the assistant chief wouldn't go against the advice of his acting head of MIT?' said Ridpath.

'He might. If he does, I won't be acting head any more. I'll have resigned and been put on the train back to Glasgow. I hear Scotland is particularly beautiful in February. Cold, wet, dark and unlivable, but beautiful.'

'Good luck, boss. It's the right thing to do.'

'Thank you, Ridpath. But being right isn't often good for your health... or your career. You of all people should know.'

'I'll wait for your call, boss.'

'Aye, and be ready to move as soon as I give the go-ahead. It's time to take down these scum.'

Chapter SIXTY-NINE

Harold Lardner checked the house one more time. He'd enjoyed a particularly good dinner. There had been nothing in the fridge of course, so, using Frank Diamond's credit card, he had ordered a delivery from Uber, washing it down with a bottle of Cabernet Sauvignon he'd found under the stairs.

The call to Ridpath had been dessert, the icing on the cake.

He'd slept well, enjoying the softness of Frank's bed after years of lying on the foam mattresses at Ashworth.

Breakfast had been a cafetière of coffee, toast and a rather pleasant raspberry jam.

No need to queue.

No need to smell the unwashed bodies of the other inmates.

No need to listen to their inane chatter.

A quiet, comfortable, civilised breakfast. God, how he enjoyed them.

Frank Diamond still lay where he had been killed last night, his head resting against the laptop, a small dribble of blood seeping out of the corner of his mouth.

A shame about Frank. Why had he become so greedy? They had worked together so long and so successfully. All the time he was in Ashworth, Frank had been his eyes and ears on the outside. Managing Sanghera and his foibles, handling the bodies, ensuring what they were doing was never discovered by the idiots at ChromaEstates or by Mathilda Staunton.

Frank had even introduced his son to Lardner before he was sent to Ashworth. The son was easy to indoctrinate; young and impressionable, all he had to do was feed the fantasies lying dormant in his mind. Fantasies of power and potency, of the need to control life and death.

A malleable mind and body which he moulded into a killer, the best he had ever created.

The young man was a believer and had been told what to do and when to do it.

There was still business to take care of for him.

He picked up the biscuit tin lid with its attached clock and placed it over the top of the packed Semtex and assorted screws and bolts, ensuring no wires were sticking out. He sealed the outside with duct tape.

The black screen, absent of lights and numbers stared back at him. All he had to do was press the button on the side and hey presto, BOOM.

He checked the time.

11.36 a.m.

Time to study the schematics of the Coroner's Court once more, enjoy a spot of lunch and a little nap afterwards.

He would get ready to leave at exactly 3.30 p.m. The drive to Stockford would take thirty minutes, forty if the traffic was heavy, leaving him plenty of time to compose himself to make the phone call and gain entry to the Coroner's Court.

At 4.15 p.m., the coroner would be approaching the end of the afternoon session of the inquest. He'd sit at the back and watch and wait.

Finally, after all these years, he would get his revenge. It was time Ridpath suffered for all the pain he had created. A pain that could never be assuaged no matter how hard one tried.

He visualised all the details one more time, enjoying the intimacy of it all; seeing the victims, blessed in their innocence, the touch of the button as he pressed it, the red light flashing, the final firebomb ascending into the dull, grey sky.

The ultimate feeling of power and control; over life and death.

Everything had been planned to the last detail, nothing could go wrong.

He looked out of the window. A thin, white drift of snow was beginning to settle on the trees and fall on the ground.

It was the perfect day for them to die.

Chapter SEVENTY

Thirty minutes later and Steve Carruthers had still not returned to MIT.

Ridpath messaged him.

> What's happening? Everybody is waiting for the go-ahead.

The answer came two minutes later.

> No answer yet from the assistant chief. He has worries. Consulting legal team.

Ridpath strode up and down between the desks, wearing a furrow into the carpet.

'Relax,' said Helen, 'the go-ahead will come soon.'

Ridpath stared at her without answering. He walked over to the window. Outside a flurry of snow was beginning to fall. In the distance, the Pennines were covered in cloud blending into the snow-covered land.

'Right people, weather conditions have changed, let's go over the details one more time.'

There was an audible groan from the assembled teams, but they still gathered round the map of Withington and the schematic of the SunnySide Residential Home as Ridpath went through both plans of attack for the third time.

At one p.m., Steve Carruthers finally returned. 'He's consulting with the director of operations on whether we need tactical involvement.'

'It's an old folks' home in Didsbury not a drug den in Moss Side,' said Emily.

'He's worried about the reaction if it goes wrong, especially after the threat of legal action from ChromaEstates.'

'Why don't we get the army involved too? I've heard a couple of Chieftain tanks are extremely effective against militant pensioners.'

'I don't need sarcasm right now, and I don't need it from you, DC Shipton.'

'Sorry, sir. It's just we've been waiting since this morning.'

'If the wait means you are no longer capable of leading your part of the operation, I'm sure I can find somebody else who is more than capable.'

'It's not… sir… sorry, I'll keep my mouth shut in future.'

'Good advice for yourself.' Carruthers raised his voice. 'Anybody else got anything to say?'

The room was quiet as everyone looked towards their DCI.

'Good, let's keep it that way.'

They ordered up sandwiches from the canteen and flasks of coffee and tea. The food and drink were consumed in silence until finally it was broken.

'City are playing Everton tomorrow at the Etihad. I think they might need ice skates not football boots,' said Stan Jones.

'They're skating on thin ice anyway this year,' answered one of his team.

'City could wear ice skates and still beat the Toffees every day of the week.' Chrissy interrupted. 'My bet is 2–0. Anybody willing to bet on Everton?'

The room stayed silent.

Finally, it was Helen Shipton who spoke, 'You know the problem with ice skating is, no matter how good you are, the hardest part is your nipples.'

They all stared at her.

She was saved from further questioning by Steve Carruthers.

'I know an ice-skating joke. A scouser decided he needed something new and different for a winter hobby. He went to the bookstore and bought every book he could find on ice fishing.

'For weeks he read and studied, hoping to become an expert in the field. Finally, he decided he knew enough and out he went for his first ice-fishing trip. He carefully gathered and packed all the tools and equipment needed for the excursion. Each piece of equipment had its own special place in his kit.'

Emily leant over, 'I've heard this before, it's good.'

'When he got to the ice, he found a quiet little area, placed his padded stool and carefully laid out his tools. Just as he was about to make his first cut into the ice, a booming voice from the sky bellowed, "There are no fish under the ice!"

'Startled, the scouser grabbed up all his belongings, moved further along the ice, poured some hot chocolate from his thermos, and started to cut a new hole.

'Again, the voice from above bellowed, "There are no fish under the ice!"

'Amazed, the scouser was not sure what to do, as this certainly was not covered in any of his books. He packed up his gear and moved to the far side of the ice. Once there, he stopped for a few moments to regain his calm. Then he was extremely careful to set everything up perfectly – tools in the right place, chair positioned exactly. Just as he was about to cut this new hole, the voice came again.

'"There are no fish under the ice!"

'Petrified, the scouser looked skyward and asked, "Is that you, Lord?"

'The voice boomed back, "NO THIS IS THE MANAGER OF THE SKATING RINK!"'

There was silence for a moment before the assembled coppers collapsed with laughter.

Carruthers looked sheepish. 'We usually tell it about Shetlanders, but I guess it works just as well for the glaikits from Liverpool.'

His phone rang.

'Yes, sir, yes, I will do. Yes, sir. Understood.' He ended the call and a broad smile crossed his face. 'We've got the go, are you ready, Ridpath?'

'All set, boss. Are we using the tacticals? We'll have to brief them if we are.'

'We'll do it without them. I don't expect trouble from the seventy-year-olds at SunnySide. Have you enough heavies to take down Frank Diamond, Helen?'

'Twelve officers from West Didsbury nick plus backup if needed. Plenty.'

'I did some more checking on Diamond, boss, while we were waiting.' Chrissy spoke over the hubbub. 'He's ex-army, twenty-two years in the Royal Engineers, three tours in Northern Ireland. Left in 2010 and seems to have immediately got into trouble; drunk driving, fighting in a public space, assault on a copper. Then in 2016, he cleaned up his act. I don't know how he met Lardner but he visited the pathologist three times in Ashworth. Employed by Genepro since 2016 and has kept his nose clean ever since. Not even a traffic or speeding ticket.'

'You sure you can handle him, Helen? I could ask tactical to release men.'

Helen Shipton was adjusting her stab vest. 'We'll be fine, boss. If myself, Stan Jones and twelve heavies can't handle Frank Diamond, nobody can.'

'Good.' Carruthers held up his airwave. 'It's Channel 3. Let's keep radio silence in case they are listening in. No useless blether. Understood?'

'Understood, boss.'

He checked his watch. 'Let's move. I want to raid both places at the same time: 3.30 p.m. exactly. One last thing people, be careful out there. Take no unnecessary risks. Everything is going to be by the book. I want nae comebacks from some mealy-mouthed advocates or our senior management. We will follow protocols to the letter. Understood?'

Carruthers' accent had become more Glaswegian as his speech had progressed.

'Awa', let's get the bawsacks.'

They all trooped down to where the cars were waiting, engines running.

'Ridpath and Emily, you're with me. You'll be in charge of the serving of the warrant and handle the interview with the Staunton woman, Ridpath.'

For a second, Ridpath wondered if Carruthers was setting him up to be the fall guy and then instantly dismissed the idea. If he wanted a patsy, he wouldn't be coming with them. He would stay in his nice warm office in Police HQ like all the other politicians.

'We interview her here or at the residential home, boss?'

'We'll do it there as we're searching. The quicker we find the answers we're looking for the better. We need to confirm a link between the home and any of the bodies found at TRACE or Genepro. If we do, Mrs Staunton can bleat to the Masons from the comfort of a prison cell.'

'And if we don't?'

'Then the assistant chief made it clear we would both be looking for new jobs. Traffic warden was one of the suggestions he made.'

'We'd better find the evidence, boss.'

'Famous last words, Ridpath.'

They jumped in the back of the car, and immediately they accelerated away, the rest of the team following behind.

In the car, nobody spoke.

Chapter SEVENTY-ONE

Lardner took one last look inside the house before closing the door. He placed the open bag containing the biscuit tin carefully on the front seat, then ran round to climb into the driver's seat.

He'd hidden the schematics and the bomb-making equipment in a cupboard upstairs. The police would search the place after discovering Frank Diamond's body but he didn't want them to discover the clues to where he was going too quickly.

But once they found the stuff, even the most stupid copper should be able to put two and two together to make four. He'd even made sure the next door neighbour saw him get into the car, waving to her as she peered through the window.

It had been a while since he had driven a manual car, Mansell's had been an automatic. It was one of the many activities they didn't allow in Ashworth.

He quickly familiarised himself with the controls, moving the gears to check their gates. Starting the engine, he put the car in reverse, letting out the clutch.

The car died.

This wasn't going to be as easy as he thought. Should he call an Uber rather than drive? He tried once more and this time the car started to inch back out of the drive onto the main road. He put it into first and drove off, signalling right at the end of the road.

He was getting used to it again. After all, he'd spent twenty years driving around Manchester from one crime scene or mortuary to another.

The car picked up speed, and he signalled right again at the lights to take himself onto Princess Road.

The lights turned green and he pulled away, braking hard as a blue Ford Mondeo ran the red light, turning left past him, followed by four police cars.

Were they going to his house? Or to another incident?

He waited for them to pass before putting the car in gear again and turning left, accelerating away from the lights.

If they were after him, they were earlier than he expected. Had he underestimated Ridpath?

Perhaps.

But it didn't matter now. All he had to do was get to the Coroner's Court and finish the job.

He smiled to himself. There were always minor hiccups in every plan but as long as the details were handled properly, the project could continue.

Thirty minutes from now, he would be parking outside the Coroner's Court in Stockford. After all these years, he would finally enjoy the revenge which had kept him alive in the darkest of nights lying in his cell staring at the ceiling.

The beauty of those dreams would be realised.

Ridpath and those closest to him would all be dead.

Chapter SEVENTY-TWO

They assembled two streets away from SunnySide, in a small unadopted and unsurfaced lane off the main road.

Outside, the snow was falling more heavily now, beginning to carpet the ground. Inside, the heater was on full, blasting out hot air into the car.

Ridpath checked his watch.

3.28 p.m.

He pressed the button at the side of the airwave, 'Ready Helen? Over.'

The machine squawked loudly before an answer came.

'In position, Ridpath, both front and back.'

He turned to Carruthers sitting in the rear of the car next to Emily. Behind them, two transit vans were filled to the brim with uniforms, a sea of blue.

They had all been briefed they were entering a residential home full of elderly people. Shouting was to be kept to a minimum and all care should be taken when dealing with the residents. The last thing they wanted was for one of the pensioners to have a heart attack.

The care assistants however were to be detained as quickly as possible and placed under guard in their staffroom to await questioning.

'She's ready to go in, boss. You want to go now?'

Carruthers checked his watch. 'No. Wait.'

Ridpath picked up the airwave. 'Hold in position, Helen.'

'Roger that.'

What was Carruthers waiting for? The longer they waited out here on the street, the more likely they would be spotted by someone at the home.

A car drove towards them down the potholed street, indicted right to turn into a driveway then honked loudly. The window rolled down. 'You can't park here. I need to get into my house.'

Ridpath glanced back towards Carruthers who was still staring at his watch. It was past three thirty already.

He told the police driver to move backward allowing the other car to enter his house. The man drove past them shaking his head.

On the back seat, Carruthers checked his watch one last time, came to a decision and said, 'Let's move, Ridpath.'

Immediately, he was on the airwave. 'Go. Go. Go.'

The car suddenly surged forward, pausing for a millisecond at the end of the street before turning left and racing down the main road. Turning left again at the second street along, sliding to a halt on the soft snow carpeting the road.

The gates to SunnySide were locked. From the front transit, a copper ran out with a pair of bolt cutters and sliced through the padlock.

Ridpath had kept the channel open on his airwave to hear what was happening with Helen Shipton's team. He heard her repeat the go order, followed by the roar of a car engine.

Then silence followed by the squeal of brakes. The crunch of running feet on snow and the crash of a battering ram against the door.

Helen shouted, 'In.'

Ridpath switched off the airwave, leapt out of the car and rushed through the now open metal gate. Followed by Carruthers, Emily and a posse of uniformed coppers.

As ordered, everybody was quiet and focused.

He went through the front door, holding up the search warrant at a startled young care worker. 'This is a warrant to search these premises, where is Mathilda Staunton?'

The female care worker simply pointed towards the door at the rear without saying a word. Ridpath strode through, down the short corridor into the day room.

A few of the elderly residents were playing cards, others were watching television, still more were doing nothing, simply staring into mid-air, dreaming of lives long lived.

'Don't be alarmed, remain where you are, this is the police. We are going to search these premises,' Ridpath announced.

A few of the residents looked at each other, whilst the card players glanced at Ridpath before returning to their game.

Nobody moved.

Ridpath's airwave squawked.

'We've found Frank Diamond in the sitting room, Ridpath. He's dead, a screwdriver in the back of his head.'

'Was Lardner there?'

'We don't know, Ridpath.'

'Search the house and report back.'

'Will do. Over.'

Ridpath pointed to one of the care assistants. 'Where is Mathilda Staunton?'

'In her office.'

'Emily, can you get the staff together in their staffroom and do a head count. We'll interview them all later.'

'What about our tea?' one of the residents bleated. 'It's time for our afternoon tea, and Friday is bourbons. We only get one biscuit each but I like my bourbons.'

Ridpath looked around. All the other residents were staring back at him. He pointed to an unlucky constable who just happened to be in his eyeline. 'You...'

'PC Grayling, sir.'

'Give these people their tea. And make sure they have three bourbons each.'

He strode down the corridor followed by Steve Carruthers. Without knocking, he burst through the door.

Mathilda Staunton was sitting behind her desk, rubbing her face with a white towel.

'What the hell are you doing in my office?'

'Mathilda Staunton, we have a warrant to search these premises and your files.'

He held the signed warrant in front of her face.

'We'll see.' She picked up the phone on her desk and began dialling a number.

Ridpath was about to stop her when Carruthers reached forward and held his arm.

'Bruce, it's Mathilda here. I have a load of ugly policemen in my office with a search warrant…'

She stopped speaking, simply nodding her head as the person at the other end of the phone talked to her.

'But… I… Are you sure? I…'

Carruthers whispered in his ear. 'She's discovering the assistant chief has just rung the boss of ChromaEstates to let him know this is happening. It's one of the reasons we had to wait. I didn't want their solicitors serving us with an injunction halfway through the search.'

Mathilda Staunton put the phone down. 'I am to help you in every way I can.'

'That's commendable, Mrs Staunton. Let me introduce myself. My name is Detective Chief Inspector Carruthers. I believe you have already had the dubious pleasure of meeting my colleague, DI Ridpath. He now has something to say to you.'

'Mathilda Staunton, I am arresting you on suspicion of being an accessory to murder. You do not have to say anything. But it may harm your defence if you do not mention when questioned something which you later rely on in court. Anything you do say may be given in evidence.'

Chapter SEVENTY-THREE

He was driving down the M60 towards Stockford, making sure he stayed well within the speed limit. It would be stupid to be stopped by traffic police now.

On one side of the road, the valley of the Mersey. On the other, the dormitory suburbs of Sale, Wythenshawe and Cheadle extended far into the distance. Row upon row of houses, all built from red brick and all exactly the same.

How many countless lives had been wasted within the walls of these square, semi-detached prisons? How many dreams destroyed? How many hopes squandered?

How many people spent their lives inside those walls waiting for a death they knew was inevitable?

The words of T. S. Eliot came back to him. 'He who was living is now dead. We who were living are now dying.'

They were already dead, they just didn't know it yet.

He laughed to himself. Manchester was full of the living dead. You only had to walk through the city centre on a Saturday afternoon to see them. Their skin dull, their eyes lifeless, their movements jerky and spasmodic as they hunted for the latest bargains to feed on with their hard-earned cash.

Hadn't he seen them for himself? Countless thousands of their bodies laid out on his stainless steel table. Some had been strangled, others stabbed, a few shot. But most had already died long before they made it onto his table.

Sad, lonely lives.

Even sadder, more lonely deaths.

He glanced down at the bomb in its open carryall on the front seat. For a second, he considered stopping, turning round and going back to Frank's house, giving himself up to the police.

What was the point of killing people who were already dead?

But another voice spoke to him.

They deserve death at your hands. They stopped your work, interfered with your experiments, placed you in a prison surrounded by madmen, drugged, treated and analysed by idiots. They all deserve to die now, not twenty years from now. And Ridpath, he needs to feel the pain of absence, the absolute hurt of loss. Just as you have suffered for the last six years.

He knew the voice was right.

He couldn't stop now.

The plan was in action. The plays had been made. The pawns pushed forward to the centre of the board.

All that remained were the final moves.

It was time to play them.

He signalled left to come off the M60 at the next slip road, the exit to Stockford.

The Coroner's Court, its jury, witnesses, barristers and staff were waiting for him, waiting for death.

They didn't know it, of course. Nobody knew when they were going to die.

Except him.

He knew he was dying. Hadn't he cut up enough people to know the signs of cancer; the loss of weight, the coughing, the tiredness.

He would die soon and so would they.

The thought made him happy.

Extremely happy.

Chapter SEVENTY-FOUR

'Now, Mrs Staunton, I need to ask you a few questions, would you like a solicitor present?'

'I'm not an accessory to murder, I don't know what you're talking about.'

Ridpath took a picture from his document bag. 'Do you know this man?'

She picked it up and glanced at it quickly. 'It's Dr Sanghera. He's the doctor who signs the death certificates whenever a resident dies.'

Ridpath noticed she used the present tense about the doctor. Was she unaware he was dead?

'Did he ever examine any of the residents before signing a certificate?'

'It's not necessary, we tell him when they die and he handles the paperwork. A death certificate is a formality anyway.'

'It isn't, Mrs Staunton, it is a legal document confirming death and the causes of death.'

Her eyes narrowed. 'Who are you? You came here before as a coroner's officer and now you're a detective?'

'Like I said before—'

Carruthers touched his arm, stopping him from speaking. 'DI Ridpath is a Greater Manchester police officer seconded to the coroner's office. Now to get back to *our* questions. Did you know this Dr Sanghera also worked for Genepro, who performed mortuary services for SunnySide Residential Home?'

'Yes, of course I did. I appointed the company.'

'You didn't see any conflict of interest?'

'Why? He was just another supplier to the home. They put in the cheapest quote. We have many service suppliers.'

Ridpath took another picture out from his document file. 'Do you recognise this man?'

She nodded straight away. 'It's Frank Diamond. He's Genepro's mortuary officer. We ring him whenever somebody dies. The most efficient man I ever worked with. Normally undertakers can take hours to arrive, it's extremely upsetting for the residents, but Frank always comes straight away, sometimes within fifteen minutes. The deceased are taken out of the home before the residents are awake.'

'Almost as if he was waiting for your call?'

'I don't know what you mean, Inspector Ridpath. Now, if there are no more questions, I'm a busy woman—'

Ridpath held up his hand. 'We still have a few more questions, Mrs Staunton, if you don't mind.'

'Please hurry up, I'm extremely busy today.'

It was time to shake this woman out of her complacency. 'Do you recognise this man?'

She picked up the picture expecting to see another headshot. Immediately, her hand went to her mouth and she looked away.

'That's… it's Albert, but he has no eyes. Why doesn't he have eyes?'

'Albert?'

'Albert Owens. He died on Wednesday morning. He came here in April 2023. Why doesn't he have eyes?'

'Can you confirm it is Mr Owens? Please look at the picture again.'

She glanced again at the image taken by the forensic photographer before quickly looking away again and simply nodding.

'Do you have Mr Owens' file?'

She searched on her desk. 'I was about to close it and send his final bill to the council. He was a DOL.'

'Deprived of Liberty?'

She nodded. 'Early onset dementia. Most days he was unresponsive. We tried to get him to talk but he wouldn't or couldn't.

He was unable to look after himself at home and had no living relatives.' She pulled out a file. 'Here it is.'

Ridpath took the file and opened it. Albert Owens' smiling picture looked out at him from his admittance form. He still had eyes.

'I see you have signed his last day as 6 February. Do you complete every form after a resident dies?'

'In triplicate. I attach the death certificate signed by the doctor. One copy to head office, one copy to the council and one copy to your office at the coroner.'

He turned the page. 'I see there is a will attached to his file.'

'Yes, we often attach wills to the resident files. It helps us to contact executors and next of kin after they pass away.'

'Did Albert have an executor or a next of kin?'

'I don't think he did.'

Ridpath read through the will. 'It appears Mr Owens had property.'

'I thought he did. It was in the process of being sold by the council.'

'To pay for the fees he was charged for staying here?'

'It is the normal practice if a resident has assets worth more than £23,250. A financial assessment was made first by the council, of course.'

'I see there's a codicil to the will, written two days before Mr Owens died, witnessed by you and one of your directors, Bruce Edwards. The codicil leaves money to the home and two of the care assistants, a William Diamond and a Carys Black. Isn't it a conflict of interest to be a witness if you are also a beneficiary?'

Mrs Staunton raised her voice. 'I am not a beneficiary.'

'Your residential home is,' added Steve Carruthers.

'*I* am not. You see, Mr Ridpath, we checked on the house and it had been donated to the RSPCA years ago. There was no point in Mr Owens willing it to anybody. He no longer owned it.'

But Ridpath was no longer listening.

333

William Diamond. Why did the name ring a bell?

Before he could find an answer to the question, his airwave squawked again.

'Hi, Helen, what it is?'

'I think we have a problem, Ridpath.'

Chapter SEVENTY-FIVE

As he neared the Coroner's Court, the anticipation was building inside his chest. He stopped at a red light and took the time to go over the plan once more.

He was exactly on time.

The red light turned green, he put the car in gear and moved off. For a second, the back wheels skidded on the thin snow before finally gripping the road. Through the windscreen he could see large flakes of snow falling from the sky, landing on the bonnet and quickly turning to liquid from the heat of the engine.

Stockford looked pretty in the snow. It would look even prettier when flames of orange, red and blue gushed out from the court.

Nearly there now. Only four hundred yards to go.

He glanced down at the bag lying next to him on the front seat. Strange, how such a small device could create so much death and destruction.

For a second, he wondered if Frank Diamond had tricked him. It wasn't a bomb at all, but a child's toy constructed from Plasticine and a few batteries.

Then he shook his head. Frank wouldn't make a toy, he was far too proud of his skills acquired in Northern Ireland.

He reached out to touch the bag then withdrew his hand.

He slowed down as a pedestrian crossed the road in front of him, head down, shoulders hunched over. An old man braving the elements to do his shopping at one of the many supermarkets in the area.

He didn't regret the deaths of the old from SunnySide. They would have died anyway soon enough. He had given them the ability to make a useful contribution to society by donating their organs. The fact he made money from their donations was not important. Somebody had to fund his work. In Ashworth, he couldn't do it himself any more.

He remembered when he had the idea. It was after a particularly gruelling week in 2015. He had performed fourteen post-mortems that week. Removed fourteen hearts. Weighed fourteen brains. Sewn up fourteen bodies.

And then they had all been placed in the ground or incinerated in a crematorium. What a waste of fabulous human flesh.

He then created Genepro. When he offered his medical and mortuary services to SunnySide practically for free, they almost snatched his arm off. It was all grist to the mill of corporate profits, never mind the potential conflict of interest.

Hiring Dr Sanghera was easy, he couldn't get a job anywhere else and he was a good surgeon, shame he couldn't keep his hands of his living patients.

Just as it was starting, Ridpath had spoilt it all. Trapping Leslie and discovering his experiments at TRACE. All those years' work down the drain because of one curious copper.

Ashworth nearly killed him. Too many stupid people and that was just the doctors. How had he survived six years? By spending every day planning his revenge.

On the Coroner's Court.

On Ridpath.

On SunnySide.

On Ashworth.

On all those who had used and betrayed him.

The Coroner's Court was to the left now. He indicated to turn into the small street next to it where Frank had reserved a parking space.

He glanced down at the clock.

4.05 p.m. Right on time.

Frank had placed two bollards on a parking spot outside the court. He chuckled to himself. The British were so law abiding, simply the presence of two yellow bollards with 'POLICE. NO PARKING' on them would prevent anybody from taking the place.

He had thought of everything.

He parked the car, pushing the bollards to one side. One last check on the bomb in its canvas holdall. It was nestling inside, quiet as a newborn baby.

He took a deep breath.

Time to go up to the Coroner's Court. He would sit at the back. Another witness to the machinery of English justice. And then, when the time was right, he would act.

Chapter SEVENTY-SIX

'What did you say?'

Helen spoke more slowly and clearly. 'We searched Diamond's house. Upstairs in a cupboard, we found a backpack, inside were some blueprints and what looked like bomb-making material. We're now outside the house, waiting for the bomb squad.'

'Have you cleared the area?'

'We're knocking on doors and getting people out of their houses. The next door neighbour reports somebody left the house in Diamond's car a few minutes ago. The description matches that of Harold Lardner. Over.'

'Did he murder Diamond?'

'Looks like it.'

'Get the registration and put out an APB for the car.'

'There's more, Ridpath.'

'What?'

'I took a look at the blueprints. They were for the East Manchester Coroner's Court.'

'Shit. Clear the area and keep me informed.'

'Will do, over.'

Ridpath stood up. 'You heard, boss?'

Carruthers nodded. 'Go, Ridpath, we'll handle it here. Emily, you go with him.'

Ridpath rushed out of Staunton's room, running past the pensioners playing their card games or watching the television. The young copper was still handing our cups of tea and extra bourbon biscuits.

Emily was close behind. 'We'll take Steve's car, I'll drive.'

He pulled out his phone. 'Control, get a tactical unit to the East Manchester Coroner's Court immediately and alert the bomb squad. We have a code red. Repeat: a code red.'

He clicked off his phone and ran down the driveway of the retirement home, searching for the car. It was on his right facing towards the exit of the street, the driver sitting in the front listening to the radio, reading the *Daily Mirror*.

'Out,' ordered Ridpath, 'we need this car.'

The man got out. Emily grabbed Ridpath's arm. 'I'm driving.'

Ridpath nodded once and ran round to the passenger side, slipping on the snow and nearly falling over.

Emily started the engine as Ridpath climbed in beside her. The wheels of the car spun before finally gripping, the car fishtailing as they accelerated towards the main road.

Ridpath stared through the windscreen.

Emily switched on the siren and the lights as they raced through the red lights at Princess Parkway, narrowly avoiding an articulated lorry as it crossed the junction.

Would they get there on time?

Ridpath rang Sophia's mobile.

No answer.

He rang her landline.

Still no answer.

Where was she? And then it hit him. There was an inquest today. They would all be in court and Sophia would be doing his job.

'Move it, Emily, move it.'

The car surged forward, overtaking a slow car on the inside lane.

Outside, the suburbs of Manchester looked cold and lonely in the falling snow.

His phone rang, the noise loud and jangling.

Chapter SEVENTY-SEVEN

Harold Lardner closed the door to the car and marched up the steps of the Coroner's Court, stopping in front of the entrance to take out his mobile phone.

He called the number on speed dial. It was answered after just one ring.

'Ridpath, by now you know where I am.'

'Who is this? Is it you Lardner?'

'It's your favourite psychopath, Ridpath, and I am about to enter the Coroner's Court. I have a bomb with me and I'm going to blow up everybody inside. Do you understand me?'

'Don't do it, Lardner. These people have done nothing to you.'

In the distance, Lardner heard the sirens of emergency vehicles. 'It seems the cavalry are on the way. Tell them not to enter the court, Ridpath, if they do, everybody will die.'

'Don't do it, I'm begging you.'

'You can stop me, Ridpath.'

'How? Tell me and I'll do it.'

'I want you to come inside. If you do, I'll let them go. All except the coroner, he has to stay. It's a shame Mrs Challinor isn't here, but I hear she's at death's door anyway. Do you understand me, Ridpath?'

'I understand, but...'

'Time to go, Ridpath. See you soon.'

He switched off the phone and opened the doors leading into the Coroner's Court. A large woman was waiting outside the main court, wearing a name tag. Jenny Oldfield.

'Hello, sir, the court is in session with an inquest at the moment.'

'I know, I'd like to enter as an observer.'

'Of course.' She took out a clipboard. 'Your name?'

'Mr Venge. Robert Edward Venge.' He coughed twice to cover his smile.

'Please sign here, Mr Venge. Please switch off your mobile phone. It is not to be used when the court is in session.'

'Of course.' He pretended to switch it off.

'I need to check your bag.'

He opened it for her. 'It's just my coat and my lunchbox. I keep the sandwiches in an old biscuit tin.' He'd put an empty tin on top of the coats with the bomb beneath just in case his holdall was searched.

She took a cursory look inside. 'Huntley and Palmers? I remember those growing up. Fine, Mr Venge. You can take a seat anywhere on the back row.'

He walked past her and then stopped. 'Is Mr Ridpath around?'

'He's not here today. Do you know him?'

'We have met before, but it was a long time ago.'

'I'll let him know you were here.'

Outside, the emergency sirens were getting louder and closer.

He opened the door to the Coroner's Court and stepped inside.

Chapter SEVENTY-EIGHT

They were nearing the Coroner's Court. Ridpath could see the road ahead had already been blocked by police vehicles. On the left, a tactical unit van was discharging heavily armed officers onto the street. They began to fan around the court building, taking up positions at the front and back doors.

The car slid to a halt in front of one of the police units.

Ridpath jumped out, calling Sophia again.

Still no answer.

He ran up to the cordon, closely followed by Emily Parkinson, badging his way past a copper at the front. 'Is the area closed off?'

'We're just doing it, sir.'

'Push the cordon back another hundred yards. We don't know what sort of bomb he is carrying.'

'Yes, sir.' The copper ran off to talk to his sergeant.

Ridpath called Jenny Oldfield this time. The call was picked up immediately.

'Jenny, has anybody entered the court recently?'

There was a slight pause. 'A man came in a few minutes ago. He asked after you.'

'Clear the court room immediately, this is an emergency.'

'What?'

'Clear the court room.'

'But Mr Montague will not be pleased, he's just doing his summation.'

'I don't care, clear the court room.'

'Will do, Ridpath.'

Ridpath stayed on the line, hearing her go through the doors of the court room. Around him the snow was falling heavily, covering the ground in a soft white fleece. Despite the flashing lights and the frenetic activity of all the coppers, the air was strangely still and peaceful.

On any other day, Ridpath would have found the scene beautiful.

'Ridpath…' It was Jenny Oldfield again, she was whispering, '…there's a man standing up in the court. He's telling everybody to stand still and not move. He says he's got a bomb. What should I do?'

'Where are you now, Jenny?'

'Outside the court. As soon as I walked in, he stood up and shouted at everybody. I left before he could block the door.'

'Where is he now?'

'Standing next to the door.'

'Okay, listen to me. Come out now. The police have the building surrounded.'

Ridpath watched as the front door of the building slowly opened. Jenny Oldfield's face appeared round the corner and she ran down the steps straight towards him.

As she did, Ridpath's phone rang again.

'I can hear your colleagues outside, Ridpath. I presume they have the building surrounded.'

'You can't get away, Lardner, there's no escape.'

'You presume I want to escape. I have the hostages here with me. If you don't step inside the court in exactly one minute, I'll blow them all up. Do you understand, Ridpath? One minute, starting from now.'

The phone went dead.

Chapter SEVENTY-NINE

I'd been hiding for an hour and was beginning to feel the cold as the snow started to fall.

I stomped my feet trying to bring some life to them. 'Come on, hurry up,' I said out loud.

At that moment, a car drew up outside the house. Eve got out carrying a large school backpack. She waved at the car and called out. 'Bye Mrs Knight. See ya tomorrow, Maisie.'

'Not if I see you first, Eve.'

An old joke, one I'd used often at school.

She walked up the driveway, took out a key and opened the door, closing it behind her as she went into the hall.

I checked my watch. The timing was just right. As ever, the Master had planned everything down to the last second.

He'd told me to give her thirty minutes. Let her settle down, begin to feel at home. Then I'd go across and complete the mission for the Master. But I didn't know if I could wait that long, it was so bloody cold out here.

Shame. I liked Eve, but he had been clear in his instructions. It was to be my last job for him. Afterwards, I would be in control of my own future, deciding when to take life and when to spare it.

He said I was now ready for the responsibility.

Praise his power.

I checked my watch again. 4.25.

He said to move at 4.35. I don't know why but those were his precise instructions.

I walked across the street and stood outside the house.

A gentle snow was falling around my feet, dusting the ground. I looked backwards seeing my footprints in the snow. I had come so far in such a short time with the Master's guidance.

Would I be able to carry on on my own?

*I heard the Master's voice in my head. 'Concentrate on the present.
Be aware of the details. Forget everything but the mission.'*

*Light shone in the hallway and kitchen. A quick look down the road.
Nobody around, everybody would be at home in this weather.*

Another quick glance at my watch.

I would wait. The Master was always right. Praise his power.

Chapter EIGHTY

The phone rang again. 'The minute is up, what are you doing, Ridpath.'

'I'm coming in, Lardner, you can let them go.'

'They can leave when you are sitting in the court room with me.'

'No, release some of them now as evidence of your good faith.'

'A classic negotiator's gambit, Ridpath. Remember, I have read all the same books as you.' A slight pause. 'But to show my good faith, here are three women. The rest will come out when you come in.'

The door to the Coroner's Court opened and three women walked out slowly, their hands in the air. Ridpath recognised none of them. They must have been witnesses at the inquest.

A medical team rushed forward with blankets and they were taken to be checked in an ambulance.

'Emily, find out what's happening inside from those hostages.'

She rushed off to the ambulance parked on a side road.

Lardner's voice again. 'I've kept my part of the bargain. Will you keep yours?'

A large BMW pulled through the cordon, stopping at the kerb. Out from it stepped an older uniformed man with a single laurel wreath on his epaulette: the assistant chief constable.

Lardner's voice came over his phone. 'Well, Ridpath, I'm waiting.'

'DI Ridpath is it? ACC Lauriston. I will be taking over as Gold Commander. Situation report.'

The senior officer was abrupt in his manner, a man renowned for being inflexible.

'We have Harold Lardner inside with an unknown number of hostages. We have communications with him.' He held up the phone. 'He's threatening to blow them up unless I go inside.'

'Give me the phone.' Ridpath passed it over. 'Mr Lardner, you are surrounded, there is no escape, give yourself up and come out quietly.'

'Who is this? I want to speak to Ridpath.'

'This is Assistant Chief Constable Lauriston, I am now in charge. I repeat, you are surrounded, give yourself up.'

'I want to speak to Ridpath not some toerag from headquarters.'

'That will not be possible, give yourself up.'

'Listen, ACC Lauriston, I will only speak to Ridpath. Unless you put him on the phone in thirty seconds, I am going to blow this court room, and everybody in it, sky high.'

'It's not an idle threat, Mr Lauriston. We found bomb-making materials in a house where he was staying.'

'Ten seconds gone.'

Emily ran back. 'The hostages say there are ten people in the court now including the coroner, two barristers and Sophia Rahman.'

ACC Lauriston's eyes moved from side to side as he tried to decide what to do.

Lardner's voice came over the phone. 'Twenty seconds.'

'Release more hostages and I will put Ridpath back on the phone.'

'No. You are in no place to bargain with me, ACC Lauriston. Five seconds left.'

The ACC handed the phone back to Ridpath.

'Lardner, it's me, I'll come in if you release more hostages.'

The ACC shook his head violently.

'Still bargaining, Ridpath. You always were a negotiator. I'll release everybody except the staff at the court… if you come in.'

'You can't agree to that, DI Ridpath.'

The detective ignored his boss. 'Release them and I'll come in.'

'Agreed.'

'You can't go in there, DI Ridpath. We're not giving anything to a convicted murderer.'

The hostages appeared at the front door of the building one by one, running down the steps as soon as they realised they were free.

'I've kept my part of the bargain. Now you, Ridpath.'

The detective handed the phone over to ACC Lauriston and began walking up the steps to the court room.

'DI Ridpath, you cannot go in there. That is a direct order from a superior officer. Do not go in there.'

Ridpath hesitated for a moment, before carrying on up the steps.

Chapter EIGHTY-ONE

I checked my watch one more time. 4.34.

The snow was still falling, but not so heavily now. The ends of the branches of the trees were beginning to droop with the weight.

The street was still quiet, not a sound from anywhere, the snow deadening every sound.

At any other time, this would have been one of those perfect moments, like the picture-perfect lid of a chocolate box Mum had given me for Christmas when I was seven.

She hadn't stayed long after that, didn't even say goodbye when she left. I'd missed her for a short time, but Dad was there for me.

I don't know where she is now. Dead hopefully. I'd kill her myself if I saw her again. Perhaps, that would be my first job after I finished this work for the Master. I'd search for my mother and kill her as painfully as I could.

I let the thoughts of strangling her fill my body with pleasure. I would make her pay for having left me all those years ago.

A sound to the left brought me back to the present. A cat crossed the road and sought refuge from the snow beneath the warm engine of a car.

In front of me, the house was quiet. The lights in the kitchen and upstairs appeared to be shining brighter as the night became darker. I'd seen movement downstairs a few minutes ago, Eve was definitely there.

It was time to begin.

I took out my phone and took a picture of the house, sending it to the Master. He always wants pictures.

I opened the gate, the hinges squawked loudly. They definitely needed oil.

I stopped for a moment, waiting to see if there would be any reaction from inside the house.

Nothing.

I walked up the narrow path and stood in front of the door, taking another picture. A selfie this time with the door and its number in the background, also sending it to the Master.

Then I pressed the bell, hearing the noise echo through the house.

The sound of steps in the hallway, and the door began to open.

Chapter EIGHTY-TWO

'Hello, Ridpath, you took your time getting here. Come in, won't you? And do lock the door behind you. We don't want ACC Lauriston to get any stupid ideas, do we?'

Ridpath did as he was told.

Lardner was sat facing the four remaining hostages: the coroner, Sophia and two men who Ridpath didn't know. But from their black jackets and pinstripe trousers, he guessed they were solicitors or barristers.

The court was the same as he always remembered it, the jury box on the right wall, the coroner's large old desk at the front with the door to her office behind it, the witness box to the left and an array of chairs at the back.

It was the same but now it felt totally different.

'Why don't you join us?' Lardner pointed to a seat on his left.

'You need to get us out of here, Ridpath. He's threatening to blow us up.' Clarence Montague was visibly shaking, his hands trembling as he pointed towards Lardner. 'I didn't sign up for this when I came from Surrey.'

Ridpath ignored him. 'Are you okay, Sophia?'

'I'm fine, Ridpath. Is this Harold Lardner?'

'That is correct, young lady. You see in front of you the renowned Beast of Manchester.'

'Why don't you let them go, Harold. I'm here as I promised.'

'So it's Harold, is it now? Trying to use my first name to make a connection, to become my friend?'

'No, calling you Lardner all the time seems so public school boyish.'

'But everybody calls you Ridpath.'

'True. I hate being called Thomas, and Tom is even worse.'

'You're definitely not a Thomas. Ridpath suits you.'

'Let them go, Harold. This is between us two, it's nothing to do with them.'

Lardner thought for a moment, patting a bag on the seat next to him. Was that the bomb?

'You're right. They can leave, but you…' he pointed at Clarence Montague, 'you have to stay.'

Ridpath waved his hand at Sophia and the legal people, indicating they should go. The two men got up and almost ran out of the court room.

Sophia stopped for a moment. 'Will you be okay, Ridpath?'

'Go, Sophia, there's no point in you staying here.' He smiled. 'You have a wedding to arrange, remember?'

'How very touching, doesn't it make you want to vomit. Unless she leaves in three seconds, she stays.'

'Go, Sophia.'

His assistant ran out of the court room and he heard her shouting as she moved down the steps outside.

'Just us two now, Ridpath.' He looked across at Montague. The man was weeping silently, his body curled up on the chair. 'And him. But he doesn't really count does he?'

'Let him leave, Harold, he's done nothing to you.'

'Let me go,' Montague bawled.

'But he's the coroner, a representative of the whole corrupt system. You know I used to stand in front of these idiots giving my evidence and none of them understood a word I was saying. Now, Mrs Challinor was different. She had actually bothered to do a forensic science degree in addition to her legal qualifications so she was well informed. But the rest; they would swallow any old tosh I told them.'

'Let me go, I've done nothing wrong,' bawled Montague again, louder this time.

'This is so tiresome.' Lardner picked up a microphone stand and brought it down on the coroner's head. The crying ceased and the man slumped forward, collapsing on the floor at Lardner's feet.

'I couldn't stand the weeping and wailing. The man had no dignity.'

Ridpath jumped forward to check on Clarence Montague. Lardner immediately reached back to place his hand on the bag next to his chair.

'Let him be. He probably has concussion or at most a fractured skull. It won't affect his mind. He didn't have one anyway.'

'I need to check on him.'

'Leave him!' The voice was a command which quickly modulated to Lardner's softer tones. 'Just us now, Ridpath. And the bag of course.' He picked up the canvas holdall, reaching inside to pull out a biscuit tin and putting it beneath his chair. Then he pulled out an old coat wrapped around another larger biscuit tin with a digital clock on top.

'I do believe it's time to play our little game.' His finger hovered over the button.

'Wait!' shouted Ridpath.

'I've waited long enough. Six years to be precise.'

Lardner pressed a button on top of the tin and the digital clock began a countdown from three minutes.

'You have just three minutes left to live, Ridpath.' He glanced down at the clock. 'I'm sorry, two minutes fifty-five seconds. How time flies when you are enjoying yourself.'

Chapter EIGHTY-THREE

Eve was making herself a sandwich from the leftover bits of lettuce, half a tomato and a slice of Kraft cheese. Dad still hadn't arranged the delivery from Ocado. She would have to remind him again. Perhaps she would walk to the Tesco Express again and get a few necessities, but he'd told her not to.

Why was he behaving so strangely these days? And what was with the trip to the Lakes, they never went away in the middle of the term. She was looking forward to visiting Elterwater again though, she loved walking in the area and shopping in Grasmere. This time, she could pick up something about the Romantic poets; they had to study them in English next term.

She checked outside the window. The garden was covered in a thin, white duvet of snow. She didn't like snow at all. She loved the look of it but didn't like the reality – it was cold, wet and inevitably turned into a dirty black mess when it thawed. Like a charcoal slushie but twice as ugly.

Perhaps, her dad was right. Better to stay at home and wait for him to come back. After all, they were going to the Lakes this weekend, no point in buying fresh food when all it would do was sit in the fridge.

She smelt what was left of the milk she bought from Tesco the other night. Not too bad, might even be vaguely drinkable.

She liked staying in the house alone, there was a quietness, a peacefulness she enjoyed. She could play her music loud without her dad getting upset. For some strange reason he didn't like Beabadoobee. His brain had been addled by too much northern soul, Bowie, Iggy Pop and Oasis.

She liked The Smiths though. Morrissey had grown up less than five minutes from where they lived and she could understand the teenage angst of 'Shoplifters of the World Unite'.

Not that she would ever shoplift. Her dad would kill her if she did. Maisie did it occasionally more for the thrill than anything else. A Twix bar here and there when her mum forgot to give her a snack.

She cut the limp sandwich in half, placing it on a plate. Quadratic equations were calling her name followed by the Welsh castles of Edward I. She'd been to Conwy once when her mum was still alive. She found the place cold and forbidding, which she guessed was Edward's whole point. The castles were a symbol of power and control after all.

She was halfway upstairs when she heard the doorbell.

Who could it be? She wasn't expecting anybody. Had her dad forgotten his key again? Or perhaps he had ordered food and they were now delivering it. But why hadn't he messaged her?

She put her sandwich and milk on the windowsill and trotted downstairs to open the door. Through the frosted glass, she could see a small shape. It wasn't her dad or the deliveryman.

Perhaps it was Maisie?

She opened the door, keeping the security chain attached.

'Billy? What are you doing here?'

Chapter EIGHTY-FOUR

'I should warn you, Ridpath, just in case you get any ideas of attacking me. The bomb has a rocker switch, once it is activated, even the slightest movement will set it off. A lovely idea, don't you think? Frank Diamond picked it up when he was working for the Royal Engineers in Northern Ireland. Join the army and see the world, huh?'

Ridpath stared at the clock on top of the tin.

2.30

The green numbers seemed to be getting faster as they counted down.

'For the last six years, I've dreamt of this moment. Having you here in front of me, a bomb by my side primed to go off. You don't know how much I've been looking forward to it.'

'You're going to die as well, Harold.'

The man laughed. 'I know that, Ridpath. We all have to die sometime, but unfortunately for me, that date with death will be earlier than most. Cancer, you see. Of the pancreas. No cure, just a long, slow painful death. I'd rather go out quickly, with a bang, you might say if you had a sense of humour.'

Ridpath could see it now. The loss of weight. The sallowness of the skin. The patchiness of the hair. He knew the signs well.

'You had cancer too, didn't you? Myeloma wasn't it? A blood cancer. You were lucky they managed to find a cure for you.'

Ridpath looked at the clock again.

2.00

'They might find a cure for you, never give up hope.'

'I think you are forgetting which one of us has the medical degree. There is no cure for pancreatic cancer, particularly when

356

it is Stage Four. I thought seeing as I was going to die, I might as well take you with me. And him of course.' He pointed to the still prostrate Clarence Montague.

'It doesn't have to be this way, Harold.'

'Oh, but it does, Ridpath. I've planned it this way. All the clues I gave you; the young boy's body dumped on Seagram Road in Withington, the capsule in the boy's mouth, all the links to TRACE and SunnySide Residential Home. I thought you'd never make the connection. I even had to have Dr Sanghera killed and left all those personal effects at Genepro, placing Andrew's stuff in there as well. You were slow this time, Ridpath. Is age creeping up on you? Are you losing your powers?'

'It was you all the time?'

'Who else? God? He doesn't exist, I replaced him long ago.'

'What about the note to the coroner?' He looked at the prone Clarence Montague still lying on the floor.

Lardner held his hands up. 'Nothing to do with me. Wish I'd thought of it though.'

Ridpath glanced at the clock.

1.20

He checked the court room. Was there anywhere he could hide before the bomb went off? Could he make it outside in time? With the rocker switch, all Lardner had to do was knock the bomb off the chair and it would explode. He'd never get out in time.

And what about Montague? Despite all his problems with the man, he couldn't leave the coroner lying there on the floor.

Lardner's phone buzzed with the arrival of a message.

'I have one more surprise for you, Ridpath.' Lardner looked at his phone and smiled. 'You might recognise this place.'

He turned the phone round so Ridpath could see the screen.

'That's my home. Why do you have a picture of my home?'

Lardner scrolled upwards revealing another picture.

Ridpath was staring at a young man. The same young man who had knocked on his door four nights ago.

'Billy? What's he doing outside my house?'

And then it hit Ridpath.

'This is Billy Diamond, aka William Diamond. Frank's son. He going to kill your daughter.'

Chapter EIGHTY-FIVE

'It's cold, Eve. Can I come in?'

'I dunno, my dad's not here and he doesn't like strangers in the house when he's not here.'

Billy rubbed his gloveless hands together and stomped his feet. 'I'm not a stranger, you know me. Even your dad knows about me. He invited me to come to your house, remember?'

She hesitated. Dad had invited Billy to come round, hadn't he? She could just invite him in and let him wait there till her dad returned. Then at least they could meet each other.

But her dad's instructions were very clear. 'Don't let anybody into the house, understand?'

'Come on Eve, it's cold. I won't stay long, just for a cuppa.'

'We don't have any tea.'

'For a coffee then, it's cold out here.'

She thought for a long while. It was snowing and his coat was awfully thin. It couldn't hurt to let him shelter until it had stopped snowing.

'I don't know, Dad was very clear about not letting anybody in. He seemed to be worried about something. I think it was to do with his work.'

'But I'm not just anybody, Eve. I'm Billy, I've even met your dad.'

He had met her dad and he wasn't just anybody. She was about to take the chain off its hook when she saw a small gold cross around his neck. Why had she never noticed that before? Did he always wear it?

She watched as he tucked the cross back into his shirt. 'Let me in, Eve,' he said, a strange anger in his voice.

Eve suddenly felt scared, that sound in his voice had frightened her. She shook her head. 'I can't, my dad he...'

He seemed to lose patience and pulled a knife from his pocket. The metal of the long blade gleamed in the light on the porch. 'Let me in, bitch,' he snarled.

She tried to slam the door but he had already put his foot in the gap. 'Billy, stop it, what are you doing?'

'Open the door, Eve.' His voice was quiet now, more in control. 'I have to come in.'

She pressed on the door, trying to close it, but his foot remained where it was. 'Go away, Billy, my dad will kill you if he finds out.'

'But you're not going to tell him, are you? You're never going to tell him.'

She could feel him leaning his weight against the door. The chain was stretched tight now, the door opening wider. Cold air rushing into the warm house.

She ran upstairs, stopping on the landing. 'Don't come in Billy, my dad will be home soon.'

'Your dad won't be home for a long time, Eve. He's at the Coroner's Court in Stockford. He's busy with the Master.'

As he spoke his small hand was sneaking round the edge of the door trying to find the chain.

Chapter EIGHTY-SIX

Eve was in trouble. Ridpath glanced at the clock on top of the bomb.

56

55

54

53

The green numerals seemed to be moving even faster.

Lardner had a smug smile on his face. 'Cat got your tongue, Ridpath? Your wife died and now none of your family will be alive after today. My mission is fulfilled.'

45

44

43

Ridpath had to do something. But what? He looked around, desperately searching for an answer.

Clarence Montague stirred, lifting his head from the ground. 'What? What happened?'

For a moment, Lardner was distracted.

Without thinking, Ridpath dived forward, throwing his whole body at the pathologist. The man fell backwards away from the bomb and the chair, with Ridpath on top of him.

A jolt of pain shot through Ridpath's shoulder. Lardner lashed out with his legs trying to get the detective off him, kicking upwards.

Ridpath pressed down with his shoulder across the man's face, struggling to stay on top.

Lardner took a bite out of his flesh. Ridpath's shoulder screamed in pain as Lardner continued to bite, refusing to let go, his legs still kicking out.

The pain was too much, Ridpath had to pull away from the jaws. As he did, Lardner's head came up and he tried to kick the bomb off the chair.

He kicked out once, twice, missing both times.

Ridpath pressed down again, this time using his forearm against the man's throat.

Lardner was reaching out for the bomb using his foot, shifting his body, trying to kick the chair.

Ridpath pressed even harder, trying to cut off the man's air supply, stop him resisting. The body went limp beneath him for a few seconds before the eyes flashed open again.

Ignoring the pain in his shoulder, Ridpath punched downwards, connecting with Lardner's head on the side of the temple. He struck again and again, feeling the crunch of his knuckles against Lardner's nose.

He hit harder and harder and harder until he collapsed across the man's body, gasping for breath, sweat dripping off his forehead.

Lardner didn't move, the man was out cold.

Behind him, Clarence Montague was slowly sitting upright rubbing his head and groaning.

Ridpath glanced across at the bomb.

15

14

13

He dragged himself to his knees. For a second, Lardner groaned audibly and then fell silent again.

Ridpath crawled over and picked up the biscuit tin carefully from the chair, desperately trying to make sure he kept it as level as possible.

11

10

9

Slowly, he rose to his feet, his hands trembling as he stepped over Lardner's unconscious body. Where should he go?

He saw the door to the coroner's office over on the far wall. It was his only chance. He walked as quickly as he could towards the front of the court, skirting the coroner's large oak desk and carefully stepping up to the raised dais.

The door was in front of him. But how could he open it?

He put the box down on the desk and twisted the door knob, his shoulder screaming in pain, opening the heavy door into the coroner's office.

5

4

3

He was running out of time. He picked up the biscuit tin.

2

1

0

A loud buzz from inside the box. No time to put it down. Instead, he launched it into the coroner's office, slammed the door shut and dived underneath the coroner's desk, covering his head with his arms.

Nothing happened.

Slowly, he raised his head. Had Lardner been faking? Was the biscuit tin and the timer all an elaborate bluff to get him to come to the Coroner's Court?

And then there was an enormous roar, the air seemed to be sucked out of his lungs and the world went black.

Chapter EIGHTY-SEVEN

Eve ran downstairs again, throwing all her weight against the door, trapping the hand.

A sharp squeal of pain, followed by, 'You bitch, you'll pay for that.'

He threw himself at the door. It shook and shuddered but held. The door rocked again. Through the frosted glass, she could see Billy's face twisted in anger and aggression.

'Go away, Billy. Please leave me alone!'

The answer was another slam of his body against the door. The chain was coming away from the jamb now.

Through the frosted glass, she saw Billy take a few steps back and then charge at the door with his shoulder.

It gave way, banging open, the frosted glass shattering from the impact. Billy fell through, landing on the floor at her feet.

She looked around her for something to hit him with.

Nothing.

Should she run to the kitchen?

He was getting up from the floor, his left arm hanging limply at his side. 'Eve, you should've let me in. It would have been so much easier and quicker.'

The knife came up and pointed directly at her. She backed away towards the hall table.

He was on his knees now, rising to his feet. 'I have to do this, Eve. I have my orders. But I'll make it painless, you won't feel a thing, I promise.'

She reached behind her, feeling something long and cylindrical on the table. She brought up the air freshener and sprayed it directly into Billy's eyes.

He flinched and screamed.

She sprayed more, aiming directly at his face.

The scent of her mother filled the hallway. A scent she remembered from her childhood. Roses. The scent of summer. Her mother's scent.

He went down, scratching at his eyes.

She vaulted Billy's prone body and ran upstairs.

He was already getting to his feet. 'You're gonna pay for that, bitch.'

Eve saw the sandwich and milk on the windowsill. She picked them both up, throwing them at his head.

He ducked as the glass full of milk shattered against the far wall.

His eyes were read and his skin blotchy. 'I'm going to enjoy making you suffer,' he snarled.

She ran up to her bedroom, slamming the door and locking it behind her. What could she do? She tried to pull her cupboard across the door but it was too heavy.

She could hear him shouting.

'You should have let me in when I asked you, Eve. Now I'm going to kill you slowly and very, very painfully.'

Chapter EIGHTY-EIGHT

Ridpath woke up, his head ringing. Emily was standing over him, her mouth was moving but he could hear no words, no sounds, just a loud, persistent ringing in his ears.

He tried to sit up but fell back down to the ground, his head hitting the floor.

He had to do something. What was it he had to do?

Emily was moving her lips again. Gradually, her voice was coming into focus, piercing through the ringing in his ears.

'Are you okay, Ridpath?'

He shook his head trying to clear it.

'What's wrong? Where does it hurt?'

Eve.

That was it. Eve was being attacked.

He tried to sit up again but Emily pushed him down.

'Need to go, Eve, she...'

'Ridpath, you've just been in an explosion. We need to get you out.'

He could smell burning. Where was he? He seemed to be on the other side of the Coroner's Court next to the door.

'These EMTs are going to help you.'

He shrugged them off. 'Need to get to Eve... She's being attacked.'

Why doesn't she understand?

'What?'

He took three deep breaths, as he was being picked up by two burly medics. 'Eve is being attacked. Lardner sent someone to kill her. We need to stop him. I—'

Emily's eyes opened wide and Ridpath knew she had finally understood.

'Take me to her. We need to go now.'

'Where Ridpath?'

'My house, she's being attacked in my house.'

As Ridpath was being carried down the stairs by the medics, Emily was on her phone. 'Control, we need an emergency team, code red, to 13 Glebe Close, attack in progress on an underaged female. That is a code red, all units to respond immediately.'

'Roger that, DS Parkinson. ETA five minutes. Over.'

At the bottom of the stairs, Ridpath shrugged off the medics again. 'I need to go to her NOW!'

Emily made a decision. 'Put him in my car.'

'But he needs medical attention. We don't know the extent of his injuries…'

'Put him in my car,' she ordered.

The phone in Ridpath's pocket began to ring.

Chapter EIGHTY-NINE

She could hear his feet stomping up the stairs and suddenly there was pounding at her door. 'Open up, Eve. You can't escape.'

She looked for her phone, finding it next to her laptop. She picked it up but her hands were shaking and it fell to the floor.

The doorknob rattled and he banged on it with his fist. 'Open up now, Eve.'

Then it went quiet. Was he still there? She needed to get help. Her phone? Where was her phone?

She looked all around her room, eventually finding it underneath her table next to the bin. What was it doing there?

She ran across the room and picked it up.

It was still quiet in the hallway. Where was Billy and what was he doing? Why was it so quiet?

Her hands were still shaking as she dialled the number.

One ring.

Two rings.

'Dad,' she whispered holding the phone close to her mouth.

'Eve.'

They spoke at the same time.

'Are you okay?'

'He's here, Dad.'

'Billy Diamond is in the house?'

She was breathing heavily. 'He's outside my bedroom. What should I do, Dad?'

'I'm coming.'

Eve could hear the high-pitched wail of the siren through the phone. 'I'm scared, Dad, he rang the bell and wanted to come in...'

As she spoke, there was a loud crash against her bedroom door, followed by another and another. The wood began to splinter.

'Dad...' she shouted into the phone.

Another crash and the metal leg of the coat stand from the hallway appeared in a hole in the door.

A thin, white hand snaked through the hole and began to turn the doorknob.

'Dad!' Eve screamed.

Chapter NINETY

The phone went dead in Ridpath's hand. Her last two screams had cut him to the quick.

He tried Eve's number again but there was no answer. Why wasn't she answering?

He banged his fist on the dashboard. 'Hurry, Emily, faster.' Every part of his body ached and his head was throbbing, but all he could think of was Eve.

He would never forgive himself if something happened to her. He should have been there protecting her. Wasn't that what a dad was supposed to do? Lardner had warned him and he had continued working, leaving Eve to fend for herself.

How could he have been so stupid?

He banged his fist on the dashboard. 'Move it, move it!'

The siren wailed as Emily slalomed through the traffic, using the hard shoulder whenever she could.

Would they get there on time?

Ridpath rang Eve's mobile again.

Still no answer.

'Faster, Emily, faster...'

Outside, the suburbs of Manchester raced by. The snow was still falling but more slowly now, the flakes drifting down to cover the trees in a white icing. Occasionally, the white snow picked up the red and blue lights from the car, reflecting the colours back.

Other cars pulled to the side, seeing the urgent blue and red lights in their rearview mirrors.

Emily's face was solemn, her jaw clenched tight, concentrating on the road in front of her.

Ridpath rang Eve's phone for the third time.

Still no answer.

'Eve!' shouted Ridpath into the mouthpiece.

But there was no response from the other end of the phone.

He recognised the roads now, they were getting near to his house. Would they be in time? Eve wasn't answering her phone. What would he do if he lost her? He'd already lost Polly, he couldn't lose Eve too.

Emily turned left at the top of his road. The car started sliding towards the fence at the corner, before finally it gripped the road and accelerated forward.

Three police vehicles were parked outside the house, lights flashing.

The car slid to a stop. Ridpath was already out of it before it stopped moving.

His front door was wide open, the frosted glass shattered.

He limped up the garden path, shouting, 'Eve, Eve.'

There was no answer.

He could hear Emily's footsteps behind him, crunching on the snow. He stepped over the broken door, shattered glass lay in the hallway. A can of air freshener lay on the floor and the coat stand was missing. A large wet stain covered the wall and the place smelt of a strange mixture of roses and stale milk.

A bulky copper came out from the kitchen, his face revealing no emotion. 'We arrived too late, we couldn't help her.'

'Eve!' Ridpath shouted.

No answer.

He climbed upstairs, every step causing a sharp pain to shoot up his leg. The door to Eve's room was open with two of the panels splintered, fragments of wood lying everywhere.

'Eve,' he shouted again.

From inside the room, he heard whimpering.

Eve was sat on the floor, her arms wrapped around her legs, her head resting on her knees. Next to her lay Billy Diamond. His body stretched out and his head leaking blood.

He rushed over to her and wrapped her in his arms.

'I didn't mean to kill him, Dad, he had a knife.'

'Shush, baby, shush.'

'I hit him with the lamp when he came through the door. The lamp Mum gave me. I think it's broken.'

He held her tight. 'Shush, Eve, it's all right, don't talk now.'

The knife was still in Billy Diamond's hand. A hand with a swallow tattoo in the gap between the index finger and the thumb.

He hugged her even tighter. 'It's alright, Eve, I'm here now.'

Emily came into the room with the burly policeman. 'The responders have called for an ambulance for Eve, it should be here in three minutes. Another one is coming for the boy. They didn't want to move him without the medics being here.'

'He's still alive?' whispered Eve.

Emily nodded. 'He's out cold. You must have given him a hell of a whack young lady.'

'Get the ambulance here before I finish him off,' Ridpath ordered.

He picked up his trembling daughter and, holding her close, slowly walked down the stairs to the kitchen. 'It's okay, Eve, it's okay.'

She held him tighter.

'You're safe now, I'm here.'

Outside the window, the snow had stopped falling and the sun had begun to peer through the clouds.

It was just another winter's day in Manchester.

Friday, February 23.

Two weeks later.

Chapter NINETY-ONE

Ridpath limped into Mrs Challinor's hospital room. Her daughter, Sarah, was already there, carrying two bags.

'You're finally leaving,' he said.

'Can't say I'll miss the place.'

Mrs Challinor folded up a white T-shirt, placing it and some toiletries in one of the bags held by her daughter.

'You didn't need to come, Ridpath.'

'I wanted to see if you needed any help leaving.'

'Thank you for the thought. Where's Eve?'

He pointed back towards the corridor. 'Outside, on her iPad, waiting for us.'

'Is she okay?'

Ridpath shrugged his shoulders. 'As well as can be expected. She's sleeping with the light on now and sometimes wakes up in the middle of the night with nightmares.'

'You're getting help for her?'

'The therapist says she's strong and focused. He hopes there won't be any long-term issues.'

'But he doesn't know?'

'They never do.'

'You haven't been to the coroner's office?'

'I'm still persona non grata. But I heard Clarence Montague was leaving, going back to the dark, satanic mills of Surrey apparently. After being hit by Lardner, he suffered concussion and when the bomb exploded, he was cut by flying shards of glass and splinters. According to him, he didn't sign up for such treatment when he came north to Manchester. Helen Moore has asked me to return when he goes at the end of the month.'

'Are you going to do it?'

'Honest?'

She nodded.

'I don't know. At the moment, I don't want to make any decisions until Eve is settled and happy. She's all that matters right now. I'm on compassionate leave from GMP for as long as I want. Both Claire Trent and Steve Carruthers have told me to take my time. They've even confirmed my Inspector rank. Four years too late but hey, it's the police.'

'What happened to Billy Whatshisname?'

'Billy Diamond? He woke up with a massive headache after Eve clouted him with the lamp. He's been charged with eight counts of murder. They found seven bodies at TRACE with his DNA on them. The same DNA was also found, with Andy Golding's, in the back of the van. He was the one who dumped the body, not his father. He's been singing like a proverbial canary. Blaming everything on Lardner of course. Said that he was ordered to kill and had to obey because the Master, aka Lardner, had told him to murder the old people.'

'The Nuremberg defence?'

'Exactly.'

'And Harold Lardner?'

'He's been moved to Broadmoor. They're holding an inquiry into how he escaped so easily from Ashworth but I'm sure nobody will be to blame. He'll spend the rest of his life there.'

'It couldn't happen to a nicer person.'

Ridpath stared into mid-air for a few moments before speaking. 'It's strange, but this whole case began with an invest-igation into a missing boy. I went to his funeral a week ago.'

'Andrew Golding?'

Ridpath nodded his head. 'According to Billy Diamond, Andy Golding saw him murder the boy's grandmother. He then began to blackmail them for money. It was Billy's father, Frank

Diamond, who killed Andy with Lardner ordering that his body be kept at TRACE in case it was needed.' A long pause. 'If the police had done their job properly, we might have solved it four years ago, prevented the deaths of so many people in that residential home.'

'You can't blame yourself, Ridpath, you did your job. You were an advocate for the dead. It's all they want.'

She stared at him for a long time. 'I'd like you to stay as the coroner's officer if you can. You're an indispensable part of the team. And when I'm not there, Helen Moore will need you even more. But I'll leave the decision to you. Eve must come first.'

'Thank you for asking, I don't know at the moment. All I care about is Eve.'

'I understand. I have about six months of rehab apparently before they'll let me work again.'

'It's good to hear you want to come back.'

'I don't know how I'm going to survive,' said Sarah.

'Neither do I,' echoed Margaret Challinor, 'it would be great to work with you again Ridpath, we still have so much to do.'

'I know, Mrs Challinor, even more than when we started.'

'But for now, I just want to get out of this bloody hospital. Where's that daughter of yours, call her in.'

'Eve, Mrs Challinor would like to see you.'

Eve appeared sheepishly at the door.

'I need somebody strong to help me get to the car, Eve, I wonder if you could help me. You're a strong person, aren't you?'

'I think so, Mrs Challinor.'

'Call me, Margaret. Now come here and let me take your arm. I'm still a bit wobbly on my feet.'

Eve walked over and stood beside her. Mrs Challinor leant in and gave her a hug. 'Now let me take your arm. Sometimes, we all need somebody to lean on.'

Do you love crime fiction and are always on the lookout for brilliant authors?

Canelo Crime is home to some of the most exciting novels around. Thousands of readers are already enjoying our compulsive stories. Are you ready to find your new favourite writer?

Find out more and sign up to our newsletter at canelocrime.com